Indu Sundaresan was born and raised in India and went to the United States for graduate studies. She is the author of the Taj trilogy: *The Twentieth Wife* (winner of the 2003 Washington State Book Award), *The Feast of Roses*, and *Shadow Princess*. She is also the author of *The Splendor of Silence* and a collection of short stories, *In the Convent of Little Flowers*.

Rights to the Taj trilogy have been acquired for a television series in India, beginning with *The Twentieth Wife*.

Visit her at: www.indusundaresan.com

Find her on Facebook: www.facebook.com/pages/Indu-Sundaresan/331750008182

Join her on Twitter: @ISundaresan

Praise for *Shadow Princess*

"Indu Sundaresan's *Shadow Princess*, the final installment in her Taj Trilogy, begs to be made into a movie…The author…diverts her gaze from the confines of the Mughal palace to the bustling markets, smoky camps, and even the construction site of Mumtaz's tomb, and…the text comes alive."—*India Today*

"An enchanting tale of treachery, fratricide, devotion, love, intrigue and obsession."—*Indian Express*

"Indu Sundaresan weaves a shimmering web of fiction around the historical facts at her disposal…The author's avid interest in history and her extensive research into her subject are evident in the convincing reconstruction of the complex political drama and the day-to-day affairs of the royal family…"—*Deccan Herald*

"Sibling rivalry, power struggles, deceit, unrequited love and secret alliances, all make this novel a compelling page turner…A treat for lovers of historical fiction."—*Elle*

"Sundaresan brings sober devotion to the dynastic tale…A mine of fabulous detail on the daily lives of the Mughal emperors…"—*Kirkus Reviews*

"From a few lines in various historic documents, Sundaresan brings to life two little-known though remarkable women who, though they lived in the shadows of great men, proved that still greater women stood behind them."—*The Oregonian*

"A perfect read for those who wish to delve deeply into the cultural struggles of Indian women and the Taj Mahal's celebrated architecture."—*Booklist*

"Sundaresan has a scholar's fascination with the period; she's at her best describing the opulent court or the construction of the Taj Mahal."—*Publishers Weekly*

Praise for *The Twentieth Wife*

"Sundaresan attempts to bring our history to us in a highly palatable form...The vignettes of court life...are opulently displayed in her pages."—*The Sunday Tribune*

"Sundaresan delightfully combines history and juicy gossip..."—*India Today*

"Indu is...a disciplined researcher, with the ability to construct a graceful narrative that at once is grand in its sweep and yet rich in the sensory detail of each specific moment."—*First City*

"*The Twentieth Wife* is a profoundly imaginative exploration of what life must have been like behind harem walls."—*Outlook*

"*The Twentieth Wife* has adeptly spliced romance with political intrigue, giving the reader a broad insight into the political climate of the Mughal period."—*The Hindu*

"Written as an epic romance against the backdrop of palace intrigues and power struggles, this is the story of one woman's rise from behind the veil..."—*The Economic Times*

"A wonderful tale of love, hate and deceit, all woven into one magnificent Mughal tapestry."—*Indian Express*

"A sweeping, carefully researched tale of desire, sexual mores and political treachery set against the backdrop of 16th and 17th-century India."—*Publishers Weekly*

"Sundaresan is a gifted storyteller with an obvious passion for history."—*USA Today*

Praise for *The Feast of Roses*

"Set against a fascinating backdrop...This intricate canvas comes to life in Indu Sundaresan's quietly casual, yet vividly descriptive prose..."—*Deccan Herald*

"Broadly sticking to historical facts, Sundaresan has woven a fascinating and an engrossing fiction, revolving around the protagonist—Mehrunnisa, who defies all norms by refusing to be confined to the duties of an Empress and dares to re-define her role as a decision-maker."—*Free Press Journal*

"In *The Feast of Roses*...[Sundaresan] continues the second half of the empress' life—and peppers it beautifully with her rich and well-informed vision of 17th-century Mughal India..."—*Seattle Weekly*

"An excellent read and a wonderful love story."—*Book Review Cafe*

"The novel's scope and ambition are impressive, as are the numerous period details and descriptions of the various cultural ceremonies that distinguish court life in royal India..."—*Publishers Weekly*

"This is a must-read for history buffs and would-be powerful consorts."—MyShelf.com

ALSO BY INDU SUNDARESAN

Shadow Princess

The Twentieth Wife

The Feast of Roses

The Splendor of Silence

In the Convent of Little Flowers

The MOUNTAIN
of
LIGHT

Indu Sundaresan

HarperCollins *Publishers* India

First published in India in 2013 by
HarperCollins *Publishers* India

Copyright © Indu Sundaresan 2013

ISBN: 978-93-5116-091-5

2 4 6 8 10 9 7 5 3 1

Indu Sundaresan asserts the moral right
to be identified as the author of this work.

HarperCollins *Publishers*
A-53, Sector 57, Noida, Uttar Pradesh 201301, India
77-85 Fulham Palace Road, London W6 8JB, United Kingdom
Hazelton Lanes, 55 Avenue Road, Suite 2900, Toronto, Ontario M5R 3L2
and 1995 Markham Road, Scarborough, Ontario M1B 5M8, Canada
25 Ryde Road, Pymble, Sydney, NSW 2073, Australia
31 View Road, Glenfield, Auckland 10, New Zealand
10 East 53rd Street, New York NY 10022, USA

Printed and bound at
Thomson Press (India) Ltd.

For my mother-in-law and father-in-law,

Sarada and Raju

and, always, always

for Sitara

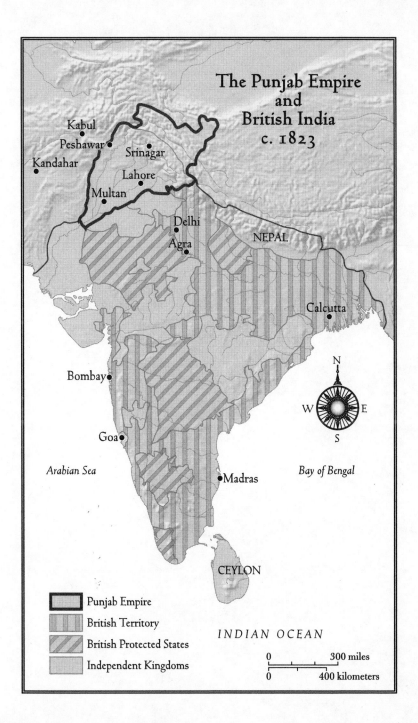

The Punjab Empire
and
British India
c. 1823

Kabul
Peshawar
Kandahar
Srinagar
Lahore
Multan
Delhi
Agra
NEPAL
Calcutta
Bombay
Goa
Arabian Sea
Madras
Bay of Bengal
CEYLON
INDIAN OCEAN

N
W   E
S

Punjab Empire
British Territory
British Protected States
Independent Kingdoms

0   300 miles
0   400 kilometers

Author's Note

In April 1850, Lord Dalhousie, the British Governor-General of India, ordered the 186-carat Kohinoor diamond secreted from Bombay to London, to adorn the arm of his sovereign, Queen Victoria. Until the diamond reached England, very few people knew it had even left India.

The reason for this furtiveness was the general discontent in India as Dalhousie annexed the lands of the Punjab Empire to those of British India, and dispossessed the boy king of the Punjab—Maharajah Dalip Singh—of his throne, his kingdom, and the massive wealth of his Toshakhana, the treasury house.

The young Maharajah was also the last Indian owner of the Kohinoor.

Although the Kohinoor has belonged to the monarchs of England for the last hundred and sixty-three years, the diamond has a deep reach into Indian history—according to legend, Lord Krishna gave it to a disciple in response to his meditations, many thousands of years ago.

More contemporarily, the first recorded mention of the Kohinoor occurs in the memoirs of Emperor Babur, who established the Mughal Empire in 1526, and received the diamond from one of the rajas whom he defeated.

The diamond then slips in and out of India—possessed, in its departures, by the kings of Persia and Afghanistan. Nadir Shah, King of Persia, gives it its name, calling it a veritable Koh-i-noor, a "Mountain of Light."

In 1809, the ruler of Afghanistan, Shah Shuja, is dethroned by his brother. Shuja turns to the ruler of the Punjab, Maharajah Ranjit Singh, for help in regaining Afghanistan, and promises Ranjit the Kohinoor in return.

This is where *The Mountain of Light* begins. And at this point—at Ranjit Singh's court—the history of the Kohinoor becomes inextricably linked with the British in India.

The first ship from the English East India Company touched Indian shores in 1608, during Mughal rule, and for the next hundred years or so, the Company fought to gain a trade treaty with the Mughal kings, excluding the already-present Portuguese and Dutch in India.

As the Mughal Empire disintegrated, the Company acquired influence. It lent armies to various independent kings as they seceded from Mughal lands, and claimed harsh compensations—indiscriminate use of the kings' armies and treasuries—that fell just a little short of actual rule. The Court of Directors of the Company grew massively rich, and corrupt, it was said, controlling vast chunks of India, nominally on behalf of their sovereign in England. In 1773, a regulating act in the British Parliament limited the Company's powers in India, and established the presence of a Crown-appointed, Court of Directors–approved governor-general.

In *The Mountain of Light*, when the Afghan ruler Shah Shuja comes to the Punjab in the early 1800s with the Kohinoor diamond, there is a flurry of interest in him. Maharajah Ranjit Singh wants the Kohinoor; the British want Shuja—to set him up as a puppet king in Afghanistan.

Years after Ranjit Singh gets the Kohinoor from Shuja, in

1838, a British embassy arrives at his court in the form of the British Governor-General of India, Lord Auckland, and his sisters Emily and Fanny Eden. Auckland wants the ailing and aging Punjab Maharajah's help in invading Afghanistan—which Ranjit Singh does not agree to, and which eventually becomes one of the most disastrous wars the British fight in Asia.

After Ranjit Singh dies, soon after Auckland's visit, four of his sons are killed in wars of succession, leaving only the six-year-old Prince Dalip Singh as heir to his father's empire—and the Kohinoor diamond. While the British did not dare to invade the Punjab under the powerful Ranjit Singh's rule, they now manage to lodge a foot into the door to the Empire, and eventually annex the Punjab to British lands in India.

Although Dalip Singh was called a maharajah until the end of his life, it was an empty title, and his was a flimsy, unsubstantial crown.

During the lengthy process of annexation, Henry Lawrence, a Company employee, comes to the Punjab as the British Resident along with his brother John. The Lawrence brothers are in charge of cataloging the wealth of the Punjab Empire, and facilitating the shift of power from Maharajah Dalip Singh to the East India Company. However dismal their duties, they both, with great diplomacy, manage cordial relations with the Indians they meet during the annexation.

Maharajah Dalip Singh loses his Punjab, and his Kohinoor diamond, which becomes the property of the Queen of England. He follows it to London when he's sixteen years old and is feted and petted there for a long while, until he realizes that all the compensation granted to him cannot make up for the loss of his lands, and his diamond.

Four years after Maharajah Dalip Singh comes to England, in 1858, the British government dissolves the East India Company, and Victoria becomes Queen-Empress of India.

Colonialism begins in India at this date; all of a sudden the British are no longer traders or "Company" men—they are the masters . . . the British Raj has begun.

Here then, in *The Mountain of Light,* are the final chapters of the Kohinoor's existence in India, and the last few years before India loses her sovereignty and becomes a British colony.

Cast of Primary Characters

Paolo Avitabile — Italian soldier; governor of Peshawar; general in Maharajah Ranjit Singh's army

Fakir Azizuddin — Foreign minister to Maharajah Ranjit Singh

Cecilia Bowles — Lady Login's relative; Maharajah Dalip Singh's love interest

Dalip Singh — Fifth Maharajah of the Punjab Empire

Emily Eden — Lord Auckland's sister

Fanny Eden — Lord Auckland's sister

George, Lord Auckland — Governor-General of India (1836–1842)

Ibrahim Khan — Shah Shuja's foster brother

Jindan Kaur — Maharajah Ranjit Singh's wife; Maharajah Dalip Singh's mother

Henry Lawrence	Resident at Lahore (and Agent of the Governor-General of India) (1846–1856); Maharajah Dalip Singh's guardian
John Lawrence	Henry Lawrence's brother; Viceroy of India (1864–1869)
Dr. John Login	Bengal army surgeon; Maharajah Dalip Singh's guardian
Lena Login	John Login's wife; Maharajah Dalip Singh's guardian
Lieutenant Colonel Frederick Mackeson	Political agent to the Governor-General of India, Lord Dalhousie
Misr Makraj	State treasurer for Maharajah Ranjit Singh
Multan Raj	Lieutenant-Colonel Mackeson's servant; Misr Makraj's son
Captain Edward Ramsay	Military secretary to the Governor-General of India, Lord Dalhousie
Ranjit Singh	First Maharajah of the Punjab Empire (1799–1839)
Roshni	Betrothed to Dalip Singh; sister of Maharajah Ranjit Singh's adopted son, Sher Singh

Shah Shuja Durrani   Ruler of Afghanistan (1803–1809 and 1839–1842)

Sophia   Bamba Sophia Jindan; Maharajah Dalip Singh's oldest daughter

Victoria   Queen of Great Britain and Ireland (1837–1901); Empress of India (1876–1901)

Victoria Gouramma   Princess of the Coorg kingdom in India; Queen Victoria's goddaughter

Wafa Begam   Shah Shuja's wife

Harry Wingate   Owner and publisher of the *Bombay Herald*

Cast of Secondary Characters

Jean-François Allard	French soldier; general in Maharajah Ranjit Singh's army
Lady Anne Elizabeth Beaumont	Passenger aboard the SS *Indus*
Bhajan Lal	Maharajah Dalip Singh's tutor
Mary Booth	Passenger aboard the SS *Indus*
Thomas Booth	Passenger aboard the SS *Indus*; Mary Booth's brother
Major Bryne	Quartermaster in the British encampment; head of the Governor-General's hous›old in Calcutta
Lord Dalhousie	Governor-General of India (1848–1856)
Josiah Harlan	American; Maharajah Ranjit Singh's ambassador to Afghanistan
Martin Honigberger	Romanian; personal physician to Maharajah Ranjit Singh

William Huthwaite	Passenger aboard the SS *Indus*
Arabella-Catherine Hyde	Passenger aboard the SS *Indus*
Jimrud	Emily Eden's *jemadar* her personal butler
Honoria Lawrence	Henry Lawrence's wife
Mir Kheema	Maharajah Dalip Singh's attendant
Sher Singh	Fourth Maharajah of the Punjab Empire; Ranjit Singh's adopted son
Mr. Taft	Clerk at the East India Company, in charge of gifts given and received
Jean-Baptiste Ventura	Italian soldier; governor of Lahore; general in Maharajah Ranjit Singh's army
Captain Richard Watkins	Maharajah Dalip Singh's friend in London
Martyn Wingate	Harry Wingate's son; passenger aboard the SS *Indus*

The Mountain of Light

Fragment of Light

June 1817

The midday sun leaned over to place its fiery kiss upon the
Shalimar Gardens in Lahore, four and a half miles east of
the fort and walled city. The blazing light wavered into a
haze around the almond, guava, and mango trees, and except
under the trees where it could not penetrate, all shadows
leached into the blistering ground.

The Shalimar Gardens—the Abode of Pleasure—was
a name taken by the Mughal Emperor Shah Jahan from the
gardens his father had built in the valley of Kashmir. In the
late 1630s, the Ravi River in Lahore flooded its banks. Angry
waters swamped and carved out new geographical features,
shifting vast quantities of mud from one place to another, leaving acclivities and declivities where none had existed before.
One such slope in the land was born after this flood. So it was
here Emperor Shah Jahan ordered the garden to be built in
three terraces that descended from the south to the north.

At high noon on this day of June 1817, two young men
tarried in the central platform of the pool in the middle terrace.

They were both bareheaded, their chests bare also. Each wore only a *kispet*—long, tight shorts of buffalo hide leather, which covered them from their waists down, the ends rucked up over their knees to facilitate ease of movement. The upper halves of their bodies, and their legs and feet, glistened with sesame oil, pungent and aromatic in the sear of the sun. Earlier in the morning—according to the rules of the game—they had smoothed the oil on each other. It was the first and last gesture of amity and goodwill.

For their referee, they had corralled an old gardener lounging in the deep shade of the nearby tamarind tree, a hand-rolled *beedi* wrapped in his fist, smoke coiling out from between his fingers.

"Him?" Ibrahim Khan had asked, thick eyebrows elevated in disbelief.

His sovereign had shrugged, lifting massive, muscled shoulders. "As good as anyone else, Ibrahim. We know the rules ourselves. The only other man around is Zaman, and he's useless, as you know. Should I have to call upon one of the flowers in my *zenana* instead?"

Ibrahim grinned. "With respect, your Majesty, the women of your harem will only support you. And they're likely to squeal or curse in horror when I defeat you. Calling on them is not conducive to an even playing field."

A small smile flitted across Shah Shuja's face. And when it did, it lightened his features, brought a sparkle to his gray eyes, erased the embedded lines of worry on his forehead. Made him, so Ibrahim thought, more like the deeply powerful man he had known all of his life.

A tiny spear of ache stabbed Ibrahim's heart. They were far removed from what they had once been. Shuja had been born of a king—Shah Timur Durrani—whose father had established the Afghan Empire in the name of the Durrani dynasty. Timur had had many sons, of many wives, as was the established custom of the time. There was no law of primogeniture—the eldest son did not automatically inherit the throne. Nor was he gifted with quiescent brothers willing to live out their lives as governors of districts or provinces. At Timur's death, the throne had changed hands four times, one son or the other claiming it for his own for a brief while, driven from it when another had amassed enough of a threatening army. And so Shuja had lost his kingdom to his half brother Shah Mahmud.

Shah Shuja put a hand on Ibrahim's shoulder. "First, you will not defeat me. How is that even possible?" When the younger man opened his mouth to protest, he stilled the words with a wave. "It's true. I might be a little older, Ibrahim, and that only means I've been wrestling longer than you have. And second, my wives dote upon you. Although"— and he grinned again, a wicked gleam in his eye—"you *will* not win, they will minister to your injuries with enough of a fuss to make you happy."

Ibrahim bowed his head. "We'll see, your Majesty."

Every now and then, Shuja and Ibrahim indulged themselves in the games and play of their childhood. There was so little else for them to do at Lahore in the Shalimar Gardens, a place where they had spent the last three years as "guests" of the wily Maharajah Ranjit Singh. This wrestling match was one such, conjured up late the night before, when the last cup of wine had been drunk, when the moon had skated downward into the dark sky, when the *nautch* girls had slunk away, and they had both been lying on their divans, twitchy with pent-up energy. What to do on the morrow? How to spend their time? Each day was like the others, the same views, the same fountains, the same watch upon the sun and the moon— to mark interminable time—gliding over that limited arc of sky above the gardens.

The gardener had still been there last night, ensconced in a hollow in the trunk of the tamarind when they had both sprung up, vigorous, shouting for him to come to them.

He was a small, old man, his face carved in deep wrinkles that spanned out around his inscrutable eyes and curved in two semicircles from his nose to his mouth. His skin was a deep, clayey brown. His lower lip was crushed inward—he had no bottom teeth—and when he spoke, it was with slow, measured words that echoed out of the cavern of that mouth. Shuja had tried Persian first. "Do you know the rules of wrestling, my friend?"

He had stared at them, his chin swaying loosely in the lower half of his face. So Ibrahim had spoken to him in Urdu. Again, nothing. "Try Pashto," Shuja had said in an undertone in that language. No luck there either. Why would he know an Afghani tongue, similar as it was to Persian, which he was more likely to understand? "Where *does* he come from?" Shah Shuja had said, exasperated. Ibrahim Khan had tried Hindustani last, having exhausted the little bit of Arabic he knew. And then, the old man's mobile mouth had deepened into his face. "*Ji,* Sahib," he'd said. And so, pulling words out of their hybrid vocabulary, they had explained that they needed him at the Shalimar Gardens at noon, to referee their wrestling match. They had taught him how to start the match, how to stop it at an illegal hold, how to impose a penalty, how to restart it.

And now they stood at either end of the marble platform in the center of the pool in the middle terrace of the gardens, arms hanging loosely by their thighs. Aware, out of the corners of their eyes, of the old man under the tamarind.

Shuja saw his hand move, and shifted quickly upon his toes. The old man put his fingers into his mouth and let out a tart, prolonged whistle. Shuja veered in surprise—this was not how he was supposed to start the match. In that brief moment of distraction, he heard Ibrahim's feet smack on the heated marble floor before he flung himself on his king. Shuja fell backward, rocked off his balance. He felt his feet slipping, strained against Ibrahim, until they were locked in an embrace.

Their breaths escaped in harsh puffs. Ibrahim was smaller than Shah Shuja, shorter by a head's length, and he used that advantage to tuck his forehead under Shuja's arm and crush his ribs. They spun around the marble platform, holding desperately on to each other.

All of a sudden, Ibrahim's clutch slackened, and his arm snaked from Shuja's back to around his right thigh. He heaved. Shuja came crashing down upon his back. As Ibrahim straightened to straddle him, Shuja kicked out with his leg. Ibrahim flew into the air, briefly, before smashing to the floor himself.

When Shuja sprang upon him, Ibrahim rolled away and bounded up. They were already sweating when they started the match, but now moisture poured down from the thick hair on their heads and their beards. Shuja grappled with the slick skin on Ibrahim's legs—he had shaved his chest and legs that morning, so that Shuja would have no hair to hold on to—and finally wedged his fingers into the waistband of Ibrahim's *kispet*. Yanked him down.

Ibrahim yelled, "That's an illegal hold, referee!"

The old man, massaging his face in bemusement, whistled again. In the thick silence of the courtyard, the sound boomed. A flock of parrots in the tamarind rose in a protesting flurry of green feathers and red beaks and disappeared into the pale sky.

Shuja and Ibrahim hurled out of the hold and went to opposite ends of the platform. Their chests heaved; their stomachs caved inward and out as they drew breath into their tired lungs, outlining their ribs and their hip bones. Agony flared in Shuja's lower back. There was a shock of burning along his right forearm, which he had put out to take the brunt of the fall. Ibrahim stood at his corner, wiping the sweat from his eyes, smiling.

Smiling? Maybe there was some truth to the fact that he was younger and so stronger, Shuja thought. Although neither was really that old; Shah Shuja was thirty-two, Ibrahim twenty-nine.

They had not talked since the first whistle; no gibes, no trash, no filling the opponent's ear—and so his brain—with debilitating words. This was one of the rules of the game. It had to be played, and fought, in complete silence, with only muscle and brawn determining the winner. But the rules said nothing about facial expressions. An intimidating glare, a supercilious grin—like the one Ibrahim wore on his face— these were unaccountable quantities. Shah Shuja's breathing quieted, he felt his body come to rest again. He flexed the muscles in his arms. A sliver of iron lodged itself in his spine.

When the two minutes had passed, the old man, keeping count of the seconds by beating his crooked foot upon the ground and raising puffs of red mud, whistled again.

Shuja hurtled across and barreled into Ibrahim's chest. The force of the movement carried them over the knee-high marble lattice railing of the platform and out into the shallow pool. It was only luck that allowed them both to land upon the flat of the pool's surface and not on one of the lotus-bud-shaped fountains that speared upward.

The pool was littered with these fountains—a hundred and fifty-two in all—each spewing droplets of water that created a thousand rainbows in the sun. Here, the light was fractured, dazzle-bright. Shah Shuja shut his eyes and grappled, following only the sound of Ibrahim's breath and his groans. At one point, Ibrahim held his king's head under the water, only six inches deep at any place, but enough to suffocate. Shuja reached out blindly with a long arm to seize his throat, squeezed his fingers tight, until Ibrahim let go and he could heave up to gulp in some air.

Almost desultorily, the old man whistled again. He was learning, Shuja thought, as he climbed wearily back onto the platform and shuffled to his corner. The pool had a pebbled base, strewn with chunks of semiprecious stones—jasper, agate, carnelian—which created a glitter of colors under the water, and which had left deep gouges on their backs and chests and arms, streaked now with blood.

Two minutes was all they got again until the old man whistled and they met at the center of the platform. The sun had burned off the water and some of the oil; their holds were more secure. As his body spiraled into a bottomless exhaustion, Shah Shuja's brain snapped alive.

The hours passed. The sun slipped westward. On the pavilion of the upper terrace—the Aiwan—a lone woman came to stand under the arches and looked down upon the two men struggling on the platform, arms fastened around each other, eyes shut against the sweat that streamed down their faces.

Wafa Begam had been married to Shah Shuja for seventeen years. The first of his wives, she was the person he knew best. His mother had been in a harem, and as a boy, he was taken from it early, put into the men's quarters. There had been no actual friendship with other members of his family. Always lurking behind his half brothers was the silhouette of their father's crown, impossible to ignore. Shuja loved Ibrahim, but it was a friendship in the outside world.

When he was fifteen, his marriage was arranged with Wafa, also fifteen that year. And all of a sudden, he had found the comfort of home in the arms of this thin girl. Here, within the walls of his harem apartments, the young Shuja had confided in her his fears, his determination, his ambitions—and she had never laughed at them, never considered them impractical. Shuja's brother Shah Zaman ascended the throne of Afghanistan first, and then Shah Mahmud tore it away from him, throwing Zaman into prison, blinding him in both eyes with a piece of hot wire. And so Shuja built up his own army to overthrow Mahmud, ruled for nine years himself . . . and in 1809, when he moved his court from Kabul to

Peshawar, Mahmud sneaked up and grabbed Kabul and then marched on to Peshawar.

Wafa moved her slender hands restlessly in front of her, entangling her fingers in a veil which came over her head to her waist. To stay on in Peshawar, with Mahmud's army battering at the door, would have been death for all of them. The only option was to flee, to retreat, to find shelter elsewhere, to regroup and come back for Afghanistan. Shuja had woken her in the middle of the night and hurried her, along with the other women of his harem, to waiting horses and palanquins. "Go safely, my dear," he had said. At that last moment, when her hand reached out to him, when she swung her head through the gap in the curtains for one more look at her husband—not knowing if she would ever see him alive again—he pressed a packet into her hand and closed her fingers over it. "This will buy my life someday. Or"—his steady gaze met hers—"if I die, it will make you rich."

When Wafa unwrapped the satin cloth four days into their journey to the lands of the Punjab and Maharajah Ranjit Singh, she saw the armlet of heavy gold Shuja wore upon his person every day. The central diamond was mammoth, built with fire and light, flanked by two smaller diamonds. Shah Shuja had given her—the wife of his heart, the only woman he trusted—the Kohinoor diamond.

Wafa watched awhile, as one man and then the other pushed and jostled, as they fell with loud thuds upon the floor, as they broke the rules by snatching at beards or hair, as Shuja cried out when one of his fingers was caught in the railing of the platform and snapped with an audible crack. She flinched at that sound, but didn't move as they dragged themselves apart to rest. Her nose quivered and then wrinkled at the old man and his whistling. Wafa's veil, of a pure silk the color of newly opened pink roses at dawn scattered with dew, lay around her lean shoulders. Underneath she wore a short *choli*, a bodice that covered her breasts and was held together on her back with two strings; her waist was bare, and she had on pink silk trousers, tight on her hips, billowing around her thighs, caught up around the ankles. This was Wafa Begam's concession to living in India, adopting a part of the dress that kept her cool in the Lahore summers, and keeping the trousers that she wore normally in Afghanistan.

She shifted against one of the pillars of the Aiwan, resting her shoulder on it, her arms clasped around her waist. Her gaze drifted over the middle terrace to the old man at one side of the pool. He was squatting in the manner of a peasant, and a minute breeze brought the acrid tang of smoke from the smoldering *beedi* held in his hand. He turned, suddenly, to look at her. She stayed where she was. Not caring that her face was uncovered, not bothering to pull the veil over her eyes. What did it matter? The old gardener had never ascended to the upper terrace and the Aiwan, where she stood, because it was the most private part of the Shalimar Gardens, one marked out for the use of Shah Shuja's *zenana*. Such an old man could hardly have his blood boil at the sight of a woman from another man's harem . . . or be capable of doing anything about it. He was nothing. Just another servant from Maharajah Ranjit Singh's court, sent here to serve them.

She lifted her chin, looked pointedly away toward her husband and Ibrahim. There was dried, caked blood on their arms and chests. They moved slower and slower, doggedly, like two animals engaged in a mortal combat.

"Your Majesty, you must eat," a slave said behind her.

Wafa sighed. There was no point waiting for the men. There were rules in the wrestling match for penalties and illegalities, and even when and how the match started, but no rules for the ending. A few years ago, while Shah Shuja had still been the ruler of Afghanistan, he had wrestled with another man for eight hours—some matches had gone on for two days, or three, until one of the opponents had dropped dead in the dirt.

She put her fingertips to her mouth, kissed them, and then upended her palm and blew the kiss across the scorching air to her husband. Shuja reared his head, as though he had felt the touch of her lips upon him, and charged into Ibrahim with renewed vigor. Please Allah, she thought, as she walked away to the *shamiana* set at one end of the upper terrace where the slaves had laid out the food, let them not kill each other. Perhaps they wouldn't kill each other in any case; Shuja loved Ibrahim with the devotion of a brother, and Ibrahim could not live with himself if he caused any harm to Shuja. For a deposed king, there was no better friend than such a one as Ibrahim. She was worried, but only mildly, because she knew that the past three years of confinement—the past three years as Maharajah Ranjit Singh's "guest"—had fretted Shuja beyond measure. He needed to do something. Anything. He needed to return to Afghanistan as a king. But Maharajah Ranjit Singh would not let them go until they gave him the Kohinoor diamond.

Wafa Begam ate her food, bending over her plate, licking her fingers clean delicately, listening to the snorts and rumbles that floated upward to the *zenana* terrace, her demeanor cool. She could have been feasting at a festival while still Queen of Afghanistan, so calm was she. But then, she was also the woman who had kept the Kohinoor safe from the greedy Ranjit Singh and not let him have it for all the long years he had held her—and her husband—in captivity.

In the end, the match lasted only until the sun set, at six o'clock. And then, only because the heated sun fell gratefully into the arms of the cool earth, and darkness pounced upon Lahore. There was no twilight to speak of, no smudging of the sun's golden rays into pale blues and blacks, this close to the center of the earth. Shuja's whole arm was aflame; in one rest period he had ripped a strip of cloth from the knee of his *kispet* and wrapped it around the broken index finger of his left hand, binding only two fingers together so that he could have the rest to hold on to Ibrahim. But it hadn't helped. The hurt had crept up his arm and sent tentacles of torture over his shoulder and neck.

Ibrahim hadn't fared any better. He had cuts and gashes all over his back and his chest, blood encrusted in some spots, fresh in others, where Shuja's nails had ripped through the wounds. He was also limping from having twisted his ankle sometime during that afternoon.

An hour before sunset, the slaves would normally light all the oil lamps, the *diyas* made of terra-cotta, the size of small and shallow cups. Some were in niches under the waterfalls that brought water down from one terrace to the other along the central pool, some along the pathways on either side of the pool, some under the trees, some in them, hung in little woven baskets of jute and silk thread. When darkness came, the whole of the gardens would live again in pinpoints of light picked out here and there like a glittering sprinkle of diamonds, mirroring the stars in the night sky above.

Shuja shouted out, "Light the lamps!" He was still shoving against Ibrahim, using force from the right side of his body—his left arm lay almost useless. Ibrahim's hair, rank with sweat, was rammed into his chest, just under his nose. But Shuja did not smell him, because he stank as much as Ibrahim did, and in any case, it was difficult to distinguish what he was smelling—blood, sweat, heated oil, the spray of water. His eyes burned and had turned red. His sight was blurred. It was time to stop the match—they were both out of shape after years of sloth and imprisonment. But Shah Shuja, the erstwhile ruler of Afghanistan, was a stubborn, tenacious man, or he would not have held that title of king, nor—as he was determined—would he become king again by giving up anything so easily.

Ibrahim, on the other hand, was simply obstinate. He was

more exhausted than he cared to acknowledge. They had missed their afternoon meal and their cup of *chai* in the evening, and he craved both. His body seemed beaten into hollowness.

"Light the lamps now!" Shuja roared. Ibrahim cringed as his master's voice exploded over his eardrums, but he did not let go. His head, slick with perspiration, moved here and there on Shuja's chest, seeking a hold, so that the grip of his fingers could be more secure. The cuts and bruises on his skin stung as sweat rolled over and into them.

In the echoing silence after Shuja's last demand, a voice, tranquil and musical, called out from above their heads. "Enough, my lord."

Shuja raised his head in the gloom, his eyes seeking the direction of his wife's voice. Ibrahim Khan shifted, and Shuja's attention, honed to a fine edge, came crashing back on his opponent. He sensed, even in that brief moment, that Ibrahim's concentration had wavered, that the younger man had lost some of his grit, that Wafa's voice had recalled to him the pleasure of a silken divan with overstuffed cushions, of a woman's soft touch, of comfort and ease. That he had been distracted and that his will to kill, to win, to defeat, had been shaken.

In that second of slackness, Shah Shuja propelled Ibrahim to the very edge of the platform and slammed him against the railing. When Ibrahim fell onto the floor, Shuja scrambled in the dark and heaved himself over him, forcing his back flat on the marble slabs. He straddled Ibrahim and said, triumphant and shaking from the effort, "Enough, Ibrahim?"

"I give up, your Majesty." Ibrahim's voice was trembling and thin.

In the Aiwan pavilion above, Wafa Begam reached behind her and uncovered an oil lantern. She held it high up above her head, and the honeyed light spilled over her arms and her face, and below, over the waters of the pool with its now silent fountains, and the two men on the platform in the middle of the pool, their heads drooping with fatigue, their chins collapsed into their chests.

"Come to the *zenana*, your Majesty," she called out. "Ibrahim, you come also," and when he wearily shook his head, she said, "Don't be silly, you need care also. And, this won't be the first time you've come into the harem quarters."

It wasn't.

To Shuja, Ibrahim Khan was more kin than his actual half brothers. They did not have the same father, but they had the same mother, or rather they had both drunk the milk of the same mother. And that tied them together in a bond that nothing else could. As with all royal families, Shuja's first taste of nourishment had come from a wet nurse's plump breast, not that of the woman who had given birth to him. Three years later, the wet nurse had given birth to another boy—Ibrahim. It would have been natural for Shuja to have chosen the child his foster mother had had just before he was born as his playmate. Instead, at three, still being fed by his foster mother, he had stood at her knee as the newborn baby wrapped his tiny palm around Shuja's little finger and held on with a might that had surprised him. Ibrahim had then trailed Shuja through his own apartments and gifted to him the devotion none of his own half brothers had.

When Shuja had crushed Mahmud to become king, it was Ibrahim who had led his armies and who had kept the crown safe for Shuja. When Mahmud had yet again come roaring back to take Afghan lands, Shuja had sent his harem to the Punjab under Ibrahim's care . . . because there was no other man he could trust with his most precious possession, more precious to him than the kingdom, the wealth of that kingdom, or even the Kohinoor diamond. Ibrahim had had entry into Shah Shuja's *zenana* from the time Wafa Begam stepped into it. He was to the women as much their brother as he was their husband's.

And so Wafa had them both brought by the stairs that

led up on either side of the Aiwan into the upper terrace, and there, under the cloak of the starlit sky, she bathed their wounds, applied poultices, watched over them as they slept, mumbling, restless, and in pain, twisting the silk sheets around their limbs. As the night wore on, she plied the peacock feather fan herself, laid a cool hand on their fiery brows, sang little songs in the dark to soothe their fevered dreams.

They had all forgotten about the old man. When the night came to claim the skies, and Wafa Begam led her husband and his foster brother away, he backed down the long central pathway that flanked the pool to the lower terrace. There, he slid down the ramp, cut across the quadrangle of skillfully trimmed lawns, and let himself out of the West Gate. The guards inside, five of them, standing shoulder to shoulder across the archway, stiffened to attention when they saw his slow, shambling figure approach.

One raised his spear and pointed the end at the old man's concave stomach, its honed tip drawing a thin splinter of blood on the skin.

The man's head snapped up. His back straightened, the muscles in his back and his legs seemed to take on new life, became plump and rigid. His eyes, which had been wandering and watery, glittered in the light of the lamps in the archway's niches.

When he spoke, his voice was sturdy, nothing like the rambling drawl he had affected in the middle terrace while in Shuja's and Ibrahim's presence. "You dare to draw *my* blood?"

The guard's hand shook. The old man wrapped a finger around the base of the spear's blade and nudged it away.

The outer door opened, and a captain in Maharajah Ranjit Singh's army poked his head in. "Retreat, you fools!"

he said quietly. When the guards fell out of formation, he came in through the gap, his hands folded across his waist. "I beg pardon, *huʐoor*. They are new, know nothing about who you are."

The old man bent his head and contemplated the line of blood on his stomach. It was nothing, a mere scratch. He mopped it away and then wiped his hand on the folds of his dirty *dhoti*. "I appreciate," he said, "the enthusiasm of these young men. It is vital that they question every person who enters and leaves the Shalimar. No harm done."

The captain bowed, the guards bowed, and the old man slipped out of the West Gate. Neither of them knew who he was, or why he had access to the Shalimar Gardens, where the Maharajah held Shah Shuja captive, only that he was someone of importance, a man it would be wise not to cross. The captain very much wanted to ask if the man would forget this little incident and not mention it to his king . . . but he did not know how to do this.

The old man strode across the expanse of beaten mud outside the West Gate to the group of horsemen waiting at the far end. One of them brought a frolicking black horse to him, and running, he put one foot in a stirrup and heaved himself over its back. Even before he had settled in the saddle, he kicked his heels into its flanks. The entire party vanished in a froth of dust west toward the fort at Lahore, the lights from their torches smearing through the darkness and then fading away.

As he rode, Fakir Azizuddin felt around the waistline of his *dhoti* and undid a small bundle. The set of lower teeth, of the purest ivory, fashioned by the Maharajah's personal physician, Martin Honigberger, he popped into his mouth and maneuvered his tongue around until they lodged into place. As he did so, his lower lip filled out, the slope of his mouth became less awkward, his jawline firmed, and the years tumbled from his face. Azizuddin, foreign minister in Maharajah Ranjit Singh's court, was as old as his king that year—thirty-seven.

He had lost his teeth when a gang of the Akalis had swooped upon him in the middle of the night in Lahore, as he was returning home from an audience with his sovereign. This was before Ranjit Singh had subdued these most unlawful and marauding of warriors and made the Akalis part of his entourage and members of his personal bodyguards.

Azizuddin's massacre of the four men who had jumped upon him in an unlit alleyway had been instrumental in bringing about this submission. The first fist into his face had knocked out his teeth. With a hanging chin, blood streaming down his neck and drenching his clothes, Azizuddin had spun around in the darkness, his quick eye noting the positions of his assailants, his ears attuned to their breathing. A quoit, the Akali's most powerful weapon, a slender circle of sharpened steel, had come whizzing through the air. Azizuddin had ducked and sent his dagger flying in the direction of the thrower. He had had only a sword left, and with it, deliberately, he'd slashed through each of the three men and left them cut up on the ground. The next morning, with a white, blood-mottled bandage securing his jaw to the upper half of his face, Azizuddin had listened as the Akali leader came to ask for a pardon. "Granted," Azizuddin had said simply, "if you lay your arms down to my sovereign."

Every now and then, minor rebellions among the Akalis flared up, were quickly squashed, the rebels killed on the spot with no trial, no thought—this was justice they understood and bowed to.

Indeed, Azizuddin thought, leaning forward in his saddle, the rush of the wind in his ears, his skin cooling after the day spent in the heated embrace of the sun, it was the Akalis who formed, now, part of his bodyguard also. As the men created a tight circle around him, matching the pace of his horse, the light from the torches glanced off their quoits, which they insisted on wearing around their necks. The inner ring of the quoit was all dulled steel, easy to grasp, and if this touched their necks it was no danger at all. When an enemy threatened, the Akali pulled it over his head without mussing his turban or his hair and flung it in one movement—in less than two seconds.

Azizuddin had no personal vanity at all, so the loss of his teeth didn't bother him. Only women ought to think of how they looked, how they smelled, whether their conversation was pleasing and pleasant. For many years, Azizuddin had served his master with a shattered jaw until he quite got used to speaking out of the side of his mouth. And then, a physician from Transylvania, Honigberger, had come to the Maharajah's court at Lahore. He was one of the many foreigners who had honed in on Ranjit Singh, having heard of his generous pay and his openness to odd men who could not make their way elsewhere. Honigberger had cured the king's headaches with a pink powder, something none of the other *hakims* at court had been able to do, and so he'd toppled them to take their position. One day he'd said, in his diffident, half-finished Persian, to Azizuddin that he could make him new teeth that would fit as well as his old. Out of a pale wood? No, ivory—it would never break and he could chew on the toughest meats in the kingdom and make a mince of them in no time. And so, Azizuddin had gotten his teeth. They had wiped years off his face, and he took the teeth out when he wanted to opt for a disguise.

The streets of Lahore were clotted with the bluish gray smoke of cooking fires, making it hard to see, but a sure sense of direction led the horsemen through one alley and then another. Dogs barked at their passing, children squealed; at one point an urchin skipped across their path, his hair flying, just missing being clipped by Azizuddin's horse's hooves. The city fell away behind them as they approached the Masti Darwaza, the easternmost entry into Lahore Fort.

Here, the reception was kinder to Fakir Azizuddin. His Akalis drew in their horses as the giant, metal-studded doors swung open, and he raced through the gateway. Before he could look back, the doors had swung shut. Azizuddin slowed his horse to a canter, rode across the courtyard of the Diwan-i-am, the Hall of Public Audience, and to the westernmost end. Here, he jumped down from the saddle and lobbed the reins to the waiting syces. He then turned right and north and went along a corridor to the northwesternmost corner of the fort, which housed the Shah Burj and the Naulakha buildings, both of which opened out into a square, red-sandstone-paved courtyard.

Just like the Shalimar Gardens, this fort had been built, some two hundred years ago, by the Mughal Emperor Shah Jahan. Now, the Mughal Empire had fallen to pieces, shrunken its boundaries to just the city of Delhi. And all the splendor of Lahore—the fort, the city, the gardens— belonged to Azizuddin's king, Ranjit Singh, who was ruler of the Punjab Empire.

Fakir Azizuddin padded on light feet through the court-yard, past the fountain, and up the steps into the Sheesh Mahal, the northernmost part of the Shah Burj. Here, lamps were lit in every niche, and true to its name, the Sheesh Mahal—the Palace of Mirrors—glittered and hurled light back into every corner from its mirrored walls. Azizuddin passed into the riverside apartments and looked down and out toward the Ravi River. The Maharajah was a lone figure on a horse in the *maidan*, the expanse of mud that crept from the walls of the fort to the banks of the river. Azizuddin stood watching until Ranjit Singh glanced up at him and raised his hand.

In the quiet of the night, the Maharajah's voice came clear and strong. "Come down, Azizuddin, you have news?"

"Yes, your Majesty," Azizuddin shouted. Then, he turned and ran back out to the Hall of Public Audience and, from there, through the western gate and around the walls of the fort, through the scrub to where his king waited for him.

The Shalimar Gardens were laid out in an elongated rectangle, south to north. There were three terraces—the highest one on the southern end, ten feet above the middle terrace, which was also ten feet above the lower terrace. This demarcation in height created the public and private spaces in the gardens. The upper terrace, which housed the pavilion of the Aiwan on its southernmost end, was for the women of the harem. The middle terrace, in the center of whose pool Shuja and Ibrahim had wrestled, was the semiprivate courtyard—here, again, while in residence, the Mughal emperors had met with the grandees of the Empire, or held amusements in the form of musical nights under the stars, and the orchestra would sit on the platform in the center of the pool, the Emperor himself on a marble throne which jutted out into the pool. The lower terrace was essentially the Hall of Public Audience. It had gateways leading into it from the northern, eastern, and western walls—the last of which Fakir Azizuddin had left through to go to Lahore Fort.

A long channel cut through the gardens in the middle from the south to the north, and thus had Emperor Shah Jahan brought his water feature into every terrace. Where the water descended from one terrace to the next, there were miniature cascades over marble walls littered with niches in which to light lamps on dark nights, and the water then flowed into the central pool in each terrace, and on its way down through the channel.

Wafa Begam had taken her husband and Ibrahim into the upper terrace to sleep. Their beds were made under the stars, close to the pool in the center. A few coal braziers were set around the quadrangle formed by the water channels. Dried *neem* leaves curled and charred in the fire of the braziers, sending pungent clouds of smoke into the air to keep away mosquitoes and insects.

A lamp, its flame shaded by glass and a wooden cap, squatted by her side. Wafa leaned against Shuja's bed, seated on the marble floor, and ate her evening meal. Every now and then, she tilted the plate toward the light so as to better see what she was eating, but it all looked the same. A mass of curry, the *naan* soggy in the gravy, the vegetables wilted in the heat, the taste unmemorable. Still, she ate it, licked her fingers, and wiped her plate clean. Then, she rose to wash her hands in the cool waters of the pool and came back to kneel by her sleeping husband's bed. She rested her elbows on the edge of the cot, her hands clasped under her chin, and watched the rise and fall of breath in his chest.

When he stirred, uneasy, she laid her face against his arm and waited for his breathing to even again. She stayed like that for a long while. Across the courtyard was Ibrahim's bed, which he had insisted on dragging to the far end. He lay on his side, faced away, trying to put as much physical distance as he could between them and him, still fretting about being in the courtyard of Shah Shuja's *zenana*.

Wafa placed a gentle kiss on Shuja's forehead and then took the lantern with her to the water channel and sat down on the sun-warmed stone. She undid the long row of diamond buttons that held her pajamas around her ankles, folded up the cloth around her shins, and put her feet in the tepid, swirling water. The servants had all retired for the night— or rather, she had sent them away, but she still looked long and hard around the courtyard, stopping at the shadows on the walls to see if they moved, listening above the noise of the water for sounds that were unnatural, man-made. Nothing. She reached into the bodice of her blouse and took out a sweat-smeared, crumpled piece of paper, which she held up to the lamplight.

It was another letter from Maharajah Ranjit Singh. It had pretty beginnings, a flowery middle, a complimentary end, but in essence it was—as so many others had been—a demand for the Kohinoor diamond.

She had promised it to the Maharajah herself, with her own mouth, so the letter said. And it was true, Wafa thought, chewing on her lower lip. Shuja had asked her to buy his freedom with the Kohinoor, and when Wafa first came to the Punjab, five years ago, she had figuratively dangled the diamond in front of Ranjit Singh. And he, ravenous, had wanted it. But, she had said, drawing it away from his avaricious grasp, she would be honored to gift the Kohinoor to the Maharajah, if only . . . she were happy enough to do so. With her husband languishing in jail in Kashmir, such joy was beyond her now.

When Wafa came to the Punjab, Shuja himself had fled east from Peshawar to Kashmir, which was also, then, part of Afghanistan. Here, he had hoped to gather an army and push back at his brother Mahmud, west into Peshawar again and then into Kabul. Instead, the wily governor of Kashmir—who had long chafed against Afghan rule—had thrown Shuja into prison and declared himself independent of Afghanistan.

Where is the Kohinoor diamond? Ranjit Singh had asked. Wafa, who had the diamond tucked into the sleeve of her blouse, had said that it was with her husband, in his prison cell, and only freeing him would free the diamond.

So Maharajah Ranjit Singh had sent an army thundering into Kashmir, annexed it to his Punjab Empire, and brought Shah Shuja to Lahore to reunite him with his wife. Shuja and his belongings were extensively searched during that journey to Lahore, and no Kohinoor came to light. This was when the Maharajah had realized the trick that had been played on him—but, no matter, a grateful Wafa, content in her husband's arms, would soon give him the diamond.

For good measure, while his armies were up north, Ran-

jit Singh had conquered and annexed Peshawar also and sent
Shah Mahmud back to a whittled Afghanistan that contained
now only the lands around Kabul.

The light from the lantern dimmed, the glass encrusted
with a swarm of moths that lit upon it and dashed away. The
cicadas, which had begun their sharp chirping when the sun
set, had increased their sounds. It was to this lullaby that
Wafa slept, if she slept at all. She put down the letter and
flicked a finger against the lantern, dislodging the moths for a
few, brief seconds.

For all the loveliness, quiet, and repose in the Shalimar,
this was merely a luxurious prison. Guards were stationed
outside its perimeter. Nothing was allowed in without
being inspected. Every servant was in the employ of the
Maharajah.

The night air cooled suddenly, and Wafa, born and
brought up among the snow-clad mountains of Afghanistan,
shivered in this little bit of chill. She lay back on the pathway
and looked up at the skies. Ranjit Singh had been very patient
with them for five years—two when she had been here in
Lahore, and these past three more since Shuja had been rescued from Kashmir and brought to her. Wafa spread her
fingers out over the stone. The Maharajah could have killed
them at any time and no one would have said nay. It was . . .
almost his right, as their jailer, to do so. She had no illusions
about Ranjit's generosity—the Kohinoor stayed his hand. If
they died without telling him where it was, chances were that
he would never find it, or that some minion would, and he
would never possess it. So they kept their lives, because their
hearts were tethered by a thin line of light to the diamond. A
tiny fragment of light.

In the meantime, when the Maharajah was out of sorts,
edgy, stopped their supplies of food or water, or sent them
testy messages, Wafa had persuaded Shah Shuja to give
up their other treasures. And so, they had sent him smaller

gemstones—diamonds, rubies, topazes; a gold- and jewel-
encrusted *hukkah;* and finally, the entire state pavilion, a tent
of the finest wool, embroidery in gold and silver thread on
every inch of the fabric, a silver chair upon which Shuja had
held court.

Wafa Begam rose from the pathway and walked up and
down, leaving wet footprints on the sandstone that seemed to
dry almost as soon as she made them. She glanced at her husband, and then at Ibrahim. As much as Ranjit Singh kept them
alive for the sake of the Kohinoor, once he had it, their lives
would be worth less than nothing. *Something* had to be done.
What? Who would help them now? Whom could they turn to?

Her head jerked up when a thin whistle fractured the
cacophony of the cicadas. The tune was familiar, one she
had heard many years ago. A horse snorted outside the garden's walls. Wafa ran to the sound. The thick brick walls rose
above her, faced with two rows of blind arches, rosebud mer-
lons on the top. It was hard to see anything. And then, she
heard a whoosh through the air, and a rock came tumbling
over the edge of the wall, fell onto the grass with a small thud.

Wafa waited, her heart pounding in her chest. What was
this? An attack? She nudged the rock with her foot. A brown
paper was tied around it with a string. She ran back to the
lamp with the rock, undid the knot, and spread out the paper
on the pathway. The letter that had thus crudely come into
the garden was in a rough Persian.

When she looked up again, her eyes were shining and all
worry had fled. Wafa went to Shuja's bed and woke him with
a kiss upon his forehead.

"Is it morning yet?" he asked.

"It might well be for us, my lord," she said, holding out
the letter to him.

* * *

Fakir Azizuddin pounded across the dry dirt of the *maidan* and came to a halt a few feet away from his king. The fort's walls loomed behind them, and golden light spilled out in a shifting pattern from the Shah Burj, from where Azizuddin had been commanded down.

Ranjit Singh's horse, Leili, snickered and bent her lovely head to nuzzle against Azizuddin's shoulder. He felt the touch of her wet, warm muzzle on his neck and patted Leili absently. She sniffed and drew back, shaking her head this way and that as the Maharajah let go of his reins and said with a laugh, "You haven't paid her enough attention, Azizuddin. She's upset with you. I suppose you have nothing to give her in that getup of yours?" When the minister shook his head, Ranjit slid his hand into the pouch hanging from his cummerbund and threw chunks of brown sugar—*jaggery*—to him.

Azizuddin caught each piece deftly, his fingers nipping at the air, and held out an open palm to the horse. Leili's rough tongue scraped the *jaggery* off his skin, and then she touched his head with hers.

The Maharajah of the Punjab rubbed Leili's arched neck with his thick hands, gentle as though he held a child. He bent to whisper in her ear, to pat her flanks, and Azizuddin felt a flood of adoration choke his chest. It was like this no matter how many times he was in his sovereign's presence, and as Ranjit Singh's foreign minister, one of the few men he trusted implicitly, Azizuddin met with and saw him almost every day. Unless he was away from Lahore on the Maharajah's business.

Azizuddin had known Ranjit since 1799, the year the nineteen-year-old boy had conquered Lahore. Azizuddin's father had been a scholar in the city—their family had long ties to its history, and had served every ruler. For the first few days of his rule, Ranjit had kept the father by his side, and one day had been asked for and granted permission to bring the sons to the king. Azizuddin could still remember that first meeting, clear as though it had been carved into his brain.

Ranjit Singh had not been—and still wasn't—a handsome man. Almost unprepossessing in fact. Short of stature, compact with thick-muscled legs and shoulders, a solid head crowned by a turban, his clothing so nondescript that he could have been a man on the street. No jewelry, no embroidery. Just a chunky dagger slipped into his cummerbund, its hilt caked with diamonds.

This was their new king, Azizuddin had thought with wonder. This child—no, that he had amended in his head, because both Aziz and Ranjit were nineteen years old—this youth with a scraggly beard had managed to subjugate the greatest city on earth? His father, sage and old, had spoken eloquently at home of their sovereign, of his intelligence, of his very presence. Azizuddin had looked down at the floor, shifted uncomfortably on his feet, felt a frisson of unease that his father had been so taken in by this . . . impostor. And then Ranjit Singh had laughed, at something another courtier said. And the sound, pure and hearty, had wrapped itself around Azizuddin's heart. Even that laugh had the confidence and the power of a king.

They had talked then. Ranjit had asked Azizuddin what he had studied; he had listened to the answers and, with a charming, self-deprecating shrug, had declared that he himself was illiterate, and so in awe of anyone with a little learning. Would Azizuddin teach him? Yes, your Majesty, anytime. Come every day then. The questions had come pounding out of the Maharajah with a force and alacrity that had surprised even the young Azizuddin. There was nothing Ranjit Singh was not curious about. The sun, the moon, the stars, the country of America, the British in Europe, the philosophies in Sanskrit, in Persian, in Arabic, in Pashto. What and why and how and when—everything began here and ended here. Azizuddin read out loud to Ranjit every night, and every morning, and while he struggled himself to remember the masses of information, it seemed to have soaked into his master's skin.

Devotion had come to rest in Fakir Azizuddin then, along with a fierce loyalty to this man who was, truly, meant to be king.

"What news?" Ranjit Singh asked now. His whisperings had brought peace to Leili, and she stood quiet, picking her feet off the ground in a gentle, rhythmic trot. On his horse, any horse, the Maharajah loomed larger than his normal self. It was as though he was one with the animal. He could persuade Leili to do almost anything; why, he had fought a war with an Afghani governor to win her, more than he had done for any of his wives. Leili was an Arabian of the purest stock, midnight black, with a white star upon her right flank and a blending of white on her high tail. When she had been brought into the Maharajah's stables, she had been finicky, demanding, snipping at her keepers with her strong, white teeth. Only Ranjit Singh had calmed her; one touch from him, one word, and her ears had quivered, her amber eyes had swung toward him, and from that day onward she would not allow anyone else to ride her.

"They wrestled, your Majesty," Azizuddin said with a smile, thinking that he was himself much like the horse. They both had the same affection for this man.

Ranjit sighed and rubbed his forehead. "Again? And where is the Kohinoor?"

Azizuddin bit his lip. "I don't know, your Majesty. I've tried to find out. Two months"—he spread out his hands— "and I still don't know. I think the wife has it hidden somewhere. Perhaps Shah Shuja himself is unaware of where."

The Maharajah ran his fingers through his beard, which was disheveled and to his waist, picked out now with strands of white hair. He was dressed as humbly as the first time Azizuddin had met him, in a long saffron-hued tunic, white pajamas, his turban white, the same dagger in his cummerbund. There was a single ring of silver upon the middle finger of his right hand with an enormous pearl set in it, and no other jewelry. At one point, a few years ago, he had said to Aziz that he would wear the Kohinoor when he got it. When, not if, Azizuddin had noted, because, as in all else, Ranjit Singh had no doubts that the diamond belonged to him. After all these years of waiting, it was rightfully his.

So, hesitantly, Azizuddin said, "Your Majesty, you have been generous, almost too generous with Shah Shuja. Why not just . . . um . . . end his life? And take the Kohinoor? It has to be somewhere in the Shalimar Gardens; we would find it, upturn every slab of stone in the gardens if need be."

Leili stepped sideways, carrying her rider out of pale light that flowed from the apartments above, and Azizuddin could no longer see his king. His voice, though, came in a slow and thoughtful rumble. "Aziz, there's no use in taking life needlessly. I've never done so before; I don't intend to do so now."

No, Aziz thought, he never had. In all the wars, the conquests, the battles, the life of every loser had been spared. Other kings in similar situations would not have been— and had not been—this kind. And, after all, Shah Shuja and his family had come to the Punjab in search of refuge, and though they had been granted it, they hadn't fulfilled the exact terms of their promise. The trophies they had sent were now stuffed into the Maharajah's overflowing Toshakhana, the treasury house. So why this hankering for the Kohinoor? He asked Ranjit Singh.

"Because it belongs here, Aziz. With me, in India. The Kohinoor *is* India—take it away from the country and the light departs along with it. You know that it was mined here, that even Hindu mythology puts it in the hands of the mortals as a gift from the gods?"

Azizuddin nodded. "But," he said, a twinkle in his eye.

Ranjit Singh laughed into the dark night, that same rich sound that had thrilled the young Aziz. "But, I want it. I want to own it. I want to be the man who had the Kohinoor in his possession. I want to be the one who breaks the curse upon it—that only a woman could own it and keep her life. Hmmm"—now he turned reflective—"maybe that is why Wafa Begam has been able to keep it from me for so long. What is she like?"

The question took Azizuddin by surprise. "Why," he said, and then stumbled over his words, "she has beauty, a strong voice—I've heard it more than once; her husband relies upon her. She halted the wrestling match today. They might have killed each other by the end of it, if she hadn't stopped it. She's a woman, your Majesty. What other terms could I possibly describe her by?"

"Shabbily done, Azizuddin. I wish I could see her myself."

"Would you want to, your Majesty?"

"No . . . perhaps. For the last five years she has sent me sweet letters with honeyed words, knowing full well that I want the Kohinoor, and yet she's managed to keep it away from me. She has the saccharine tongue of a diplomat, Azizuddin. You'd do well to learn from this."

Azizuddin nodded somberly. If it hadn't been for his disguise as the old gardener, he himself would never have seen Shuja's wife. For someone who had been brought up cloistered, who spent her whole life within the harem's walls, she had a knife-edge brain.

His attention was distracted when a torch flared to life on the outer edge of the *maidan*. The sudden flame stabbed the dark night sky before it settled into a more steady blaze. The man holding it walked toward them and then bent to the ground and set his torch upon a wooden peg, which caught fire. He kept on, heading in their direction, until a line of gold, from pegs hammered into the ground, created a blazing stroke upon the dry earth.

"What is—"

"You'll see," the Maharajah said. "Now!" he shouted.

At his voice, a man emerged from the darkness, astride a horse, riding hard toward the pegs. He had a spear in his outflung right hand, holding it well away from his body. As his horse charged, kicking up a blur of dust, he bent from his waist, his head level with the horse's head, and aimed the shining tip of his spear at the first peg. The tip went through the peg, and he lifted it into the air as he rode away and disappeared beyond the perimeter of light. Before a bemused Azizuddin could see a soldier on the side pull the flaming peg off the spear, the sound of horses' hooves thundered over the *maidan* and another man came into view.

In all, there were three men, and one by one, they sliced the pegs cleanly from the mud, not lessening the speed of their gallop, and riding away to divest their spears of the pegs before returning again. At the end of the demonstration, as each speared peg was extinguished, darkness pounced back over them. There was only the reek of spent fire, a bluish gray haze of smoke, and the tired canter of horses being led away.

It had been impeccably done. Tent pegging was not a sport for the faint of heart; it required tremendous concentration, a gimlet eye, an unshakable seat. Tumbling from the horse at that speed, spear in hand, or mistakenly plunging the spear into the earth and ricocheting from the saddle—either of these could mean death or a grievous maiming.

"Did they pass the test, your Majesty?" Azizuddin asked with a grin. He had identified the third man—Paolo Avitabile; difficult not to do so, Aziz thought, he was some seven feet tall, thickset, broad-shouldered, and when he rode his horse—although he rode it well—it looked like a dog between his legs.

"Will you hire them?"

Ranjit Singh tapped his right thumb into the palm of his left hand, as he always did, unconsciously, when he was deep in thought, and Azizuddin heard this—the dull thwack of skin against skin.

As the Maharajah's foreign minister, Fakir Azizuddin had a motley bunch of spies embedded in all parts of the Punjab Empire. And it was his job, and so consequently the job of his spies, to ferret out all foreigners on Ranjit Singh's land and send notice of them to the court. One such message had come a few months ago from Peshawar. That there were *firangis* looking for employ. And so Azizuddin had gone to Peshawar and found three tough, rough men. Paolo Avitabile, he of the huge height, was Italian. So also was Jean-Baptiste Ventura; and their friend, Jean-François Allard, was French. All the three men had been soldiers, adventurers, in Napoleon Bonaparte's armies and had set out east in the early days when Napoleon had cast his gaze toward an Indian empire.

They had halted at Persia and found positions in the Shah's army. As a consequence, they all spoke fluent Persian but also—and this came as a surprise to Azizuddin—more than a smattering of Hindustani. Why they had left the Shah of Persia's services, Azizuddin did not inquire. He did not care, and neither did Maharajah Ranjit Singh.

Aziz had escorted the men to Lahore, introduced them to Ranjit Singh, watched and listened to all of their conversations with his sovereign. The men were not mere soldiers—they were leaders, and they came in search of generalships in the Punjab army; nothing else would do for them.

"I'm going to send Avitabile to Peshawar, Aziz," the Maharajah said. "It's a city filled with dissidents, maybe he can cut them down to shape, create some order in that wild land."

"A good idea, your Majesty. Perhaps his very size will intimidate most of Peshawar. And the others?"

Ranjit Singh clicked his tongue. "They will be useful also. Here, training the armies. Send an imperial order to them, will you? Avitabile goes to Peshawar; make him a governor, some title of authority, so he can actually be useful there. He should have control over the revenues also. And choose a regiment for Allard and Ventura—they begin tomorrow, at dawn. I want to see maneuvers from their men in ten days."

"Yes, your Majesty." Azizuddin brushed his nape, easing the ache there. His shoulders hurt also from all the hunching, and being in the guise of the old man all day long. He twisted his head this way and that, wishing he weren't so exhausted. Because there was something he wanted to say to Ranjit; it was important, or could be. But what? He sifted, in his weary head, through all the communications that had come to his desk that morning, before he left for the Shalimar Gardens. Something to do with . . . someone in Lahore. An errant handful of breeze waved the smoke of the tent peg fires under the minister's nose. He inhaled, was reminded of the *firangis* who had sped down the *maidan* . . . and thought then of another *firangi*.

The Maharajah had swung off his horse meanwhile and come up to him. He put his hand on Aziz's shoulder. Standing thus, they were the same height. His voice was gentle. "Go home, my friend. I will see you tomorrow."

"Your Majesty!" Azizuddin clutched at his sovereign's hand. "The Englishman, Elphinstone, is here in Lahore. He arrived two days ago."

The Maharajah of the Punjab was blind in one eye—his left one, from a childhood bout of smallpox, which had also pitted the skin on his face. When Aziz looked at his king, he saw a handsome, sharply cut face, the bottom half enveloped in an unkempt beard, the eyebrows thick but cleanly arched, the expanse of forehead smooth, as though nary a thought had ruffled it. Even the blind eye was not evident really. Both of the Maharajah's eyes were a very pale shade of gray, the

irises ringed in black, brilliant like polished silver. The blind
eye was fixed in one direction, which gave Ranjit a mild
squint, but this Aziz always forgot, because when his good
eye gazed upon him, blazed upon him, he was drawn into the
man who possessed it.

"Why didn't you tell me earlier?" Ranjit Singh's voice
was biting. His eye still flared at his minister, who now had
his head bent miserably, the deep hues of a blush darkening
his already brown skin.

There were many reasons why, of course. He had known
only this morning, and he had been at the Shalimar all day,
and for a brief moment there, Azizuddin had not remembered
who Elphinstone was. Not until now. He said, "I have no
excuse, your Majesty."

Ranjit Singh began to pace the *maidan*, hands clasped
behind his back. He kicked at pebbles and sent them skittering through the dust. He slapped his hands against his thighs.
He tapped his thumb into the palm of his other hand. Azizuddin watched him, his own brain flocking with thoughts.

"Aziz," the Maharajah called.

He went sprinting over the field.

"Tell me again about this Elphinstone. He took an
embassy from the English East India Company to Shah
Shuja's court?"

Azizuddin nodded. This was something he knew, also
something the Maharajah knew—because his recall was
prodigious—but it was always useful to refresh both of
their memories. Quickly, and succinctly, Fakir Azizuddin
spoke into Ranjit's ear while the king stood courteously by,
motionless and listening.

Some eight years ago, in 1809, Mountstuart Elphinstone
had traveled through the Punjab Empire on his way to Afghanistan. Peshawar was still part of Afghan lands, and Shah Shuja
had come to that city to meet Elphinstone from Kabul—a
monstrous mistake, because it was then Shuja's half brother

Mahmud had occupied Kabul and taken the throne from Shuja. The British had been worried about Napoleon's possible invasion of—and so their holdings in—India, and the embassy had been to seek Shuja's assurance that he would repel Bonaparte. That treaty was never signed; before it could be, Shuja himself had been deposed, and the British had retreated back to India. Both of the comings and goings through the Punjab, Maharajah Ranjit Singh had allowed, seemingly distant, but in truth, very much interested. He had been content to watch and wait.

An ousted Shuja was of no importance to the British, they had let him be for the last eight years, and yet . . . here was this Elphinstone back in the Punjab.

By an 1806 Treaty of Lahore, Ranjit Singh had agreed with the English East India Company that the lands north of the Sutlej River belonged to him, and those south of the river to the British in India. However, the Maharajah not only gave them free rein to travel through his Empire but also made sure that his bazaars and merchants provided them with the means to do so at low prices and with immaculate hospitality.

Why? Azizuddin had asked him once, and the Maharajah had replied that it was always a good policy to keep enemies well fed, contented, and close to the heart.

So, Elphinstone's presence at Lahore was not a surprise. What was unusual was that he had sneaked into the city. And that he had been the man who met Shuja in Afghanistan.

The Maharajah spoke first. "Napoleon Bonaparte has been defeated? And so, our tent-pegging *firangis* came here for a job?"

Azizuddin bobbed his head. "At Waterloo. He will not escape again; they've taken him to some island in the middle of the Atlantic Ocean. The British will not make the Elba mistake again."

"Who then?"

"The Russians, your Majesty," Azizuddin said slowly. "Rumor is that the Russian envoy in Kabul is very friendly with Shah Mahmud. Yes"—he nodded more furiously, sure now of himself—"the British fear a Russian invasion of India."

An almost full moon had risen over the cusp of the horizon, and sent its hoary light across the *maidan*. In the plummy dark, Azizuddin had not been able to see the Akali guards on the periphery of the field, although he had known they were there. Ranjit Singh had not been king of the Punjab Empire for so long, and with so much success, by wandering alone even in his own lands. Now, the silver glow glittered over the rings of the quoits, marking each Akali as an obvious target for anyone who would care to raise a musket in their direction—although few would and live to tell of it.

The Maharajah put back his well-shaped head and laughed up at the moon. The sound reverberated around the *maidan*, echoed off the walls of the fort. "Our British friends are very nervous people. They worried about Bonaparte invading India, but to do so, he would have had to defeat *me*. Now they worry about the Russians? I'm still the Maharajah of the Punjab."

Azizuddin smiled. It was true. Ranjit Singh was only thirty-seven years old. Allah willing, he would live for many more years, and he, who had halted the rapacious East India Company south of the Sutlej, would not give up his empire for another foreign invader, whether he was French, or Russian, or anybody else.

"Elphinstone, your Majesty," he said.

The Maharajah sobered, combing through the hair of his beard with long fingers. "Ah, yes, the problem of Elphinstone. Double the guard around the Shalimar Gardens. If the British want to steal Shuja from me and put him on the Afghan throne instead of Mahmud, they will have to ask me first. That's why they want him, don't they, Aziz?"

"Yes, your Majesty."

"Double the guard now. Before first light."

Azizuddin bowed, his hand touching his forehead in a *taslim*. He turned to leave, and Ranjit Singh's voice, lazy, casual, came to him. "Besides, Shuja still has to give me the Kohinoor. He's not going anywhere until he does so."

There was only one gateway, one entrance from the outside into the upper terrace of the Shalimar Gardens, set in the middle of the southern wall. The south entrance was also surrounded by the soldiers of the Maharajah. Though the guard was to protect every inch of the exterior walls of the Shalimar, after three years, the rotation had slackened.

And so, every night around the first hour of the next day, the guard outside the Khwabagh, Wafa Begam's sleeping quarters on the western side of the upper terrace, took a long hike through the scrub toward the fire that burned in the distance.

An old woman, toothless and haggard, had set up her *chai* shop here for the soldiers—this far, because she wasn't allowed to come any closer. Her "shop" consisted merely of two stones dragged together to hold a fire, a terra-cotta vessel atop, in which the water boiled, tea leaves she threw into the simmer, a brass pot of day-old milk, a mound of sugar tied into a knot at the end of her sari's *pallu*. For one cup of *chai*, she charged the men one *anna*. When they had drunk their *chai*, she wiped the cups out with a dirty rag and set them to dry in the heated dark. If she had been closer to the river, she would have washed out the cups. All night long, she stirred the *chai* and doled out cups, and when morning came, she packed up her things and went home to sleep. She had a young and comely daughter, who took over the *chai* duty during the day in the bazaar on the outskirts of Lahore, but she would not send that child to the deserted land around the Shalimar Gardens, to be at the mercy of these foulmouthed soldiers. She came herself.

The guard, a thin, swarthy man, came to squat by the woman and grunted. He held a shining *anna* piece in his grubby hand, but he was one of those who liked to toy with her, not paying for his cup of tea until he had drunk at least three. He sat facing her, with his back to the Shalimar. She ladled out the muddy liquid, put the cup on the ground, and prodded it toward him with her knuckles.

He picked it up with both his hands and drank noisily. "It's awful today, Maji." He called her Mother, as did the other soldiers, because she was old, not out of respect.

She shrugged. Awful today, awful yesterday, it was all the same to her. This was the only *chai* shop for miles, and in the middle of the night, they would take what they got. At least, the *chai* was hot.

Her attention was caught by a movement on the Shalimar's walls, near the upper terrace. The moon had risen, and the walls stood starkly black. Something snaked up into the lighter sky beyond the walls, once, twice, a third time, until a figure showed, its arm raised to catch the rope. Then, the figure disappeared for a while, as the old woman watched intently. It came back, hesitated for a moment, and then a man swung over the edge of the wall and began to let himself down with the rope.

The old woman grinned, showing a gaping mouth; she had only two teeth left in her upper and lower jaws.

The guard eyed her suspiciously. "What's so funny? What did you put in the *chai*?"

"Drink it," she snapped. "And give me my money."

He leaned over and knocked her on the side of her head. As she lay in the dirt, arms around her breasts, crooning in pain, he helped himself to another cup of *chai*. He took a sip and spat it out. Then another, which he also spat out, as if to show her how easily he wasted the *chai*. The third he drank. The woman sat up, massaging her head, and watched as another man stood briefly in the light of the moon above the garden's walls and then began climbing down. His *kurta* was a patch of white against the murky walls, moving surely and speedily.

The guard deliberately drank his *chai*, and then he stood up, lodged his toe under the lip of the vessel on the fire, and upended it. The old woman sat there, rocking and moaning, her eyes flashing with hatred. A smile gathered around her mouth. She let him go, with the *anna* coin folded into the cloth of his turban, and saw him pick his way through the land, gaze downward, stepping carefully to avoid snakes and scorpions.

By the time the guard had kicked at the *chai* urn, the second man had descended to the ground.

Shah Shuja jumped the last three yards, landing on the balls of his feet, the shock sending a jar of pain through his sore legs. He flitted closer to the wall. "Where is she?" he hissed into the gloom.

Ibrahim Khan limped up, trailing a foot; he had crushed an ankle during his fall from the rope and eaten up the yelp that had come bursting from him. His face was wan in the moonlight, his hair shining in a cloud of curls. "It's a bad night to escape, your Majesty. Too much light. Are these people to be trusted?"

They turned to the two men standing against the wall, their clothing blurred and indistinct in the shadows, the cloths of their turbans wrapped around the lower halves of their faces. One of them had pitched the rope to Shuja, and he had heard quiet grunts as he heaved upward. Since, neither of the men had spoken, or helped them descend.

The letter tied around the rock that Wafa Begam had read and shown to her husband had come from Elphinstone. In it, he had offered to rescue them from the Shalimar Gardens, but it had to be tonight, in a few hours. Elphinstone had already spent too much time in Lahore, any longer and the Maharajah would begin to get inquisitive. Would his Majesty, Shah Shuja, trust that the British had his best interests at heart?

For once, Wafa, more suspicious about almost anything than her husband, had not advised caution. "We must go tonight," she said. Shuja, awakened from a dreamy sleep, the muscles of his arms, legs, and shoulders fiery raw from the wrestling, had shaken his head to clear the fog. All those years of plotting, scheming, wondering who would help them, how that help would appear . . . had come to this. An imperative in the middle of the night. Leave now. How? he had asked. But the letter only said in two hours, not how.

They had woken Ibrahim, drawn him from his cot, doused his head in the waters of the central pool in the upper terrace, and whispered the news in his ear. Shuja and he had padded all around the upper and middle terraces in search of an escape route, or some indication that, suddenly, there was one. They did not descend into the lower terrace, where the Maharajah's guards kept watch, and all their movements were stealthy, quiet, so that no noise filtered downward.

Then that whistle had come again from beyond the walls, sweet and lucid, like the song of a bird. A violinist had accompanied Elphinstone's embassy to Peshawar, and one spring evening, Shuja had invited this man's music into his palace. The music had a strange yet beguiling sound for all of them—a violin concerto by a composer named Bach—and he had asked for it to be played often, and tried to get his own court musicians to imitate that sound.

"Here," Wafa had said, pulling them up the stairs to the top of the wall. They couldn't see anything of the men below, but they heard them throwing the rope and saw it a moment

later, twisting temptingly just beyond reach. Both Shuja and
Ibrahim had held back, too exhausted to make real sense of
what was happening, and it was Wafa who had leaned over
the parapet and caught the rope. She who had yanked it to
one of the pillars and wrapped it around. But she could not
tie the knot and sat there, trembling, her face drenched with
tears. "Come, my lord. Are we going to stay here forever?
Do you want to lose the Kohinoor to Ranjit Singh?"

At that word, Shuja ran to her, knotted the rope, and
tugged at it to check that it was secure.

"Where is the diamond?" he asked.

In response, she bent to kiss his hand, used his fingers to
wipe away her tears. "Go, Ibrahim and you must go first.
Even if they catch us doing this, I will be safe; they will not
dare touch me. Go!"

As she pushed him away, Shuja resisted. Go without her?
What was she saying?

She sensed his hesitation. "I will follow right after. After
I get the Kohinoor, that is. Go now!" And with that she fled
out of the pavilion. He heard her running down the stone
pathway alongside the long water channel, and then heard the
soft, successive thuds of her feet as she descended the stairs to
the middle terrace.

Shuja had never given a thought to where his wife had
hidden the diamond; better not to know until he actually
wanted it. If he had considered it at all, if he had been asked
where, he would have thought it was somewhere in her
harem quarters. But, to conceal it in the middle terrace, with
the gardeners working there, the guards roaming around
every now and then, in so public a place . . . why, it was brilliant. Galvanized into action, he shoved Ibrahim over the
edge of the wall and listened as he made his way down. Just
for a moment, before he went over himself, he tarried again.
Where was Wafa? Why was she taking so long? Then, he
swung over, wrapped his hands around the rope, and slid

down the wall, his toes grabbing onto footholds in the dark, the rope ending far too soon, leaving him swaying above nothing.

"Where is she?" he whispered now, glancing up with a growing worry. He said to one of the two men, "Whistle that song again."

The man shook his head, didn't seem inclined to speak at first, and then he said, in a hoarse voice, "Too dangerous, your Majesty."

Just then, Shah Shuja saw his wife dangle a leg over the parapet. She hung over the edge on her stomach for a sickening moment, and Shuja urged her in a whisper, "Grab on to the rope, Wafa."

She reached for the rope and let her weight down. It took her a long time to descend, almost five minutes; at times she hung in the moonlight, at times her body banged into the wall, but slowly she came down to the end of the rope and swung there in a circle. "What do I do now?" she asked, terrified.

"Let go," Shuja said firmly. Ibrahim and he linked their arms under Wafa, and when Shuja waved to the two men to help them, one shook his head. Wafa Begam undid her tight grasp around the rope and fell into the net formed by her husband and Ibrahim. She was shaking, teary-eyed, and trembling. But she still smiled. Her thin chiffon veil was pulled tight around her face and tied at her nape, enclosing her head in a pale blue.

"Do you have it?" Shuja said in her ear, holding his wife tight by his side.

She nodded.

And then, one of the men said in a deep, cultured voice, "Perhaps then you will allow me to take it from you, your Majesty, and give it to my Maharajah."

* * *

As dawn cleaved a line of lilac on the horizon, slitting open another day, a row of slaves toted loads of firewood upon their backs toward the Shalimar Gardens. The slaves were bent under the weight of the sticks, which were swaddled in cloth, strung with ropes around the tops of their heads like headbands.

They flung each stack near the door at the southeastern corner of the middle terrace, by the side of a huge brick stove. The firewood was shoved into the stove's black and yawning mouth, burning balls of newspapers were thrown in, each setting fire to one part until the whole roared to life.

Water from the Hasli Canal, which fed the fountains and pools in the gardens, was diverted in a little stream to the top of the stove and into a permanently built brick-dome-covered stone cauldron. Pipes ran from this dome into the Shalimar, releasing clouds of steam into a series of closed pavilions on the southeastern corner of the middle terrace. This was the bathhouse, the *hammam* that Emperor Shah Jahan had built for the pleasure of both the ladies of his harem and himself. The only entrance into the *hammam* was from inside the gardens, in a series of three pointed archways that were tucked into the corner.

Shah Shuja lay on the wet floor near the pool in the center of the *hammam*, stripped down to a small pair of shorts and nothing else. His face rested against the stone, his left arm hung into the pale and green waters of the pool. Wafa Begam sat astride his back, clad in very little herself, merely a small cloth covering her breasts and another piece of cloth fashioned into underwear.

She dug the heels of her palms into Shuja's back and ran them over the length of it, from his waist to his hairline. She made fists and pummeled the spent muscles. She kneaded his arms, pulled the strain out of every finger, bent to kiss his sweaty cheek, the hair on his beard scratching her face.

Smudged light streamed around them in sharp bars from

each of the skylights above. One lit the center of the pool, and the water glowed like a gathering of emeralds. Others cast their radiance around, lighting up the steam as it swirled through, taking on ghostly shapes at one moment, dispersing into flatness the next.

Shuja and Wafa lay in the path of one such shaft of light, which glanced off her slender shoulders, dabbed at Shuja's hair, turning it into glittering ebony, painted its way over his outflung arm, and dripped into the pool.

He made a movement, and Wafa rose on her knees and allowed him to flip onto his back before settling down over him again. They gazed at each other for a long while, not speaking, not knowing, perhaps, what to say. They had tried to escape in the middle of the previous night, had been captured and brought back into the Shalimar soon after—merely a few hours had passed before they ordered the *hammam* fires lit.

"What now?" Shuja said, cupping his palm over his wife's cheek.

She leaned into his hand, her eyebrows meeting in distress. "Now," she said slowly and clearly, "we wait and see what the Maharajah will do."

Shuja felt an ache blossom inside his chest, and he rubbed at it unconsciously. Seeing that, Wafa caressed him, taking his hand away, replacing it with her own. He kissed her hand, felt the warm skin on his lips, felt a well of tears rise behind his eyes. Even Wafa had lost hope.

In these past five years, whether in the dungeons under the Hari Parbat Fort in Kashmir, or here in the golden cage of the Shalimar, it had always been Shuja who had been doubtful, or pessimistic. Wafa, with her laughter, her joy, her belief that everything would go her way or no way at all, had a spark of hope lighting her from within. Oh, she had cried before, in distress, or frustration, or hatred, but she had never swerved from their purpose—Shuja would be freed and one day he would return to Afghanistan to be king.

Shah Shuja swiped at the tears that ran in thin lines around the edges of his face and hoped that his wife wouldn't notice them. "Sweat in my eyes," he said hoarsely.

She nodded, wrapped her arms around his, brought his palm back to her face again, and buried her nose in it.

What had happened last night had devastated them. Only because it was so unexpected, something they were so little prepared for. The shock was not of the unanticipated but of the fact that they ought to have known better.

At first, when the voice had come out of the darkness, Shuja had propelled Wafa behind him, his eyes roving around, wondering where it had come from and who had spoken.

And then, one of the peasants hired by Elphinstone to help them escape had stepped forward and, with great deliberateness, stripped the turban cloth from the lower half of his face. In the distorted play of light—the silver from the moonlight, the dimness of the walls, the dull white glow of the turbans— for just a moment, Shuja had strained to see the man's face and, for another moment, hadn't recognized him.

He had whipped around to Ibrahim, who said quietly, "It's the old gardener, your Majesty. We've been hoodwinked."

Shuja had felt a strain around his chest then. *All* of this had been a trick? Nothing but a ruse to bring them out of the Shalimar Gardens with the Kohinoor? And, who was this man who had played at being a gardener in their midst?

He'd raised his chin with a pointed, silent question.

The man had bowed. "I am Fakir Azizuddin."

Ah, Shuja had thought, the Maharajah's foreign minister— this was no ordinary minion but one of his most powerful courtiers. At his side, he'd felt Wafa shaking and he'd put an arm around her, turned his back upon Azizuddin so that he could hug his wife. When he lifted her face to his, he had realized that she was laughing, not crying.

"What?" he had whispered.

"Let me handle this," she'd said. "I'll talk to the fakir."

He had turned to face Fakir Azizuddin.

"Your Majesty," the other man had said, "we could make this very easy, dignified for all of us, if you will only permit yourselves to be searched. After that, you are free to return to the Shalimar Gardens. With the Kohinoor in his possession, the Maharajah will be delighted to outline some very lavish terms for you; he has already spoken to me of an annuity, and a substantial lump sum."

"What about me, Fakir Azizuddin?" Wafa Begam had said in a strong voice, stepping out from behind her husband. The light was faint, Wafa's veil was swathed around her head; all Azizuddin could see was a shape, nose, the bones above the eyes, the jut of cheekbones—and he'd seen much more before of Shuja's favorite wife in his guise as a gardener—yet etiquette demanded, so he'd bent his gaze to the ground.

"You too, your Majesty." His voice had been deferential, but trailed into something very like indecision.

Wafa Begam had pounced on that uncertainty and cut Maharajah Ranjit Singh's famous and powerful foreign minister into tiny pieces and strewed his carcass around. "You don't have a woman on staff, do you? I refuse to be searched by a man—you wouldn't dare do this to me." She had straightened her back, become queenly, regal, her pale hands fluttering in the semidarkness. "In fact, I refuse to submit to a search by any woman." Easy to say because there wasn't any woman around, unless Azizuddin counted the *chai* lady, even now packing up her belongings and getting ready to close for the night, since her tea had been spilled by the guard.

With that, Wafa Begam had strolled past all of them—a line opened in the middle of the group of silent soldiers guarding the southern gateway into the upper terrace—and went back inside the Shalimar Gardens.

Shah Shuja had begun to laugh, mirth shaking his frame.

He still hadn't said a word to Azizuddin, and Ibrahim hadn't spoken either.

The minister had bowed to the erstwhile ruler of Afghanistan, and gestured toward the entrance to the gardens. He didn't want to search them at all, because he was sure that Wafa Begam had the Kohinoor.

While the night had eaten up the rest of the hours, there were two groups of people awake, one on either side of the Shalimar's walls. Inside, Shuja and Wafa knew that this small victory meant nothing, that this was the beginning of the end for them.

And outside, Fakir Azizuddin pondered and paced. He had come back to the Shalimar with another set of guards, only to find the escape was already in progress. For a brief few seconds, a cold hand had wrapped around his heart. Mentioning Elphinstone to the Maharajah had been almost an afterthought; he hadn't thought it important then. Even an hour ago, preparing the guard, during the trip through the scrub, a journey he had already made twice today, Aziz had doubted the wisdom of haste. But when Ranjit Singh gave an order, it was obeyed. As simple as that. And then, to see the two men in Elphinstone's employ whistling a snatch of a violin concerto, the blows on their heads, bundling them out of the way before Ibrahim Khan came snaking down the rope . . . waiting for Wafa Begam to also descend . . . Azizuddin had thought himself brilliant in allowing it to happen so that he could corner them and snatch the Kohinoor and end all these years of futile waiting.

But then Wafa had walked away with the diamond, and Azizuddin knew that it was *she* who was brilliant. He was just a fool who had thought only to the edge of the pit, not beyond it, and so had fallen in.

The wily Wafa would have hidden the Kohinoor again by now. They had searched the gardens many times in the past few years, and it had never been discovered. He knew how much his king wanted the diamond. And Azizuddin wanted to be the man who brought it to him. He had thought for a while longer, and then walked around the perimeter of the Shalimar Gardens, looking up at the walls as the light rose, giving a new set of orders to the guards.

"I'm hungry," Wafa Begam said. All of their worries seemed to have leached away with the steam; the tiredness had left their bodies, and they both lay back on the edge of the pool, their feet in the water, looking up at the skylights.

Shuja ordered the steam to be stopped, and the hiss died down into a quiet nothingness. The light from the sun seemed to burn away the mist and created dark shadows in the shade, a golden transparency where it touched.

Perhaps things were not so bad after all, Shuja thought, his fingers entwined with his wife's. He had one more thing left to give Ranjit Singh if he became too demanding. He didn't know anymore if Elphinstone was truly in Lahore, if his offer to help was genuine, if the night's adventures had been an elaborate ruse.

"Let's go have breakfast," he said, rising from the floor and helping Wafa up.

They went out into the middle terrace, paused for a moment at the pool. The fountains were silent now, and water lay without a ripple, placid, the tinted stones underneath the surface throwing rainbows of glittering color upon the face of the water.

When they ascended to the upper terrace, all was quiet. No smoke from the kitchen fires, no aroma of cooked chicken and lamb, no fragrance of freshly baked *naans*. Every morning, through the south entrance of the upper terrace, Maharajah Ranjit Singh sent in a mass of supplies—clucking hens driven in a cluster, fresh vegetables, spices in covered jars, butter and *ghee* in urns. But today, the gates had been firmly shut. The Maharajah of the Punjab intended to starve them until Shah Shuja gave him the Kohinoor diamond.

For the next two days, Shuja, Ibrahim, and Wafa ate the ripening guavas in the trees, and then the unripe ones, their stomachs protesting. When the guavas were gone, they washed the green mangoes, cut them into slices, sprinkled on salt and chilli powder, ate them until their tongues became sour.

Desperate, Shuja sent the Maharajah his last jewel, a stone as big as his fist, hued in pale yellow, and said that it was the Kohinoor. A long eight hours passed on that third day as they waited. Ranjit Singh had never seen the Kohinoor; he did not know what it looked like, or how big it actually was, or anything about it at all.

A letter came from the king to Shah Shuja in which he thanked him for the *pukraj*, the wonderful topaz, he had sent him, but it wasn't the Kohinoor, was it?

On the fourth day, a slew of gardeners came into the Shalimar and cut down every tree. They drained the pools, shut off the water source from the Hasli Canal, and the stones in the central pool of the middle terrace lay twinkling reproachfully at them in the harsh sun.

A few hours later, Wafa Begam picked her way over the stones in the pool, went to the fountain spout that was the third one from the northwest corner, toward the wrestling platform, bent down, and picked up the armlet hidden there.

She was weak, rabidly hungry, shaking from a want of water and food. Shuja took the armlet himself to Fakir Azizuddin, who waited at the northernmost end of the middle terrace, his face turned away from Wafa Begam. Shuja's steps were halting, dragged on the ground.

Azizuddin examined the armlet and the enormous stone in the center, which caught fire in the light from the sun and shed its lovely glow over his dark face.

"Thank you, your Majesty," he said.

Within the hour, servants had brought in covered dishes wrapped in red satin cloth and laid them out on a carpet in the Aiwan pavilion. Shuja, Wafa, and Ibrahim ate everything in sight, drank cups of wine, and fell onto the carpets sated and full.

The next day, they found all the entrances to the Shalimar thrown wide open, no guards around, the heated air from the plains rolling in. Freedom, Shah Shuja thought, as he watched the Englishman, Mountstuart Elphinstone, ride his horse into the lower terrace and bow his head. More horses were brought in; they jumped into the saddles and rode away south toward the Sutlej River. When they had crossed the river and entered the lands of British India, they were guided to a splendid *haveli* in Ludhiana.

Roses for Emily

December 1838
Twenty years later

What is her name?"

A doubtful silence tarried behind her, until she almost turned—unused to not being answered immediately—and then thought better of it.

Fakir Azizuddin said, "Imli."

Her voice was resonant with laughter. "She's named for the tamarind?"

"No," he said, "surely not, your Majesty. It's just that . . . these English names . . . they are so difficult. So short, sometimes so meaningless. I've only seen it written down, and my English, you know, is of such newness. Perhaps Em-ee-lee."

Maharani Jindan Kaur pondered on that, tapping her slender foot upon the ground. She, and the fakir, stood on the northern bank of the Sutlej River, on the very boundary of the lands ruled by Maharajah Ranjit Singh. Behind her, and him, spread the royal encampment, some hundred thousand souls, tents laid out in a refined grid, dirt pathways hammered and smoothed in the dust, bazaar streets that sold spices, oranges, *ghee,* and copper vessels. In front of her was the mighty Sutlej itself, which found its source thousands of miles away to the east and north, in the Himalayan mountains and the kingdom of Tibet. Here, in the Punjab, the same river that had earlier thundered through rock and mud, carving out sheer gorges, plummeting in deep waterfalls, had spent its force and lay in a wide, tranquil band of water. So serene was the Sutlej on her way to joining the Indus River and emptying out into the Arabian Sea, that the land grew lush and green in parallel stripes around the waters, buffaloes nibbled in the grass and waded in the river to rest upon sudden sandbanks, their black heads bowed under the weight of their curved horns.

"It's a funny name," Jindan said. "But then all these English names are incomprehensible to me."

Fakir Azizuddin was half-turned from his Queen, almost facing into his own king's camp, but not quite, because he couldn't look obviously upon the woman, and couldn't present his back to her. So, he shifted in little semicircles, swinging his body this way and that. He allowed his gaze only to fall upon the skirts of her *ghagara,* noted the smooth heel that lifted one edge of it, the sole painted orange with henna. She was young, this wife of his Maharajah, perhaps not even eighteen years old yet. And Ranjit Singh, this year, was fifty-eight years old. Aziz let his eyes move upward, taking in her graceful figure under the gossamer, sea-green veil, that tight waist, that thinly muscled back bared beneath the strings of her *choli,* that long, curved neck bent under a mass of opaque indigo hair. On her right arm, just above the elbow, and gathered in the fabric of the veil, the Kohinoor diamond glowed softly. The ties of the armlet were pink-tasseled and hung to her waist. Aziz, who had seen and held the diamond in his hand when he took it from Shah Shuja over two decades ago, was mesmerized as the radiance of the sun percolated through the green of the veil and set the stone on fire. The

two surrounding diamonds were like paste beside it. She had
ensnared the heart of his king, this woman, so firmly that he
had given her the Kohinoor to wear. And, there was another
reason. The baby she held, whom Ranjit Singh had named
Dalip Singh, Prince of the Punjab Empire. A baby who could
one day be king.

"This Emily, she is the Governor-General's lady?"

He didn't answer immediately, and a young girl standing beside the Maharani turned and poked him in his chest.
Azizuddin, who hadn't really noticed her until then—because
the women of the harem insisted upon having so many people
hanging on to them—frowned and bent down to peer into
her face. She grinned, flashing pristine white teeth at him, her
cheeks deepening on both sides into dimples. Her blue-gray
eyes were long and sloping, but it was her eyelashes that fascinated him—thick and so long that they brushed the tops of
her arched eyebrows. She couldn't have been more than ten
or twelve years old. Wah Allah, Aziz thought, this child will
grow up to break many men's hearts. Who was she?

She tugged hard at his beard, within her reach now, and
whispered, "Answer the Maharani."

Aziz yanked his hair from her grasp; there was almost no
one in the Punjab Empire who would dare to touch his person; he was the man who had the Maharajah's ear, some said
his affections also. He rubbed his burning chin and said, hurriedly, "Yes, your Majesty. He has another one, named"—
that faltering again as he tried to decipher the word in his
brain, "Fan-ee."

"He's a brave man to bring both of them along with him
to meet the Maharajah. He doesn't worry about them fighting? Or wanting his attention?"

Jindan Kaur had been the only one of Maharajah Ranjit
Singh's wives who had accompanied him to the Sutlej River
for this encounter with Lord Auckland, Governor-General of
India. The others he had left behind at the fort at Lahore—

time enough for them to satisfy any curiosity they might have about the British embassy to the Punjab, because the British encampment was to travel through Punjab lands to Lahore, and perhaps beyond, as Ranjit Singh's guests. The British wanted something from Ranjit, and it would take more than a mere meeting over the muddy waters of the Sutlej for that; this was diplomacy at its lengthiest best. In any case, in India, no decision was made either quickly or lightly, and it was often delayed so much as to not be necessary at all in the end, and the demanding side would be left with not a smidgen of discourtesy to be angry at, only a bafflement that it had all taken so long and yet they were where they had first begun . . . and damn it, everyone had still been *so* nice.

"He doesn't, it would seem," Azizuddin said with a trace of humor in his voice. The Maharani understood the politics of the harem well. And he knew, and she knew also, that it was the child Dalip who had been responsible for bringing her here with his king.

The young Maharani swayed, rocking her baby. The infant pursed his lips, and turned his head to burrow into his mother's breast, his arms and legs suddenly loose and puppet-like in sleep. She rested her nose upon his fragrant hair, thick and sleek already, just three months after his birth, in long fingers of ebony silk around his oval face, one cluster spearing downward on either side of his plump cheeks.

The little girl by her side sneaked a hand under the veil, and under Jindan's arm, and clasped the baby's tiny foot. Aziz stood watching them surreptitiously—this girl was very familiar with the Maharajah's new wife. Who was she? It seemed to him that he knew, or had heard, and as Jindan cooed to her baby, he rummaged through his memory.

Maharajah Ranjit Singh had arrived at the river a month ago, the English two days ago. A fog of dust hung over the British encampment, surrounding it and some hundred feet skyward, blurring the sharp December blue of the sky, the outlines of the tents, its thickness added to by the campfires, which sent their smoke straight up in pockets of white and gray. It would take a few days to settle, once the horses were tethered and comfortable, the tents were fully upright, the business of living begun. There wasn't even the murmur of a breeze, and so the British side of the Sutlej was like an oil painting left to molder in a stable, covered with dust, its outlines indistinct.

Jindan had waited for these last two days to make the long trek through the Maharajah's camp and come to the riverside, hoping that she would be able to take a measure of these English people, even from this far. But she wanted something more. So she said, "Fakir Azizuddin, make arrangements for the ladies of the Governor-General to come see me, will you?"

"When, your Majesty?" He had managed to speak fast enough to cover his surprise, not much hesitation there, but his voice came out in a revealing squeak.

She grinned, and when she spoke it was in the coarse Urdu of the camp soldiers, deliberately reminding him of her so-common origins. "In a couple of days. At my convenience, not theirs."

The girl by the Maharani's side turned again to Aziz and stuck her tongue out at him. So there, Fakir Azizuddin, she seemed to be saying. Aziz knew that the very young could be very stupid, that this girl didn't know just how important he was, or she would be more afraid of him. And then he saw the small gold disc suspended on a gold chain around her neck. The medallion, more like a gold sovereign, was the size of a small dinner plate against her stomach, and on it was impressed the coat of arms of the Punjab Empire—two curving daggers, a double-edged sword, a quoit in the center. So, this girl had the Maharajah's favor, he thought. Ranjit Singh had a propensity for taking into his fort, his harem, anyone who came to him for help, or could claim any kinship to him. The Maharajah also loved children, and so he had adopted a boy, Sher Singh, from a distant branch of his family, and a few years ago brought this girl, Roshni, who was Sher Singh's much younger sister, into the safety and shelter of his *zenana* quarters.

Aziz formed the sound of her name with his mouth, exaggerating a little. *Rosh-ni. I know who you are.* She mimed back. *So what?* And then. *Ha-ha.*

He watched the agility of her expressions, the flash in those light blue eyes, the pantomime, and smiled to himself. He could see why the Maharajah was taken with this brilliant child; she was an entertaining minx. With a very apt name. Roshni. Light. Illumination.

Maharani Jindan Kaur swung around and began walking back to her tent. The Maharajah's foreign minister flushed, bowed, scuttled out of her way, and followed her through the streets, cursing himself. Until that last sentence, they had spoken Persian, a language she was less than fluent in but something she had taught herself, so it had come out stilted, without finesse. But the Urdu of the camps was something she had grown up with, it slid off her tongue easily, and it was a slap in his face for his surprise that the queen of the Punjab would want to meet her counterpart in the British embassy. See, Fakir Azizuddin, she had seemed to be saying, there's a reason there are no other queens here at the Sutlej. I might have grown up among soldiers, but I am now your sovereign's wife, and have your king's love . . . not to mention his child.

As they passed, men turned their faces from her, women raised their hands to foreheads in the salaam, the blacksmith stilled the pounding on his anvil, the cries of the bazaar died down. And Jindan, veiled and covered, carried Prince Dalip Singh and showed him to his people. They saw his face, they marveled at his plumpness, the cast of black in his hair, the tiny fingers that curled around the chiffon of his mother's veil, and they wiped the audacity from their expressions.

There were no sneers, no sniggers, just an awe that the bundle in the woman's arms, finally, and deliberately, made her queen.

If he had been asked, Fakir Azizuddin would have advised against this ramble through the long camp to stand on the embankment and stare at the British on the other side. At the very least, she ought to have had an entourage around her, a gaggle of veiled ladies, a sprinkling of soldiers, a clearing of the paths, a shouting of discouragement toward anyone who dared to raise their eyes toward the Maharani. Oh, and a maid to hold the child. Why would a queen carry her own son like this? It made no sense to Aziz. There were rumors eddying around that she even nursed the child herself. These were all actions of a low-class woman who had no one to do such things for her; Aziz would have thought that, if anything, she would intentionally be more regal than the other ranis of the Maharajah, to put lie to who she was and where she came from.

And then, he saw the melting faces of the soldiers and their womenfolk, watched them bow in the *taslim* or the *konish*, touch their hearts at the sight of the child, his prince. The diamond shone in the sunlight, like a star plucked out of the night sky, but the infant seemed more brilliant than a rock that could feed the world's millions. Aziz shook his head in disbelief and in admiration.

When Jindan had reached the outside of the tents that formed the royal enclosure, she waited. He said, "It shall be as you say, your Majesty."

She inclined her head, *now* she was imperious, and went inside.

Jindan Kaur had asked for, and got, the rooms beside the Maharajah's, a privilege a few of his wives had had, in his youth, perhaps, but not for a long while now. The tent, spare and white, with no embellishments in gold and silver *zari*, no beaten gold pillars holding up the awnings, no abundant Persian and Turkish carpets of thick, knotted wool, was, even so, large and contained canvas partitions that divided one space from another. It had high doorways, tall ceilings, windows of a fine white mesh that kept out insects and filtered in the sweet air birthed above the Sutlej's waters. The floors were covered with crudely woven *dhurries* in white; the furniture was simple, white cotton divans with cushions and bolsters, a sleek wooden chair in every room for Ranjit Singh.

The Maharani paused at the entrance to the main sitting room, staying just beyond the doorway, unseen by the occupants of the room. When the Maharajah met with the British delegation, his own person would be modest, as always, but the courtiers would be dressed in their dazzling silks, would glitter with jewels—*there* would be all of the pomp and the enormous wealth of the Punjab Empire. For show, Jindan, Ranjit Singh had said. I myself need none of it. Jindan smiled, looking around her at all that pristine white. In an empire where dust and mud ruled, where the rains fell sparingly and sometimes not at all, where the green of verdure flourished only around the hearts of rivers and streams, white was a luxury that only a king could command. Not so humble after all.

Roshni, sticking to her as usual, beckoned Jindan's head down, and the Maharani felt the child's warm, moist breath tickle her ear. "Shall I go?"

"Wait in my room, Roshan."

The girl reached on tiptoe and kissed Jindan's arm, somewhere above the Kohinoor, and then she fled, the sound of her footsteps sucked into the pile of the *dhurries* on the floor.

Jindan leaned against the wooden doorframe and listened as the Granthi read out passages from the Guru Granth Sahib to his Maharajah. In the last few years, as he had grown older and two strokes had frozen the left part of his body, Ranjit had asked for a learned man at his court, a different one each time, to sing out hymns from the scripture at all times of the day, whenever he had felt the need for it. She moved slowly until she filled the doorway and watched her husband in his chair, the Granthi seated on a stool next to a wooden table on which the holy book lay. Ranjit's right hand cupped his face, and when she appeared, he moved that hand so that his face moved also and his bright eye gazed at her. He smiled, a half smile that curved the right part of his mouth, left the other side immobile.

She felt a painful swelling in her breasts; it was time for another feed, but the baby slept on, his fist tucked under his chin, all crumpled up in his mother's arms. She tickled him gently on his ribs, and he opened his glittering eyes and screwed up his mouth in a lusty cry.

Maharani Jindan Kaur held him close, her fingers already undoing the buttons of her *choli*, as she vanished in a swirl of skirts, the child's cry loud and then dying into contentment as his mouth found her breast.

In the sitting room, Maharajah Ranjit Singh cleared his throat. The Granthi heard him but finished the verse he was reciting and waited, his head bowed, looking down upon his hands.

"Enough for now," Ranjit said.

"Tomorrow, your Majesty?" the man asked.

"Maybe not. Fakir Azizuddin will send word. Thank you."

When the man had left, after touching his forehead to the ground in front of the Guru Granth Sahib, and gathering the book reverently into his arms, Ranjit called for his servants. They carried his chair out, moving sideways through the doorway, into the main area, and from there they went into the bedroom of the Maharani.

When the servants had departed, Jindan pulled the veil from over her head and the suckling child, and sat there smiling upon the Maharajah. The golden light from the waning sun slanted in from the windows, caressed her shining hair and that of her child, cast a honeyed warmth upon her bare skin.

Ranjit Singh sighed. He set his right hand down carefully upon the arm of his chair and moved his head with an effort until it rested against the back. He never tired of looking upon her, this girl he had plucked from the banks of the Ravi River one heated summer afternoon in Lahore, just outside the fort's walls. And, eventually, brought her into his harem as his wife. His gaze then drifted to Roshni, sitting on the floor near Jindan, her legs crossed in front of her, her head leaning against Jindan's shoulder. Every now and then, she put out a small hand to caress Dalip's head.

"Why do you do that yourself?" His voice was rasping; speech was still troublesome, and he couldn't get as many words out as he wanted; his brain was always crammed with questions now that could find no answers.

But Jindan understood, as she had always seemed to. "This?" she said, glancing down upon the concentrated face of the baby, eyes now shut, mouth working busily. "I lost one, you know."

He nodded, as much as that petrified left part of his neck would allow. There had been a child before this one; at five months along, Jindan had tripped over the wooden horse cart of one of the other children in the harem—not his own, one of the many others of the various women to whom he gave shelter, cousins and friends—and had collapsed sharply upon the ground. It had been such a simple fall; she had not twisted an ankle, or injured a bone, but she had been taken to her bed, and that night the bleeding had started.

Jindan began to speak and then turned to Roshni. "Roshan, child, leave the room. I want to speak to the Maharajah of matters that are not for your ears."

Roshni twisted her nose. "Why, Ma?"

In his chair, Ranjit tipped forward as much as his shattered body would allow him to. He had hoped that Jindan would form friendships among at least some of the women in his harem; he knew that her life would be miserable if she didn't. But Jindan had become fond not of one of his other wives, or his cousins, but of this little girl who had come from Sher Singh's house in Amritsar almost on the same day as Jindan. In his, the Maharajah's *zenana*, Roshni was in the place of his child, because he had unofficially adopted her, much as he had adopted her brother Sher Singh and made him one of the heirs to his throne. But Jindan, who at eighteen was only six years older than Roshni, was Ranjit's wife. And so, Roshni called Jindan Ma.

"Go," Jindan said again. This time when Roshni rose, muttering under her breath, she came up to the Maharajah and nestled against his chin and his beard. And then, she ran from the room.

Jindan smiled. "She's a good girl, even helpful with Dalip."

"What were we speaking of just now?"

"I prayed that if I were given the chance for another child, I would not leave it to the care of others. Just that, your Majesty."

He watched her for a long while with a feeling of peace that he never found elsewhere, not even in the saddle. While the strokes, one after another, had decimated the movement of most of his body, he could still ride a horse, and for that he was grateful. Just as he was grateful for this young woman who had come into his life to be his wife, to share his bed, and to give him another child.

Jindan Kaur was the daughter of one of the court's *bhistis*—

the water carriers. These were the men to be found in every town and city in India, hunched under the weight of their goat-skin bags. Goats were skinned almost whole for their skins, the inside scoured, polished, and hammered into a smoothness, the outside left with short, brown and white fuzz, and then sewn into a bag with only one seam. Even that one seam had to have stitches that disappeared into the pelt, else water, with its inva-sive, fluid form would leak out. One end had a small copper mouth with a lid, the other a larger mouth. The *bhistis* filled their bags through the larger mouths and slung them over their shoulders with the smaller openings downward, near their hips. Jute cords, toughly woven, joined the two ends together and were strapped over their chests. When they sold water, they let open the smaller mouth into whatever container was offered to them, capped it, and then collected the money. Water had a sur-prising weight, and the *bhistis* were easily identified as the men who walked around bent down with a permanent stoop, even after they had put their bags away for the night.

The Maharani put the baby up on her shoulder and tapped on his back until he burped and then, sated, his eyes closed again and his breathing evened.

"He sleeps a lot," Maharajah Ranjit Singh said.

She laughed, rubbing her face against the child's side. "All babies do."

"I wouldn't know," he said, suddenly grave. "I was too busy conquering kingdoms and kings when my other sons were younger."

If the initial stroke hadn't left him immobile in a chair, he would not have seen Jindan, or noticed her. It was during those first long days, when he had chafed at his inability to move his hand, his leg, his mouth, his face, when the words came garbled and nonsensical out of his mouth even though his brain was on fire with what he wanted to say, that he had insisted upon being taken to the Shah Burj tower every afternoon. He refused to take a nap, it seemed too much like defeat, especially since he lay looking up at the night sky, worrying about what had happened to him, and what would happen to his empire with the British clustering over the southern doorstep at the Sutlej. True, he had signed a treaty with them to stay away, but that was many decades ago. A few Afghani spies had also been caught within the Punjab from the north. Ranjit Singh knew that he was the one who held the Empire together. And word of his stroke had already filtered out, so the scouts came snuffling around to find out the truth.

One afternoon, he had asked to be left at the Shah Burj, leaning from his chair against the marble latticework *jali,* his forehead resting against the carving, which left its imprint upon his skin because he couldn't move away easily by himself. Looking over the trees, the fields of rice and wheat, the crows leaving black footprints on the sky, he had seen the girl bend into the river, plunge in a goatskin bag, fill it, cap it, and lift it over her head and shoulders onto her back. The wet bag had sprinkled water into the air around her, each drop creating a tiny rainbow, until she had seemed to be suspended in light. Her clothing was shabby, her *ghagara* wet up to her knees, frayed at the edges, her *choli* faded from so many washes that it was a dull shade of gray. He had watched, imprisoned as he was, as she staggered when the weight of the bag first settled on her shoulders.

She'd righted herself painfully and begun the long, shambling trek back to the fort.

Ranjit Singh still hadn't seen her face, but something in that measured determination of a girl who was hardly strong enough to carry a *bhisti*'s load had captured his heart. He'd asked Fakir Azizuddin to send for her. She had come to stand in front of him, a little shy, mostly frightened. Carrying water was men's work. But her father was too ill, and had been in his bed for some days now—money had to be made, and there was only one way she knew how to make it. Her speech was crude, not appealing, and she was prickly with resentment. The Maharajah had offered her some learning, some lessons.

"What would I do with it?" she had asked, her hand churning in a contemptuous movement.

"Bah," he had shouted. "What everyone else does with it. I wouldn't know; ask Fakir Azizuddin. He was the one who grew up interred in books and the alphabet." He had turned to his astonished foreign minister. "Tell her. I will pension off your father; you'll never need to work for a living again. Tell her."

Fakir Azizuddin had stammered out something meaningless. He had taken the girl into the harem, asked for her to be bathed and dressed and sent to the tutors.

A month later, the Maharajah of the Punjab had fallen in love with the child of a *bhisti*. She had talked to him, sung to him, looked at him with such devotion that he couldn't bring himself to part with her. And so, he had married her.

Jindan Kaur laid the sleeping child in his cradle. In that clean, frugal room, the baby's bed was made of a gleaming gold, embedded with diamonds that twinkled, the sheets were of silk, the canopy had studded on the inside a thousand jewels of every color with silk-tasseled fringes. She had been willing to accede to the Maharajah's love for white and minimalism, as long as she could put her son in a bed of gold. She then came up to Ranjit Singh, knelt by his chair, and wrapped her arms around him.

He could hear the thud of her heart, smell the faint aroma of roses from her perfume, feel the caress of her fingers upon his neck. They stayed like that until the sun set, and darkness came tumbling down upon the tent, and the cradle with the child glowed in multicolored points of light, and one luminous fragment of light smoldered from the heart of the Kohinoor on the sleeve of her *choli*.

"I'm sorry," he said.

Maharajah Ranjit Singh had two other sons who were in

line for the throne, Kharak Singh and Sher Singh, grown men both, with children and wives. Dalip Singh was only three months old.

Jindan knew this, although they had never talked about the succession, for it would mean that Ranjit Singh was dead. She nodded and kissed his mottled cheek.

He felt a tightness in his stomach at the touch of her lips. How much longer could he live? Which was why he had allowed Lord Auckland to come to the Punjab to meet him.

"What does he want, this Auckland?" Jindan asked softly.

"My help in invading Afghanistan."

"And will you give it to him?"

She heard the roll of laughter in the Maharajah's chest. "Of course not. But with this"—he moved his right hand ineffectually to gesture at his wasted body—"I thought it best to hear him out, pull it along, and then not say no, but not do anything."

"He wants to put Shah Shuja on the throne of Afghanistan?"

"Yes," Ranjit said, grinning. "How do you know?"

She moved her shoulders. "Who else is there? Who else would listen to the British? Shuja's been in Ludhiana as their guest, under their protection, panting for this opportunity."

Ranjit Singh stroked her brow, which was creased with worry. She was wondering what this meant for her, for her son, their son.

She shifted, fretful. "You're too generous with them, your Majesty. The British embassy is now twenty-five thousand men"—when he raised his right eyebrow, she waved—"Azizuddin told me. Well, I asked. He said that you're taking care of everything for them—that thousands of hens go for their pots every morning along with flour and rice, spices; that their bazaars only sell what you send and that the shopkeepers have been told to sell anything and take nothing, and all their bills come to you. Is it even necessary?"

He touched the diamond on her arm, his fingers shutting out the glow for a brief moment, before he let the light seep in again. "My purse is bottomless, Jindan. My treasury is even larger. So, why not? But, there's always an underlying purpose to this . . . generosity. When I refuse to send my army into Afghanistan, because I consider it to be a futile attempt, the British will not be able to accuse me of a lack of charity."

"You're really saving the Punjab," she said slowly.

"If it comes to that, yes. On the day the Governor-General crosses the Sutlej to come for his first official visit, he will be greeted by my soldiers in formation. My hand may be open, but it also holds the sword." He nodded. "It has always held the sword, but now it has learned to temper aggression with money, diplomacy."

She squatted on the floor beside her husband and leaned her head against his knee. Ranjit Singh hadn't said this time, although he'd said it before, that taking care of the guest was the host's first duty. It was something the British had not learned in India. This entire diplomatic dance had been taking place for about a year now. Fakir Azizuddin had led a contingent from Ranjit Singh's court first to Calcutta to meet Lord Auckland and then, this past summer, to Simla, where the Governor-General had halted in his up-country tour. When the political secretary, McNaghten, had come at the head of his own group from the Governor-General to the Maharajah's court in Adeenagar soon after, it had been the same. They were met at the Punjab border, escorted by Ranjit Singh's cavalry and infantry, no food or drink that passed their lips had been paid for by the British. When they returned to Simla again, they were burdened with gifts from the Punjab.

The reception of Fakir Azizuddin's embassy at Simla had not been quite as enthusiastic. They had set up an encampment on the lower slopes of the valley, and an hour later a thunderstorm had come booming in over all of them. The tents had been shattered, the downpours dug deep gouges into the hillsides, and it had rained for two days and two nights. At the end of the storm had come a polite note from Lord Auckland's office asking if they were all right, and of course, Azizuddin had written back saying that the bond between the British and the Punjab had created a shelter for them from the storm. In reality, he had rented a mansion in Simla within the first hour of the storm, after the tents collapsed. When the Maharajah had heard of this, he'd sent for the state treasurer, Misr Makraj, and had him count out sovereigns into Azizuddin's hands until his palms curved around a pile of shimmering gold.

Maharani Jindan Kaur sighed. She didn't think that the British were a threat to the Punjab. Wanting to see Emily and Fanny Eden was just . . . curiosity; if nothing else, asserting her right as the Maharajah's wife, as the mother of his child.

"I will be meeting the Governor-General's women," she said.

"I will also," Ranjit Singh said. "They are very free and open with their women, these British. I hear General Avitabile is . . . interested in the older one. I don't see—"

"And this Lord Auckland does not mind?"

"She's his sister, my dear, perhaps he's looking for a way to get rid of her."

"Ah," Jindan said, and then her frown cleared. "They're both his *sisters*? What man travels with his sisters to India? Where are his wives? What kind of a man does not have a wife?" There was a genuine perplexity in her questions. In India, everyone married. It was as simple as that. There was no question of falling in love, of course, unless you were fortunate enough to do so after you were married, as Jindan herself had, but every man had a woman—someone, somewhere, anyhow—who fitted into his life.

The Maharajah's mouth deepened into its lopsided smile. "I will ask him."

Prince Dalip Singh gurgled in his sleep. Jindan rose, ran to the cradle, and placed a soothing touch on her child's brow. Ranjit Singh could hear a hiss of breath from his son, and a chomping of his gums before he settled down again. He watched his young wife, saw the intent look on her face as she gazed down upon the boy, and felt a pang in his heart. He had had two strokes already, and another one would finish him off—this was Honigberger's studied opinion. He had one useless heir in Kharak Singh, weak of face, weak of character, with a marked weakness for wine and the women of his harem. He had another son, and Kharak had a son with an ambitious mother, and they would all fight one another for the throne, and perhaps one of them would hold it long enough for the Punjab Empire to survive. There was already an intense jealousy among his sons and their wives, that he had allowed Jindan to wear the Kohinoor. Since he had taken it from Shuja, no one, other than Misr Makraj, who was treasurer, had been allowed to touch it. But he liked seeing the massive diamond upon the arm of the woman who had attempted to carry a water bag up from the Ravi, who wore with such grace a stone whose value was, even now, to her unimaginable and impossible. Who had, after all these years when he had considered himself old, desiccated, given him a son. A new boy. A new life.

He smiled to himself. If there was a curse upon the diamond, that no man could keep it and retain his kingdom, he had shattered the curse, looked upon it and spat at it, stomped it into the ground. The Lion of the Punjab had kept the Kohinoor within his mammoth paws for twenty years. The smile faded from his mouth and he grew grave. He had built his empire and he meant for it to endure. Would it?

And what of that child in the cradle? What would become of him? Would he be a pawn in someone's game? Would this young wife of his, who had given him such immense joy at a time when he most needed it, would she survive also?

* * *

The lamp spluttered, and a thin spiral of smoke curled its way upward. Emily Eden laid down her pen on the blotting paper and scrubbed her forehead tiredly. The flame wavered once, and again, and extinguished itself with a sigh. The outlines of the tent disappeared, and then reemerged, lit faintly from the glow of torches in the camp outside. The roses in the silver vases on her desk seemed to come abloom in the dark, heavy-scented, padding the air with their aroma. Emily touched the supple petals, bent in to breathe the perfume, thought of the man who had sent them to her.

"Not asleep?"

She moved quickly, straightened from the flowers, yanked the top page from her desk and burrowed it under other papers. When he had reached her, he sat down heavily upon the carpets, near her chair.

"Not on the floor, dear. Jimrud swept, but snakes . . ." and scorpions, insects and spiders, in fact, all of India on many, varied legs would ooze into a darkened tent, gnaw at the furniture, leave malodorous droppings.

"I don't care," George said, his body slackening. A blurred tangerine glow trickled through the white canvas. Her desk lay flush along the wall, in front of a window. Their mother had given it to Emily for her tenth birthday, the first substantial gift she had received in her young life. At sixteen, she'd moved into an attic bedroom by herself and tucked it under the steep slope of the roof, knocking her head each time she rose. When they came to India, they had been told to take *everything* with them—servants, furniture, clothing, shoes, books, pens, paper, knitting, wool. Once they got here, she realized that things were not quite so dire, but she was still glad for the desk—its amber-hued oak, its scarred legs—because it tethered her to home, to England.

Emily trawled her fingers through George's thinning brush of hair. India had done this. When they left home, his hair had been a rich brown, now it was heavily woven through with strands of white. "I used to think that bringing my old room to India would make it England. So everyone told us, you remember, when we first embarked—take the comforts of home with you."

He glanced up. "Who are you writing to? Mary?"

"Eleanor," she said, falteringly, glad that he couldn't see the flush that crept up her neck. "Although by the time this letter gets to her, it will be May or June, and her garden will be in full bloom."

George wrapped his arms around her leg, and she felt the warmth of his face seeping in through the thin cotton of her nightgown. She dabbed at her nape and her hand came away damp with sweat. In Greenwich, at Park Lodge, where George had been Commissioner of Greenwich Hospital, the garden would have gone into its quiet hibernation, now, in December. Frost would carve patterns on the thick glass of the casement windows; the branches of the birches would be rimmed with ice, trunks stripped of bark, lying about in paper curls of white; the grass would crackle with frozen dew. There had been other houses, other gardens, but the memory of the Park Lodge garden—where Emily had planted the rosebushes, the elms, the rhododendrons—was the one that came swooping clear to her when life in India troubled.

When their mother had died, Emily and Fanny, the only unmarried girls in the brood of fourteen, had left Eden Farm and gone to George. If George had been married, Emily and Fanny would have had to live by themselves—two mistresses in George's home were already one too many, but *three* . . . unthinkable. Fanny was three years younger than Emily, George thirteen years older. And so they had muddled along now, for what, some twenty years almost, Emily thought with surprise—in this triangular marriage.

Outside, a horse coughed. In a sick horse, this was a painful whine, a hoarse and labored drawing in of breath. Emily said, "What's the matter with that animal?"

"Pneumonia, I think. He won't last long; there's no cure for it."

Emily sank her chin into her chest and whispered into the lace collar of her nightgown. "I *hate* it here."

George did not speak for a long time. They just listened to the tortured hacking of the horse and watched as the shadow of its neck and head flailed across the tent's walls.

"How long have we been in India?" George's voice was subdued.

"Two and a half years," Emily said tiredly. "We arrived at Government House in Calcutta on March fourth, my birthday."

"They weren't expecting us," George said, with a dash of unexpected humor.

The then acting Governor-General of India, Sir Charles Metcalfe, had known that Lord Auckland and his sisters had arrived at the mouth of the Hooghly River, and had boarded a ferry on their way to Calcutta to relieve him of his duties. That by itself meant nothing—in India, a ferry ride of a few hours could become a journey of days, or the boat could capsize, or become stuck on the bank . . . or . . . So Metcalfe had gone on with his dinner party on the night of the fourth of March 1836. In the meantime, George, Emily, and Fanny had landed at the port at Calcutta to a small band playing an abbreviated and surprised welcome, and a convoy of horse-drawn buggies to rush them through the plummeting dusk of the crowded streets. After traveling through a vast park, they had confronted Government House, set on the banks of the river, with its Ionic pillars, its central dome, its twenty-seven acres . . . it was like a blessed piece of England, this mammoth house. Later, Emily would learn that it *was* England, more specifically, Kedleston Hall in Derbyshire, built according to the same plan at the turn of the century by an ambitious Governor-General. They had climbed the steep steps leading up to the front door of Government House, gone through the reception area and into the dining room.

Metcalfe, caught at the head of the table with his wineglass rising to his mouth, had set it down carefully and hailed the travelers, who were still teetering on their land legs after so many months at sea. He had caught hold of George, Lord Auckland's arm, dragged him to his place peremptorily, sworn him in as the new Governor-General of India, demanded that one of the waiters move his plate—with the remains of the fish he had been eating—to another setting down the table, and sat down to enjoy his meal again.

"Happy birthday to me," Emily said.

George agreed. "It was a frightful introduction to India." Disoriented, his mind filled with the flash-by images of the Calcutta docks, the sweating trumpeters of the band, the ramshackle slums of the native quarter, he had stared at the eighty-five guests his predecessor had amassed in the dining room for a casual night—as Metcalfe had said, nothing special. George loathed making speeches, and he'd wondered what kind of a crowd a formal event demanded if this was just a few friends to dinner. He had swallowed air, he'd stumbled through the words, he'd toasted the King, his voice had failed, he'd collapsed into his chair and been watched as each forkful of tough goat meat went to his mouth and he chewed.

"Poor George," Emily said softly, kissing the top of his head.

Things didn't get better, because the Governor-General of India was the representative of the Crown and the East India Company. He had to stand up to talk at every occasion, stiff and uneasy with a stultifying formality to his language; he had to be seen everywhere, his frock coat cut at the right angles, his hair brushed, his collar pristine, his boots shining. That was usually in the evenings. In the mornings, at Government House in Calcutta, where his offices were downstairs in the front, George was buried under the weight of papers that came in the red dispatch boxes from every corner of British India. He had a staff of seventy people, most of whom were snappy, blindingly rich young men—younger sons of earls and dukes all eager for their India experience and with little else to do back home—who were his ADCs, his aides-de-camp.

Government House was an open house. Emily had privacy only in her bedroom upstairs; once she opened the door, she was likely to find almost anyone around: ladies come for a visit, the native servants creeping about, the ADCs running down hallways. She had a personal staff of thirty servants, including one whose job was only to pick up her handkerchief, if she dropped it.

"It's a difficult life," Emily said quietly, "but no one who had come to India before told us it would be easy."

"And we came for the money," George said, surprising even himself by the honesty. When Emily moved in her chair in protest, he said, "It's true, Em. Macaulay was only a member of the Governor-General's council, remember, and he came back home with a purse of twenty thousand pounds, enough for him and his sister to live on for the rest of their lives. I make that amount every year. When we return, we will be rich. This is why we came to India. Why *I* came to India. Fanny and you were very good to accompany me. I wouldn't have known what to do without you."

Emily gave a half laugh, embarrassed. Well, it *was* true, but they'd never talked about it before. And how could they have let George come here alone, without them? It was their duty, no matter how frightful the prospect had been.

"Go to bed," she said. "Or do you want to sleep here tonight?"

"No," he said, rising. A sheet of paper fell onto the carpet from the pocket of his nightshirt and lay there, glowing white on the dark of the wool. "Oh, this came today." He held it out. "Runjeet's wife wants to meet you. And Fanny, I suppose."

Emily flipped open the letter and held it up to the faint light that glowed around them. "It's in Persian. Did McNaghten translate? But, this wife, George"—a small frown gathered on her forehead—"she's common, isn't she? The daughter of a cleaner or some such?"

This also was the unfortunate part of India to Emily. Even among the British inhabitants of the country, there was no telling who came from where. Some of them had money; some had the advantage of a long enough residence in India that their origins were forgotten; some were simply people Emily, Fanny, and George would not have met or talked with in England. Here, the social order was in a dreadful jumble.

George put his hands around her face and bent down until their breaths mingled. "You've got to see her, Em. Every raja's wife is common, by our standards anyway. And this royalty in India is common also—they're not usually born to the title, they snatch it from their brothers, fathers, and friends. It doesn't matter. I want Runjeet to help us in Afghanistan. So, you've got to see his . . . er . . . wife, or whatever she is. She'll probably give you a heap of jewels as a gift, you know how ridiculously generous Runjeet has been."

"What are we giving them?"

"Wait." He ran out of the tent and came back with a rectangular package enfolded in newspaper. Emily tore open the wrappings and gazed upon the portrait she had painted of Queen Victoria in her coronation robes. She had taken the face from a newspaper clipping, the gown from a very bad description, the jewels from her imagination, because they had been in India when Victoria was crowned sovereign of England; in fact, news of the king's death and the new queen had come to them only in October, four months later. George had had the portrait framed in gold, embedded with rubies and diamonds, and shells.

"Is it enough? We don't want to seem mean . . . and, Runjeet keeps his women in a harem, would he care to see our Queen thus?"

"She's our ruler, Emily." His mouth drooped in distaste. "One day she might well rule over the Punjab. I don't care what the native rajas think. And, I thought of giving him this also, along with some guns and cannons." From the lower pocket of his nightshirt, he pulled out a clatter of green stones, smoothly rounded, linked with tiny gold chains. Pure emeralds, fashioned into a cluster of grapes, so realistic that Emily's mouth had watered when she'd first seen them in Calcutta.

"It's beautiful," Emily said. "But Runjeet has the Kohinoor, you know; these will seem like paltry gems to him."

"Maybe he'll give us the Kohinoor in return."

They were silent, listening as the unwell horse shifted about on its feet, trying to be comfortable.

"Imagine that," Emily said softly, "you could be the Governor-General who sent the diamond to the Queen."

George grunted. "Mr. Taft would snap it out of my hand before we even had a chance to look at it and bear it away to the Company's treasure house."

George, Lord Auckland, had been appointed Governor-General of India by the King of England and the Prime Minister of England. And, though the British government could offer the highest post in India to any man it chose, the English East India Company, a private trading concern, still ruled over most of India. Every gift, every honor paid to the Governor-General, or the members of his council, had to pass through the hands of the Company.

Mr. Taft was merely a clerk in the Company's employ. But his job was to attach himself to the Governor-General's office, to follow him around, to catalog and list every offering from a native king—and to send them all to fill the Company's coffers.

"True," Emily said. "Nothing's really ours here, except what we pay for. Mr. Taft is most scrupulous about that. But, George, think of the glory—if you managed to get the Kohinoor away from Runjeet and gave it to her Majesty. No one would ever forget that . . . or you."

He gave her a thin smile that vanished as quickly as it came. George had no illusions about himself or what he could do. He had thought for a very long while about this invasion of Afghanistan, hesitant to stir up too much trouble during his tenure as Governor-General, but McNaghten, his political secretary, was insistent . . . and it *would* be splendid to conquer Afghanistan, make it a vassal to British India . . . there could be no harm, surely? Nothing but success in this venture?

While Emily talked, George put a fastidious finger on the triangular edge of the paper jutting out from the others on her desk. He saw her writing, and rubbed out the blot of ink on the end of the last word. "This is to General Avitabile?"

She nodded.

"That Italian who is in Runjeet's employ? Why, Emily?"

She turned away. "He's been very kind. You know, after he came with Fakir Azizuddin to Calcutta, as part of Runjeet's first embassy, well, at that time, he promised me shawls, some gowns, embroidered in the finest wool from Kashmir. They came yesterday, a year and a half after I'd met him in Calcutta. It was good of him to remember after so long. I want to thank him . . ."

There was a whiteness around George's nostrils, and his cheeks had drawn into his bones. He did not look at her either. "He's been writing to you all the while."

"Not *all* the while, some of the time," Emily said. She glanced at his finely wrought face—that sharp, hooked nose, that slender jaw, those arched eyebrows—and thought that her brother was, even at fifty-three, an attractive man. But he was a cold, dull creature, eminently suited for this position as Governor-General of India. George had the looks of a poet, maybe he was even as handsome as Lord Byron, who had wreaked havoc on the periphery of their lives, but he hadn't the heart of one. How would she explain this to him, about General Avitabile, a man she had seen only a year and a half ago but who had . . . taken her fancy. Emily flushed, buried her face into the gloom of the tent. She was forty-one years old and had never yet met a man she had been attracted to, until she met the giant Monsieur Avitabile.

"But you have no . . . understanding with this Avitabile. Do you?" George tapped his fingers on the desk and the letter. "You can't write to him, or any man. Do you, Em?" This last came with a plea.

She clicked her tongue. "Don't be ridiculous, George. He did Fanny and me a favor, I responded with thanks. As for only being able to write to a man I am betrothed to . . . it's such a wild and old-fashioned notion. I write to Melbourne, he writes to me, and you know there's nothing there between us."

George kicked the leg of the desk lightly and felt his way out of the room. He paused for a bit. "You *could* have had Melbourne if you wanted. He's Prime Minister of England. I don't doubt that he offered me this post as Governor-General of India because of you, once it was his for the giving. Flirt, if you like, with General Avitabile. But you cannot leave me." He turned. "You can't be so silly, Em."

She opened her mouth to protest, shut it again, and listened to him fumble his way through the tented corridor that led to his own room, which he had dubbed "Foully Palace."

They had left Calcutta soon after Runjeet's embassy, and had been on the road for a year and a half now, wandering up-country through British territories, visiting Company regiments at various cities and towns. It was the duty of every

Governor-General of India to travel through his lands; else, shut away in the relative splendor of Government House in Calcutta, he wouldn't know anything about the real India. Or so, at least, the Court of Directors of East India Company thought. And all the while, this—the encounter with the Maharajah of the Punjab—had been the main objective. Now, they were here on the banks of the Sutlej.

This morning, Jimrud had toted into Emily's tent an armful of yellow and pink roses, long-stemmed, freshly cut, dew upon the petals that fell in a shimmering glitter of silver drops when she arranged the blooms in the vases. There was a note of welcome from Avitabile. And General Avitabile was finally, finally on the other bank, a short two miles away.

The British encampment straggled along a short length of the Sutlej River, for the most part, tents flung haphazardly into the flat ground, wide and unused spaces in between. The privies lay behind the tents, landward, and the trip at night would have to be made with a lot of weaving and maneuvering around the horses, cattle, sheep, and goats that were penned wherever there was a place. So the intention to use the privies had to come well before the actual need for it. George Auckland's tent lay somewhere in the middle; Emily's and Fanny's were connected to this by a series of chintz-covered corridors. Ten-foot-high red screens, in calico, adorned with geometric shapes, enclosed their sets of tents. To Emily, it was like being in a *zenana* of the Mughal kings who had ruled India (and still, technically ruled India, although the British were, surely, supreme now), with only a postage-stamp-size view of the unruffled waters of the river through a tear in the screens.

Major Bryne, supervisor of the Governor-General's household at Calcutta and in charge of their living arrangements dur-

ing the long march in the Upper Provinces of India, had pored
over the *Ain-i-Akbari* of Abul Fazl, written during the time of
Emperor Akbar's rule in the late 1500s. It was difficult going at
first—Bryne's Persian was assured, and of some twenty years
standing, learned when he first came to India as a civil servant
(as one of the required languages), but Abul Fazl had spoken
the tongue on his father's knee, had written his *Ain* in a dense
scholarly manner, and some three hundred years earlier. Picking through the manuscript during the whole year before the
Governor-General's march, Bryne had nonetheless managed
to jot down some important details. A few days before Emily,
George, and Fanny left Calcutta, the Paish-khana, the advance
camp, had set off on the journey itself, first on the flats, towed
by steamer up the Ganges all the way to Kanpur, and from then
on by foot, horseback, carriage, elephant back, camel back, in
a slow progression over the last few months until they had
arrived at the banks of the Sutlej.

It was Bryne who, in his enthusiastic imitation of the
Ain, had put Emily, Fanny, and George in the *zenana* enclosure, just as Akbar had in his day enclosed his women. It was
Bryne who had laid out the camp in a faithful reproduction
of the Emperor's camp—there was a Diwan-i-am, a Hall of
Public Audience; a Diwan-i-khas, a Hall of Private Audience;
three hundred yards of plain dirt separating the Governor-
General's enclosures and offices from the accompanying regiments of the British army; a wax-cloth-covered tower, which
housed the band, overlooking the *zenana* quarters; even an
Akash-diya, "light in the sky," a hundred-foot-high pole atop
which sat an equally large paraffin lamp, lit all night through
as an indication of the Governor-General's presence at camp.

Bryne made some changes, of course. The bazaar for the
soldiers and the servants was, as per the *Ain,* on the four outside corners of the camp. But a few shops were installed inside
at regular intervals. They sold hats, pins, petticoats, the odd
book or novel from the belongings of a recently dead Com-

pany man, brooches, necklaces, yards of indifferent fabric, needles, thread, thimbles, and the like. Food came from the kitchen house at the rear, and this only for the three hundred or so inhabitants—the aides-de-camp; the various secretaries, political and civil; the military commanders; the medical men; the civil servants attached to the Governor-General's office in the capacity of advisers or listeners; and all of their families.

The *Ain*'s tent for worship had been replaced by, well, a tent for worship presided over by the chaplain, Mr. Hurley, in which, every Sunday morning, he gave long, sonorous sermons unmindful of the heat, or the clanking *punkah* that merely moved the sluggish air around. The streets were laid out at right angles, in tight and sharp turns, not more than a few hundred yards long, and this became the promenade. Here, on somewhat cool evenings, the ladies came out to walk alongside their men, arm in arm, nodding their heads at friends and acquaintances they had seen every day for the last year and a half, showing off their oft-shown finery—vastly out of fashion in London by now.

Across the Sutlej, there was no such haphazardness in Maharajah Ranjit Singh's camp. Major Bryne's counterpart, Mahabat Arif, was equally well versed in the *Ain*, perhaps better so, since like the author of the *Ain*, he had learned his Persian early on and well. More important, he was quartermaster of a moving camp under a nomadic ruler. For although the Maharajah's empire stretched from Kashmir in the north to the Sutlej in the south and pushed against Afghanistan in the west, Ranjit Singh had had no capital city, no place to rest, for all of his ruling years—he lived in the camp, and delegated administration of the cities to his various generals.

Ranjit Singh's encampment reached out in orderly concentric rectangles—the Maharajah's tent in the very middle, surrounded by the women of his *zenana;* these separated by screens from the offices of the court, a *darbar* hall, a meeting room, an eating room, and beyond them the army. The generals of the army lived among their men and had lushly decorated tents, much like that of their king.

It was in one such tent, on the northeastern corner of the camp, about half a mile from the water's edge, that lights still burned, even this late at night.

General Paolo Avitabile drank, moved his hand down, and a silver platter held by a manservant found its way under the base of the goblet and it landed, deft as a kiss, with barely a sound.

"So the Maharajah is finally to meet Lord Auckland tomorrow," Avitabile said in Persian.

By his side, the doctor, Martin Honigberger, nodded. "What did you think of this new Governor-General?"

"Speak English, won't you?" This came harshly from the man seated on their far right on the semicircular divan. Josiah Harlan, the American in the group.

Avitabile turned to gaze at him. Harlan was always a little crass, a little too loud, his consonants grating, his vowels never quite achieving the sound of music. Though he too could speak Persian (and perfectly understood what had been said), he butchered the beauty of the language in his mouth well before it found its way to a listener's ear. At court, everyone—Indian and not—cringed when Harlan spoke his chopped Persian or Hindustani, and Avitabile could see their minds processing the words before they could be, even remotely, understood.

"Why?" Avitabile asked, his hand out for the wine, which swung down from the bearer's arms on the platter before he had reached too far. The crushed grapes from Kabul sang on his tongue, sweet, tart, fruity, honeyed. He raised his wineglass toward Harlan in appreciation, for it was this man who had brought the cases of Kabul wines from Afghanistan a few months ago, and his efforts had filled the Maharajah's cellars to choking.

"The servants," Harlan mumbled. "They understand too much."

At this, all the men in Avitabile's tent roared with a gentle laughter.

"It's only the British who believe that the Indians do not understand English, Josiah," General Ventura said. "No doubt their servants do, and make use of the fact to their advantage."

"Still . . ." Harlan muttered. His was the brightest eye in the room, among these most decorated foreign generals and ministers in Maharajah Ranjit Singh's employ. Josiah Harlan had never let a fermented drink pass through his lips in all his years, whether here in Hindustan or at home in Philadelphia. His father had been a merchant trader; his brothers were in the same business, and the sea was in their blood. But of all of his siblings, it was Josiah who had sailed off American shores early on, to Calcutta and to a small port in China. Returning home had seemed like being in a bland, one-stroked canvas. Still, Josiah had fallen in love with a woman with fair hands that moved in a blur against her black Puritan gown; but she had later married someone else. "You're too bloody pious, Josiah," she'd said. "I couldn't well have my hearth plagued with such grimness all my living days." So Harlan had boarded another ship and come back to India, vowing never to set foot on American soil again. He was a thick-shouldered man, heavy on top, with a black beard that plunged to his belt. The hair on his head was equally thick, and at a passing glance, if he was dressed in his court robes, he could be taken for a Sikh, a native of the Punjab.

There was a single ambition that simmered within Harlan. He wanted to be king. He hoped sometime, somehow, any-how, to rule over some peoples. He did not care if they were black, white, green, or blue, he just wanted to be king. Per-haps even of Afghanistan? After all, the British were eyeing Dost Mohammad with disfavor, meant to invade his coun-try and put a puppet king on the throne instead, so why not Josiah Harlan of Pennsylvania? They could call him . . .

". . . the Prince of Ghor," Avitabile said.

Again, there was that placid laughter from Honigberger and Ventura, who knew that Harlan had already loosely styled himself such, taking the name of the province of Ghor in Afghanistan, this after just a few visits to that country on behalf of Ranjit Singh, and after finding in Dost Mohammad a ruler who had no intention of being deposed.

Harlan flushed and subsided onto the cushions of the divan. On the far side of the tent, the *nautch* girls still danced, the music from the sitars still played, and the singer's voice, though hoarse from overuse through the long night, still trilled out the same songs.

"Send them away, Avitabile," Honigberger begged in his guttural voice, his eyelids drooping with fatigue. "The Maharajah makes us watch his *nautch* girls interminably, should we have to in your tent also? Besides, they're tired."

Avitabile raised an eyebrow toward his *jemadar*, Babu. The man stood all the way near the flap of the tent, out of earshot surely, and Honigberger had spoken in English, but in a wailing, fretful, above all carrying voice, and Babu understood, bowed, clapped his hands softly, and ushered the orchestra and the dancing girls out.

"Why does Auckland want to invade Afghanistan?" Honigberger asked when the tent was empty of everyone but the five men.

"Auckland doesn't," Avitabile said, lighting a thin, brown cigarette, cupping his hands over the flame. His lean, brown face lit up briefly, gray eyes long-lashed, the skin smooth and clean-shaven with barely a wrinkle marring it. When he raised his head toward his companions, no laugh lines cut along the edges of his mouth. Avitabile had rarely laughed enough to create them. He flung the matchstick into the air, and it came to rest, smoke winding upward, upon the rich red Persian carpet. But Avitabile did not care. His warehouse in Peshawar contained many more such carpets, silver and gold platters, jugs, goblets, and pots. "McNaghten does," he said now. "That political secretary. Auckland is too timid to venture into anything remotely resembling a war or conquest."

Ventura's teeth flashed in a white gleam. Like Avitabile, Ventura was a soldier, a general in Ranjit Singh's army, also, an Italian. In fact, it was Ventura who had drawn Avitabile this far out east, and the two men, of like temperament, like personality, could trace their friendship back all the way to the first day they had signed up as soldiers outside the tiny town of Agerola on the Amalfi coast, at the age of sixteen.

"He is a bear, that McNaghten," Ventura said. "He is the reason there is going to be a war with Afghanistan, and he is the reason Auckland is here, hat in hand, imploring our Maharajah for troops and money."

Honigberger wiped his bald head thoughtfully. He was the official surgeon in Ranjit Singh's court, from the principality of Transylvania in Romania. His primary job was personal physician to the Maharajah. And, because Ranjit Singh could not imagine a man intelligent in one way not to have *some* acumen in another, Honigberger was also put in charge of the Empire's gunpowder factory and the stock of guns for the imperial army. He might have known how to treat the ailing horse that had disturbed Emily's sleep for many nights now, if he had known of its existence or been asked for help—at one time, Honigberger had made a poultice to treat the ulcerated legs of the Maharajah's favorite horse, Leili.

Avitabile felt in the pocket of his short cotton coat for the pair of dice he kept there always, and flung them upon the carpet. They rolled smoothly on the pile and came to rest against the base of the lantern with a quiet click. The men bent to peer at the dice, ivory-clear, glowing like little nuggets of snow.

"What did you throw this time, my friend?" Allard asked. Jean-François Allard had been the earliest—before Avitabile and Ventura—at the Maharajah Ranjit Singh's court, and had blazed the trail for them, so to speak, landing first at the court of Persia, and then taking them with him to Lahore. Allard was French, born at Saint-Tropez, and like Avitabile had grown up with the blue of the sea in his heart.

The Maharajah had been impressed by Allard's credentials, by the decorations heaped on him by the Persian Shah, and Allard had been given the city of Lahore to govern. In Maharajah Ranjit Singh's court, at times, the risks were high, but the rewards equally so.

"Two fours," Avitabile responded in the same language Allard had spoken in, French.

"It is true?" Honigberger asked.

"Always," Harlan said with a small smile that lost itself in his midnight beard. "Avitabile has the . . . the best luck of any man I've known." He had meant to say the devil's own luck, but Harlan had never taken the devil's name in jest or in seriousness.

Paolo Avitabile lay back on the cushions of the divan and let his long legs hang over the edge. Stretched out like this, he was a giant of a man, as indeed he was standing also, an inch shy of seven feet. He had won the dice from a boy in the army, and won exactly that, the dice themselves, not the money from the game. He had won because he had cast the dice perfectly each time, calling out how the cubes would roll before he threw. On his way back, Paolo had bought a single rose from a street seller, crushed the petals in a small canteen of water, and immersed the sweaty dice into this. His tent mate had laughed. Making perfume, my Paoluccio? No, just my luck, Paolo had replied, rubbing off the offensive odor of that other boy.

Paolo had been seventeen at that time, one year into his army service, already roughened and hardened into a man his parents had not recognized when he returned home on leave to Agerola. All of a sudden, the house he had grown up in with his four brothers and sisters had seemed small, confining, the roof too low, the doorframes no longer accommodating his sprouting figure. He had never gone back to Agerola again but had spent every subsequent leave, and his money, on books. He read day and night when not on the march or the drill grounds. And like Ventura and Allard, he had joined the imperial army under Napoleon Bonaparte, for that little man had fired something in all of their imaginations with his bold and published ambitions, his very presence, even his name, which came to represent all that was hallowed in military life.

And eventually Ventura and Avitabile had met in the army, and each had risen through the ranks. And then, Napoleon was imprisoned at Elba, he escaped from Elba, he fought at Waterloo, he was defeated at Waterloo, he was sent to Saint Helena. They all knew that this was the final setback—that there was no escaping from Saint Helena and that, having once let Napoleon get away, the British were not about to make that mistake again.

The imperial army disbanded, but not Napoleon's most cherished ambition. For although he had fought at various battlefields and in various countries, even in Egypt, what Napoleon Bonaparte had most wanted was to be Emperor of India. Just that. Every other battle was in preparation for this one, last encounter that would make him king of India's millions, and master of her treasures. He had heard of Maharajah Ranjit Singh, of course, and possibly knew that he might have to defeat him to make his dreams a reality. Bonaparte had also heard of the Persian Shah, who if he wanted to take the land route to India, would be inflexibly in the way—but he had thought of Persia as another country to conquer, that's all.

General Paolo Avitabile lifted himself off the divan and crawled on his hands and knees to the lantern and the dice that lay against its base. The two fours lay faceup. He picked them up, put them back into his pocket, and waved at his friends.

"To home, to bed, *mes amis*," he said. "Tomorrow the Auckland meets the Maharajah. And I have other people to see. The *chère* mademoiselle Emily."

"You're going hunting, Avitabile," Harlan said thoughtfully, chewing on a piece of straw.

"I've already chased down my prey, Josiah."

The men left. In a few hours they would be up again, bathed and groomed, sharp as ever, with no trace of the night's excess upon their faces or their persons. Avitabile, Ventura, and Allard were the hardest-working and most effective of the Maharajah's generals. If the British did not dare to cross the Sutlej to invade the Punjab, or if the Afghan King Dost Mohammad was content not to push too hard against his southern boundaries to anger Ranjit Singh, it was due to these men.

They were nothing loath to do this; they had talents, the Maharajah paid amply for them, and they were all, already, men of stupendous fortune, their beggarly soldier days long forgotten. As long as Ranjit Singh lived, he had their devotion. But he was ill, ailing, aged even, and all five men had begun thinking about what it would mean if their foreign king died and they were left unmoored in this alien land, after so many years.

Why not reach out to the mighty British Empire, which had already pounced upon, and pinned down the Union Jack on so much of the map of India?

As the late-night revelers in both camps went to bed, lights were doused, and shimmering, blue-flamed night lanterns picked out the streets and the guardhouses. In the skies above, clouds came to blot out the stars in mammoth handfuls until, at dawn, only a single beam of the sun's rays cut an opening in all that gray and sent a spear of gold cleaving into the middle of the Sutlej. The clouds also held the warmth in, smothering the land below, and when the skies opened and let loose their fury, it was a heated downpour that fell upon the banks of the river.

Emily woke to the sound of the rain crashing upon the roof of her tent. One edge had caved in, and water streamed down the tent pole and puddled on the carpet. Chance sniffed around the pole, his long tongue lapping moisture from the pile. His fur was sprayed with wet, and when he came to push his nose into her lap, she said, "Away, Chance. Jimrud!"

Her *jemadar* filled the doorway to the tent, his eyes bent downward. "You called, Ladyship?"

"Take Chance to Bhushan."

"*Ji*, Ladyship." He hesitated though, his gaunt, brown hands moving in distress upon the white shirtfront of his tunic, worrying the gilt buttons. "Bhushan is . . . um . . . occupied right now. He will be back in twenty minutes. Can the dog stay here until then? You know that only he can manage Chance."

Bhushan was, well, he was Chance's butler. When they left England, Emily had refused to leave her dog behind. And at Calcutta, Chance had had three men hired exclusively to look after him. One cooked his meat, added spices to it, made a stew, and poured it over rice for his meals. Another bathed him every day, dried his fur, combed it smooth and shining. A third, Bhushan, entertained him, took him out to the pond at the end of the garden at Government House and allowed him to leap after the pale yellow and green frogs.

"Where is he?"

Jimrud blushed, his brown skin darkening even more. He mumbled, "He has gone to the river, Lady Sahib. With his *lota*. The rain . . . it will take him a while to return. A letter came this morning to the Lord Sahib, Ladyship, and he sent you a note. Here." Jimrud shuffled into the room and laid the paper on the edge of Emily's bed.

Emily coughed and grabbed at the letter. What Jimrud was saying, in his discreet way, was that Bhushan had gone to use the public privies near the bank, and he would rather not have had to say that. She wouldn't have allowed a manservant into her bedroom in England, but here, in India, he was one of the few people who actually spoke English, and besides, he was a native. He didn't count as a man, and she didn't care if the neckline of her nightgown fell open, or her silhouette showed through the flimsy cotton. Jimrud had no emotions toward her. He came, he obeyed, he rarely raised his eyes to her, he left. He was so perfect that at one point Major Bryne, who had been looking for a replacement for George's butler, had tried to wrangle Jimrud away from Emily. Bryne's argument was that a new *jemadar* could be found for Emily, and how wonderful it would be for the next Governor-General's wife to find a personal manservant already trained and fluent in English. But Emily had held on to Jimrud's arm tenaciously—and let George muddle his way with a new *jemadar* himself, and left all the training to Major Bryne. It was a small victory, but a victory nonetheless.

She opened the letter. It was dated an hour before the rains had begun. George said that the Maharajah had canceled the official meeting because of the weather and that they would have to wait for the sun to smile upon them, but the Maharani had set up a welcome tent upriver, would the ladies of the Governor-General's party favor her with a visit later this afternoon?

Fanny had already gone out into the rain to inspect the Queen's Buff regiment along with their nephew Bill, who was military secretary to George—he had come with them from England, because his mother had asked George to take him to India and keep him out of trouble for a while at least. Emily called for her maid Wright, dressed slowly, ate her breakfast, and thought about General Avitabile, who had wound through her dreams. Would he be there?

And so, a few hours later, they set out on their horses with a small contingent of ladies from the camp—McNaghten's wife; the chaplain's wife, Mrs. Hurley; a sprinkling of other women who all made up the society at Calcutta. George's aides-de-camp had their native wives, but they kept them hidden in *zenanas* of their own, tucked away, pensioned off when the actual wife came in from England. Mr. Taft was with them also, his red dispatch case slung over his saddle, his brain, doubtless, already classifying each item that the Maharani Jindan Kaur would present to Emily and Fanny. The soldiers of the Sixth Hussars followed behind.

The rain had abated its ferocity, and now, as they picked through the sludgy ground into a grove of guava, it splashed silently over the lime-green leaves and slid across the curve of Emily's bonnet and down her neck. She hunched above her reins, one knee wedged around the hump in the saddle, her boots grimy, her hands fiery inside her leather gloves.

Fanny laughed. And in that silent wood, where the only sound came from the sucking of their horses' hooves in the muck and the twitter of the parrots as they flew low, rustling the leaves and sending showers of water upon their unprotected heads, the laugh was a clean, pure noise. Glass cutting through the humid air.

Emily turned to look at her sister. At Park Lodge, while Emily was in the garden, her gloves caked with dirt, a smear of soil upon her cheek where she had pushed her hair out of the way, the cool wind burnishing her skin into a healthy crimson, Fanny had lain on the sofa in the drawing room, her head stuffed with perpetual colds, her chest hollow, her voice hoarse with a cough. Fanny had always been a picture of balled-up handkerchiefs, a red nose, and complaints in a wheezing voice.

And then, they had stepped onto the docks at Calcutta. Here, with the thermometer nudging the low one hundreds, Emily lay flattened in a public corridor at Government House in a cane chair, her stays loosened, her fingers ink-stained, letters strewn in her lap, hoping to snag the little crosscurrent of breeze that sneaked in through the front door and out the back. And Fanny? She had returned to her nubile, hopping youth. The heat never seemed to bother her. While their skins had taken on the yellow pallor of the interminably long Indian summers, Fanny's was brown and lush. She woke in the early mornings, rode out with Bill or another officer, brought home a veritable menagerie of animals she had found wounded; she wrote letters, she visited rajas, she knitted and embroidered and painted.

Even now, her bonnet traveled down her back, held at her throat with two strings, and her black hair glittered with drops of rain. In India, Fanny had become Emily. There was nothing she wouldn't try. She had gone out camping in the Rajkot hills, shot at a tiger, and come back to camp with her face peppered with gunpowder. At the parties at Government House, she tried all the dances on the floor, she drank wine and did not water it down; her face had opened up, her smile had brightened.

Fanny held up her hand, the sleeves of her gown puckered to the elbow, and pulled down a branch of the guava tree nearest to her. Emily ducked, but it was too late, and water tumbled upon them both. "Isn't this glorious?" Fanny shouted.

"Fanny, stop," Emily said. "You haven't even bothered to change after your outing this morning. We're going to get to the Maharani's tent looking like beggars."

"I haven't?" Fanny said in surprise, looking down at her morning gown. There was a small rend in the muslin at the hem, a smudge of grime along her thigh. "Well, the Maharani commanded us without notice; she'll have to take us as we are. I'm sure she only wants to see us, not our clothes. I haven't had the luxury of bathing and preparing for this all morning, Em, wallowing in the roses that General Avitabile sends to fill my tent."

"Hush," Emily said, glancing back quickly. But the pathway had narrowed, and the other women, a little way away, were talking among themselves; just for the moment, Emily and Fanny were alone in this sea of green light and humidity.

And then Fanny said, a curious gleam in her eye, "Why didn't you accept our ponderous friend Melbourne, Emily? He asked you, didn't he? Lady Cowper said he had and she should know; he's ludicrously fond of his sister." And slyly, "Just as George is with you."

Emily reddened. "Lady Cowper talked to you about it? It was none of your business."

"Ah," Fanny said, throwing back her head and laughing, "but it was, my dear. If you married that old stodge, I would have George to myself. I was *immensely* interested. And you wouldn't tell me anything, so I had to go searching for the other woman in Melbourne's life. You know, you could have been the wife of the Prime Minister of England today; imagine that, being received by the Queen"—she waved her hand in a slow circle—"none of this trucking through the rain and mud to meet a native woman who styles herself as such. None of this being commanded by one of them."

"We haven't been commanded," Emily said automatically.

But Fanny wouldn't stop. "But we have been, my dear. Else we wouldn't be in this forest, me wet, you miserable, both of us thinking about that comely Monsieur Avitabile, with his fluid French ways, the masses of roses he grows in his greenhouses in Peshawar."

"He wouldn't have done, you know," Emily said finally. Her horse had come to a halt, its nose bowed doggedly into the earth. She urged it on, prodded its sides, rattled her reins, until Fanny's cool hand, in its lace fingerless glove, came on its head and she said, *"Chalo."*

They were riding in a single line now, the path had narrowed even more, and the branches of the trees came quickening down upon them. Emily was in front, Fanny's mare a short hand span behind.

"Melbourne?" Fanny asked.

Emily sighed. "Yes, Melbourne." When she thought at all about it, this last proposal of marriage when she was thirty-five years old, it wasn't with a tumbling regret.

When Melbourne had come to her, his first wife had been dead for four years; it was the summer they had spent at Lady Cowper's country house. Humming rumors had said that he was the next man to be prime minister; it would have been a good marriage. There was really nothing against it, nobody but herself to consult—Lady Cowper had encouraged it; George would have been mildly happy; and Fanny would have been ecstatic at, as she put it, having George to herself.

"What was wrong with him?" Fanny asked.

Emily turned to speak sideways into the air. "I don't know. Nothing. Perhaps everything." Her mouth twisted in a wry downturn. "I thought too, you know, of my . . . our . . . *my* life with George, and then the one I could possibly have with Melbourne. It wouldn't have done."

"You're too fastidious, Emily. It was his first wife you were thinking of and the glorious scandal, and that he stood by her despite it."

"Perhaps . . ." Emily had read Galt's *The Life of Lord Byron* also, as had all of London, inquisitive about a man she'd met only once, but more curious about what had been his immense charm. For Lady Caroline Lamb had made an absolute ass of herself over Byron, and she had left her husband to do so; and her long-suffering husband, who had taken her back after the violent end of the affair, was none other than Lord Melbourne. Emily had not thought much of Lady Caroline Lamb, who was beautiful, though in an untidy way with those quantities of wispy hair, that constant look of openmouthed surprise, that flighty mind.

"We are so unlike," Emily said slowly. "That, I suppose, is what stopped me. I couldn't imagine a man who had once been in love with *her*, to be in love with me."

"Were *you* in love with him?"

"Perhaps . . ." Emily said again. "I could have been. Maybe . . ."

"It didn't stop him from becoming prime minister though," Fanny said.

"People forget."

A parrot shrieked, and they both looked up, startled.

Fanny pointed her whip at the bird, and it moved on the branch, muttering, its head slanted to one side and then the other as it gazed at them with its beady eyes.

"We should hurry, Miss Eden," Mr. Taft called out from behind them. "We must not keep the Maharajah's wife waiting."

They moved out from the shelter of the grove into open land. Here, the eye stretched into the vast distance, flat everywhere, a few rocks and boulders to break the monotony of the landscape. The rain had slackened into a gentle mist, speckling the waters of the Sutlej with tiny circles. Under the shade of her bonnet, Emily felt sweat gather in her hair, curve rivulets down the sides of her face. She mopped her skin with a handkerchief, and then tucked it back between the third and fourth buttons of her gown. She felt hot, and heavy, sluggish.

For the past few days, since their arrival at the river, during the setting up of the camp and the settling in, Avitabile had sent her baskets of roses and little notes. He didn't say much of consequence—he, and she, had never said much, for what was there to say, after all? They had met a few times at Calcutta, they had talked, he had sent her roses then, as now, and he had remembered his promise of shawls and gowns from Kashmir, ordered them, supervised the work, had them packed carefully and delivered to their tent.

Mr. Taft, worrying the face of his watch by looking at it too many times as he rode beside them, had been lingering outside, notebook in hand to take an inventory of the gift from Avitabile. Four shawls and four gowns of the finest wool and silk embroidery, perhaps six months of painstaking work by at least two embroiderers—everything had been registered, the price assessed after he had calculated the labor, the material, the cost of living in Kashmir. And then he had looked up at Emily, expressionless, his skeletal, white face immobile, only his pinched nostrils flaring in and out as he breathed. I'll pay for them all, she had said. They are expensive, Miss Eden. All right, Emily had said, reaching for her purse, how much?

They had reached a small makeshift pier on the southern bank of the Sutlej. Here, the river narrowed as two spits of sand and rock pushed their way inward on both sides. Through the haze of rain, Emily and Fanny saw a royal tent in red set up on the northern spit. It was a small tent, with crimson screens erected around, and the main tent pole flew the triangular flag of the Punjab Empire—amber yellow, embroidered in black with a double-edged sword, two other daggers curving left and right around it, the center of the sword encircled by something that looked very much like the quoits, the thin bands of steel that the Akalis used as their weapon.

"It must mean that the Maharani is in residence," Fanny said at Emily's elbow.

They dismounted and waited as the barge was readied with a barrage of shouting and cursing. The women went down the rocks carefully and were hauled aboard.

"The roses didn't come today," Fanny said.

Emily turned, and for a moment her face crumpled with distress, an emotion she had never shown before to Fanny. "No." She could barely say the word.

They had neither of them really known George until their mother died and they moved in with him. He had already left for school when she was born. And yet, even growing up together, Fanny and Emily had kept apart—they were so dissimilar, just how much they'd realized only when they went to George. Because Emily and George always had something to talk about; when Emily had fallen ill ten years ago, it was George, not Fanny, who had come home from work every day, fed her beef broth, wiped her brow, read to her at night until the candle guttered in the saucer.

At Government House in Calcutta, Fanny and Emily had chosen rooms in opposite wings—Emily's room was next door to George's; Fanny's was down the corridor, some twenty yards away. They met at the table; they went together to visit the ladies of the cantonment sometimes, and to church. That was all. And, for the first time—with that brief conversation about Lord Melbourne, six years after the event—Emily had let Fanny see what was in her heart.

"Tell him to come and see you, Em," Fanny said, reaching out and touching her sister's thick-gloved hand. "And take that off, it's too hot here."

"It would not be proper," Emily mumbled.

Mr. Taft gestured to them from the barge and they picked their way over, holding up the hems of their dresses so that their boots and ankles showed. Emily realized with a mild shock that Fanny was not wearing her stockings. The Company clerk averted his head, although he held out his hand, and the boatmen stared, stony-faced. The boat was nothing but a flat piece of wood, with no seating, water lapping over the edges. They stood clustered around the middle. Half-naked boatmen, clad only in loincloths, their feet bare, rain streaming over their muscular bodies, ran up and down the length of long poles that they used to propel the flat over the Sutlej.

Maharani Jindan Kaur met them under a gold awning, her back straight, her hands clasped in front. Of her face, they could see little; a veil swung over her head and fell almost to her feet in a swathe of shimmering white seed pearls.

They bowed to each other. A man standing near her, Fakir Azizuddin, murmured greetings on behalf of his queen, Mr. Taft translated for them, and then they went inside.

Within, Azizuddin and Taft were banished to the far corner, behind a chintz screen, both scrunched uncomfortably into a small space. Of Mr. Taft, Emily could see nothing—the screen swallowed his figure, but the heron feather on Fakir Azizuddin's turban bobbed above as he shifted around.

They all sat in a tight circle. It was close inside the tent, even though the cloth was rolled up over the white mesh screens; the mesh itself was clogged with drops of rainwater. Servant girls brought goblets of pomegranate sherbet, palely pink, shards of ice clinking against the glass. There were trays of sweet *burfis* sprinkled with shavings of coconut, made of wheat flour, glistening with *ghee*. Fanny took off her gloves and ate everything; Emily sat on her divan, her knees drawn up to her chest, and took small sips of only the sherbet.

The Maharani could not speak English, so whatever she said, Fakir Azizuddin translated from behind the screen, his voice booming over the confines of the tent, his language ungrammatical, incorrect, but still comprehensible.

They talked thus, complimenting each other, welcoming each other, and saying nothing much. Then, Jindan leaned back and whispered something into the ear of one of her ladies-in-waiting, who rose and went to a small table in the corner and brought back a tray covered with a white cloth.

"The Maharani is pleased to welcome her British sisters to the Punjab," Fakir Azizuddin said, "and she begs that you will consider these paltry gifts and wear them with joy."

Jindan whisked away the cloth, and revealed two perfect diamond and emerald necklaces lying shimmering on the dark wood.

McNaghten's wife sucked in a breath, and they all leaned forward.

One of the Company's clerks had gone on the East India Company's business to . . . somewhere, some native raja's kingdom, to talk about water rights of a river that flowed through the Company's lands, which were downstream from the raja's.

Emily couldn't remember much about the actual business, but the clerk's wife had come back to Calcutta with stories of entertainments at the raja's harem, and boasted of a shawl, a gold necklace, earrings, and bangles that the principal queen had given her. When she had displayed them at the next ball at Government House, Emily had pitied the poor woman. The gold was real, all right, but so chunky, so unimaginatively constructed, good enough only to be smelted into something new. Even Mr. Taft—or rather his counterpart in the Company—had disdained to snatch the jewelry from the clerk's wife.

"One for each of you," Aziz said. "Miss Eden and Miss Fanny Eden."

These pieces were impeccable, rose-cut diamonds, embedded in shining gold, emeralds with the heart of a forest in the rain, luminously green and radiating a wet light.

Fanny nudged Emily. "Taft is probably hopping around behind there." She took out her handkerchief from her right sleeve, wiped her hands on it, and laid a gentle finger on the stones. She laughed with pure wonder, and they heard Mr. Taft clear his throat many times, meaningfully.

A little girl had been standing beside the Queen, her arm around Jindan's shoulder, half-leaning on the older woman. She was a pretty little thing, with solemn, light-colored eyes and a stoic face. Now, a smile curved her mouth upward, and she bent to Jindan and whispered something in her ear.

Jindan held her hand out to Fanny, and when Fanny reciprocated, she shook her head.

"Her Majesty would like to see your handkerchief, Miss Fanny."

"This?" Fanny asked in surprise, and then she knelt on the carpet and smoothed out the piece of fabric, with its lace edging.

"Does anyone else have one?" Fakir Azizuddin asked.

"We all do," Fanny said. She reached into Emily's dress and took out her handkerchief, then signaled to the other

women to give her theirs. Each square she laid carefully on
the carpet, and they all watched as the Maharani and her
ladies crowded over, exclaiming about the lace, dabbing
reverently at the cloth. The girl moved the handkerchiefs
around, gazing at the Maharani with delight.

"Could we leave these with you, your Majesty?" Fanny
asked.

Jindan Kaur nodded, and Aziz said, "It would give my
Queen a great deal of pleasure; she thanks you very much."

A baby cried from somewhere at the back of the tent,
and Maharani Jindan Kaur rose hurriedly, as though that
wail had coiled outward and tethered onto her. The little girl
had already run out to the back, and Emily saw her standing there, almost bowed under by the weight of the child in
her thin arms. The baby was the Maharajah's son, so much
McNaghten, or perhaps Bill, had mentioned to her. But who
was this little girl in the lushly embroidered *ghagara* and
choli, her hair plaited behind her back, almost down to her
knees, the medallion of solid gold around her neck. Who was
she?

Another figure blotted out the child's at the back flap of
the tent, and Emily realized that Jindan Kaur was leaving.

"Thank you," Azizuddin said. The audience was over.

Mr. Taft was led out from a side entrance and came lop-
ing over the soggy ground to grab the tray with the diamond
necklaces, which he wrapped in soft muslin and put into his
dispatch case. Then, holding the case snug under his arm, the
tray itself in his other hand, he followed them to the riverbank.

On the way back, Fanny was grim. The rain had let up
almost completely, although thin, gray clouds still tarried
in the sky, and the sun shed its light upon them as though
through a veil—translucent and golden.

Halfway through the guava grove, Emily's horse refused
to budge. They tried cajoling it, kicking it, feeding it lumps of

brown and raw *jaggery*, but nothing would work. So Fanny dismounted from her horse and said, "Let's walk back."

They did, Emily hesitant at first, following her sister's example of tucking the hem of her gown into her waistband—only long after the others had disappeared toward the British encampment.

Fanny said suddenly, "Did you see the Kohinoor?"

"The Maharani was wearing it?"

"On her arm. He must really love her, that Runjeet."

Emily was disdainful. "It cannot have been that big after all. Even though"—here a doubt crept into her voice—"Bill said it was." Then she remembered the joyful face of Runjeet's young bride. Emily sucked on her tongue. "He's so old, Fanny. I cannot . . . think of them together. And that child who cried, it was their son. He won't ever become Maharajah of the Punjab, will he? There are other, older sons."

"And us," Fanny said. The grimness had come back to her expression now.

Emily knew what she meant, but she didn't respond. What was there to say? Fanny and she saw things differently, just as they had when they were younger. What was there to say?

"Why does George want to invade Afghanistan, Em?"

She shrugged and waved her hand in a vague motion. "I think . . . the Russians. Shuja's there to be put on the throne; we could do with a friend in Afghanistan. George doesn't think . . . that Dost Mohammad is . . . er . . . friendly toward the British Empire."

Fanny slashed at the nearest tree with her whip, and the parrots rose in a mass of green and red, scolded her, and vanished into the sky. "We're not a very friendly people, are we? Look at what we did to the King of Oude; we annexed his kingdom. And if Runjeet's heirs are not careful, we'll do that to the Punjab also."

At another time, before their talk of this morning, Emily would have shouted at Fanny. Something short, something biting, and ended the conversation. But now, as their boots were sucked into the mud, as they walked together, alone, for almost the first time in their lives, she put a warning hand on her sister's arm.

"Don't say this in public, Fanny. Not even to George— it makes a mockery of why we are here in India. It's preposterous, this kind of talking. The East India Company has a right . . . *we* have a right—"

Fanny's eyebrows arched until they were lost in her dark hair. "A divine right, Em?"

"Why not?" This, doggedly.

"I wonder," Fanny said slowly, "if we consulted the Indians at all in this matter. The East India Company has eaten up great big chunks of India; you're right, we will not spit it out without a fight."

Emily laughed, and Fanny looked at her in surprise. "Perhaps you're not so different from George and me after all, Fan. You take advantage of George's position as Governor-General of India, of the money he makes, and then you complain about it."

A voice came to them through the forest. George, squelching in the mud, his shirt sticking to his chest and back, brown riding up his trousers. How was the visit? What did the Maharani say? Anything about the meeting with Runjeet? And so, they walked back together, each of them hanging off one of their brother's arms, thankful for the support after the long, damp day. When they parted within their tents, it was as though the day had not happened, they had not talked, not delved into their hearts and held out secrets to each other. It was as though that twenty yards of corridor had come to stretch between them again.

But Emily forgot all of that, for when she stepped into her tent, there, on the little footstool by the bed, was a wicker basket crammed with white roses. And a letter, on custard-thick paper, filled with elegant, sloping writing.

On the day they were to meet Maharajah Ranjit Singh, the comings and goings between the two camps began well before the break of dawn.

At five o'clock, a British emissary went across the Sutlej, on a raft, alone, rowing himself blindly in the heavy, cotton-like mist that skimmed the river's waters. He had been expected, of course, but that didn't stop the Maharajah's men from sending a few harmless rifle shots zinging through the fog around him. So he arrived sweating and shaking, the air still redolent with the stench of gunpowder. The Maharajah's emissary met him at the banks. They bowed to each other, drank a few cups of steaming *chai,* and the British man ate two or three gluey sweets he could not give name to and did not want in his mouth.

"His Excellency, Lord Auckland of the British Empire wishes to visit the great Maharajah Runjeet Singh and present his compliments in person," he said, wiping his teeth with his tongue and worrying bits of stickiness from them.

The Maharajah's man nodded. "The great and *glorious* Maharajah Ranjit Singh, Lion of the Punjab, Maharajah of Lahore, Head of State, and Lord of the Five Rivers, will be happy to receive the Lord Auckland."

A line of the Maharajah's soldiers, dressed in white and gold, with flimsy gold gauze scarves wrapped around their long beards, came smartly to attention behind. Auckland's emissary bowed again, and again, until he could get on the raft and row himself back to the British encampment. The mist had lifted in all of the talking as the sun sliced over the horizon, and if the Maharajah's men had wanted to practice their shooting, he would have been an open, and standing target. But he arrived back south safely.

An hour later, another emissary rowed from the Maharajah's side to the British side to thank the first one for his visit and to assure the British of Ranjit Singh's acute keenness in meeting Lord Auckland and how much he was looking forward to it. This went on, back and forth, a few times in the morning, and the Sutlej was muddied with all the traffic.

Finally, around ten o'clock, Mr. McNaghten himself went over to the Punjab side, and he was met halfway on the river by Sher Singh, Maharajah Ranjit Singh's adopted son. The two men conversed in the middle, standing upright on their rafts, maintaining their balance precariously while the rowers struggled to keep them afloat. It was agreed by all that the time had finally come for Lord Auckland to make his way to the Sikh encampment.

So at eleven o'clock, Emily and Fanny came out into the warm morning air. George was standing by William McNaghten; Bill, their nephew; and the ADCs. The Queen's Buff regiment stretched out to the riverbank in two solid and parallel lines, rifles held up above their heads and slanted inward, forming a tent of armament.

George stepped forward and put out his arm for Emily, who slipped her small hand through it, and they went down the line of soldiers. Emily could feel the stiffness in George's movements, his sudden intake of breath when he saw the row of caparisoned elephants lined up on the other bank, and the lone, white horse prancing in front. The figure atop the horse was small, hunched, and yet he rode as though born on that elegant horse.

"That is the Maharajah?" Emily asked, patting her brother's arm.

"Must be," he muttered. "Must say he makes a finer figure than I expected. Oh, Emily"—he stumbled, and she held him tight until he had regained his stride—"two months of this to get through."

She glanced at her brother. His black velvet tailcoat fitted about his shoulders, emblazoned with ribbons and decorations, the epaulets rimmed in gold braid. His linen, high-waisted trousers had been dusted off just five minutes before by his *jemadar* in his tent, but they had already become sullied with dirt; his knee-length boots were dull. George wore a white shirt with a short collar, and a red velvet vest. Above his collar, his thin face was taut and shiny with sweat, his hair lying flat against his skull.

Behind them, Fanny murmured something in a low voice into Bill's ear, and his muted laughter followed them all the way.

Emily and George climbed into a sumptuously decorated howdah on an elephant's back—after two years on the move, she could do this without much effort. George, who had never become used to anything in India, tripped and finally heaved himself over to fall onto the cushions. When they had settled themselves, Emily turned to watch the rest of their party climb onto the backs of other elephants.

The mahout, a slim, dark man clad in only a *dhoti* covering him from the waist down, knocked with his ankh on the elephant's head and it rose laboriously. First on its hind legs, tipping them forward, and then on its forelegs. Emily held on to her hat with one hand and the pillars of the howdah with the other. They could not have rowed over the Sutlej, or ridden on horses, or even walked on foot. Nothing less than an elephant and a howdah would do for the Governor-General of India to meet the Maharajah of the Punjab Empire.

The elephant trudged slowly into the Sutlej, drops of water splashing upward. Emily and George ducked and shielded their faces. She took out her handkerchief and wiped the mud from George's cravat as best she could.

And then, the elephant halted in the middle of the river, its trunk punching through the air, its huge ears fluttering at the edges. The mahout banged on its head, prodded the heavy, gray skin with his ankh, spoke into its ear. But it stood there, obstinate. And then, its trunk sneaked downward, they heard an intake of harsh breath, and before Emily or George could react, the elephant had raised its trunk over its head and bathed them with a rush of warm water.

The mahout turned, took off his turban, and wiped his forehead with the cloth. His voice was filled with a hidden laughter. "I'm sorry, Lord Sahib, he will not move."

The other elephants and camels trudged through the Sutlej, passing them by, uncontrolled for the most part by their mahouts and drivers. Fanny waved. "We're going to get there first, George!"

George sank back and hid his face in Emily's lap. "We should have taken a damn boat. It was McNaghten who insisted upon these animals. He knew, from Fakir Azizuddin, that Runjeet meant to meet us with his entire stable of elephants, so we could do no less, McNaghten said."

"And it's his war also, isn't it, George?" Emily said, looking around her in despair. Fanny was hanging half out of her howdah, and at that moment, a fistful of wind blew her hat onto the waters. Emily followed its path and saw it float for a moment before it sank. And then she searched for the man who was responsible for this fracas—William McNaghten, George's political secretary. In the normal course of things, to meet a native king, George would have brought along his foreign secretary, but the visit to the Punjab Empire was a political one, for the purpose of embarking on a war, and McNaghten had kidnapped the foreign secretary's duties for his own.

On the other bank, the lone figure on the horse threw his right hand up into the air, and then he jerked at his reins. The more orderly elephants on the northern bank of the Sutlej opened their ranks and gave way to their king. When he had galloped out of sight, the elephants moved back into formation, solid and unyielding.

Emily and George sat on their elephant in the middle of

the Sutlej River for an hour. Each time a raft was rowed near
the animal, it trumpeted and bumped it away with its trunk.
The mahout jumped into the waters and disappeared in the
crowd and the shouting. If he had stayed, he would have
felt the lashes of a whip on his shoulders before the end of
the day. The elephant had no such compunction. He doused
his trunk into the Sutlej and sprayed them with water again
and again. On the other bank, the reception committee went
back to their quarters, and only the Maharajah's normal guard
remained, lounging on rocks, smoking *beedis* and watching
them with avid curiosity.

McNaghten and the other members of George's council
scurried up and down in the sand, like so many crabs. Some
of them had guided their elephants safely back to land, some
had splashed back through the water.

Finally, Emily dangled over the edge of the howdah and
clambered down the elephant's broad torso, using the ropes
that tethered the howdah to its back as a ladder. The Sutlej
ran shallow here, only some three or four feet deep. A flurry
of ADCs, stripped to their shirts, made a chair with their arms
and carried her back. Emily flushed, acutely conscious of
their heated breaths upon her neck, of their arms around her
waist, under the backs of her thighs; she had never been so
close to these young men, not even when dancing with them.
And so, George and she returned to their camp, bedraggled
and filthy, her gray velvet gown ruined forever.

When darkness dropped, an infantryman waded into
the waters up to the stubborn beast, raised his rifle, and shot
it between the eyes. Within the hour, the carcass had been
towed away.

In her tent, Emily lay in her bed. A kind message had come
from the Maharajah that since they had been . . . ah . . . unable
to meet today, would tomorrow work equally well? Same
time? Same place? McNaghten said yes, yes, yes, of course,
your Majesty; the Governor-General of India will be there.

George slept early, mopping up the frightful day with the fabric of the night. Emily could hear Fanny and Bill playing a noisy game of cards in her room—it had all just been a great deal of fun for Fanny. We've given the Maharajah some rollicking entertainment, she had said, that's all. Emily held the note that had accompanied this morning's roses.

Je pense souvent à Calcutta, Avitabile had said. *Vous aussi?*

I think often of Calcutta. Do you also?

She did. When they had settled into life at Government House at Calcutta in some fashion, ambassadors began coming and going from the courts of the lesser maharajahs and leaders of inconsequential states—all of whom wanted something from the East India Company. And then came the contingent from Maharajah Ranjit Singh's court in the Punjab. He was no petty ruler, and *they* wanted something from him. Along with that contingent came a seven-foot-tall, gravely handsome Neapolitan named Paolo Avitabile.

Emily first met Avitabile at the grand ball thrown in honor of Ranjit Singh's deputation in the Marble Hall. Earlier that afternoon, George had given them a small luncheon, which Emily had missed, lying down in her room upstairs with a headache and chills. For the ball, she forced herself out of bed, had Wright assist her with her corset, pull her pink muslin gown over her head, allowed her English maid to fan out the roses trimmed on the edges of the dress. It was an old gown, two years out of fashion in Paris, the colors muted, but the best one she had.

Some seven hundred people attended the ball. The Maharajah's party was large by itself, eighty people, and they stood out in the very English crowd with their magnificent silk turbans, long beards, the diamonds, rubies, and emeralds studded on their coats, belts, and enameled daggers.

The enormous chandeliers in Marble Hall, hugging close to its ornate ceiling, were shimmering lit, footmen glided in red plush trousers and white gloves, the tables were pushed back against the walls, and when the band struck up its first quadrille, Paolo Avitabile bent his long length over Emily's hand and asked her for a dance.

The room suddenly faded around her, and all Emily could see was his gentle, lean face, those thickly arched eyebrows, the hint of a smile about his lips. His hand was clasped warmly about hers. "I don't dance, monsieur," she stammered in French, the language he had used. He had spoken it impeccably, without even a hint of an accent. "Thank you, but I don't, really."

Avitabile pulled out a chair, with a curt bow to Eliza Fane, who was seated nearby, her eyes gleaming with curiosity, turned his back, and settled next to Emily. "Then I shall not also, Mademoiselle Emily. If I cannot, with the most beautiful woman in this room, it's hardly worth the effort."

Eliza Fane chortled and Emily flushed, deeply uncomfortable at the praise. Lord Melbourne, in his lucid moments, or even in his most romantic ones, had never used the word *beautiful* in referring to her. And Melbourne had been proposing marriage to Emily.

"You have been with the Maharajah for a while, monsieur?" she asked. The room was suddenly hot, the noise was unbearable, the colors of the women's clothing blurred in front of her eyes. Her head throbbed.

"Twenty years," he replied, neatly flicking a glass of champagne from a passing footman's salver. "Would you like one also?" He bent a finger to beckon. The footman, Baigley, hesitated at the imperious summons, with a mutinous fold around his mouth. The parties for the native rajah were an inevitable part of the Governor-General's duties, but the servants did not take to them easily, or obediently. And Avitabile, though not a native, was in the pay of one. To Baigley, brought out to India from the London slums to work at Government House, however, they were all the same.

Before Emily could react, Avitabile snapped his fingers. "Now." She could not see his expression, Baigley could, and he skipped over with the champagne and presented it, trembling, to the general.

"I apologize," Avitabile said smoothly, setting the flute upon the table. "There's only one way to deal with these brigands. Forgive me, but if he were in my house, I would have cut off his fingers by sundown." He took a sip of his drink, swirled it around so that it caught a golden light from the candles, and looked at it reflectively. His amused gaze rested upon Emily. "Well, perhaps not all of his fingers, and no, not his thumb, he would be useless without it, but maybe just one little one."

Behind him, there was the scraping of a chair as Eliza Fane rose.

"Who is she?" Avitabile asked.

Emily stared at him. Melbourne had seemed coarse to her, bumbling, unable to form a sentence of love, although grandiosely eloquent in Parliament—that last had got him elected Prime Minister. Avitabile, this fastidious man in his impeccably cut frock coat, the long length of his legs stretched out and crossed at the ankles in front of her gown, was, for all his raw talk, fascinating.

"Eliza Fane is the Commander in Chief's daughter," she said.

"Ah, Mr. Fane's child," Avitabile said. He glanced at her deliberately. "Not so much of a child anymore though, I see."

Emily watched as Eliza paled, white to her fingertips, and moved heavily away.

"She has been . . . cruel," Emily said, more to herself than to him.

"I know women, mademoiselle," Avitabile replied. "I have known many women." He leaned forward to rest his forearms on the table. "Was it cruelty, really? From someone whom you would not consort with in London?"

"No." Emily shook her head. "It's true, what you say. We wouldn't have had any reason . . . Her father moves in different circles. But she's some nine years younger than me, Monsieur Avitabile."

"You are honest, Mademoiselle Emily." Avitabile spread out his hands. "I have known many women, but none as honest as you. None who have told me how old they are."

"I haven't."

"Ah, but nine years is a lot of time to admit as a difference. A year, maybe two, even better just a few months would lead to a lot of muddled speculation." He put his hand out to her again. "Will you dance with me now at least?"

"Yes," she said.

The quadrille had long ended, the orchestra was tuning up for a new song, and when it came, the floor cleared as the women fled to the ends of the room. It was a waltz, newly brought down from England. Her heart thumping in her chest, Emily allowed Avitabile to lead her through the dance.

She could not lift her eyes to his, and knew that everyone was watching them. Her head was bowed under the weight of a neck that was suddenly heavy, her right hand was laid down, holding a clutch of her gown, her left was clasped in Avitabile's right, and his other hand lay warm around her waist. And so they moved.

The next morning came a bouquet of roses and the very first letter from Avitabile. In it he asked, *Voudriez-vous me montrer votre ménagerie, chère mademoiselle Emily?* Will you show me your zoo?

Mr. Taft came in on the heels of Jimrud, Emily's *jemadar*, who bore both the red roses and the letter. He flitted past the open door to her bedroom in his short coat and trousers that never met his ankles, punctuating his movements with dry coughs.

She ignored him, and instead held out her arms and filled them with the scent and color of the flowers. It was the month of June, a steaming, stewing June in Calcutta, and roses were not to be found anywhere. And yet, these were limpid, just in full bloom, still patterned with dew, and exquisite. Jimrud then silently offered the letter. Emily slit it open with a silver letter opener and read the few words it contained. She felt a warmth rise to cover her face.

It was ridiculous to feel like this. All their lives, the Eden girls had been pursued, in one form or another, in the marriage market. If Emily and Fanny were the only two unmarried sisters in the outsize Eden clan, it was by choice. They had a place with George, some income of their own, and the reasons for marrying—if not for love, maybe then for security, for a home—didn't exist for them. The proposals, when they came, were also from men of some power and esteem. Eleanor, the oldest, now married for some forty years, had once enamored William Pitt, who had gone on to become Prime Minister of England. Nothing came of it. When the second man knelt in front of Eleanor, hand on his heart, she hadn't done badly either and was now the Countess of Buckinghamshire. And yet, why was she, Emily, moved by this Paolo Avitabile?

Mr. Taft made a gargling sound in his throat. "Miss Eden, I must ask for a look at the gift."

"Protocol, Mr. Taft?" Emily asked with a sigh.

"Yes, you never know with these native kings, they strew so many diamonds around, and everything you get must go into the Toshakhana." He had the grace to look embarrassed for once. "Company rules." The Toshakhana was the East India Company's treasure house, a term it had borrowed from the native rajas and their *toshakhanas*. Because in India, the treasures were so vast, so unimaginably rich, merely calling it a treasure would almost be . . . a misnomer.

"Here." Emily proffered the roses and watched as his

stubby fingers parted the petals of each flower and he peered in, suspicious even of the dew which might well be the diamonds he had talked about. He upturned the bouquet and shook it out; nothing fell from it other than a rush of water. He pricked his finger on the thorns, wrapped it in a handkerchief, and continued his examination. When he had finished, he held the roses out to her, and then drew back his arm. "But . . ." he said.

Emily laughed. "They're just roses, Mr. Taft. If you put them into the Toshakhana, they will eventually wither and die—no money can be made out of them."

Taft looked hopefully at the folded letter in Emily's hands. She shook her head. "I won't show it to you; it's private. Now"—she held out her hand—"can I have my roses back?"

He returned them, reluctantly, and when he had left, Emily sat down to read the letter again, and again.

Later that week, the Governor-General and his sisters took their official yacht, the *Sonamukhi*, fifteen miles up the river Hooghly to Barrackpore, along with some members of Maharajah Ranjit Singh's party. Lord Wellesley, who had built Government House at Calcutta, had constructed a building of the same name in Barrackpore, the summer residence of the Governor-General. This was nowhere as grand as the Calcutta residence, but it boasted, in its park, a complete menagerie.

The Barrackpore zoo had a pelican, Java pigeons, a rhinoceros, cranes, tigers, elephants, and bears. Here, for two days, Emily and Avitabile paraded the grounds, their servants never too far behind. They sat by the cage of the tiger and spoke in low voices; they walked among the pathways at night and listened to the wild, haunting cries of the birds in the aviary.

When the party left for the Punjab, Avitabile bowed and

kissed Emily's hand. It was the first time he had attempted to make any sort of contact with her. He said, "I will order the cashmere shawls for you, mademoiselle, and have them sent to Government House."

"Thank you," she said. "But I'm afraid Mr. Taft will not allow us to keep them."

"I must have a talk with your Mr. Taft."

"No," she said, smiling, a hand on his arm. "He does his duty, that's all. We would be glad of the shawls, General Avitabile."

"Until Lahore then," he said.

Emily nodded, suddenly overcome with sadness. It would be a while before they arrived at Maharajah Runjeet Singh's court, and there was no guarantee that Avitabile would be there—he was Governor of Peshawar, and if his duties kept him in that province, there he would stay.

Over the next year and a half, Avitabile had written to Emily, something about Peshawar, something about the shawls. She had responded lightly, telling him of their travels, of the native rajas they had met, of the schools for British orphans that she had gone to, of the Hindu College, where the natives were being taught medicine.

When each letter came, George said something new to her about General Avitabile. That he was a mercenary, a soldier, a warrior, that he hadn't had a formal education. That when he had first gone to Peshawar as governor, he had had stakes erected all around the city's walls, and every morning, before breakfast, ninety men were hung from those stakes. They were all miscreants, true, and by the end of a couple of weeks, the only men who walked the streets of Peshawar were the honest, the upright, the decent.

"It's a good thing then, George?" Emily asked, puzzled.

"If you think it is, Em. We have a justice system in England, trials, appeals, that sort of thing, meant to weed out

the bad from society. This kind of summary judgment is . . .
appalling."

"I see," Emily said. But it didn't change her mind about
Avitabile.

She waited, with an undefined yearning, to come to meet
the Maharajah. She wondered if Avitabile would be there. On
the first morning, the roses came again. He was there. That
was all she could think about. That she would meet him soon.
Again. And, soon.

Emily pulled off the bedclothes, thrust her feet into slippers, and padded to her desk. She dipped her pen into the inkpot, drained it on the lip of the pot, and held it over the paper.
She hesitated so long that a blob of ink formed at the tip of
the nib and hung trembling there. She touched the nib to the
blotting paper and then began to write.

Emily didn't often heed—perhaps had never heeded—
what Fanny had to say. For once, she did. If Paolo Avitabile would not make a move in coming to see her, she would
invite him.

*A dinner, Monsieur Avitabile? I would like to thank you in
person for the shawls and the gowns; they were much more than
I expected.* Then, greatly daring. *And . . . we could pick up our
friendship from where we left off at Calcutta.*

She blew out her lantern and burrowed under the sheets,
resting her feet on Chance's warm body, rounded and snug-
gled at the bottom of the bed. When she was almost asleep,
the sickly horse outside coughed again. She listened to the
sound growing feebler and feebler until it stopped, and all
she could hear was the rasping of the animal's breath, sieved
through worn-out lungs. The *punkah* creaked, the night wore
on, and before dawn, the mist had taken on a coldness that
caused the guards to wrap mufflers around their throats and
shove their hands into their pockets.

The previous day had been one of stultifying heat; this

next one brought the long-awaited winter to the Punjab with a sudden ferocity known only in India.

The skies were a mottled gray on the next day, heavy, leaden. In England, they would have carried in their wombs a hint of snow—here it was all just a dry, spotless cold. By the time Jimrud brought her a morning cup of chocolate, muddied with goat's milk, Emily was sitting up in bed, the covers drawn over her knees and feet.

"Thank you," she said, holding the warm cup between chilled fingers.

Jimrud bowed. "You are welcome very much, Ladyship."

And that was the type of English he had learned, and so earned his position in the Governor-General's residence in Calcutta as the personal butler to the lady of the house. Soon after the dinner party on the first day of their arrival at Calcutta, in the small hours of the night, the three hundred indoor servants had been lined up in the front hallway for an introduction. Emily and Fanny, along with George, had solemnly shaken every person's hand as their name was called and they came up to present themselves, much to Major Bryne's amusement.

"You don't have to, you know," he had said in an undertone to Emily. "You shouldn't, in fact; these natives don't know what to do with a proffered hand. They're not like the ones back home."

But Emily knew what etiquette required of her. She would do this twice, once upon meeting the servants for the first time, a second time when they left Calcutta for England. Only, they had never had so many hands to shake.

The advantage of having a male attendant had come to Emily when the first of Avitabile's letters arrived, for Jimrud

was not unlike the eunuch in a Mughal emperor's *zenana*—
only the male servants could move out of, and between, the
two camps.

She glanced up at him now, her heart beating a little
faster. "Anything more, Jimrud?"

"This, Ladyship," he said and drew from the folds of his
cloth coat a perfect peach-colored rose with a long, pale stem.
He set it upon her bed, where Chance sniffed at it and turned
away.

"Thank you," Emily said faintly and waited until he had
bowed his way out before reaching for the flower. In the dull
gray of the tent, the rose bloomed with the colors of a sunrise,
the tips of its petals a darker shade, packed with perfume. Just
the one rose, she thought, and no accompanying note. What
did it mean? Had Avitabile received her note from the previous night? They all left their letters on a little table outside
their tents, in the corridor, and it was Jimrud's job to gather
them, send them on their way, and bring in the mailbags.

When Wright, her English maid, and Rosina, her half-
Indian, half-Portuguese maid, came in to help her dress, they
pulled out one of the gowns Avitabile had sent for her, in
shades of russet that cast a glow on her face, made her skin
look less yellow, and clasped about her neck the rubies that
George had bought for her in Calcutta. Irons, heated in the
coal brazier that now warmed the tent, were twisted around
her hair. When they had finished, Emily looked into the oval
mirror and touched her reflection briefly. In the muted light,
she looked . . . younger.

Today, they crossed over on a boat—their elephants were
left standing on the southern bank. And again, the Maharajah
of the Punjab waited for them on his horse, a steady, upright
figure, his hand resting on the reins, the horse obedient to his
command.

Behind him, on the large, flat *maidan* that stretched to the
horizon, unfettered by trees or hillocks, was what looked like

a solid white wall, topped with red capping, four miles long. Ranjit Singh cantered in front of this wall, alone and dressed in crimson. George nudged Emily as they neared, and she drew in a heavy breath. The "wall" was a line of foot soldiers, in white uniforms and red turbans, thirty thousand men in all.

"I don't think we can take the Punjab Empire as we did Oude, George," Fanny said.

Her brother smiled. The night's rest had done him some good. He surprised both his sisters by saying, "Not with all this show of might. Runjeet does know how to impress."

When they disembarked, they waited until the whole group—the political, private, and military secretaries of the Governor-General's office and the ADCs—was gathered. Then, McNaghten went over to the Maharajah and received his permission to introduce Lord Auckland. Ranjit Singh brought his horse ahead a few steps, George went forward a few on his own, and they met somewhere in the middle, bowed to each other, and then proceeded to the mammoth red tent pitched behind the line of the Maharajah's soldiers.

Coal braziers, smoking with frankincense and jasmine, created a thick, warm fug. Two silver chairs had been set in the center on a dais raised a few feet from the ground, and the floor around was thickly carpeted in Persian rugs in shades of red and green. The central pillar that held up the tent was encased in a thick sheet of gold encrusted with diamonds, rubies, and emeralds.

George, Emily, and Fanny went down the long length of Punjab soldiers to the platform. Emily's eyes clouded in that jumble of color. Silks in every shade imaginable, daggers, swords, and turbans littered with jewels that seemed to rival the light from the oil-wick lanterns suspended from the dome of the tent. The British party was dreary in comparison, blots of blacks, grays, and white. The men gazed at them, especially at Emily and Fanny.

At the ball in Government House, Avitabile and she had

been the only ones who had danced the waltz. The other ladies wouldn't—they said that the natives stared at them, as though in twirling around a dance floor they had all lowered themselves to the level of *nautch* girls. And it was true enough. There had been no women from the Punjab embassy at the ball, and there were no women here in the tent today. Maharajah Ranjit Singh's wives, and the wives of his men, were all safely tucked into their *zenana* tents, awaiting news of the encounter from their husbands and the servants they had sent over.

Emily concentrated on the figure of the Maharajah in front of her. He was a small man, tiny as a woman, not as imposing as he had been on the horse. A king, amid all the splendor of his courtiers, he was clad only in a crimson coat, white pajamas, and a white turban on his small head. His left foot dragged over the pile of the carpets; his left arm dangled useless by his side.

When he had reached one of the silver chairs, he indicated with a nod that George should take the other one. A few more were brought out, and one was set for Emily on the Maharajah's left. Seated, he seemed to shrink into the velvet upholstery of the chair, and seemed to age anew. His left eye was a very light gray; he was said to be blind in that eye. The muscles of his face had loosened their hold after the stroke—pulling at his beard and setting his white mustache askew. But the right eye, the one that turned toward Emily, was intense, penetrating.

In the haze of the tent, the medley of colors, the flash of brilliant stones, the warm breathing of the hundreds of men, the sweat that gathered in the neckline of her gown, Emily felt faint for a moment and under the spell of this little man, injured and maimed, who ruled over the largest and most profitable mass of land in India. Fanny, on the Maharajah's right, leaned over the back of her chair and behind Ranjit Singh, and whispered, "This man is a king, Em."

He was. Unexpectedly so; even though Bill had returned

from Adeenagar—his earlier visit to the Punjab court—
with tales of the Maharajah's magnificence, somehow, Emily
hadn't believed in them. Or hadn't cared; it was Avitabile she
had thought of. The audience had barely begun; they were
all to travel to Lahore as Runjeet's guests, and over the next
two months, the true business of the asking would begin. But,
Emily thought suddenly, Runjeet would not agree to help
them invade Afghanistan. She glanced at George, who was
running a finger around his collar, wiping his face of perspiration, and then his damp hands.

She looked around, but she hadn't worn her glasses. If
General Avitabile was present in that throng, she couldn't
identify him.

Ranjit Singh pulled off his left shoe and tucked his left
foot over his right thigh, holding and massaging his toes as
he did so. Emily's gaze was suddenly caught by the twinkle
of a fire on the Maharajah's wasted left arm. Clasped around
the cheap red stuff of his coat was a golden armlet with three
stones, two lesser ones on either side and in the middle, a
pigeon's-egg-size stone, clear, flawless, valued at the price of
a handful of kingdoms.

The Maharajah spoke first, in a low, slurred voice. Fakir
Azizuddin leaned over the back of his chair and listened.
Azizuddin then transferred the Persian into Hindustani and
tested out the meaning in conference with Sher Singh, the
Maharajah's adopted son and the man who had headed the
contingent to Calcutta. Sher Singh bent toward McNaghten and the British translator. Ten minutes later, Dr. Drummond, the Governor-General's private surgeon, said in a loud
voice, "The Maharajah wishes to know if you are admiring
his Kohinoor diamond, Miss Eden."

George sighed, and Emily started. The first words in this
historic meeting had been addressed to her.

She said, faltering, "It's beautiful, your Majesty."

Dr. Drummond pounced on the words, and they went

through a reverse pantomime until, another ten minutes later, Ranjit Singh slanted his head to listen to what Emily had said.

For the next three hours they conversed thus, from one mouth to another ear. They jumped into the sentences of diplomacy. Flowers had bloomed in the garden of friendship now that the representative of Queen Victoria had met with the Lion of the Punjab. May that garden never suffer the vicissitudes of a drought, and be forever watered by the golden stream of camaraderie. Hark, are those not the sweet voices of nightingales singing in the bowers of the affection between England and the Punjab? And when that was over, and Emily saw George comfortable in the meaningless extravagance of language that he practiced in the course of his duties with every native raja in India, Ranjit Singh turned his bright eye upon her brother and asked, "Where is your wife? Your lovely sisters are surely welcome, but where is your wife, Governor-General?"

"I'm not married, your Majesty," Lord Auckland murmured, tripping over the words. "Never found the need to do so."

Ranjit Singh waved his hand. "Never did, eh? Not even one?"

"In England, we can have only one, Maharajah, and what if she was not to my liking by the end of it? I could not get rid of her."

Oh, George, Emily thought, what a response that was. But it seemed to delight the Maharajah, who nodded and said, "Perhaps our way is better then. We have many wives, so if one is not pleasant, there are others to take her place." He laughed, a thin, rasping sound. "It keeps them all amenable."

At that point, an attendant brought in a baby wrapped in a silk shawl and laid him on the carpet at the Maharajah's feet.

"My son," Maharajah Ranjit Singh said, "my latest boy,

Prince Dalip Singh. Is he not magnificent? I would say he has the look of his lovely mother, but I think he looks more like me. Such, Governor-General," he said to George, "are the pleasures a woman grants to a man. You have never wished for this?"

George muttered a reply that no one could hear. Little glasses of the Maharajah's special wine—brewed of wheat alcohol, raisins, meat juice, cardamom, musk, opium with a sprinkling of powdered pearls—were now brought in and offered all around. Bill had warned them about this potion, and a drop burned the inside of Emily's mouth. When Ranjit Singh had turned to see Fanny drink half the glass, and choke upon it in a fit of coughing, Emily let her hand fall to her side and poured the wine down into the carpet. A hissing puff of steam rose from the pile. The Maharajah's head whipped around to her.

"You've enjoyed it, I see? Finished already? Another one for Lord Auckland's sister." He raised his glass and poured the rest of his wine down his throat. "I like a woman who enjoys her wine."

When Emily had had her glass filled and sat looking down at the clear liquid in misery, a voice said by her side, "Keep it in your hand, mademoiselle; you can set it down when you leave. The Maharajah dislikes seeing an empty glass."

She could not raise her gaze to look at the speaker. Under cover of the noise in the tent, she said quietly, "Thank you, Monsieur Avitabile."

The baby cried, and an attendant came to whisk him away. Other children were brought in to play in the space in front of the platform, and the Maharajah introduced each of them—this one was a niece, this a nephew, this was Sher Singh's son, and so Ranjit's grandson. The little girl they had met with Jindan had led the youngest children in by the hand, and she stood by, smiling at the Maharajah, luminous in that twinkling light. The children of the British encampment were safely ensconced in their tents and the arms of their native *ayahs;* here, the children of the Punjab ran free among the assembly, shoving their wooden horses and carts against the boots of the courtiers, giggling when tickled.

Fanny drank a second glass of the blistering wine, and then she laughed, and everyone seemed to join in. Emily felt her neck heavy on her shoulders. Avitabile was close by, but where?

At that moment, the Maharajah's head swung around, and his one, dazzling eye gazed upon her speculatively. "I have seen you admiring the Kohinoor, sister of the Governor-General, perhaps my General Avitabile could bring it over to your tent and show it to you?"

Mr. McNaghten crushed his fingers together until his knuckles cracked. "Your Majesty," he began, "Lord Auckland would be glad to host General Avitabile himself—"

"Tomorrow, then?" Maharajah Ranjit Singh said, breaking gently into McNaghten's tirade.

She nodded, wordless.

Avitabile came in the evening with a tray of jewels from the Maharajah's Toshakhana, accompanied by a posse of the Akalis. They ranged themselves outside the sitting room in the Governor-General's set of tents, each carrying a flaring torch, which outlined their figures inside—the towers of their turbans, the sharp curves of their swords, the tight cinches of the cummerbunds around their waists, and the deadly circles of the quoits hanging from them.

All that day, Emily had paced her tent, restless. She could not write her letters, could barely eat anything; she sat in the armchair, she stood, she flitted around. George had gone out, early in the morning, for a review of troops—both British and from the Punjab. Fanny, fearless, had accompanied him, and watched all day long from atop a howdah, dipping her hand into a bag of sandwiches when she was hungry.

Emily fretted, shifting the papers around on her desk. Ranjit Singh must have known something of what had happened in Calcutta, and in his own way had engineered Avitabile's visit to her tent. It was a disconcerting feeling. At home, in England, Emily would not have cared, as she had not when the gossip surrounded Melbourne and her at Lady Cowper's, for this was part of the dance of courtship—if, she thought wryly, Melbourne's mumblings could be called that. Here, in India, there was no such notion at all. If a man wanted a wife, or was attracted to a woman (though how he would actually see her first was a wonder), he married her . . . and married as many others as he wanted. If a king wanted another king's wife, he killed the husband and took the wife. But this was not Calcutta—and while the rules of England could have been employed in their little piece of property at Government House, here, at the Sutlej, was a rawness and roughness that bespoke a foreign land.

Emily hesitated to call this a courtship, even though she was forty-one years old and felt at times like a giddy young girl in the throes of a first love. It was not, even, a love. For what had it been? A few letters, a walk in the park, a waltz in Marble Hall. Shawls and gowns sent to her in the fulfillment of a promise. That was all.

She wore another one of the gowns—this one in pink, embroidered with fully caparisoned elephants along the bottom—and a shawl when she greeted General Paolo Avitabile, her gaze steady upon his face. He had grown older, a few more lines along his forehead, a small stoop to his shoulders, some grays painted in his dark hair. For all that she had read his letters carefully, and many times, she knew nothing of this man. And yet, when he kissed her hand, she had a sudden and deep yearning to caress his face. She moved, flushing, her heart thumping with a rhythm of excitement it had not known for years. In the light from the many silver candlesticks around the tent, tallow falling thickly down their sides, his eyes were a light gray.

The general followed Emily to a sideboard with curved legs and set the tray down. She took a deep breath. Diamonds, rubies, emeralds, and pearls sparkled against the black velvet covering on the tray. There were heavy necklaces of emeralds surrounded with tiny, faceted diamonds, matching earrings, bangles. Rubies the size of pomegranate seeds, and one, set in a bracelet, the size of a cherry. A tiny model of Leili, the horse, was fashioned out of a pure white ivory, its saddle and harness studded with diamonds. But in the center of the tray reposed the armlet that contained the Kohinoor.

Emily reached for it, and Avitabile's warm hand closed over hers. "My life depends on bringing these back to my king safely, Mademoiselle Emily."

The shadows of the Akali soldiers shifted across the wall of the tent.

"What would they do? Kill me?" she asked, smiling.

Avitabile shook his head gravely. "No." He picked up the armlet and held it out to her. "I would not let them, mademoiselle. They are a crude sort of people, no real understanding of any sophistication and throw that thing there"—he jerked his thumb backward—"without thinking. It's a disc, and travels at great speed, and when it reaches its object, it slices off his neck." He made a motion under his chin. "And he's dead. One cannot breathe when one's nose is no longer attached to one's torso."

Emily shuddered. She took the armlet from Avitabile. It was wider than she had thought, and heavy, with thick gold links, a diamond-studded clasp, and two silk tassels. Only a king, she thought, would think of putting diamonds on a clasp, which would not show when he wore the armlet around the upper part of his arm. But the real beauty of the piece lay in that central diamond. She ran her fingers over its surface, and felt a cool power in the stone. Avitabile took it from her and, holding her hand, draped it around her wrist so that the light from the diamond glowed.

This touching seemed natural with him, even though the servants were ranged around the room. It was casual, not anything to make much of. They both looked down upon the Kohinoor, and Emily's hand began to tremble in his grasp. It was a moment so intimate, so sudden and unexpected. Inside, Emily began to struggle for words to speak. Finally they came.

"What is its history?" she asked, in a hushed voice.

Avitabile shrugged. "My king got it from Shah Shuja—you know, the man you are all attempting to put on the Afghan throne as king, replacing Dost Mohammad. Shuja was driven out of Afghanistan and came to the Maharajah for help, which he gave him, and then he had to give him the Kohinoor in return. But it belonged, once, to the Mughal kings."

On their way to the Punjab from Calcutta, they had stopped in Delhi to see the last Mughal king, Bahadur Shah Zafar, in his palaces at the fort. Most of the rooms of the fort were open to visitors, British and foreign visitors only, since the King of Delhi was now under the "protection" of the East India Company. His empire had diminished to the environs of his fort at Delhi, and even that was invaded by picnic parties when they wanted. George had not come with them, he could not as Governor-General of India, for it would then have seemed to be an official visit and the Mughal king was not to be acknowledged as any sort of a sovereign at all—McNaghten had been very adamant about this. So Emily and Fanny had gone, visited the ruined marble halls and hallways, and seen the king on a distant terrace overlooking the Yamuna River, his balding head bared to the sun, the smoke from his *hukkah* spiraling upward, a lone attendant squatting at his feet.

"It has, though, been a long time since it belonged to the Mughals."

Avitabile nodded, a gleam of appreciation in his glance. "True, you know your Indian history, mademoiselle. And, as long as my Maharajah is alive, it will remain an Indian diamond. After him"—he shrugged—"who knows."

Ever since they had come to India, Emily had been almost surfeited with the range and breadth of jewelry and precious stones she had seen—pearls of an impossible luster; diamonds glittering like a new-hewn moon; rubies to rival sunrises; emeralds that evoked the cool hush of a rained-upon forest. And crude as the setting was for the Kohinoor, with its rudimentary gold work and the two lesser diamonds, one on either side, it still took her breath away.

"Is there really a curse upon it?" she asked.

Avitabile took the armlet from her and laid it back upon the tray. "There is a legend, certainly," he agreed, "that the Kohinoor must never be worn upon a ruler's crown. The Mughal king Shah Jahan had it embedded into his Peacock Throne; my master has it in an armlet and wears it well away from his head. Other than that . . . I don't know, mademoiselle. But diamonds of a fabulous worth have a way of bringing misfortune upon all those who possess them."

Emily turned away; the moment had passed. "Shall we eat, Monsieur Avitabile? St. Cloup has been immensely bothered about this meal; he intends to rival all the cooks in your kitchen at Peshawar."

"That," Avitabile said comfortably, "is something I doubt he can do, mademoiselle. I have the best. It's a simple truth. Someday, perhaps, you will eat at my home. That would truly be a pleasure."

Major Bryne had hung a chandelier in this sitting room, to one side, and the little, round table was set directly underneath it, the light from the chandelier casting its flickering flame around but not on the table. The tablecloth was white damask, the fabric lush in the muted light; a crystal vase stood in the middle filled with the white roses that Avitabile had sent in the morning. The china was from Government House, and came from an original set that served a hundred people. The plates were white with a pink and gold edging, the cutlery was pure silver, and the napkins were again damask. In the year and a half that George, Emily, and Fanny had progressed, in great state, through the Upper Provinces of India, this whole set had traveled with them, cushioned in hay, nestled in tin boxes made for this purpose, and toted on camel back.

"You brought this along with you?" Avitabile asked, drawing out Emily's chair and waiting for her to be seated.

"We are like the Mughal kings, Monsieur Avitabile," Emily replied, laughing. "We were told that if we left one stick of furniture in Government House, the white ants would reduce them to a crumble before we returned, and if we left one candlestick, it would be burgled. So, we brought it all along."

"And now your encampment is some twenty-five thousand people?"

"Yes, it's difficult to imagine." Emily nodded toward the head bearer, lurking in the entry to the tent. He came in with a bottle of claret, wrapped in a white napkin, and deftly filled their glasses. She flung out her napkin and put it on her lap as she picked up her wineglass. "Thank you for showing me the Kohinoor," she said.

He smiled. "It is my master you must thank. The Maharajah is a generous man."

Their glasses touched lightly and they drank.

Outside the tent they heard the slow, hacking cough of the ill horse. Once, twice, a third and tired time. The *khitmatgar* put two bowls of soup in front of them—shrimp balls in a clear, cinnamon-flavored broth. There was nothing but a little salt and pepper for the flavoring, but the shrimp was perfectly cooked, the broth flavored just right, and the soup sang on their tongues.

"Tell me about Peshawar," Emily said, putting down her soup spoon. Here, for the first time, she had an opportunity to really talk with General Avitabile, to watch his face as they did so, to consider him . . . for what? A husband? "But before that, are you married?"

He waved his spoon in the air. "Many times, mademoiselle. They are all native women, you understand. The Maharajah made us all sign a contract with him when we joined his service—we had to learn an Indian language, which was not a problem for me, for I spoke Persian before. And we had to marry a Punjabi woman." He rubbed his chin, his gaze intent upon her face. "I married several."

"Ah." At least, he was honest. But an ache caught Emily between her ribs, and she rubbed her side, over the corset. What did it matter, really? This was life in India. A man could not be expected to be . . . celibate. And all of George's ADCs had these native wives, women who were not to take the place of a real Englishwoman.

"Tell me about Peshawar," she said again, faintly, as the fish was brought in—lake trout in an almond jacket. All morning long, St. Cloup, the French cook they had brought along with them from England, had clattered around the camp, complaining that his oven would not heat properly. Coals had come from the northern side of the Sutlej to pile on top of the oven, and a man had been employed in keeping them smoking at just the right temperature, so that St. Cloup could finish this dish in time. When the bearer lifted the cover, the thin slivers of almonds were precisely browned all over; the mousse had seeped into the flaky skin of the trout; the mushroom sauce was burnished with a hint of sherry; and the whole lay upon a bed of pureed watercress, palely green.

"Peshawar was . . . is a city of hooligans," Avitabile said, lifting a slice of trout and setting it on Emily's plate.

He served himself and then pointed at his plate with a fork. "Not bad; not what I would have expected. I wonder if it tastes as good as it looks." He slipped a piece into his mouth and chewed. "They ran riot over the people, killing as they wished, a law unto themselves. I changed all that for the Maharajah."

The light from the chandelier cast Avitabile's face in a shadow, and all Emily could see was the burning fire in his eyes. "Your St. Cloup is indeed a marvel, Mademoiselle Emily." When he had finished the fish on his plate, he continued, "There's no lawlessness in Peshawar now, not anymore. I widened the streets, and men and women walk abroad in the middle of the night without fear." A smile, wicked and enticing to Emily. "There's no one left to fear."

"Will you go back to Italy, monsieur?"

"Someday, yes. My Maharajah will not live forever . . . After him, there's really no one left to rule. Perhaps you British will take over the Punjab Empire then."

"Perhaps," Emily said.

They ate the chicken Alabaster, doused in a cream sauce, in silence, and all the while Emily watched his hands move fluidly over the table. His cutlery did not clink on his plate, and he ate and drank with a quietness she had never seen in a man. St. Cloup gave them a mango fool for dessert, simple and elegant, with a smear of cream on top.

"I see why your chef does this little dessert," Avitabile said, "to tell me that he can get ripe mangoes in December."

"He has been nursing these in hay since the summer, picked green, ripened over the last six months."

When the food was cleared away and a glass of port lay before Avitabile, he sat back and folded his hands in his lap. "This has been a very pleasant interlude, Mademoiselle Emily."

"Yes," Emily said slowly. "Yes." It had been just that, an interlude. Nothing more.

"I return to Peshawar tomorrow, mademoiselle," he said, rising as he spoke. He pushed his chair back in to the table and came around the other side to hold Emily's as she rose. "You see, only I can maintain order there. I might find a few more men to hang before breakfast. Such is my life."

"I see that," she said, putting out her hand to him. He kissed it again, and she felt the warmth of his breath upon her skin. He raised a hand in farewell at the door to the tent, and when he had gone out, she doused the candles, leaving only the jeweled light from the chandelier near the ceiling.

She stood there, alone, arms wrapped tightly around herself. She heard the horse stretch the sound of its lengthy cough. A shot blasted through the sound, and through the white canvas of the tent, Emily saw the horse collapse on the dirt, and die.

The next day the Governor-General's party broke camp and crossed over the Sutlej into Punjab territory, to begin the leisurely waltz of asking and being refused.

Emily did not accompany them. She went back to Simla to await George and Fanny's return, before they could all head back to Calcutta. There, in the rented cottage, she watched snow dust the mountains, completed her sketches, wrote long letters to Eleanor, Robert, and Mary. Late at night, when Jim-rud and her maids were asleep, alone by the flickering fire in the hearth, she thought of home, of England.

She did not think of Monsieur Avitabile.

Love in Lahore

September 1846
Eight years later

A gigantic harvest moon rose over the ramparts of Lahore
Fort, tangerine-hued in the just-darkened night sky. It was
a hot moon—a great big ball of fire, with no illusion of
coolness—as heated as the day had been. Henry Lawrence
had seen the mercury rise trembling in the thermometer until,
late in the afternoon, it had hit a hundred and ten degrees. As
a consequence, it had been a quiet day, for which Henry was
grateful.

He sat, legs splayed, on the floor of the northern end of
Jahangir's Quadrangle, against the base of the flat-roofed
building that hugged the outer, riverfront rim of the courtyard. The wall behind his back was warm, and heat seeped
in through the thin cotton of his trousers. Reaching into
the inner pocket of his khaki shirt, he took out a packet of
beedis—native cigarettes. His fingers caught in the lacings of
his shirt's collar and the packet fell to the ground, the *beedis*
spilling in all directions. He picked one up, struck a match,
cupped his fist around the flame although no breeze budged

the thick night air, lit the squat end of the *beedi*. Inhaled. The tobacco was harsh, unfiltered, and the smoke scraped down his throat to his lungs.

It had been many years since Henry had smoked the pallid, insipid cigarettes that came from England, not after his first taste of a *beedi*. That had happened in the middle of the jungles in the Northwest Provinces, where he had been sent as a revenue surveyor—difficult work that meant tramping through the wilderness of unmapped, uncharted territory, peopled with natives and villages who had never seen an Englishman before. Who could not understand that their land was now part of the British Empire. Or that land tax payments were due, every quarter, to a foreign lord, where once it had been at the whimsy of whichever raja or emperor had ruled over them—this king sitting far away in Delhi, or Agra, or Lahore.

It had been tough, exacting work. There were no hotels to be had, no *dak* bungalows (since the survey took place far from the *dak*—postal—routes), no chicken curries with gleaming white rice, certainly no tinned sausages and ham. Henry and his group—which was composed of him, a horse which he rode when it was amenable, three donkeys to carry the load of his tent and his belongings, four servants, two to guard, two to look after his needs—had traversed the hilly, shrub-clad land for months. Once in a very rare while, they would stumble upon another British civil servant, also with his survey papers, his native servants, his tent, donkeys, and horses. That night they would each break out their cigarettes and their brandy, drink a tot before a crackling fire, talk the hours away, glad to hear the sound of English spoken as it should be. The campfires were kept burning all through the night, and Henry's sleep would often be fractured by the frustrated roar of a tiger or the cry of a jackal.

Henry's cigarettes ran out in two months, and quaking with need, he watched his servant pull out a pouch of tobacco flakes, a notebook with dried *tendu* leaves carefully inter-spersed between its pages, and a square of jute cloth. First, the man worried the frayed edges of the jute cloth, until his stumpy fingers delicately picked out a string of thread. Then, he laid out a rectangular piece of *tendu* leaf, filled it with the tobacco, and furled it on a diagonal into a cylinder. He rolled this several times between the palms of his hands, with a deli-cate touch, not crushing the leaf. The jute thread went twice around the base of the *beedi,* and the man twisted the ends before stubbing in the bigger edge to keep the tobacco from falling out. It was simple, it was easy.

Looking up at Henry's eager face, his servant offered it to him. "Here, Sahib."

Henry took it gingerly, bent to have it lit, took a drag. "Is it safe?"

The man shrugged, lifting emaciated shoulders. "I have smoked these, Larens Sahib, since I was twelve years old." The semblance of a smile cracked across his wizened face. "Safer than being here, surely."

When he returned to what passed for civilization in India, Henry Lawrence could not put an English cigarette in his mouth; he had gone unfortunately native in the matter.

The *beedi* in Henry's hand burned down until the tip of glowing embers seared his fingers. He dropped it on the ground, moved his foot to stamp it out, and ran his hand through the abundant darkness of his hair. How many days had he been here in Lahore, as Resident? Some sixty-five, and it was, for an artillery soldier, a promotion beyond his best dreams. Such choice posts went only to the civil servants of the Indian Civil Service, and Henry Lawrence had come to India twenty-three years ago, at the age of sixteen, to join the Bengal Artillery in Dum Dum near Calcutta.

All his postings since then had been in the Northwest Provinces of British India, outside the boundaries of the Pun-jab Empire, the last one—as Assistant Agent—at Firozpur, just south of the Sutlej River, which had been deemed by the Treaty of Amritsar in 1809 the southern bastion of the Empire, beyond which the British army redcoats would not travel.

And yet, here they were at Lahore, Henry thought with a dry irony. Maharajah Ranjit had been dead for some seven years. The Punjab Empire had disintegrated into a veritable bloodbath. Three, maybe four of Ranjit's descendants had since died by the sword of a brother, a cousin, a friend, and only one young boy was left to reign over the lands of the Punjab. He had been crowned king with the help of the British army, another irony. And that child's name was Maharajah Dalip Singh.

As the moon flooded the courtyard of Jahangir's Quadrangle with its flaming glow, Henry gathered the *beedis* strewn over the floor. He took off his boots. His bare feet slapped against the stone of the pathway that led to a square pool in the center of the courtyard, with its marble platform.

Once, not so long ago, this courtyard had been part of the most private quarters at Lahore Fort. Lord Auckland, author of that devastating war in Afghanistan, a past Governor-General, had come to Lahore Fort as a guest of Ranjit Singh. But he wouldn't have been permitted into Jahangir's Quadrangle, then part of the *zenana*—harem—space. Auckland would have been received in the courtyard just south, the Diwan-i-Am, the Hall of Public Audience, perhaps in the adjoining Shah Burj, which was still part of the *zenana*, but Maharajah Ranjit Singh had used it as his own, not allowed his women there.

Henry rubbed his right side as he walked, dulling the pain there. Three days ago, while he was riding through the local bazaar outside the fort, a piece of brick had come flying out of nowhere and glanced off his shoulder. The soldiers accompanying him, and his private secretary, Herbert Edwardes, had scurried around, shouted, pounded into *zenana* apartments in the buildings overhanging the narrow street in search of the miscreant. They had found only gaggles of sloe-eyed, bold women, veils over their noses and mouths, ogling children, men belligerent at having been disturbed in their rest, or their *chai*, or their gossip.

"I saw nothing," they all variously said, when questioned in Punjabi, Urdu, Hindustani, and Persian. "But the Resident Sahib must take care, eh?"

Another warning, a very mild one, that the British were not wanted.

Although the child Dalip Singh had been proclaimed Maharajah of the Punjab, it was harshly evident that the British ruled instead.

Henry breathed in the silvered air, filled with the aroma of night blooms of the *rath-ki-rani*. After twenty-three years in India, England was a distant dream, even, the few times he had gone back, an unfamiliar country. Cold, damp, the skies knitted close with clouds, clinging moss on flagstones. He thought at times that if and when he died, it would be here in the Punjab, in this heated land with its churning passions, its strange tongues—not so unfamiliar anymore; he spoke all of them fluently—its luscious landscapes with open skies, rivers, streams, gullies, the abundantly fertile fields.

Henry lit another *beedi* and squatted on the marble floor of the platform in the center of the pool. Maharajah Ranjit Singh had owned the fort at Lahore, as the conqueror of the city, but it had its origins and its embellishments from some two or three hundred years in the past. Jahangir's Quadrangle was attributed to Emperor Jahangir of the Mughal Empire, who had ruled in the early 1600s. Immediately west was Shah Jahan's Quadrangle, also part of the riverfront residences, and beyond another series of courtyards and rooms, including the Shah Burj, which Henry had not seen yet. When he had been appointed Resident at Lahore, he had stopped his men from evacuating the women of Ranjit Singh's harem from the rest of the apartments. For his own use, he had kept Jahangir's and Shah Jahan's Quadrangles.

The last Mughal king lay moldering in Delhi, for forty years Maharajah Ranjit Singh had occupied the fort at Lahore, and now, the Punjab Empire was also dead.

When he thought of that—the death of the Punjab Empire—Henry smiled grimly into his fist, even as his mouth closed over the *beedi*. He *knew* this to be true; he was here in Lahore to make it happen. They might all talk of the British helping the Punjab rise and ride again as a northwestern power in India, with Dalip as Maharajah, or talk of the British army retreating when Dalip hit his majority. But it wouldn't happen. Why would it? There was talk of Dalhousie being made Governor-General of India; and Lord Dalhousie would annex the Punjab, throw Dalip Singh into prison, and trample over everyone's hearts until hatred and revenge bloomed. Henry and Dalhousie had an antagonistic relationship; there were childhood slights, and a vast, yawning gap of misunderstanding as adults between them. Somehow, John, Henry's brother, was a jewel to Dalhousie; Henry, not so much of one. As long as one of the Lawrence brothers is liked, Henry thought, we'll all do well in India.

Through the dense hush came the low melody of a song. A girl came into the courtyard from the south, through the archways that led into the Diwan-i-am, and flitted down the steps, two kid goats following her, their bleats insistent, their long ears flapping. She moved gently across the stone, the skirts of her *ghagara* swishing, the moonlight picking out the sparkle of a hundred diamonds strewn over her clothing. She wore a veil, also studded with diamonds, but it only covered her head to her hairline and then flowed behind her like a glittering cloud. The goats leapt at the bushes and began nibbling, the girl sang on. Henry strained to hear the words—in Persian—and he caught "my lover," "in the light of the moon," "a meeting," "a parting," and wondered if he had heard it before.

The cool whites of a *rath-ki-rani* bush's flowers covered the southwestern end of the courtyard, and the girl raked in the blooms with one hand and filled a basket hanging by her side. She shooed the goats away. "Go chew on something else, something useless." They bounced around, as though they understood what she was saying.

On the platform, in the middle of the courtyard's pool, Henry sat perfectly still, mesmerized. Who was she? Where had she come from? She had to be one of the Maharajah's entourage, but she was too young to have been Ranjit Singh's wife, surely?

The girl turned then and saw Henry. The moon was now high in the sky, a small pearl among the stars, nothing like its early, immense self, and drenched them all with a silver light that was as clear as a vivid day. From where he sat, Henry could see the girl's face, the consternation upon it, the lovely mouth opening in an "oh." She set down her basket, unhurriedly, and just as deliberately put up her hands to frame her face. It was a pantomime of surprise, and Henry felt mirth bubble up in him.

He rose, and as he did, a door opened on the western end of the courtyard and a man came through, an oil lantern held out in front of him, its loop of golden light reaching only up his arm and no further. "Pat?"

Henry waited a long moment until his brother John's eyes adjusted to the pale light in the courtyard and found him. "I'm here, John," he said resignedly. "On the platform."

"What are you doing there? It's time for bed. All good residents need their night's sleep." John Lawrence's boots smacked loudly on the pathway. Out of the corner of his eye, Henry watched the girl melt into the shadows of the building on the south; the two goats had long skipped to her side, but the basket lay in the moonlight, and from where he stood, Henry could smell the heady fragrance of the flowers.

"Come," John said. He turned his head, as did Henry, when the girl vanished beyond the arches, the diamonds on her veil giving off a flash of dull glitter, one bell in her anklets, not muffled by her skirts, ringing a sharp, clear note. "Who's that?"

"No one. I don't know who."

John frowned. "The women of the *zenana* are not allowed here. They're to keep to their quarters—they have enough space as it is . . . why can't they stay there? I'll send an order out tomorrow."

"No such thing," Henry said, as the two men walked back toward their quarters and through the door that John had come from, which led to the original Diwan-i-khas, the Hall of Private Audience, of the Mughal Emperors. Also called Shah Jahan's Quadrangle. "They have a right to it all; we're the usurpers here, John."

"You think so?" John halted and held the lantern up to the face of his brother, older than he by five years. When he met Henry's determined gaze, he shook his head. "You do think so, you've always thought so." He grinned. "Father destined me for the Civil Service and you for the army, Pat, well, you and George and Alexander. At one time I burned for it too, but Papa would not agree, and I think he was right after all. And yet, you are the one with the soft heart."

"I care for the people, John," Henry said hesitantly, knowing he sounded pompous. He was a mere captain in the army, and had not risen much beyond this rank because most of his other duties, ones he had taken on—which could be loosely termed as those of a civil servant, John's in fact— had kept him from regular promotions. As a result, Resident of Lahore or not, John's salary far exceeded Henry's, even though John had only joined Indian service five years after Henry.

"So do I," said John, quickly, hotly.

"I know." Henry put his arm around his brother's shoulders as they moved on. John had the soldier's heart, the conquering warrior's heart, and Henry had the one that should have been given to an administrator. John's motives for conquest were pure, well intentioned, but the brothers had never been able to agree on the direction these intentions should take. Henry did not think—had never thought—that the Punjab should be annexed. John had always believed so. Because he thought that the British were best-suited to rule over a fragmented kingdom; the native kings had no order, no method, no real love for taxes, revenues, wide streets, and social justice that kept a people happy and prosperous.

If Dalhousie came to India as Governor-General—*when* he came—he would choose John as his representative in the Punjab, and send Henry away elsewhere.

They entered the courtyard of the Diwan-i-khas, and it was now just before dinnertime. Oil lamps and lanterns were scattered on the edges of the pathways, lighting up their way; a table had been set in the pavilion—where once a mighty Mughal Emperor had given audience to a select few nobles, a party of British men sat down to eat on rough-hewn chairs with a bench-like table. Their candlesticks were beer bottles, candles stuck into the openings, wax piling down the thick, brown glass. The men talked, they ate, they drank some more beer, and the bottles were carefully stored away by the servants to help light up other dark nights.

Their cots were laid out in the center of the courtyard, makeshift army beds of strung and knitted jute that sagged as it took their weight; cool, cotton sheets on top, bags of hay for pillows. Feather-stuffed pillows, as back home, they had discovered, were breeding houses for lice and other vermin. The hay was thrown out, or dried in the hot sun every morning before being stuffed into a pillowcase at night.

Tomorrow, Henry thought, as he closed his eyes, he had

the unlovely duty of going through the items in Maharajah Ranjit Singh's Toshakhana—the treasury house. But, along with other distasteful duties, this one had to be done. A list of jewels and precious stones from Maharajah Ranjit Singh's Toshakhana had come by *dak* a few days ago from the Governor-General, Sir Henry Hardinge, in Calcutta.

That list had been compiled meticulously over the last thirty years, long before the British were considering annexing the Punjab. It was just a matter of routine, of protocol— this cataloging of native wealth. For you never knew when the raja might fall ill, die, or ask for aid from the East India Company, and when the time came for the Company to give its help—in whatever form—it wanted to know what treasures were hidden in that kingdom. In other words, just how much help to give.

Since the 1809 Treaty of Amritsar with Maharajah Ranjit Singh, there had been some scattered British presence in the Punjab—a secretary of the Governor-General's come to visit, a soldier, a commander in chief, and each had been shown some part of the vast wealth of the Maharajah, and each had documented what he saw. And sent these secret notes back to Calcutta. That he had been immensely wealthy had not been in doubt, because Ranjit Singh had also been ridiculously generous to everyone who visited. They had all returned burdened with cashmere shawls of immense value; pearls, diamonds, emeralds, and rubies set in every kind of jewelry imaginable; carriages, carts, fans, silks, and horses of such upstanding pedigree and paces that they had put their English Thoroughbreds to shame.

If the Maharajah could give away so much, how much more would he have had in his coffers? The British were determined to find out, and so Henry had to begin sorting through the Toshakhana.

When he finally slept, though, he did not dream of the jewels; he dreamed instead of a girl under a veil of diamonds who had mocked him. And then disappeared into the night.

The next morning, Henry went west along the public spaces of the fort, skirting Maharani Jindan Kaur's quarters—the *zenana* apartments that he had left untouched to their original occupants. In the last two months, he had met the indomitable mother of Maharajah Dalip Singh some ten times, and each meeting had ended with her making demands, and his trying to ward them off as best he could. Among his many duties, he had had to add that of a diplomat, one with the silkiest tongue, which wagged much but said nothing of any avail. It didn't deter the young Maharani, though; when she couldn't meet Henry herself, she sent her lover, Lal Singh, whom she had insisted upon making *wazir* of the Sikh Empire.

After the First Anglo-Sikh War, into which Maharani Jindan Kaur had brought the British herself, asking for their help in setting her son on the throne, the concept of a Punjab *Empire* was laughable. It did exist, but whittled away at the borders. The British had demanded, and got, Jalandar Doab, the land between the Sutlej and the Beas Rivers where various petty chieftains had championed for secession from the Empire. Kashmir had been broken away and sold to a Hindu noble at Ranjit Singh's court, Raja Gulab Singh, for one million pounds sterling. The British had levied a fine on the Punjab upon defeating them; they could not pay it, and so Kashmir was sold. The lands north of Jalandar Doab, including Lahore and up to Peshawar, still belonged to the boy king, Maharajah Dalip Singh.

Two guards came to attention and slapped at their rifles in salute. Henry nodded to them. As he ducked through the low archways leading into the northwestern end of the fort, which now housed the Toshakhana, he thought it laughable to consider the child king of anything at all. They were here, weren't they? The fort was guarded by the redcoats of the British army; Henry, John, and various others of his team occupied some of the best apartments in the fort; the Maharani had been tucked away into her little corner of the *zenana*. Even this section, housing the Naulakha and the Sheesh Mahal, had once been part of the *zenana*. Now, no longer.

Henry went through the dark gloom of the arches and out into the blinding sunshine that seared everything around into a sharp, unrelenting white. He tugged the rim of his sola *topi* over his eyes and, when that didn't suffice, shaded them with his hand and gazed around in wonder. The courtyard itself was smaller than the one in Jahangir's Quadrangle, the space much more intimate, each of the buildings on the four sides crowding upon the center. Which was divided into four quadrants by two water channels that bisected in the middle, where a fountain whispered, drops turning into rainbows and then melting away. But unlike the other courtyards, there was no grass here, just yellow, black, and white stones laid out in a repeating pattern.

The Naulakha, on his left, had a curved roof in white marble, and through its double-cusped archways Henry could see the thin marble latticework screens that kept prying eyes out and let light in for the ladies of the harem. Sometime in the mid-1600s, Emperor Shah Jahan had built this pavilion and spent nine lakhs, nine hundred thousand rupees, on it—hence its name, Nau-lakha. But then Shah Jahan had also spent five million rupees on the Taj Mahal, and a hundred and twenty million rupees on his Peacock Throne, and he had six other thrones he could sit upon. The Kohinoor diamond, in the Toshakhana of Maharajah Ranjit Singh, had once adorned the iridescent breast of the main peacock on Shah Jahan's throne. Ranjit Singh had taken Lahore, and along with it Shah Jahan's fort, and then he had taken the Kohinoor diamond. Now, Henry was here, in possession of the fort, and soon to be in possession of the diamond.

Henry turned to the building opposite him, the Sheesh Mahal, the Palace of Mirrors. From the outside, it was very simple, with its arches and its unblemished, unadorned marble—almost disappointing—but he knew that the inside would exceed every tale he had heard about it. Two months ago, when Henry had first come to Lahore, he had had this entire courtyard boarded up and locked, and stationed a twenty-four-hour-guard outside. He had ordered heavy wooden doors fitted onto the archways of the Sheesh Mahal and secured these with large locks, until he had the time to inventory its contents.

Against all wisdom, he gave the keys to the man who stood in front of the Sheesh Mahal, the keys looped around an iron ring which hung from his cummerbund. As Henry walked toward him, his feet kicked up dust in a fine plume that set him coughing. And in that dust were the smaller footprints of the man—the only ones leading to the doorway of the Sheesh Mahal, clearly made just a few minutes before. He had been right, Henry thought, in giving Misr Makraj the keys.

Misr Makraj had been treasurer to Maharajah Ranjit Singh for thirty-five years, an honored servant in whose hands, literally, had rested the vast wealth of the Punjab Empire. He was a short man, small in frame, his skin a rich mahogany. His hair was all white, cut down to stubble on his head. In his thin face, his chin jutted out, his cheeks sank in, and his eyes were clouded with the beginnings of cataracts, but his skin was smooth, unlined, belying his seventy-odd years. He was dressed as meticulously as Henry had always seen him. His hands and nails were clean, manicured. His *dhoti* was a splendid affair in lustrous white cotton, looped between his legs to tuck in at the back, its folds ironed and neat, falling down to his ankles with a row of pleats in front. His feet were bare; Misr Makraj had never entered the Toshakhana with the soil of the outside streets upon his feet. He wore a white cotton *kurta*, unembroidered and plain; in his ears were two gold rings, and on the ring finger of his right hand was a thick gold ring emblazoned with the seal of Maharajah Ranjit Singh.

"You are early, Henry Sahib," Misr Makraj said in Persian as he neared.

"So are you, Misr Makraj," Henry replied in the same language, reaching out a hand to the man. He found his grasped between Misr Makraj's two hands as he bowed. The treasurer's hands were shaking, Henry realized, and he put his other hand over their clasp. Behind Henry, the two clerks he had brought along with him snorted. It wouldn't do to shake the hands of the natives, that was what they thought. These were the Howard brothers, themselves thin men with shrunken faces and skin that had never taken the brown hues of an Indian sun, because they spent all of their time indoors in the service of the East India Company.

"It has to be done, you know," Henry said gently.

"Yes, this is true," Misr Makraj said shakily. "I had thought it would be the Maharajah Dalip Singh who would ask me for an accounting . . . not . . ." He reached for the keys, chose one, and slid it into the lock. "But I would rather it be you than anyone else, Henry Sahib."

"Thank you," Henry said.

The lock took a while to yield. The monsoon rains had come all through the months of July and August, and turned the fields around the fort into a lavish green almost overnight. Humidity hung in the air like a smothering veil, crept into lungs, created mold and mildew. Every piece of metal grew a film of rust; even the edges of mirrors were dusted brown. The lock had rusted, and as Misr Makraj struggled to turn the key, Henry had all the proof he needed that he had selected the guardian of the Toshakhana well, much as the Maharajah had for thirty-five years.

Herbert Edwardes, Henry's private secretary, had balked at his choice, and had brought John along to strengthen his argument as Henry worked over some papers one night by the light of a flickering candle. Rain had pounded down on the roof of the stone pavilion, the pond which housed the fountain had overflowed, and water had spilled merrily out of the shallow channels that bisected the yard outside.

"It's not right. How can Misr Makraj be trusted?" Edwardes had said.

"How can he not?" Henry had asked. "After all, it's a job he knows well and has done for a great many years."

"Henry"—this from John—"give me the keys, or Edwardes, or someone else. We'll keep it safe. Why this man, who has no master, and no allegiance to us. How are we going to explain this to Lord Hardinge?"

"I'll explain it," Henry had said. "In fact"—he had pointed at the paper on his desk—"I'm in the process of doing so, and cannot finish if you keep up this chatter. Hardinge made me Resident for a reason." He'd looked at their grim faces and sighed. "You must understand our position here. We are in the place of conquerors, have put their child king on the throne, but keep a hard hand upon his shoulder. We can topple him when we want. The people know this; they don't trust us. This . . . gesture of giving the keys to an old retainer of the Maharajah will go a long way, some way at least, toward building trust. You must see this."

They had remained stubborn, severe, unconvinced. "He can have no allegiance to us," John had said again. "Only to his master."

"His master is dead," Henry had replied. *And we are now his masters.* This, he had left unsaid, and watched them walk out into the rain, their shoulders stooped with dissatisfaction. But on this point, Henry himself would not yield. What would have happened if Misr Makraj had vanished with a part

of, or the whole of the Toshakhana, Henry had not wanted
to think about. It would have been the end of his career; it
would have been the end of India for him.

Now, as the lock fell open under Misr Makraj's aged
hands, Henry knew he had done right. The treasurer pushed
open the doors, leaning against them when the hinges, as
much rusted as the lock had been, creaked and protested.

Henry stepped into the murk, and his breath stilled in his
chest. Every wall was covered in minute chips of mirror, inter-
spersed with blue, green, red, and yellow tiles. The mirrors rose
to the ceiling, and Henry tilted his head to follow their line up,
around, and back down again. There were five arches in the
front entrance, four boarded up, the one in the center—the one
they had entered from—provided with the door. The reflection
of the sun on the marble floors of the courtyard kissed the mirrors on the wall, setting them on fire, so bright that it hurt his
eyes. The mirror work began from hip height on every wall;
below that were simple, marble dado panels, almost shabby in
execution, but frames for the glory above.

The four of them stood quietly, looking at the wedge of
the rooms that was visible in the light from the doorway. Misr
Makraj moved beyond the archway in the center, into the
darkness of the second room, fumbled with latches, and threw
open a set of windows. All at once, the light flooded through,
and lit up the treasures of the Toshakhana. Henry heard one
of the Howards stir, reach up to loosen his collar by running
a finger around the inside of it. He thought of the stories of
the Arabian Nights, of every myth he had ever heard about
the East, and gave thanks for this opportunity to have stepped
into one of them.

There were silver and gold chairs, stacked haphazardly.
Every surface contained cooking vessels, plates, spoons, serving ladles, serving dishes, and water pots—*ghadhis*—in solid
gold, embedded with twinkling stones. Henry blinked. He

lifted a *ghadhi*, clasping its mouth with his fingers; it almost slipped out of his hold—it was so heavy. Misr Makraj now moved around the furniture and the jewels, reaching his hand beyond them to the wall, where there were carved niches, their top arches mimicking the archways of the Toshakhana. An oil lamp sat in each niche, and Misr Makraj laboriously cleaned the wicks with a piece of cloth from the pocket of his *kurta* and lit a lucifer match, striking it on a slice of sandpaper. The sharp tang of sulfur speared through the still air.

"Where would we sit?" Henry asked, when he had found his voice. It rustled through his throat.

"Where . . ." Misr Makraj turned to him. "In the court-yard would be best, Henry Sahib. I will bring out each item, and if your men could set up their books and their pens and ink, they can then write out the lists."

"Outside then," Henry said over his shoulder, and the clerks moved away, dragging their feet.

He saw the old treasurer touch a dagger that lay atop a gold plate. Its hilt was solid gold, embedded with chips of precious stones in a rainbow of colors, and its scabbard was plain red leather with no ornamentation.

"What is that?"

"Oh." Misr Makraj turned hurriedly. "I thought you had left the room, Sahib." He glanced down at the dagger. "It belonged to the Maharajah; he had two made, exactly the same." His voice faded.

"Where's the other one now?"

"With me, Sahib. Maharajah Ranjit Singh gave it to me when I was a young man—it was a reward." His eyes had filled. "In Peshawar . . . we were out in an encampment . . . but, that was very long ago."

Henry stepped up to the plate, picked up the dagger, and went over to the windows so that he could see it in the light. The hilt was solid in the palm of his hand, and when he tugged, the blade came out easily, shining sharp and curved at the tip. "Why did the Maharajah give it to you, Misr Makraj?"

The old man blew his nose on a cotton handkerchief and tucked the handkerchief under the sleeve of his *kurta*. He took a deep breath. "Too many years have passed, Sahib, since that day. It was for . . . nothing at all. I was a farmer's son; I met the Maharajah, he gave this"—he pointed at the dagger in Henry's hands—"one like this." He murmured to himself. "A long time ago."

"Let's begin, Misr Makraj," Henry said briskly. There was a story here behind the dagger—but then stories abounded in India, steeped as she was in a varied history that went back many thousands of years, and if Henry Lawrence stopped to hear each one of them, well, he would get no work done.

For the next four hours, the treasures in the Toshakhana came out to the courtyard, and Henry and the clerks moved often, seeking shade under the wide marble eaves of the buildings, fleeing from one spot to another. There were some ten bags of gold finger rings—just that, crammed chaotically into the cloth, strewn with diamonds, rubies, topaz, emeralds, and stones Henry could not even name. He put "unknown" next to them on the list.

Misr Makraj carted enormous bundles of cashmere shawls, with embroidery, with gems embedded into them, with gold and silver *zari*, and each had been carefully packed in a thin leather pouch with the leaves of the *neem* tree tucked between the folds to keep out insects and white ants. Henry had one fine coat, made of thin wool, with golden buttons (not really gold; he was not a Maharajah), which although kept in a san-dalwood trunk made especially for his most precious items, already had four moth holes in it. The treasurer had wrought a miracle.

He then brought out delicate, filmy rock-crystal wine

cups, ninety-nine in all, the hundredth, he said, had been broken by Sher Singh, the Maharajah's adopted son, who had briefly sat on the throne of the Punjab in the long melee after Ranjit Singh's death.

One dirty rag in the palm of Misr Makraj's hand was unwrapped to reveal a pale yellow stone with a heart of fire, its facets cutting deeply into the middle, and every way the old man turned the stone in the light, it reflected it back a hundred times.

Henry reached for it hastily. "The Kohinoor?"

Misr Makraj shook his head, amused. "No, Sahib. Merely a *pukraj*. Valuable, no doubt, but not the Kohinoor. It did masquerade as the Kohinoor once though."

"Pook . . . raj," Henry said slowly. "What is that . . . oh, a topaz?"

"If you say so." Misr Makraj bent his head. "There is a humorous story about it, if you wish to hear."

They had work to do, a lot of it, but Henry said suddenly, "I wish to hear every story, Misr Makraj, everything you have to tell me."

"In a moment, Henry Sahib." The treasurer returned to the Toshakhana and returned in less than a minute, tucking a rag into the pocket of his *kurta* as he came down the stairs.

They retreated to the far end of the courtyard, away from the Howard brothers, who had barely shown any interest upon hearing that the topaz had a history. One of them had brought out his calipers and had the stone tenderly clutched between the two arms. It glowed like a piece of the sun, held in the dull gray tentacles of the tool.

"They have no soul, those two men," Misr Makraj said. "To hold a jewel like that, and feel no emotion." He smiled down at Henry, who was already sitting. "But they are good at writing and adding numbers, eh, Henry Sahib?"

"That they are," Henry said. He brought out his *beedis* and patted the stone beside him. "Please sit."

"If you say so, Sahib." Misr Makraj would never have sat down in the presence of his Maharajah; in fact, he never had, for all the years of his service, no matter how long the audiences had lasted—two, three, six hours or more. He squatted beside Henry easily enough, although tiredly. He was an old man, and his heart had been damaged many times since the death of his king.

They smoked a *beedi* each, another bit of etiquette breached, the smoke curling out from their fingers gray in the deep shadows, blue as it wandered into the sunlight and then dissipated.

"The *pukraj* belonged to the king Shah Shuja," Misr began.

"This too?" Henry said involuntarily. He had promised himself to listen with patience. Every tale had its long beginnings, middles, and even more elongated endings, no matter what it was about. A magistrate, a judge, a postmaster, or now a resident, had to have an extensive ear in India, capable of being filled with protracted sagas. He also had to have a mind like a pernickety sieve—able to strain out the superfluous, and concentrate on the fundamental.

"Yes." Another smile, this one sly. "Shah Shuja had many jewels. My Maharajah wrestled all of them from him. This too, Henry Sahib, along with the Kohinoor. But you know, don't you, that Shah Shuja was driven out of Afghanistan by his own people, and his own general in Kashmir—which was once part of Shuja's lands—imprisoned him in a dungeon there. Shuja had sent his primary wife, Wafa Begam, to Lahore a long while ago, when all these civil rebellions began on his land. She begged my king for help, promised him Peshawar in return—although Peshawar was neither Shuja's nor hers to give away. The Maharajah sent his troops to Kashmir, rescued Shuja, and returned him under guard to the arms of his wife, kept Kashmir for himself and made it part of the Punjab Empire." A shrug. "Only Peshawar was part of the original bargain, but . . . if Shuja could not rule Afghani-stan, there was no way he would have been able to rule Kash-mir. He was a weakling."

Henry nodded. "We had him for a while, you know."

"I do, and what a disaster it was for you, Henry Sahib, although I think the disaster was not of Amir Shuja's making but very much yours—the British, I mean."

Bold words from a mere retainer, Henry thought. How would Edwardes and John have reacted to this—which was after all nothing but a stark truth that could not bear to be ignored? The First Anglo-Afghan War, fought to put Shuja back on the throne of Afghanistan with the help of the Brit-ish army—with only the British army to help; Shuja had no support from his own, scattered men—had been a gut-curdling catastrophe. Henry rubbed his forehead and wiped the sweat on his fingers onto his trousers, where it darkened into a patch. He threw the burned-down end of his *beedi* into the courtyard, and it came to rest upon the stone, smoking itself into oblivion.

In the silence that stretched out between the two men— one who was on the path to being made a peer of England, the other who was nothing more than a servant without employ—Henry wondered where all the fury of his youth had gone. Whether the Indian sun had burned it all out into nothingness. He had always had a temper, much like John, and all through his school life he had jumped into scraps, feet-first, thinking later. Although invariably, he had realized later that he ought to have been more thoughtful. And Henry had never been afraid of giving an apology where he had thought he was wrong, where he had inadvertently done wrong. This, in the thirty-ninth year of his life, as he tarried in a courtyard in Lahore Fort, listening to a story, was what had matured him into the man he was today.

Shah Shuja had been as much of a curse to the British as the Kohinoor he'd once possessed was said to have a curse upon it. But Shuja had been an excuse to invade Afghanistan—the folly of that first intention, and the doggedness in following through with it belonged to one man who had unfortunately been appointed Governor-General of India, George, Lord Auckland.

"So Wafa Begam, Amir Shuja's wife, had also promised the Kohinoor to my Maharajah," Misr continued. "Or rather, he made it a condition for his help. After Shuja was in Lahore, and though under heavy guard, he had all the luxuries of a king—the food, the accommodations (the whole of the Shalimar Gardens was put at his disposal), the *nautch* girls, the picnic parties, the pleasures of his harem. My king sent him polite requests over the months to ask for the Kohinoor."

"Polite?" Henry asked ironically.

"Always polite, Henry Sahib. Maharajah Ranjit Singh was a man of great patience, and a levelheaded man. He never put to death any person unreasonably. He was also vastly generous to Shuja; he waited years for the Kohinoor."

A *bhisti* came to the door of the courtyard, with his goatskin bag slung over one arm and a tower of earthenware cups. He filled the cups for Henry and the treasurer, and one of the Howards rose to bring the water in a tray that had been set just inside the door. No one else was allowed in.

Henry drank the water thirstily, allowing it to flow down his chin and drench his shirt. In the heated courtyard, he felt a sense of blessed coolness. When he was done, he raised his cup to the man next to him.

Misr Makraj nodded, accepting the compliment. "At first, Shuja said he did not have the Kohinoor, that he had lost it while fleeing Peshawar. Then he said he had misplaced it. For a few months, he said he had searched very hard among his belongings for it. Your man Elphinstone came to Lahore to help Shuja escape, but there was nothing in the Punjab that my Maharajah did not know."

"He didn't escape?"

"No, and then he sent a message to my master saying that he had miraculously found the diamond, praise be to Allah, and that he was ready to hand it over."

Henry laughed, throwing his head back. The two Howards tilted their heads inquiringly, peered at him, and then bent back down toward their work. "He sent the topaz."

"He sent the topaz back with Fakir Azizuddin, the foreign minister. We had none of us seen the Kohinoor before, and didn't know if it was blue or white or yellow, but the court jewelers said that it wasn't a diamond at all, but a *pukraj*. The Maharajah kept the topaz—"

Henry grinned. "Of course he would."

Misr Makraj turned in surprise. "Of course; it was a silly trick to play on a great Maharajah. Shah Shuja should have sent him a fake stone, instead of a real one. So the Maharajah then cut off all his supplies again. He sent men to drain the ponds and fountains in Shalimar Bagh, and strip the trees of all fruit."

"How long did Shah Shuja last?"

Misr Makraj held up fists and began unfolding fingers. "One . . . two . . . five . . . six . . . eight."

Henry raised his eyebrows. "Eight days?"

"Eight hours, Henry Sahib." He made a spitting sound with his mouth. "And this man was once Amir of Afghanistan. A mere eight hours, and when he asked for an emissary from the Maharajah's court, Fakir Azizuddin went again. This time he came back with the Kohinoor. It was brought to my king in a box lined with red velvet, a little depression made in the cloth so that it could be shown against it. It was just the Kohinoor by itself, one stone, and a couple of strings tied to its base so that it could be worn as an armlet. For a few years, my king wore it thus."

Henry had heard, though not yet seen, that the Kohinoor was now in an arm ornament of three stones—the Kohinoor itself, flanked by two smaller diamonds, with gold links to complete the armlet. It was in his notes from the Governor-General's office in Calcutta, and the last confirming entry had been in the hand of Lord Auckland.

"And then?"

"Then he had it put into a *sarpech* for his turban. It was set in gold and had a teardrop diamond depending from it. A very small stone, Henry Sahib, this other diamond was, only forty-five carats." Here, Misr Makraj reached into his pocket and brought out the grimy piece of cloth for which he had gone into the Toshakhana. Henry watched as he opened the folds of the cloth. In his palm lay a flawless diamond, lightly faceted, about an inch and a half in length.

Only forty-five carats, Misr Makraj said, incredibly. The Kohinoor was said to be some four times the weight of this little diamond, able to feed the world's population for a whole day. This bauble would send many a man into a comfortable retirement and take care of a few more future generations.

"Beautiful, isn't it?" Misr Makraj asked, dreamily. "It takes a lot of competence to facet a diamond into a teardrop, but the Maharajah's jewelers always had skill."

Henry nodded. He felt for his watch in his vest. He had to leave soon. Tomorrow, perhaps next week, he would be back again to document all the effects of the Toshakhana and he *had* to be here—this was not work he would entrust to the sole discretion of the Howards, although he would to the man next to him, who gazed at the diamond with such adoration, it was impossible to think he would ever imagine stealing it. Or anything else in the treasury.

"Shuja, as you know," Misr Makraj continued, the stone glowing bright in his dark hand, "escaped eventually from Maharajah Ranjit Singh. He could not go back to Afghanistan, so he went instead to Ludhiana, well south of the Sutlej, into British territory."

"He was our guest, true."

Misr Makraj folded the cloth again and stood up. The corners of his mouth turned upward in a dry smile. "As much your guest as he had been ours, Henry Sahib. And then a pawn in your Afghan war."

He walked away, his bare feet creeping over the dust. In the last four hours, he had become more and more bent, his shoulders falling, his back curved, the weight of what he was doing bearing down upon him. Misr Makraj set the teardrop diamond on the book of one of the clerks, who opened up the cloth eagerly and reached for his calipers.

"What about the Kohinoor, Misr Makraj?" Henry called.

The man put out his hands. "It was eventually set in an armlet with a gold chain, flanked by two smaller diamonds. This was early on, Henry Sahib; for the last twenty years of the Maharajah's life, this is how he wore his Kohinoor."

"I mean," Henry said deliberately, "where is the Kohinoor now?"

Misr Makraj lifted his shoulders and turned to his right.

"Where it should be," said a voice from the entrance to the courtyard. "With his Majesty, Maharajah Dalip Singh."

Henry rose to his feet slowly. The woman who stood there was veiled, her *ghagara* and *choli* a crimson red, like a splash of blood against the sandstone. The thin chiffon covering her face was almost transparent, but so heavily embroidered that nothing showed, except her hands, fretting away the edge of the fabric. She stood erect, with a queenly bearing, her skirts full and lush. Even through the veil Henry could see that she was slim, with a tiny waist, and tall enough for her head to almost hit the entrance archways—he had had to duck through, but then Henry Lawrence was a tall man even among the British.

He noticed Misr Makraj bowing, and the two Howards rising from their places.

"How did you get in here?"

She moved one hand out; it was an imperious gesture. "In

my palaces, Henry Lawrence, you ask me how I go anywhere and why?"

She had spoken Persian, and Henry had responded alike; the only difficulty she had was with his name. She called him *Henny Larens*.

"It is not allowed, your . . . er . . . your," Henry stuttered and stopped, cursing under his breath. Who *was* she? One of the numerous widows of Maharajah Ranjit Singh? Not the Maharani Jindan Kaur; her voice was seared in his brain; he had heard her talk many times. When Ranjit Singh had died, he had been cremated, and five of his wives had chosen to commit Sati along with him on his funeral pyre. But he had had a quiverful of others—twenty-three that Henry knew of and, in his meticulous fashion, had documented, demanding from them proof of date of birth, their ancestry, the dates of their marriages to the Maharajah, whether they had had any children from him. This, after having been confronted with an astounding number of royal "widows" when he had first come to Lahore. The British government and the East India Company intended to grant pensions to these women—from the coffers of the Punjab Toshakhana, of course, after taking what they considered right, just, and the spoils of the conqueror.

"Not allowed." She put as much mockery as she could into those two words. "*You* are not allowed to have the Kohinoor diamond."

Henry turned helplessly to Misr Makraj, who was watching him with a gleam in his eyes. "Who is she, Misr Makraj?"

"A . . . princess, Henry Sahib," he said quietly. "She is the sister of Maharajah Sher Singh."

Henry turned again to the woman in the archway and saw her back stiffen, and her chin come up under the veil. Princess? Queen? These titles had been idly bandied about by the twenty-three remaining wives, and the hundred and thirty concubines Ranjit Singh had left behind. She was really nobody, he thought. Sher Singh had been Ranjit Singh's adopted son, and had been assassinated at the behest of Dalip Singh's mother . . . or someone else; the histories, just a few years later, were so muddied with legend. And none of those alive who had witnessed the events spoke of them. Sher Singh's antecedents were murky also; some said he was truly Ranjit Singh's son, though born without the benefit of his parents being married; some said he was a cousin. And this girl was the sister of the man who had pretended to be the son of the Lion of the Punjab, a man who had sat on the throne for a few short days before someone had walked up to him in open court, pulled out a pistol, and shot him between the eyes.

"I'm sorry—" Henry began.

"Don't be," she said harshly. "If you want the Kohinoor back, ask for me, Roshni. If you want to be sorry for me, don't be; I'm betrothed to Maharajah Dalip Singh."

"Tomorrow then," Henry said quickly. "In Jahangir's Quadrangle, at noon. Please come."

He saw her pondering his words, shaking her head at first, and then she said, "All right." She turned to go, and said over her shoulder, "You are here for protection, are you not, Henry Lawrence?"

"Yes," he said. "And to be fair, you must believe that."

She looked at him for a long while. "Why then, in all the time that you have been in Lahore, have you not made an attempt to meet with your charge? Have you seen Maharajah Dalip Singh?"

Henry felt blood warm his skin. He hadn't. The biggest part of his duties as Resident was the care of the young Maharajah, but thus far he had met only the members of the Sikh Durbar—the men who were advisors to the Maharajah's court—his mother and her lover, and the various other men who were in charge of arrangements at Lahore Fort. Henry had the city to deal with also, with all its myriad troubles— water, the lack of it; the hooligans who paraded abroad at night. And then, he had the administration of the whole of the Punjab Empire—what was left of it, ponderous enough for a man not born to rule. He had spent the last two months writing copious letters to every man of note he had served with during all his years with the artillery, inviting them to Lahore to serve under him, giving them governorships of Peshawar and Multan and other places smaller, all with the injunction that their hand must not be too heavy, their wisdom sage indeed, and the people under their guardianship happy.

In all this—days and nights spent in all this—Henry had pushed away the care of the boy king toward his retainers. As long as he had heard reports that Dalip Singh was cheerful, riding his horse every day, learning from his Urdu and Persian masters, keeping his hawks and falcons—he had not bothered to contact him.

The girl, the woman, mocked him, as though she knew his thoughts. "The Maharajah must be your *first* charge, must he not, Henry Lawrence? What else does the Resident of Lahore really have to do?"

"I . . ." Henry began, and then stopped, abashed. She was right.

She went out through the archways, and to Henry it seemed as though the light in the courtyard had dimmed. She had said that she was betrothed to Maharajah Dalip Singh, and she was twenty years old at least—there was none of that adolescent gawkiness in her walk, her talk. And Dalip Singh was eight years old.

And Henry had finally recognized her as the girl he had seen last night in Jahangir's Quadrangle.

The next morning, at four o'clock, before night had slackened its grip over the city of Lahore, the crackle of gunshots resounded off the ramparts.

Henry, John, Edwardes, and the others scrambled from their cots, flung on trousers and shirts, grabbed guns, and sprinted toward the sound. They could see flashes of light beyond the walls, near the stables just outside the Diwan-i-am, the Hall of Public Audience.

"What's happening?" Edwardes yelled, his breathing harsh. He had been in the Bengal Artillery at Dum Dum with Henry; they had arrived in India together, bunked together, spent many a night drinking and exchanging stories. Whereas Henry's figure was slim, almost gaunt after a bout of malaria in a Burma campaign, Edwardes had steadily been putting on bulk. He kept up with the Lawrence brothers, but just barely.

They clattered down the steep set of stairs of the Hathi Pol, the Elephant Gate, and out into the night. To meet with chaos.

Handheld lanterns swung their beams in wild arcs as men dashed around. Fifty or so camels strained in their harnesses, cows bellowed in pain, curses puckered the air, and a small contingent of British soldiers fired into the fabric of the sky.

"Stop," Henry roared. His eyes moved over the scene quickly—no one was dead, although a few cows had collapsed on the dirt, no one was actually shooting at someone else, and everyone was shouting. In a few moments, even this comparative peace would escalate into something worse. "John." He whipped around to his brother. "Get to the back of this crowd, show yourself to the soldiers, and get them to stop shooting—they're frightening the animals. Lake"—this to another lieutenant—"to the right, calm down the natives, find out why. Nicholson, put on your uniform jacket, man, how will they know who you are otherwise?"

Henry pounded back up the stairs leading to the Hathi Pol, grabbed a torch from its holder, and held it aloft.

John, preparing to follow his brother's orders, stopped and turned back. "Put that down, Pat, for God's sake. You're a sitting target; some of these men have guns."

"Only the British soldiers have guns," Henry shouted back. "And no one will shoot at me. Go now."

For ten minutes the racket continued; then slowly, the gunshots stopped, and the natives subsided, muttering under their breath. The only sounds heard for a while were the lowing of the cows, and the distressed snorting of the camels. Henry waited, his arm tiring as he held the light up.

"Who's in charge here?"

"I am, sir." A sergeant came up, his face blackened with gunpowder, his rifle's spout wreathed in smoke. He stood below Henry, his eyes screwed up in a defiant glitter.

"What happened?"

A downward look and an explanation that came out in a mumble. The camel artillery had been on its way to Lahore Fort, to be housed in the stables there. They had chosen this hour of the morning so that there would be no interference from the natives, so that the road would be clear. The camels were hitched onto cannons and large guns, and they had a difficult enough time towing their burdens without the natives running across their paths. But a couple of cowherds had decided to let their herds of cows—some twenty of them—pass by just as the sergeant had shouted at them to stand back. The camels had reared, some of their harnesses had come loose; the camel drivers had bellowed at the cowherds, the cowherds had yelled back. And then the sergeant had drawn his sword and jumped in between the cows and slashed out indiscriminately. He hadn't hit the cowherds—he was careful of that, he said to Henry—but a few of the cows were bleeding from their shoulders and their ears and faces.

"I'm sorry," Henry called out to the cowherds, who were quaking with rage, their *kurtas* drenched in sweat. "Go home now; you will be compensated for the cows. Tell your masters that I will come and visit them later to make amends."

The two men shook their heads. One of them spoke. "It is

indecent to harm a cow; she is like a mother to us. This man"—
he pointed at the sergeant—"has destroyed our mother."

"John," Henry said, "escort these men away, please, right
now. Send them on to their pasture."

As the men left they looked back, muttered to each other,
and one of them called out a word that Henry had come to
dread, that had signaled trouble for him in the past, *"Hartal."*

And sure enough, when the cows' blood had been wiped
off and the dirt resettled in the yard outside the Hathi Pol so
that no other native could make a pilgrimage here, the city of
Lahore woke to a strike, a *hartal*. Shops were shut down even
before they opened, schools were given the day off; women
crept out to the communal wells in fear, returning with their
pots of water held in front of their bellies, covered by their
veils. Vegetables brought fresh from the countryside baked
in the carts; no buyer dared to step outside while a gang of
ruffians roamed the streets, beating up whomever they saw,
smashing the windows of the houses, setting fires that spread
through one neighborhood, and then another.

All morning long, Henry listened with growing dismay to
the news from the outside. He called for the *wazir*, Lal Singh,
and ordered him to lift the strike.

Lal Singh was a short, fair man, with a large mole on his
chin, which he worried with his fingers as he talked. He had
shifty eyes, never met Henry's gaze, and bent his head from
one direction to another in birdlike movements. "What can I
do?" he said, touching his chin with a fat hand.

Henry looked at him with distaste. It was rumored that
Lal Singh's father had been a shopkeeper in Lahore, and it
was true that he was Maharani Jindan Kaur's lover, and the
two of them had engineered the whole coup that led to Dalip
Singh's being on the throne. It was also rumored that perhaps
Lal Singh, and not Maharajah Ranjit Singh, was Dalip Singh's
father, that their affair was one of long standing. This last
Henry did not pay heed to, or care about.

"Go talk to the people, Lal Singh," he said. "They will listen to you."

"Ah." Lal Singh pretended to ponder this. His glittering gaze rested upon the top button on Henry's shirt. "They do not listen to *you*, do they? What can *I* do? The people have a mind of their own and are demanding restitution for a wrong. You must instruct your soldiers not to touch any Indian cows, Resident Henry; it is against my religion."

"They know this." And it was true. Henry, John, Edwardes—all of them—had continually dinned this message of tolerance into the uneducated foot soldiers of the armies of the Queen and the East India Company. Especially here, in Lahore, where they were on such a tentative footing with the natives—not rulers yet, not vassals of their Maharajah either.

Then Henry pleaded with Lal Singh, something he had never done so far. But the *wazir* refused to leave the safety of the fort and step into the raging fire outside. The people would come to a resolution themselves, he said, over and over again. He could not interfere.

So, at noon, Henry, John, and Edwardes set out on horseback with five soldiers as a guard and went down the deserted, ghostly streets to the houses of the two Hindu men who owned the herds. As they passed through the barren bazaars, many eyes viewed them through shutters and just-ajar windows. Doors opened softly in their wake, and from each house, a man stepped out and joined the growing throng following them. Their horses' hooves rattled on the deserted cobblestones of the streets, along with the muted flip-flop of the men's feet behind. By the time they had reached their destination, the crowd had grown to some seven hundred men.

John nudged his horse closer to Henry's and said, "We should turn back; this is not safe. Better to come with a larger escort."

"No," Henry said, just as quietly. "We come in peace."

"Henry—"

"John," Henry said, his face rigid, "do as I say."

They arrived outside the house of one of the herd owners. It was really a mansion, Henry realized, large, whitewashed, set well back from the road and hidden behind the foliage of a grove of fruit trees—guavas, tamarinds, jamuns. They dismounted, left their horses outside the gates, reins flung on the dirt, and put the soldiers on guard.

On the front verandah, seated in balloon cane chairs, were two corpulent men in pristine white *dhotis* and *kurtas*. They nodded at the three Englishmen and, not rising from their places, indicated to the servants that more chairs be brought out. The five men sat in an uneasy circle as *chai* was served, along with a plate of purple coconut *burfis*. They ate and drank in silence—even in turbulent times such as these, niceties had to be observed—and at the end, Henry gulped down his *chai*, to wash away the sticky sugar of the sweets in his mouth.

He set his cup down and waved off a persistent fly buzzing about his ear. "The British government will compensate you for the loss of your cows. We are truly sorry about the incident."

One of the two men—and they were friends, and owners of the herds, this Henry understood even though no introductions had been made—sank deeper into his chair. A fine sheen of sweat glittered on his forehead and on the folds of his chin. He gazed at his hands, linked over a comfortable stomach, and said, in a low, muffled voice, "This is a travesty, Henry Sahib."

Henry was distracted for a moment by a harsh curse that came floating over the gardens to them from the vicinity of the gates. "I agree," he said. "The soldier responsible is an *unpad*—illiterate—and he does not understand the value you have for your cows. He will be reprimanded, and demoted immediately."

"That is good," the man replied. "But is it enough?"

"Enough for now. We will all talk to our men later today, and teach them to be more careful."

The two men glanced at each other, their eyes tiny in the many folds of flesh on their cheeks, and seemed to come to an agreement.

"Thank you," said the man who had spoken so far.

The house, the gardens, the sheer repose of the two herd owners meant that they were also rich, and men of some influence in the city. Henry said, "Will you call off the *hartal*? Everyone suffers."

The man agreed. "Everyone does. Good-bye."

The three Englishmen rose but did not shake hands. Just as they had pushed their chairs back, a loud clatter came from the gates. Curses were flung into the heated air, the horses began neighing in distress, and the men fled out of the gardens toward the sounds. Another altercation had begun, this time between Henry's five soldiers and the mob outside. The soldiers had been stripped of their rifles, and these were passed on from hand to hand until they disappeared into the mass of bodies. Bricks, stones, and sticks were lobbed upward just as Henry, Edwardes, and John launched themselves into the mob.

They fought as best they could, pushing, jostling, trampled upon by hundreds of feet. A few men that Henry grabbed out to hold slipped away from his grasp, their bodies slick with sweat. He saw a brick crash down upon Edwardes's head, and the secretary disappeared into the crowd. Henry shoved his way to him and pulled him back up onto his feet. Of John there was no sight. He had vanished also. Someone yanked at Henry's arm, and he felt an immense pain as it pulled out of his shoulder socket. His eyes blurred, his mouth went dry, and in a few seconds he would have fallen into unconsciousness.

But just at that moment, a calm voice said, *"Bas."*

Just that, just one word, at almost a whisper. *Bas.* Enough.

The throng melted away, leaving the road littered with the debris of its weapons—pieces of broken earthenware, stones, chipped bricks, sticks. Henry and his men gathered together, their faces bloodied, their uniforms soiled and torn, and stood looking at the fat herd owner who leaned upon the gate to his mansion, and who had broken up the fight.

"Go home now, Henry Sahib," he said, weary from the long walk from his verandah to the road. The gold rings on his plump hand flashed in the sunlight. "You will be safe. Go back to the fort now." With that, he turned and waddled away.

Henry cradled his sore arm, his horse picking its way back through the bazaar streets. Edwardes lay forward on his horse, half-unconscious, his face buried against the horse's mane. Only John seemed to have escaped much damage—his clothes were torn also, his collar soaked with blood from a cut above his ear, but he, the civil servant Lawrence brother, had enjoyed his foray into a minor battle with the gusto of a soldier.

Back at the fort, Dr. Kingsley, the surgeon attached to the Resident's staff, popped Henry's arm back into its socket, put a few stitches in Edwardes's face, wiped the blood from above John's ear, and attended to the soldiers.

Henry went to speak to his men.

The horde of native men had cursed and called them names, bitter names in Hindustani, Persian, and Punjabi, Henry's soldiers said to him. And you must know, sir, that English were never as expressive a language as these native ones.

Did they throw the first stone? Henry asked.

No, but they opened their filthy mouths so wide and Gus 'ere felt constrained to smack one of them on 'is bloody head . . . and that started it all. Sir.

Henry grimaced, promptly demoted the five soldiers, and set them to work cleaning out the latrines. He then sent a message to the cantonment of Firozpur, where the largest British presence was stationed in the form of five regiments, and where Henry had once been Assistant Agent. Firozpur was forty-seven miles from Lahore, south of the Sutlej River, and very much in British territory even well before the death of Maharajah Ranjit Singh.

By the middle of that night, two cavalry regiments, of a hundred and fifty soldiers each—both English and Indian—thundered into Lahore and took up their stations around the walled city and outside the Hathi Pol of the Lahore Fort.

The residents of Lahore woke to a forbidding army of redcoats, who forced the shops open at gunpoint and kept them open through the day. They rounded up the miscreants involved in the previous day's fracas one by one, and brought five native men to face Henry in the fort. He questioned them for two hours, listened to their stories, and set four of them free. The fifth man was hanged in a public bazaar that night, in front of the population of Lahore—this had been announced by drummers all over the city earlier, soon after Henry had made his decision.

And so, a shaky peace returned to the city. Henry went to bed, sick at heart about everything. He had missed his meeting with the young girl; he still did not have the Kohinoor; he had not yet met Maharajah Dalip Singh. What, he wondered, did the king think of this conflict? And what could he even think about it? He was only eight years old.

Henry woke the next morning to a sudden, unusual blindness—everything bleached pale before his eyes—a raging fever, an inferno of ache in his shoulder.

The fever ran rampant, coming and going as it pleased, whittling away flesh from Henry's bones, until he lay in his cot a slight, wasted ghost of his former self.

For the first week, Dr. Kingsley ministered to him. The fever was puzzling. Was it a recurrence of the malaria he had contracted in Burma, some twenty years ago? John thought yes—Henry had always suffered from fevers since then. Kingsley prodded at Henry's liver, just under his ribs, but it was not enlarged. Still, he fed Henry tonic water laced with quinine.

As Henry thrashed about in his narrow cot, his arm slipped out of the socket again and again, until that whole side was inflamed and swollen. Kingsley bled him, opening a vein near his elbow, and let the blood pool into a dish several times a day. At the end of the week, a pulse beat only faintly at Henry's wrist; his skin was white, paper-thin; bruises bloomed all over his body. His thick, dark hair, which he had to cut every week to keep some semblance of a soldier's appearance, ran a riot of black curls over the pillow and framed the ashen gray of his face.

When the moon was cleaved in half in the jeweled night sky, and John knelt by his brother's bed in prayer, a hand touched his shoulder. It was the girl from the Toshakhana, whom John recognized, even though she was veiled. No other woman had approached the British party before, especially not with the offer of the Kohinoor.

"What do you want?" he said roughly in Persian.

"Leave him to me," she said. "I will take care of him."

They had moved Henry's bed to the courtyard of Jahangir's Quadrangle—Kingsley being unsure of whether his fever was contagious or not. And there Henry had been alone, shifted into the coolness of the adjoining pavilion during the day, brought out under the sky at night.

"Go away," John said, raising a pale, haunted face to her.

"Is he getting better, Jan Larens?" she asked.

"No," John moaned. "Oh, God, no." Then more quietly, "I could not bear to lose him like this. What will I tell Lettice . . . and Honoria?"

"Your sister? Your mother?" she said. "Strange fashion you English have of calling your mother by name. You will tell her that Henny Larens survived his fever. And he will, if you let me." As John knelt doggedly by Henry's side, she said in a clear voice, "Do you want him to die?"

He moved away then to the edge of the lawn and sat down on the warm stone. The night passed and he watched, smoking cigarette after cigarette, the stubs thrown around him.

She had brought in ten attendants and spoke only when it was necessary. A gesture, a movement from her head, and they seemed to understand what needed to be done. They lifted Henry's quiescent figure from the cot and laid it on the ground upon a white sheet. Then they changed out all of the bedclothing, piling new sheets upon the cot, restuffing the pillowcase, erecting a rectangular frame around on which they slung a thin, white, and airy mosquito net. They put Henry's cot in the middle and set four lanterns on the floor.

The girl, the woman, stripped off Henry's clothes, and not flinching, she washed his body with a silk cloth dipped in rosewater, camphor, and cinnamon. She clicked her tongue when she saw the unhealed gashes along his arms, where Kingsley had bled him copiously, called for a jar of iridescent paste, applied it on the wounds, and bound them loosely in muslin. The men then dressed Henry and pulled a sheet over his inert form. Henry took in a deep, rasping breath, and the sound caused a stab of pain inside John.

She had a golden box brought to her, selected a cherry-size, round ball of some dark stuff, and forced it between Henry's lips. He resisted, but she leaned down and talked to him gently, and he allowed his mouth to close over it and began to chew. Fifteen minutes later, he was in a profound sleep, his chest rising and falling with a constant rhythm that John hadn't seen in the past week.

"What was that?" he asked from his spot near the pavilion, his voice carrying loud over the courtyard.

"Opium," she said. She rose and came up to him. "You must go and get some sleep also, Jan Larens. He will get better, not soon, but definitely."

"What is wrong with him?"

She shrugged, a graceful movement. "Who knows? A fever, chills, the arm . . . it could be one of any number of things. But, if he eats, and sleeps, his body will fight it. Tomorrow, I will bind his shoulder; it must not be moved while it heals. I have not"—and here he heard a smile in her voice—"the benefit of an English medical education, but I have looked after many women in the *zenana*."

"I'll stay."

"As you wish. I will be awake through the night."

And if she was, he did not know, for a few minutes after this conversation, fatigue felled him too, and he slept as he sat, head hung over his lap. In the morning, discomfort rode down the back of his spine; his dreams had been colored by images of his brother's death, but when he awoke it was to find the woman gone and Henry still deeply, sweetly asleep.

From that day onward, John Lawrence went back to the work Henry and he had left undone. Misr Makraj mentioned casually that all the heavier Toshakhana items—tent hangings, curtains, coverings, poles—were in one part of the stables, and John went thumping out into the Diwan-i-am and beyond to the stables. Sure enough, one of the stalls had a cheap wooden door, and a creaky padlock. John had this opened and stood there in awe as the camels from the artillery peered in curiously over his shoulder, their rancid breath fanning his hair. The tent poles were encased in gold and silver, studded with diamonds and emeralds. The tent hangings were perfectly matched—carpets underfoot, curtains, throws, covers, embroidered on every inch of downy and very expensive cashmere fabric. A painting stood facing the wall. John picked it up. It had a solid gold frame, shells and rubies embedded in it, and out of the painting Queen Victoria, slim, doe-eyed, looked at John in her coronation robes. He wiped the dust off and set it down—how had Ranjit Singh got this painting? Who gave it to him? Memory stirred. John remembered that the Governor-General's sister, Emily Eden, had painted a portrait for the Maharajah Ranjit Singh. Was this it?

This other Toshakhana, scented with the aroma of camel droppings and damp hay, absorbed all of his interest as he unearthed treasure after treasure. Strange, inexplicable ones, like a copy of the New Testament that Henry Martyn, an Anglican priest, had translated into Persian forty years ago. The flyleaf was inscribed "From Lady William Bentinck to Joseph Wolff." Bentinck had been Governor-General of India, but who was Joseph Wolff, and how had he come to present his Persian testament to the Maharajah?

Every now and then, John lifted his head and wondered how his brother was doing.

A desk and a chair had been brought to Jahangir's Quadrangle and set up against the latticework sandstone screens of the pavilion, which looked out over the Ravi River. Once, the river had flowed a few feet from this northern edge of the fort, but in the late 1600s, after continual flooding of the lower apartments, Emperor Aurangzeb had had a bund, an embankment, built along the whole north wall. And he had diverted the river's flow to a couple of miles farther north, leaving just a slim canal in its original path to route water for the fort's use.

July's and August's monsoon rains had filled the canal, but it was already fast drying up—great sandbanks silting its edges and a silk floss tree inclined over the canal as though seeking more water to store in the spiny thorns that climbed its trunk. The silk floss was in full bloom; it had been undeterred by the long wait for the monsoons, fiercely drought-resistant, and at the first sprinkle of rain, the whole cap of the tree had mushroomed into pink, fleshy flowers.

This was the view Henry saw every day when he lifted his head from his work. If he half-closed his eyes and blurred his gaze, sections of the latticework screen became pink with flowers of the silk floss behind, brown with the scrub of the bank, green where the broad-leaved shrubs had taken hold after the rains, blue in the upper reaches, where the sky was.

Behind him, on the very edge of the platform of the pavilion, stood a line of red dispatch boxes like a row of soldiers on guard. Henry glanced back at them, and the bright sunshine of the courtyard beyond, and sighed. He had to look through the mass of papers in each one of them, put his initials on some, a signature on others, an official stamp on yet others. Two weeks in bed with a fever and a delirium had piled up the paperwork—no one in Calcutta knew that he had tarried at the edge of death, and once he was better, they wouldn't care that he had, only that the papers needed to be attended to.

As it should be, Henry thought, in India especially. In Calcutta there was a tradition of leaving calling cards in boxes hung on gates after the summer had been passed in the cooler hills by those fortunate enough to get away from its steamy, unhealthy heat. The cards informed friends and acquaintances not just of your return but of your well-being, more specifically that another summer had passed and you were still, very much, alive.

John sat against one of the red sandstone pillars of the pavilion, half in the sun, half in the shade, his head bent over the mail which had been brought in from Firozpur, which had in its turn traveled all along the breadth of India from Calcutta, and by ship from England—via France, Egypt, Ceylon, up the Bay of Bengal to Calcutta.

Henry put his pen down. "Who was she, John?" He could hear his brother sifting through the letters.

John said, "Here's one for you. Lettice, I think; it looks like her handwriting. What's this, September? Then she wrote it in January at the latest—snow, cold, fires, fog, a white landscape. How I miss those!"

Henry laughed, the sound surprising him when it came out of his chest. "What bosh, John. You've been in India how long? Eighteen years? Something like that. What do you remember of an English fire or landscape? Could you even live in England now?"

John grinned. "It would be dull. Where else would we have the excitement of battling about cattle?"

Henry sobered and turned in his chair, its legs scraping the inlaid marble floor of the pavilion. "Who was she?"

"Here," John said in reply, sending the packet flying through the air to land at his feet. "Read it; I see Letitia hasn't written to me; you were always the favorite brother. I wonder how she fares with that dreary husband of hers. She's now Mrs. Hayes, isn't she? And he's fifteen years older than her—what *does* she see in him?"

"She fell in love with him," Henry said mildly. He bent to pick up the letter, slid a knife under the seal, and laid the pages open on his lap, but felt no inclination to read. He glanced at John, absorbed in one of his own, holding it up to the light as though he couldn't see very well.

Henry's sight had returned gradually, after the first night when he had fallen asleep and woken without a dry mouth, a pounding ache in his shoulder, or sweat-sodden bedsheets. Everything around him in the gardens had taken on a new hue, no longer a blinding white, not even gray. He could see the blue of the sky above, the greens of the trees, the pale jade of the pond in the center of the gardens, the fresh whites of the marble platform. It had felt, for the first time since his illness, as though he was alive, breathing, and conscious of the world he inhabited.

The fever had come back during the day, and at night.

He hadn't opened his eyes but could feel the cool, soft hands of a woman smoothing his hair, her fingers firm as she lifted his shoulder and bound it, over and over again until the pain had lessened into a dull throb. He had felt her feed him a ball of opium again; it had tasted tart on his tongue, and even for this sensation he was grateful. He could identify—forced his sluggish brain to identify—the tang of tamarind, the grit of coarsely ground sugar, a wedge of cashew, the ridges of dried raisins and apricots.

A few days later—when, he couldn't rightly remember— he had looked up and seen the moon in the sky as a tiny sliver of a crescent, the rest of the circle outlined in a ghostly white, and knew that it was nearly time for the new moon—two whole weeks since he'd seen the harvest moon. That was how he had counted time each night, by the shape of the moon.

The woman had been veiled most of the time, but one night, as she was bending over to wipe his face with a cloth dipped in rosewater, the edge of her veil had caught on one of the buttons of his shirt. She'd cursed softly, wrestled with the silk, and tore at it with an impatient gesture. And then, she'd pulled it from her head and pitched it away. And Henry, still not knowing if he was dreaming, or alive, or awake, had seen her face in the light of the lanterns. His heart had almost stopped at her beauty, and he'd felt hilarity bubble inside him. He was, indeed, alive, if he could react to the sight of a wom-an's beautiful face, and he could see very well also—there was nothing wrong with his eyes.

She had an oval face, velvety skin that took on the sheen of gold in the lantern's glow, carefully arched eyebrows, and pale blue eyes, colored like springtime skies. Her eye-lids were lined with kohl that swung out toward the tips of her brows. There was a dusting of gold glitter on her cheeks, which caught the light as she turned, and a flush brought on from the cursing and the flinging of the veil. Her mouth was sweet, lush, her teeth perfectly straight when she caught her lower lip between them. His mind had cataloged every bit of what he could see, and he'd begun to think that, perhaps, he *was* dreaming. His gaze had then dropped down her smooth throat, to the diamond and emerald necklace around her neck, to the edges of her embroidered *choli*.

She had drawn back then, suddenly, and when she'd reappeared in his range of vision, she was veiled again. He must have made a disappointed sound, for she'd leaned over, flooding his nose with the scent of frangipani under a hot sun, and said, "You must sleep now."

"I've slept enough," he'd said, the sound cracking through his lips. They were the first words he had spoken since the night he fell ill—all else had been the mutterings of a delirious man. "I'm hungry."

"You are?" It was a sound of pure delight. "Of course you are."

She had clapped her hands, and when an attendant leaned over, had said something to him. He'd returned with a bowl of stew—tender chicken pieces cooked in a clear broth, flavored with pepper, salt, cumin, and some ground ginger.

Henry's pillows had been piled up against the bed and she'd raised him herself, wouldn't let him even lean on his left hand for support. And then she'd fed him, her head tilted under the veil as he chewed, wiping a drop of the stew from his chin.

"More," he'd said, greedy, ravenous.

"No more," she'd said firmly, sending the bowl away with the servant. "More tomorrow perhaps. We'll see. Sleep now?" This time there was laughter in her voice.

Henry had slept. He'd woken during the night and seen her there, some distance from his cot, her knees drawn up to her chest, her chin resting on them. She'd been unveiled, her eyes gleaming in the half-darkness, her gaze steady upon him. He'd gone to sleep again.

She'd come only during the night, Henry had realized

as the days passed and he grew stronger, even able to walk with his hand on John's shoulder, most of his weight on his brother as though not trusting his own feet. As he'd become more alert, he had watched her carefully, waiting for her veil to slip, peering under its edge when he could. And then one night, she did not come, but it was a night when Henry did not need a caretaker anymore. And after that, he hadn't seen her again.

"Who was she, John?" he asked for the third time.

His brother was looking at him with a strange, closed expression. "You should read Letitia's letter."

"Why?"

"She's written me one also. Read yours, will you?"

Henry smoothed out the pages on his lap, and the very first line said, "My dearest Henry and Honoria." He let it fall back. "What news of Honoria, John?"

Again, that frown. "She's on her way here from Calcutta, Pat. She arrived at the mouth of the Hooghly two months ago, and the Batterseas put her on a *dak* route to the Punjab. It's taken her a long time to get to India—there was some problem with the ship sailing from Aden, if you remember"—Henry nodded here—"but she finally got onto one, and it took her to Calcutta."

"You've heard from Major Battersea then?" Henry asked gently.

"I have." John held up one of his letters. "He says Honoria has written also; her letter should come soon. I've left my Harriet at Firozpur; perhaps it would be better . . . if Honoria went there instead? I mean, what could a woman do here in Lahore, with things as they stand?"

Henry Lawrence sat back in his chair and stared out into the gardens of the courtyard, framed in the archways of the pavilion. The fountains sparkled in the sunlight, seen from this far, not quite heard. The Howard clerks passed through his line of vision, hurrying on some important errand or the other. They glanced simultaneously at the pavilion, ducked their heads, and went on, as though guilty at having done so. One day, soon, he would have to go back to cataloging the Toshakhana. They were reminding him of their idleness.

And then, with some difficulty, he thought about Honoria, worrying the outer seam of his trousers with his fingers. Theirs had been a long betrothal, some ten years. It had been an even more peculiar courtship. Henry had met Honoria Marshall in Ireland, on his first home leave from India and his regiment in Dum Dum. John had still been in England, and Henry, John, and their sister Letitia had gone for a holiday on the Irish coast and stayed in a small village. There, walking along a windswept beach Lettice had seen Honoria and called out to her in delight. They were old schoolmates. They'd soon found out where Honoria was lodging, and from that day on the four of them had gone out together on walking trips and picnics when the weather permitted. A month later, Honoria had come to London. They had gone to a few balls together, and some nights at the opera and at the theater. Once, when Honoria had needed an escort back to her aunt's house, Henry had accompanied her in the cab, but so also had Lettice—it wouldn't have been correct for the two of them to have been alone with each other.

In those seven days that Henry had seen Honoria, he had fallen in love with her. She was soft-spoken, she was kind, she was graceful, she walked well—everything a good English-woman should be. He thought of his lonely nights in Bengal, the sheer lack of unmarried, unattached Englishwomen in India, and fell in love with her.

He had been twenty-five years old, still a lieutenant in the artillery, with a pay that was abysmally small to maintain a wife. Besides, a few years ago, when his older brothers and he had gone to India, they had decided to start a "Lawrence Fund" to support their mother, now that their father, who had lived and died a poor soldier in the

King's army, was gone. John was then sitting for his civil service examinations—Henry had been teaching him Bengali for this—and would soon after follow them to India. He was also going to contribute to the fund, deposited in their mother's name in her bank every month, so she need never be put in the embarrassing position of asking them for money.

Simply put, Henry could not afford a wife. John, when he came to India in a few months, had entered the Civil Service at Delhi, and had been made assistant magistrate and collector, lording over eight hundred square miles of district and half a million inhabitants. John was then nineteen years old and earned the princely sum of two thousand five hundred rupees a month—about three times Henry's salary after six years of working in India. John could have married *before* he came out to India, merely on the promise of what he was about to make.

Five years had passed, and Henry had gotten a promotion. Their mother was better set up by now, the fund had grown quite large, and her letters to Henry had contained the constant complaints of a lack of a daughter-in-law from him. She'd mentioned Lettice's friend Honoria from time to time. And in reading her letters, all of Henry's old love for Honoria had returned.

It was Lettice, eventually, who had acted as a go-between and told Honoria of Henry's love for her. Her next letter to her brother had told him that his feelings were reciprocated. Henry had written a first, and very formal, letter to Honoria proposing marriage, and she had accepted.

She had begun gathering her trousseau soon after, and news from her was of her excitement, her deep love for him, her longing to see him—much as Henry had felt himself, and he'd slept with those letters under his pillow. But then, her mother had fallen ill and died and she could not leave her father so soon after her mother's death. And then her father had begun ailing and while he was ill, she could not leave him. For a long while, Henry and Honoria had written to each other, filling pages with news of England, of India, of all his postings, of his work, of her father. Until the day the news came that her father had died and she could now, finally, come to India and marry him.

Henry had sent her the money for the passage—that had been almost eight months ago. He was to have gone to Calcutta to meet her ship and married her right off the dock, so to speak, but the residency had intervened, and he could not, in good conscience, have taken personal leave at such a crucial time in Lahore's history. So he'd gone on to Lahore, and made arrangements with one of John's friends, Major Battersea, to meet Honoria at the boat, to keep her in their house in Calcutta, and to find a safe passage for her across the Northwest Provinces until she could come to Lahore. To be his wife.

"Shall I ask for her to be escorted to Firozpur, Pat?" John said again.

"Honoria has traveled alone, and far, to find me, John," Henry said quietly. "The first thing she will do is stand up with me in front of God and take me as her husband. Then, if necessary, she can go to Firozpur." He smiled. "I think she will stay here at Lahore, though, after all of her travels and adventures, we will seem very tame indeed."

John's face lightened. For the first time Henry realized that he had been afraid—no, perhaps apprehensive was more apt—of the woman who had taken care of Henry, that he might have fallen in love with her. A statement came to Henry's mind that he almost spoke out loud—*Jan Larens sab janta*—John Lawrence knows everything. The natives in Delhi had said this of the nineteen-year-old John, nosy, fussy, in the throes of ambition and inquisitiveness in his first job.

He asked John, for the fourth time, "Who was she?"

"Princess Roshni," he said. "She insisted upon looking after you, and she did a damned good job of it too."

As his brother turned to leave, Henry's voice stopped him again. "Bring the Maharajah to see me tomorrow, will you please?"

The time that had been set for the meeting was nine o'clock, again in Jahangir's Quadrangle. Maharajah Dalip Singh came with sixty-five attendants. They entered from the southern doorway, which gave out onto the pavilion and the throne *jharoka*, the balcony of the Diwan-i-am beyond.

Henry, who had been expecting to see the boy alone, or perhaps with just one or two men as an escort who would drop him off and leave them, hadn't bothered to gather an entourage around him. Both Edwardes and John had made some noises about being there, about this being an official visit, but from the very beginning Henry was determined that this was not to be so. The boy was a child; he was a grown man in the somewhat loose capacity of the boy's guardian—if any true understanding was to be reached between them, other people were unnecessary.

Now, leaning against one of the pillars of the pavilion in which he spent his day, Henry began to wish he had asked for the British contingent to be present.

The sixty-five men entered first, all dressed splendidly in robes of state and the parade ground. There were the cavalrymen in red, short jackets, blue trousers with red stripes running down the sides, and red turbans. The lancers were distinguished only by their French gray jackets, all else the same as the cavalry, and they held their lances beautifully, one hand grasping on top of, another below, the vamplate. The infantry had red jackets, white trousers, and black belts. The Gurkhas had green jackets and caps. The gunners had black waistcoats, white trousers, and crossbelts adorned with cartridges.

Henry straightened and came to attention. He stepped from the shade of the pavilion into the sunshine and began to walk toward them, wondering whether he was to meet the Maharajah halfway, or wait for him to approach, or go up to him. He decided that the best would be for them both to come up to the center of the marble platform in the middle of the pool. But to do that, he had to maneuver around the gardens to his right, where lay the only path across the pool. Unlike most other *charbaghs,* this one did not have four bisecting pathways leading to it.

The soldiers watched stoically as Henry rushed to his right and then up to the marble platform. He stood there, panting; even that effort had been too much. Then, he felt foolish, for the Maharajah would have to come to his right to get to the platform, so in the end, Henry strolled back under the watchful gaze of the soldiers and stood in the open piece of yard just under the stairs.

The courtiers came in next. They had long sherwani coats with mandarin collars; under them they wore white silk pajamas tight around their ankles and shins, with jewel-studded cummerbunds, flashy daggers, well-groomed beards wrapped in sheer gold gauze.

One of them stepped forward and announced, *"Maharajah Dalip Singh hazir hai!"* Hail to the Maharajah Dalip Singh.

The men all bowed their heads, and through the open archway appeared a slight figure, his clothing an exact, miniature replica of that of his courtiers, the diamond on his aigrette brilliant, his short dagger encrusted with emeralds. Henry could barely see any gold in the hilt or the scabbard. The boy had upturned Jodhpuri slippers on his feet, embroidered with gold and silver, the details picked out in rubies and diamonds.

And Henry stood there alone.

The courtiers shifted about on their feet—they had not expected this and didn't know what the etiquette was now. Dalip Singh bounded down the stairs, tripped and fell on the third one down, and was up before anyone could reach out a hand to him. He threw off his slippers and, barefoot, came running down to stand next to Henry.

A smile, dazzling, eager, lit up his eyes. He put a hand into Henry's and said in Persian, "I have wanted to meet you so much, Henry Lawrence. The Sikh Durbar has talked much of your kindness to my people."

Henry shook the little hand in his and held the boy at arm's length. "You are splendid yourself, your Highness. The pleasure is all mine. But we should speak Urdu, or Punjabi?"

"You know both also then? All right, either one. But I'm to be addressed as your Majesty, you know, I *am* the Maharajah of the Punjab."

Every missive from the Governor-General's office in Calcutta had been to remind Henry, in subtle terms or blatant, that none of the native princes were to be accorded the right to be addressed as Majesty—that belonged to their Queen in England; the highest honor to be paid to a native ruler was his Highness.

However, there was no one around to hear or see Henry's infraction, so he said gravely, "As you wish, your Majesty."

Dalip Singh turned and clapped his plump hands together. "Away!" he shouted at the men in the entrance. "Captain Henry and I have many things to discuss. We wish to be left alone."

Mir Kheema, Dalip's butler, came forward and bowed. "Your Majesty, this is not possible. You will need us with you. The translator—"

"Away! We do not need a translator. Now. Please." The heron's feather in his turban bobbed in the sunlight. Henry grinned; this child was indeed a king.

When the entourage had dispersed, Maharajah Dalip Singh put his hand into Henry's again, trustingly, and they walked together into the cool, dark shade of the pavilion. Dalip Singh sat on Henry's desk, Henry on the chair, and they gazed at each other for a long while.

"Oh," Dalip said, "I almost forgot." He dug into the pocket of his gold brocade sherwani, brought out a bunch of green grapes, and set it on the table. "This is for you. I thought that I should not visit you empty-handed. My father never did."

Henry reached out for the fruit, and when he held it in his hands, it was surprisingly heavy. Not grapes after all, but thirty-six emeralds fashioned into grapes, the stones smooth and unmarred, each with a green fire within; the top layer of stones were about the size of jamun fruit, the second layer smaller, the size of cherries, and so on until the tiny, last stone, which was the size of a dewdrop. In the light that streamed in through the latticework screen behind, the emeralds glowed. Little gold links connected the gems loosely so that they draped over the palm of his hand just like real fruit.

"It's exquisite," he said, in a hushed voice. "Thank you, but I cannot keep it."

Dalip shrugged, lifting his small shoulders. He swung his feet against the wood of the desk. "I know. You'll have to give it to your Company's Toshakhana. I hear"—his voice was bland—"that you've been going through the items of *my* Toshakhana?"

"Yes."

"Well, this is from my personal collection, not from the state jewels. Although"—here was a wicked gleam in his eyes—"that is also my personal collection. I *am*"—he puffed out his chest—"the Maharajah of the Punjab."

Henry Lawrence sat back in his chair and stared at the boy, a pang in his heart. Wars he understood, the making of them, the conquest of a people, the division of the spoils after.

And there had been a war—the Anglo-Sikh War—that had brought him here to Lahore. But the terms of the treaty were so . . . nebulous. The British government had promised Punjab that once their young Maharajah reached his majority, at sixteen years of age, they would retire from the land. Somehow, this insistence upon cataloging the Toshakhana didn't seem the right step in that direction; it implied only the path to full annexation. But this Henry could not say to the Maharajah; he wondered if the boy even understood this much.

Dalip Singh had a child's round face, curved cheeks, bright eyes, a rosebud mouth that was ever ready to smile. His hair, long no doubt, since the Sikhs did not cut their hair, would be braided and tucked under his turban. Tiny wisps curled out on his nape. The collar of his sherwani lay tight against his neck, and its sleeves closed about his chubby wrists. He had a little stomach that strained against his pearl and silver *zari*-embroidered cummerbund.

"What are you studying now, your Majesty?" Henry asked.

Dalip made a clicking sound with his mouth. "Captain Henry, you are here as a representative of your wonderful Queen, and I *am* the Maharajah of the Punjab." Henry grinned at this insistence, and Dalip said sharply, "It's true!"

"True enough, your Majesty, but repeating it will not make it truer."

"What I mean to say is that I'm not here to talk about my education. Tell me instead about your Afghan War. You lost, didn't you?"

There was no cunning in that ingenuous gaze. Henry did not wonder that this child was asking him a question about the war, because he was no ordinary eight-year-old; he was the Maharajah of the Punjab, and as such, he would have been schooled in the politics of his frontiers.

Dalip put a hand on Henry's arm, stopping his narrative even as he began. "Your Lord Auckland was Governor-

General then? He was the one who gave the orders for the war?"

Henry nodded. "It was his . . . fault, his responsibility."

"And why did you jump into it then?"

Henry pondered this for a long while. "No reason at all; at least, in retrospect it seems so, but Lord Auckland must have found something else that was compelling."

"I'm thirsty," Dalip said, his mouth screwed up into a pout.

Henry rose from his chair. "I'll find someone."

Just then, a servant came in with a gold tray and two golden goblets with a sweet, cool watermelon sherbet. Henry did not ask where the man had come from, or if he had been close enough to overhear the conversation. Dalip would not have been left alone, for all of his imperious posturing—there was no privacy for kings, but then again, nothing the king said would ever be repeated in public or in private.

When the attendant had retreated, Dalip got down from the desk and came to lean against Henry's chair, behind him, close enough so Henry could feel the Maharajah's warm breath on his ear. And so, Henry began his tale.

Long after Shah Shuja had been driven away from Afghanistan, Dost Mohammad had ascended the throne at Kabul. Russia had then sent an embassy to Dost Mohammad. The British, to counteract this Russian influence, had also sent their embassy, but it had seemed as though the Amir's ear had bent more toward the Russian at court than toward the Englishman.

There was still the whole of the Punjab Empire between Afghanistan and British India—for Russia to invade India, they would have to go through Persia, Afghanistan, and Punjab. But Lord Auckland had feared such an eventuality—the thing to do then was to depose Dost Mohammad and put on the throne a puppet king, who would protect British India from invasion.

And then the Persians had begun knocking on the western borders of Afghanistan, and Dost Mohammad had actually turned to the English for assistance. This, Lord Auckland had ignored, and gone on with his plans to invade Afghanistan. He had come to Maharajah Ranjit Singh for help—troops, provisions, guns, and passage through the lands of the Punjab to Peshawar (in Punjab territory) and through the Khyber Pass from there to Kabul . . . and victory.

Ranjit Singh had feted the Governor-General and his sisters, piled them with gifts, looked after the entire British encampment for a whole two months, and agreed only to the last—they would be given safe passage through his lands to Peshawar, but no guns, no provisions, no troops. The Maharajah had been too canny to indulge in a pointless war, and Shah Shuja, whom the British intended to put on the throne instead of Dost Mohammad, could never hold it—there was a reason why he had been driven out of the country in the first place.

Sorry, Ranjit Singh had said, but he'd said it so nicely, with so much generosity, even paying their way all the way to Peshawar, it was difficult to be quarrelsome with the old, one-eyed king.

"So you won Kabul then, and put Shah Shuja on the throne?" The little voice at Henry's shoulder was filled with contempt.

"Yes," Henry said. "But the rumblings of a rebellion began soon after—the people of Afghanistan hated Shuja, and adored Dost Mohammad. And, they disliked seeing British regiments more or less permanently stationed in Kabul. Although we were supposed to stay only until Shuja had attained some stability in his land."

"Just as you have promised here, Captain Henry?"

"Yes," Henry said again, discomfort filling him.

The Afghans had rebelled. Spectacularly. Key British officials had been cut down in the streets one after another; Shuja had been killed also. Dost Mohammad had been put back on the throne by the rebels. The message was clear—the British were no longer welcome in Afghanistan, they had to leave and they had to leave *now*. So in December of 1841, sixteen thousand British soldiers, their wives, children, and camp followers were driven out east toward the snow-clotted Khyber Pass, which would lead them to Peshawar, and shelter in the Punjab. The Afghanis had promised them safe passage . . . and did not keep their word. They'd massacred everyone, indiscriminately, until, a day before Christmas, only *one* man had staggered into Jalalabad, the British outpost on the Afghan side of the Khyber Pass.

His name was Dr. Brydon and though he'd spoken of the horrors of the slaughter, he had also given some hope to Henry—his brother George had been taken prisoner, not killed. Of the sixteen thousand, apart from Dr. Brydon, another four or five men had been taken prisoner.

The young Maharajah had been wandering about the pavilion, picking up Henry's inkpot, rifling through his papers, leaning against his desk to watch him, or simply skipping. He was a child; keeping quiet was not something he had learned yet. But at this point in the story he asked Henry, "Your brother George was taken prisoner? Did you go in to rescue him?"

Henry smiled grimly. "It was a while before anyone could take action; the news of the carnage shattered all of us. And Lord Auckland was a few months from the end of his term as Governor-General; he did not want to make the decision to invade Afghanistan again, not after all this had happened."

"But you did," Dalip Singh said.

"We did. The new Governor-General supported the plan, thanks be to God, and the British armies succeeded in retaking Kabul and freeing the prisoners."

"Who's on the throne of Afghanistan now, Captain Henry?" This came in a mocking tone.

So the child had known all of this before, Henry thought. He looked at him with admiration.

"Dost Mohammad," Henry said. "There was no one left, no one powerful enough to be accepted by the Afghanis, to be our ally, and to rule over the people. Dost Mohammad," he said again, laughter shaking his thin frame, "whom we set out to depose in the first instance."

"I'm bored," Dalip Singh said suddenly, and Henry waited for a juggler to appear from behind the pillars of the pavilion.

When that didn't happen, he put out a hand to the boy. "Enough of a history lesson, your Majesty. But I hope you learned that if you persist, everything will give way before you. Come, let's play cricket."

"What's that?" Dalip asked, running out to the edge of the pavilion.

"You don't know? You're in for a treat."

A few days later, the Maharajah sent his men into Henry's courtyard when he was away and had a slim, rectangular strip of grass carved out from the lawns. The men hammered at the dirt until it was glass-smooth and shiny. The cricket pitch thus came into being, and every afternoon as his strength increased, Henry taught the boy to bowl, to bat, to watch the trajectory of the ball as it left the bowler's hand and came pounding down the pitch toward him. If the ball went over the edge of the fort, toward the Ravi River, short though that distance was, it was a six—worth six runs. The four was hitting the face of a pavilion on any side of the courtyard. Dalip ordered uniforms sewn overnight, in white silk, embedded with diamond buttons, with even his turban white. When he came every day in his pristine clothes, Henry expressed surprise at how clean they were—hadn't Dalip leapt for the ball and fallen on the wet grass just yesterday?

The answer came equally surprised and exaggeratedly

wide-eyed from the boy. This was a new uniform. He wore new cricket whites *every* day. What else did Henry expect from him? After all, he *was* the Maharajah of the Punjab.

A regular cricket team came into being, with John, Edwardes, Nicholson, and the Maharajah's attendants as fielders. Henry had a new cricket set brought in from the Army & Navy stores in Calcutta, and he had to convince Dalip Singh not to embellish the handles of the bat, or the wickets, with precious stones.

Henry oversaw Dalip's studies also, making him bring his tutors to the pavilion and correcting his spelling, grammar, and his handwriting in Urdu, Punjabi, Hindustani, and Persian. He taught him a smattering of English and every morning, much to his amusement, was greeted with "Good morning, I trust you had a restful night. It looks like it's going to be a fine day, isn't it, old chap?"

Dalip didn't mention his mother, Maharani Jindan Kaur, at all. Ever since Ranjit Singh's death she had fought, ferociously, to put her son on the throne, but she had forgotten to be the child's mother. She didn't put him to bed at night, wake him in the morning with a kiss, bind his minor scratches. In the fort, she stayed in her harem apartments; Dalip in his own quarters. Since Henry had come to Lahore, the Maharani had been a niggling burr in his side. He heard complaints from her daily—orders of precedence, the number of guards around her apartments, the food from the kitchens, the use of her jewelry, the need to dip into the Toshakhana . . . they were endless. Eventually, he found her embroiled in a plot to poison him and the other British soldiers in the fort. That evening, he sent her away to the fortress at Sheikhpura, northwest of Lahore. He waited with a pounding heart for Dalip to say something to him about it. But the Maharajah said nothing.

For a moment, Henry felt a blasting ache in his chest. What had the fates done to this boy? His mother could not scheme, plot, avenge, and be his mother at the same time. And Dalip, who had lost his father before he even came to know him, was put in the care of strangers.

Another letter came from Lettice one day, when Henry was hunched over papers at his desk and Dalip was sitting on the ground, leaning against Henry's legs, laying out a cricket team on the floor with clay figures that one of his servants had made for him. The letter began, as the previous one had, with "My dearest Henry and Honoria," because his sister assumed that Honoria would be with Henry by now, and that they would be married—she didn't know about the delay at Aden. Henry read on, flipping page after page, his bewilderment growing, until he turned the last page and saw that it was signed by an Adele. Adele who? He searched through his head among all their friends, acquaintances, cousins, near and distant, and could find no one of that name who was intimate enough with him—and Honoria—to actually write to him. Then, he started laughing, and retied the letter.

Dalip looked up, curious. "Tell me," he said, "what does our sister say, Henry?"

"*Our* sister," Henry said, chuckling, "did not write this letter. In fact, it isn't even to me, but to another Henry Lawrence in the Bengal army. He's also a captain, it would seem, and . . . he also seems to have married a woman named Honoria."

A frown creased Dalip's forehead. "But you are not married, Henry."

"No, but I will be soon."

Dalip clapped his hands. "How wonderful, who is she, this Honoria? When does she come to marry you? Will it be here, in Lahore? I will throw you splendid parties to celebrate."

Henry put a hand on his charge's shoulder as he attempted to rise and rush off to make wedding arrangements. "No, stay, Dalip. My . . . Honoria is on her way; she left Calcutta a few months ago. When she gets here, I think we both will want a quiet ceremony. You can come, though, and stand up beside me if you want."

"I can? John will not mind?"

"I don't think so."

For a while, Dalip rearranged his cricket pieces on the floor as Henry wrote a note to the other Henry Lawrence, explaining his mistake and apologizing for having opened his letter. This done, he looked down at the Maharajah, who had his cheeks puffed out, his brow furrowed, as his little hands moved the pieces around with an under-the-breath running commentary. Here comes the bowler, here the batter swings, the ball flies into the wicket keeper's gloves with a thwack, they all turn to the umpire. *"Howz that?"* No, the umpire shakes his head, his eyes stony, not to be swayed by any amount of pleading . . . and so on.

Henry took out his handkerchief and dabbed the sweat from Dalip's forehead. In response, he got a brilliant, distracted smile. He cursed the sixty-odd days he had wasted in not getting to know this child, and the loss was his, Henry knew. For there was something endearing about this boy who had been born just shortly before his powerful father died, and had been a babe in the nursery all the while that his half brothers ascended the throne and were, one by one, cut down from it in a deluge of blood. No one would even have thought of, dreamed of, this child eventually wearing the imperial turban on his head. And even that turban wobbled; Henry was here, the British were here to stay.

There may be other compensations for Dalip, Henry thought, and he said, "Dalip, are you going to marry Princess Roshni?"

"Uh-huh." The Maharajah did not take his attention from the game.

"Really?" Henry persisted. "Why?"

Now Dalip did sit back to gaze at his guardian, perfectly

serious when he replied, "I'm betrothed to her, that's why, Henry."

"But . . . you're so young." What he meant to say was that there was, must be at least, a twelve-year age difference between them. And what could it have meant to this girl, who at twenty had to consider an eight-year-old child as a husband?

"Oh, Henry," Dalip said, wise beyond his years, "I will grow up, you know. I won't marry her until I'm at least sixteen, or eighteen."

"And will she wait?"

Dalip smiled, a dimple deepening his chin. "She can marry no one else now. If she doesn't wait—whatever *that* means—she will die unmarried. After all, I am—"

"The Maharajah of the Punjab," Henry cut in with a smile. "I know." Then, more serious. "I know."

Dalip jumped up from his place on the floor and, to Henry's surprise, flung himself into his arms, his small hands clasped tight around Henry's neck. Henry held him, felt the soft, flushed cheek against his, the thud of the boy's beating heart, and felt a pang of warmth stifle his chest, as though this young, foreign Maharajah was one of his own sons, born of his flesh. The feeling overwhelmed him. He hadn't expected to fall in love in Lahore. Twice.

Dalip's voice, muffled by Henry's hair, echoed in his ear. "Whoever that other Henry Lawrence is, he cannot be anywhere as nice as you are."

He drew back, his dark eyes bright and beautiful, just like his mother's. "I'm glad you're here." Then, he wrenched his arms away and ran out of the pavilion into the bright sunshine, and all the way back to his own apartments in the Lahore Fort.

* * *

The festival of Diwali came to Lahore that year on the night of the new moon. For days, gigantic gunnysacks with cheaply made terra-cotta lamps—*diyas*—had been toted into the fort and set up on the long line of the ramparts by the attendants. A day before, the servants had put oil in each of the lamps and strung into the oil a single cotton wick. The kitchens were busy all day and night with huge cauldrons bubbling over with sweets and savories, and trays of them had been sent by Dalip Singh to the British contingent until Henry, gorging himself to a stomachache, had to beg his young Maharajah to stop being so generous—it was near killing him. So Dalip sent him fine silks, daggers, turban ornaments, diamond buttons, anything else he thought was appropriate, including five Thoroughbreds from Ranjit Singh's stables—feisty horses with such elegant lines that Henry put his old nag into retirement.

The Howard brothers promptly noted everything on a list and made arrangements for the items to be transported on to Calcutta. They were disappointed when Henry sent an order to Dalip—no more gifts. *Bas.* Enough.

Two hours before sunset, attendants roamed the fort, thick cords of jute slung over their shoulders, one end smoldering and smoking, and used these long-burning matches to light all the lamps. Henry stood on the ramparts overlooking the walled city, and marveled at the houses, the gardens, the trees, the streets all lit up in pinpoints of light. When he looked up at the clear night sky, bejeweled with millions of stars, it seemed a poor imitation of the ground below. The earth was alive, gilded with illumination, and for this one night, the sky had been put to bed, put to shame.

He went back to Jahangir's Quadrangle and sat there alone after dinner, smoking a *beedi*, his eyes closed as his hand went unerringly to his mouth for a drag and then fell down. Through his closed lids he could see the radiance of the *diyas* all around the pathways, picking out the square outlines of the pool's platform, the pool itself, the arches in the buildings, the straight lines of their eaves. Then, the fireworks began. Shower after shower of pale blue, purple, pink, and green light in the sky, appearing one moment, disappearing the next, leaving the aroma of spent gunpowder hanging in a pall over the city, until the lights of the *diyas* were dimmed.

It was then the girl came into the courtyard, as she had the first time, from the southern end, and stood looking down its length at Henry Lawrence.

He rose from his place, sent his half-smoked *beedi* skittering across the stone, and waited for her to come up to him. The pale white skirts of her full *ghagara* murmured over the pathway; her back was erect, as though a hand touched the small of it; and Henry could see, through the sheer white veil, the diamonds glittering on the short *choli* she wore, which left her waist and her arms bare.

He bowed his head to her.

"So, Henny Larens," she said. "You are well, I hear. The fever has passed?"

A small breeze sighed through the courtyard and set the flames of the hundreds of *diyas* wavering, casting scurrying shadows over the hexagonal bricks. The breeze brushed against her face and molded the veil against its outlines. She reached up to pull the fabric free.

"Don't," Henry said, his hand in the air, falling to his side helplessly. "Please, let me look at you . . . and thank you for all you've done."

There was a flash of teeth as her lips parted. "You talk, and I listen. You don't need to look at me for this."

"But you don't know how disconcerting it is to have a conversation with someone you cannot properly see— whose face does not . . . change for you as you talk, tell them things." She smiled again, and Henry said, "Ah, I see you *do* understand this."

"The veil has always been an advantage for a woman, for the very reason you mention. Not for us perhaps, the naked face of the Englishwoman, every thought visible, every mystery revealed. But"—she looked up at him—"this is what you are used to. We . . . I, am foreign to you."

Henry gestured toward the stairs of the pavilion, and they went up halfway and sat on the same step. He looked down at his hands, and then at hers, clasped around her knees, the wrists slung with diamond bangles, the skin decorated with henna for Diwali. They were small hands, but powerful enough to lift him and bind his shoulder, and Henry, though a thin man, was not a light man.

"You could never be foreign to me," he said simply. "I would not have lived if it hadn't been for you. I've had this mysterious fever, these chills, before, but coupled with the torn shoulder, they would have been the end of me. Kingsley couldn't—"

"I'm sure your doctor is an able man, but there are some ailments that have no real diagnosis, no specific treatment. It's a matter of just trying everything." She laughed, a low, opulent sound. "I told your brother that."

He smiled, exhilarated at her nearness, happy even that she had come after so many messages sent to the *zenana* for just one meeting. His heart banged painfully in his chest, as though he was going to ask for her to be his . . . And yet it was just a simple conversation. Nothing more.

"I'm surprised that John listened," he said carefully, keeping a quaver out of his voice, concentrating on his words, and the sound of them. "He's not very good at that, never has been, although he's one of the most fair, most upright men I know."

"And he loves you very much, Henny Larens," she said softly, "that was why he agreed to let me take care of you." She picked at the embroidery on her *ghagara,* and with each movement, the bangles on her wrists tinkled with music. "I hear your betrothed comes to Lahore soon, to marry you. This is true?"

He nodded.

"You are old, no, to be married?"

Henry grinned. Any other woman would not so bluntly have stated the obvious. He *was* old, and looked every one of his thirty-nine years, and some more—the fevers had robbed him of the plushness of youth. His skin was thin, the bones on his face protruded, his forehead jutted out, and under his shirts his shoulders were knobby. Only his hair had been, mercifully, left alone, as thick as in his adolescence, as dark as the day it had turned that color from an original sandy brown.

"It is a betrothal of long standing."

"Then you've known her for a while." There was no inflection in her voice; it was flatly said, a comment as much as a question.

Henry told her, and all of a sudden felt the words tumble from his mouth about the whole courtship—how he had met Honoria, when he had professed his love for her, how she hadn't been able to come to India before, and for ten years. Why he did this, spoke so intimately to a woman he had barely seen, barely knew—he couldn't understand. But he felt a comfort in her presence as he had when he was ill and fevered. For the first time in India, he felt a sense of contentment that had nothing to do with his work.

She stayed silent. He asked, "Have I said too much?"

"No," she said slowly, "you hardly talked when you were unwell, you were so quiet, such an ideal patient. I worried that you had never learned to speak of what was in your soul to anyone . . . a wife, a sister, a mother . . . and all this held tight in a man's chest can only implode one day. Troubles when voiced are carried away on the wind; they have no place upon which to perch."

"I have three brothers in India," Henry said.

She shook her head and laughed. "They're men. I'm glad

your wife comes, Henny Larens. Will you marry her here, in Lahore?"

"Yes."

"Then"—she hesitated—"if she has no place to stay . . . until you are married, that is, she is welcome to be with me in the *zenana*."

The night sky lit up around them again in a burst of fireworks. It was impossible to talk with all that noise, the screams from a delighted city, the fainter sounds of gunshots in the distance. Earlier in the month, Henry and his contingent had seriously debated on whether they ought to allow Diwali to be observed—whether there wouldn't be an opportunity for rebellion under cover of all the sound and smog created by the gunpowder. But it would have been impolitic to stop the city from celebrating a tradition that went back thousands of years, and putting a stop to it would have probably created its own form of rebellion. So they had said nothing, even participated in paying for the fireworks set off from the ramparts of the fort, and looking up at the sky and hearing those gunshots, Henry hoped very much that it was just some miscreants shooting into the air, and not at someone else. He would find out in the morning.

"I think," Henry said, when he could speak, and rolls of acrid smoke drifted over the courtyard and draped themselves in folds around them, "Honoria would like that very much."

She rose then, and Henry rose with her. "Let me see you out," he said.

A tilt of her head, and that mocking voice. "I know my way around the fort very well, Henny Larens."

He watched her walk away through the haze. He would have only memories of her that he could hold in a part of his heart—nothing more. Even had he not been engaged to marry Honoria, nothing could have come out of this. Perhaps a hundred years ago in India, it would have been reasonable,

acceptable, for an Englishman to have a native wife . . . and
to know that he could never return to England with her. The
ADCs at the Governor-General's office were notorious for
their Indian "wives" even now, until the English missus came
along.

She stopped, swung around, and came running up the
pathway again, wrestling with her arm all the while. When
she had reached him, she held out her hand and said, "I
almost forgot."

In her palm was a gold armlet, a diamond on either side
of the main diamond, which was as big as a robin's egg, oval,
ablaze with radiance.

"It's yours," she said.

He took the Kohinoor and slipped it into the pocket of his
trousers but kept a hold of her hand. "Thank you," he said,
"for everything." And then, he said, "Why?"

"You're a good man. At least, I think so."

She bent her head for a brief moment, carried his hand to
her cheek and held it there. Henry felt the heat of her skin and
the flutter of a pulse. Then, she turned, picked up the skirts of
her *ghagara*, and went out into the night.

Honoria came to Lahore two days later, having traveled by
the *dak* roads from Calcutta through the Upper Provinces.
Major Battersea, who had made all the arrangements, had
written to the Postmaster General outlining her route—
where she would stop each night, where she would eat her
meals, how many guards she needed along the way, how
many torchbearers to light the way at night, how the horses
would be paid for. He had tried to get her to stay on at Calcutta until Henry was free to come to her, but she wouldn't
listen. So, alone in a country that was new to her, she got into

the *dak palki,* essentially a palanquin on wheels drawn by horses, and lumbered over thirteen hundred miles to the man she was to marry.

Henry rode to the outskirts of Lahore to meet her. She descended from the *palki* in a faded blue gown, the lace at her collar and the edges of her sleeves fraying, her face brown under a straw hat. Her skin was pitted with prickly heat. She was thinner than he remembered, older also—but then so was he.

He held her hands, and felt an overwhelming rush of emotion for this woman who had braved seas, squalls, heat, and a dangerous journey to find her way to him.

"You'll still marry me, Honoria?"

"That is why I'm here, darling Henry," she said, her eyes shining with love.

He sent her to the *zenana* at the fort. The next day the vicar rode in from Firozpur. And in Jahangir's Quadrangle, with his brother John on one side, the Maharajah of the Punjab on the other, he waited for her to walk up to him in a pale green gown, a spray of tiny white jasmines in her hair, and took her for his wife.

Once, many years later, after their children had been born, he asked her how that first day at Lahore had been.

"The girl in the *zenana* was very kind," she said. "If you hadn't loved me, Henry, I think you could have been in love with her."

An Alexandria Moon

April, 1850

Four years later

The whole third page of the *Bombay Herald,* almost all of it actually, was taken up with the advertisement by Dossabhoy Merwanjee and Co., addresses at 6, Parsee Bazaar Street, in Bombay. They were "American" importers, purveyors of all things American, from the basest—kerosene oil, navy stores, ropes, canvas, lumber—to the finest—tobacco, bar soaps, Waltham watches, and Dr. Townsend's famed and celebrated sarsaparilla, a tonic for the purification of the blood and for curing dullness or lassitude.

Having had his weekly paper all laid out—and to accommodate this relatively late-breaking story—Mr. Wingate, the publisher, cut out a small corner at the bottom right of the full-page advertisement and inserted the story there. It looked odd enough that people noticed it, and consequently the advertisement. And Mr. Dossabhoy, bathed, his beard spruce, fresh and cool in his white vest at the entrance to his store, was gratified to see large crowds who cleaned out his stock of the sarsaparilla.

The story, by "our local correspondent," read simply,

*Under other circumstances, the visit of a Governor-General would
be nothing less than royal, but not if we are to believe that Lord
Dalhousie slipped into Bombay two days ago, under cover of
dark, without notice to Lord Falkland, who as Governor of this
city, has sorely missed an opportunity to parade the other Lord
around with a plenitude of pomp.*

*Why, one wonders, all this secrecy? Would it have something
to do with the annexation of the lands of the Maharajah Ranjit
Singh? Or with the jewels of his famed Toshakhana? Or with one
specific stone—large as a woman's clenched fist, the ransom of a
king . . . on its way, perhaps, to a Queen?*

Mr. Wingate had once been sued for libel and slander by a
man who had offended him, and about whom, previously, he
had not been flattering in his *Bombay Herald.* But this story,
with its innuendos and delighted whisperings, *had* to have
some truth in it. The Government of India and the East India
Company could hardly call him out in public without revealing at least some of those truths.

Two nights ago, driving back in his horse-drawn carriage,
Wingate had passed the Treasury part of Fort George, and who
should be coming out of it but Lord Dalhousie—with a smile
on his face! Now, everyone knew that the dour Governor-
General never found occasion for mirth. A smile would spoil
that handsome façade of which he was possessed; even perhaps, ruffle that coolly blond hair so carefully brushed across
his noble forehead.

So, sitting in his carriage, wrapped in a cigar-smoke fug,
his mind pleasantly blurred by an evening of port, brandy,
sherry, Madeira, and a splendid dinner, Mr. Wingate was sure
that this man was none other than Dalhousie. He had been
last reported in the Punjab, in Lahore; for him to appear in
Bombay could only mean that he had brought here something
from the Punjab. Something so secret, so valuable, it had to
be deposited into the Treasury building. Why else would he
be here? Dalhousie surely had a furtive air about him.

The next morning, behind his cluttered and paper-strewn desk, Mr. Wingate was reading the ship lists that his *Herald* published every six months. His blunt, nicotine-yellow finger rubbed its way down the columns. Ah, here it was. On the first of April 1850, on regular schedule, the P & O paddle steamer the SS *Indus* was to depart from Bombay to Suez. From Suez to Alexandria, via Cairo, would be a three- or four-day journey at the most, and by the twenty-second or so, one of the P & O steamers that plied the Mediterranean route—Alexandria to Southampton or Portsmouth—would pick up Indian passengers and take them to England by the end of the month.

The list of warships at the Government Docks in Bombay was not so readily available to the public, but Mr. Wingate nonetheless received a copy of it at the beginning of each month. The frigate HMS *Megaera*, commissioned as a troopship, was due to arrive in two days, and . . . the HMS *Medea* was already at dock. This last, as Mr. Wingate read, was a second-class sloop, a warship, troops and cannons and other fine things, he assumed.

He glanced up at the tear-off calendar he had got as a gift from Dossabhoy Merwanjee & Co. when buying—of all things non-American—a couple of Persian carpets from them. There had been very little discount on the carpets, even though Mr. Wingate had given Dossabhoy a quarter rate cut on a full-page advertisement in the *Herald* for a whole three months. Mr. Wingate groaned. Twelve weekly page spaces to that well-fed and slick Dossabhoy, all for two Persian carpets and a cheap paper calendar with no colored paintings on it. However, the Persian carpets had kept his wife from complaining, and she happily massaged the plush pile with her toe while chatting desultorily with visitors during her "at homes." And the calendar now told him that it was the twenty-fifth of March, some six days before the *Indus*'s departure.

He sent his *chai* boy to smoke English cigarettes at the Government Docks and distribute them liberally in exchange for information. The HMS *Megaera* would be leaving tomorrow night, and she was headed to the Andaman and Nicobar Islands in the Bay of Bengal. Curious, Mr. Wingate said. Why there? The jail is there, Sahib, the boy said. A penal colony in the Andamans, thought Mr. Wingate. He was quite certain the Bay of Bengal and the islands were not in the direction of England, but to make doubly sure, he pulled out his Victoria Regina Atlas and traced over Madras and then out into the Indian Ocean. There they were, scattered in a tattered line in the middle of the waters, far, far away from England.

And the *Medea?* he asked the *chai* boy. It goes to England, Sahib, very soon, even the deckhands did not seem to know when. The man commanding the ship, Captain Lockyer, has orders to take onboard two men from some . . . government office, and to follow their orders. The captain is not very happy about leaving the fate of his ship in the hands of two nonnaval men.

Mr. Wingate gazed with adoration at the sweaty, scrawny face of his *chai* boy. He was an unprepossessing lad, long of nose, big of mouth, knobby about the knees that showed under his khaki uniform shorts. His hair was always thick with oil, and he reeked of the coconut. But he had performed a veritable miracle.

Would he, Mr. Wingate inquired delicately, happen to know the names of the two, um, nonnaval men? Co-lo-nel Mac Gragor and a Cap-i-tane Ramsay, the boys at the dock said that this second man had the same name as the Governor-General.

Colonel McGregor and Captain Ramsay, Mr. Wingate decided. He went for his *Burke's Peerage,* and again, his finger laboriously moved over the pages until he came to the current Earl of Dalhousie, who had a given name (among many) of Ramsay, and who was the head of the clan of Ramsay, and whose father was a Sir William Ramsay. Why, thought Mr. Wingate with sheer delight—Dalhousie's family was littered with Ramsays! So this captain was surely, as the *chai* boy said, a kinsman.

He searched assiduously through the military lists and found a few McGregors, a few MacGregors, but none of them seemed important enough—subalterns, or lieutenants, one a captain. It made no sense. Who *was* this McGregor?

Mr. Wingate thought about this for a long while. The *punkah* in his room flapped forward and backward, braiding the warm air into thick cords around him, setting some of the papers on his desk aflutter. The *chai* boy breathed through his mouth, wiped his running nose on the back of his hand, and then smeared that on his shorts. But surely, the HMS *Medea* would be carrying Dalhousie's precious cargo, whatever it was that he had deposited from Lahore into the Bombay Treasury, and these two men were in charge of it. The newspaperman chewed on the end of his pencil and hawked out the wood fragments into a dustbin conveniently placed within spitting distance.

The *chai* boy snorted and took in a deep, noisy breath that gargled the phlegm in his chest.

Mr. Wingate dug in his waistcoat pocket for an *anna* coin, glanced at it briefly, and then took out a rupee coin— a whole sixteen *annas*—and flipped it to the boy. The lad's smile, when he had caught the coin and weighed its value in his palm (he was too polite to actually look at it) was wide, showed all of his teeth and a good deal of the inside of his mouth.

"You're a marvel," Mr. Wingate said. "You really are."

"Thank you, Sahib." The boy bowed and backed out of the door, salaaming furiously.

What should he do with this information? Mr. Wingate wondered. No other paper in town knew of Dalhousie's visit—or they would have been buzzing with the news—

there had been no talk in the Bombay Club, or the Navy or Army Club. No mention in the theater last night during the intermission; a lot of inconsequential chatter, which he always kept his ear open to, but something as big as this would have been bandied about for months—with every person in the city trying to get onto the party lists at Government House, the morning rides lists, the tiffin lists, or trying to invite Dalhousie's wife to open a club here, a swimming bath there, a charity ball or an orphanage.

Now, if only the item in the Treasury was going to travel by the commercial P & O steamer, Mr. Wingate would have considered buying a ticket to England, or sending someone else on his behalf . . . for what he did not know yet. But it was surely being taken aboard the British Navy's HMS *Medea*, impossible to board with a captain already livid at the rattling of his authority.

What *should* he do with this information? Mr. Wingate pored over the copy for the next edition of his *Herald*, shouted at a few editors about the headlines on a couple of the pages. At the end of the day, he took his hat off the hook behind the door and went home to his wife and his children in the comfortably luxurious neighborhood of Colabah, with its lush palm trees, its bright bougainvilleas, its *chunam*-washed bungalows and neat tile roofs.

After dinner, Mary and he went for a drive in the nearby park. Mr. Wingate normally enjoyed the daily parade of nations in Bombay—the only city in the world where this could be possible. The Chinese man in his satin jacket with thin braided hair wrapped around his head; the Hindu with his fat wife and equally fat kids, their hair oil-slicked; the Portuguese with their olive complexions, short, curly hair, and white cotton shirts, looking more Indian than the Indians; the Roman Catholic priests, pale and ascetic in their flapping gray cassocks; the stiff military Englishman, quite from another country than the casual civil service English-

man, so dissimilar that they might speak different languages;
the Muslims, the Bengalis, the Gujaratis, the Jains, the Bud-
dhists, all in their distinctive outfits; and the Parsi, quiet,
composed, his beard trimmed with a precise hand . . . the
Parsi! Mr. Wingate turned his head around as the Parsi's
carriage passed, and in it, resplendent in his white vest, was
none other than Dossabhoy Merwanjee.

"You're preoccupied today, Harry," his wife said. "You
hardly noticed that nice Mr. Dossabhoy's bow; he's the one
who sold us the carpets, you know. And I've got my eye on
one of those American toy pistols for little Harry's birthday.
Will you be nice to him next time, please?"

"A lot on my mind, Mer," Mr. Wingate mumbled. "I
was thinking about poor Lucius, struck with cholera in those
dreadful barracks at Calcutta."

Mrs. Wingate shuddered; it was a delicate movement of
her massive shoulders.

"He died, you know, my brother's only son. Horace had
specifically asked me to look after him, and I thought, since I
am the publisher of the fine *Bombay Herald*, a letter of introduction from me to the Governor-General would get Lucius
a post in the Council at least. What I had in mind for him was
that military secretary title. How fine he would have been in
his uniform then, eh, Mary?"

Mrs. Wingate nodded without enthusiasm. Lucius had
been a spotty-faced boy of seventeen, who had somehow
wrangled his way as an infantryman into the Forty-third
regiment of the East India Company, and he had been happy
enough there until her husband had decided that a boy with
his charm and intelligence needed to be in Calcutta, not
languishing under a burning Indian sun on march to some
outpost. Or rather, his brother Horace had written to Harry
Wingate to tell him he ought to think so and, to help him
think so, had brought up a long-held debt. So Wingate had
written to Lord Dalhousie, and the Governor-General had

thrown that letter into the garbage, and sent its deliverer, Lucius, to the jailhouse of the nearest regiment until he could be sent back to his own—as he was AWOL from it. The Persian carpets, the ivory-inlaid tea table, the fine china tea set that Harry Wingate had also sent along—he, Wingate, was sure had gone to fatten the personal treasury of the Governor-General.

Lucius had died within a week, having caught cholera— and literally not having been able to run from it—in the jail.

This Captain Ramsay who was to travel to England at Lord Dalhousie's behest was the military secretary—the very post Mr. Wingate had coveted for his nephew had gone to Dalhousie's nephew.

The next morning, before the *Bombay Herald* went to press, Mr. Wingate cheated Mr. Dossabhoy by carving out the bottom right-hand side of his advertisement, and took his revenge upon Lord Dalhousie by printing notice of his presence in Bombay—when, why, et cetera. He had finally decided to release this information because he couldn't see how it could be of any use to him at all since he couldn't get onto the HMS *Medea*—that ship was under a tight and rigorous guard.

Three hours after the paper came out there was an accident in the steam room of the HMS *Medea;* a fire began, and half the machinery was burned before the fire could be brought under control. That put the *Medea* out of commission. There were then no ships leaving the Bombay docks— civil or military—other than the SS *Indus,* a P & O steamer, winding its leisurely way up the Red Sea to Suez, where passengers would then go across the desert, and by the Nile to Alexandria, from there across the Mediterranean on another steamer, the SS *Oriental,* almost perfectly synchronized with the Bombay–Suez route, so that there would be no delay in arriving in England.

The article in the *Herald* appeared on one day; on the next another paper carried the news of the fire on the *Medea.*

Most of Bombay read both the papers. It wasn't *that* difficult to connect the two articles and form the same impression Mr. Wingate had.

As the days passed, W. C. Symes, principal agent at the Bombay offices of the Peninsular & Oriental Steam Navigation Company, sold a few more last-minute passages to England on the SS *Indus*.

Bombay Harbor lay on the eastern side of the group of seven islands that made up the city. Some sixty years ago, the islands had been coalesced into one with a series of causeways, creating a single landmass and making travel between the islands much easier. Bombay, and its various islands, had a deep history of various owners, one after another, until the Portuguese (whose presence in India predated even the Mughal emperors, let alone the British) acquired it. They built their Roman Catholic churches in earnest, brought their language into the city, and their culture and costumes. And all during Mughal rule in India, the Portuguese and the British butted against each other, jostling for supremacy at the Mughal court, deeply suspicious of the *other* foreigners in this alien land.

And then, in 1661, Charles II married the Portuguese Catherine of Braganza, and she brought the city of Bombay with her to England as part of her dowry. It was that simple. The British in India at that time, under Emperor Aurangzeb's Mughal rule, had had no need to fight for Bombay. The Emperor hadn't cared—his main Arabian Sea port, from which his ships traded and took Indian pilgrims on the Haj to Mecca and Medina, was at Surat, north of Bombay, and afforded enough deep-water moorage for all of his, and his nobles' needs.

Charles II agreed to rent out the city of Bombay—which

he had no intention of visiting and could barely dab at on a map—to the East India Company for the awesome sum of ten pounds sterling a year. The Company offices were established in Bombay soon after the Court of Directors signed the lease for the city.

The port at Bombay Harbor was called Apollo Bandar— its name as much of a hybrid as were the people of Bombay. The British anglicized the Portuguese *pollem,* for the palla fish sold at the docks, and adopted the *Bandar,* which meant port, from Persian.

Here, on the eastern side of Bombay Island, spreading north up its face, were the P & O landing docks, the Bombay Yacht Club, the cotton baling stations, the Customs House, the quarantine area, Fort George and its Treasury, which held, at the moment, the Kohinoor diamond. Only a few people knew where exactly the Kohinoor was in Bombay, and Mr. Wingate was one. But thanks to him, almost everyone in Bombay who read the *Herald* knew that it was somewhere in the city.

At the P & O dock in Apollo Bandar, the SS *Indus* lay quiet at her moorings two nights before she was due to sail to Suez. She was one of the Company's biggest paddle steamers, weighing about seventeen hundred tons, with engines at twelve hundred horsepower, and a maximum speed of eight knots. She had one large smokestack rising from the center of her deck, imprinted with the P & O motto—*Quis separabit*— who shall separate us.

The *Indus* had been built in the dry docks at Glasgow by a local shipbuilding company, to the P & O's specifications. From the very beginning, she had been intended for use in India and so given her name—that of a mighty river in the Punjab and, some four thousand years ago, of an even mightier civilization in the valley of that river. Her first voyage had been her longest, and it had taken her from her frigid birthplace south into the warm waters off the coasts of Africa, around the Cape of Good Hope, until she had traveled up the Arabian Sea to the dock at Bombay.

The *Indus* was a trim two hundred and eight feet in length, forty feet wide, twenty-three feet deep. At full capacity, she could carry twenty-one first-class passengers and fifty-three second-class passengers. Her captain and crew made up another thirty-six people onboard.

As night fell over Bombay—almost at the same time every day of the year—no twilight dawdled in the sky and darkness plunged down to claim all of India. Lamps and lanterns flared all around the dock and on the deck of the *Indus*. It had been blisteringly hot during the day, with a white heat that had driven everyone inside, but with the coming of the night, activity began. Three large gangplanks, on wheels, were guided to the ship.

The night watchman, an old man with a sea-roughened face, sat on his haunches against the shadowed wall of the Customs House and lit a *beedi*. His lantern was attached to the end of a long wooden stick, which now lay on the ground, the lantern's wick turned so low as to be just a spot of wavering blue and gold. Every twenty-five days or so came the nights when the *Indus* was laden with provisions for her trip to the Suez, and at those times, he left off walking his rounds around the dock, or dozing quietly by the main gate, and sat here, watching over the men and the ship.

He could not see very well anymore. Old age, he thought, stroking his free hand over the contours of his bald head with a half ring of hair around the bottom. The workers were a mere blur, the lights much brighter, dimming briefly as the men moved between him and them, carrying large sacks of food and supplies. He hadn't told the dockmaster about his eyesight, especially at night, and how the shadows melded one into another. But he had worked on these docks fifty-five years, ever since he was a boy of fifteen, and knew every pier, every landing, every building old and new—for he had explored them during the day and during the night—every smell, every sound, and every shape that didn't belong. The map of the docks was engraved in his heart. Here he had lived, and here he would die. There was no retirement for this man.

"Chachaji," a voice said softly next to him.

He canted his head toward the sound and grunted. "So you are here, finally?"

The younger man bent to find and touch his uncle's feet, and then raised his hand to daub at his eyes. *"Pranam,"* he said.

"Sit," the uncle said. He still hadn't turned his head to look at his nephew. Instead, he listened as his brother's son settled comfortably on the floor, his shoulders thumping against the wall, his breath even and youthful. The older man sniffed in the air. His nephew smelled clean, and so healthy— fed on the purest butter from the Lahore cows which grazed on the banks of the Ravi River; milk from their udders, fresh and warm and frothy; the wheat that had ripened in his brother's fields, threshed in wholesome winds, ground into flour by his sister-in-law in the courtyard of the house. This boy was their last child, born late into the marriage; his confinement had caused his sister-in-law, who was then an ancient thirty-five years old, a great deal of embarrassment.

"Are you married?" he asked.

"*Ji,* Chachaji," the younger man replied. "Thirty years now—four sons and two daughters. The girls are married into the village, good houses. And my sons farm the land. They did not . . . want to go into my profession."

The night watchman nodded, his heart heavy. "I never understood why your father wanted to be a servant—"

"That was only at the beginning; when he learned of gems and jewels, he became one of the most respected men in Lahore."

"True. And I left the Punjab when I was fifteen, ran away from home because I had a fight with your grandfather and"—he spread a hand outward—"came here to Bombay. Every day the city gets more crowded; every person is unusual, comes from elsewhere, has a varied history, looks different, speaks in a foreign tongue." He sighed and with shaking fingers took out a *beedi* he had rolled in a cloth and tied around his waist. He did not offer one to his nephew, who though a man, a husband, a father of many years, was still much too young to smoke in front of him, and he would not allow such disrespect.

"I've only been here for two days, Chachaji." The younger man shifted about, his gaze fixed on the ship across the expanse of concrete where figures scurried onto the gangplanks, backs bent under the weight of gunnysacks, grumbles audible, the flap of their bare feet loud until they crested the deck, where they paused, outlined against the blue-black of the sky and the glitter of the stars, and then disappeared down the holds. "It's a"—he hesitated, searching for the word in his unlettered vocabulary—"city of . . . unbelievers."

"There's no soul here," his uncle agreed. "A lot of places for worship, but no place a heart can call a home." He drew in a lungful of smoke, exhaled, and listened as his nephew's breathing quickened in the thin gray fog that surrounded them. The boy wanted a *beedi,* but he wouldn't ask for one, or take one out of his own pocket.

"You have been happy here, Chachaji?"

"After a fashion," the old man said in comfortable rumble. "I could not go back to the Punjab after fighting with your grandfather; I had too much pride in my chest. And so, I haven't seen your father . . . or my other brothers for so many years now. A letter every now and then has been the most I've had, like the one that informed me of your coming here. Written by your father's own hand. We have never learned to read and write in our family—how proud your grandfather must have been. How is he? How is my brother?"

"Old," the younger man said with a smile that was lost

in the darkness, but not in the inflection of his voice. "And dying. My father's heart has been broken, shattered—there's no mending it."

The night watchman allowed the *beedi* to burn down between his thumb and index finger. And so death must come to all of them, he thought. Displaced, dislocated, dislodged here in Bombay, he still remembered the sweet, clean aroma of a summer morning in the fertile plains around the Ravi River, the song of the *koyal*, the calluses cutting through the young skin of his hands as he reaped the wheat. Of the fight with his father, he remembered nothing at all; only that he had had a point to make and had made it by exiling himself from his birth land and his family. His brothers had stayed on, grown up, married, had children . . . their children had married and had their own children, and in the last few years the Punjab had burned down from an Empire into a holding of the British. Much as Bombay had always been. They all had the white Sahib for a master now.

And so, each engrossed in his own thoughts, the old man and his nephew watched the steady stream of goods into the *Indus's* hold. To anyone else, these provisions would have seemed gross, a flagrant amassing of food and drink for a few weeks spent at sea, enough to feed many armies, frittered away on just a few. But the night watchman had guarded the docks for many years, and had seen many steamers boarded with mounds of groceries; his nephew had worked in the court of the Maharajah Ranjit Singh, who had owned the Kohinoor diamond as just one of his luxurious possessions among lands, rivers, streams, gullies, mountains, and palaces.

Three thousand pounds of flour, bread, hops, and malt. Oxtails, sides of beef, pork, mutton, calves' heads, and enormous blocks of ice clad in jute heaved over the steep gangplank to keep the meat fresh. Two hundred head of livestock—hens, geese, ducks, sheep, pigs—which were kept in a pen belowdecks, brought up to the bow in the middle of the night, slaughtered there, bled over the edge of the ship's bulwark. The decks were then washed down and disinfected before the first shard of dawn streaked over the horizon, so although the passengers of the *Indus* would sit down to freshly made sausages at breakfast in the stateroom, they wouldn't realize that the meat had lived and breathed, and eventually died, just a few feet away on the very deck they would promenade on after the meal.

There were bottles of champagne, claret, Madeira, port and sherry, brandy, rum, whiskey, and pale ale, soda water and lemonade for the ladies. Bags of tea, coffee, sugar, curry powder, made their way up the gangplank. And then came the jams, jellies, marmalade, macaroni, olive oil, catsup, vinegar, salted tripe, vermicelli, eggs, butter, and bacon.

The kitchens—there were two of them on the *Indus*, one for the passengers and one for the crew—were below the foredeck, and each had its set of cooks and provisions. P & O policy strictly forbade the crew cooks from dipping into the passengers' rations.

When the last of the goods had been stowed aboard—and this was the second night of the loading—the old man finally turned the wick of his lantern on high, waited for flame to flare, picked up his stick, and held the lantern, swinging, over the face of his nephew, whom he had never before seen. His breath caught in his chest—this was his brother's face, the one he would have had if the watchman had stayed on in the Punjab to see his younger brother grow up into manhood. How much he had missed because of his stupid fight with this boy's grandfather.

"I must go back now, Chachaji," his nephew said. "My master will wake soon; he cannot quite manage without me."

The watchman set the lantern down and reached out to touch his nephew's shoulder. How firm and strong he felt, how successful he had already been in his life—children he had brought up and given the family lands to, daughters he had married to good people and good families, a wife . . .

"Where is your wife?" he asked.

"She died, Chachaji," the other replied. "Four years ago." He turned to look at the *Indus,* lying a little lower in the waters of the bay, the waves lapping against her bow in a rhythmic motion, setting her rocking slightly. "So I decided to take this job. My father thought I should."

"You have been a good son," the old man said ruminatively. His brother had always had an ease of control over many things—people, his family—but then his brother had had a great responsibility in the court of Maharajah Ranjit Singh, and he had held that job for years, trusted and comfortable in the imperial presence. Bringing up his children to listen to him well into their adulthoods would also have been easy for him.

"Then you leave on this boat?" the watchman asked, nudging his chin outward.

"With my master, yes."

"You cannot come back, *beta,*" the uncle said. "Can you? After you have crossed the black waters, after you've lost caste doing so. Who will you be? What can you be?"

The younger man bowed his head. When he spoke, though, there was no bitterness in his voice. "I have been asked to go along with my master to England, there to serve him as I have here. He will not return, I think; he has other plans. And so I cannot also; I could not afford to pay my way back. But"—his mouth hardened and his eyes glittered—"it will not be so bad after all. I have work to do, Chachaji. Much work."

He rose, bent down again to touch his uncle's feet, and moved that hand to his forehead and eyes, then walked away into the gloom of the dockyard. The night watchman listened to his footsteps fading away and knew that he would not see his nephew again. They could, either of them, die before that meeting would happen.

*   *   *

While the city of Bombay slept, lamplighters roamed about, flames held aloft, their quick eyes seeking out a smoking or doused streetlamp. The street sweepers and cleaners came by, pulling their carts, and the whish-whoosh of their brushes, and sluice of water from their buckets, set the roads gleaming by dawn. Police constables walked their beats, striking the ground with their thick *lathis*. Here and there, a night watchman called out the hour in a song-filled voice.

A brisk breeze settled in from the sea, whisking around the buildings and towers, bringing cool relief to the poor, the homeless, shrouded in cotton sheets on the pavements under the star-thronged sky.

At Watson's Hotel in the Esplanade, a five-minute walk from the docks at Apollo Bandar, Lieutenant Colonel Frederick Mackeson lay on his bed in the very center of the room. It was on the fourth floor, the topmost, and at one corner, so the room had windows, or rather a series of half-glass doors, perforating two walls. A wrought-iron balcony wrapped around the outside of each floor of the hotel, common to all the rooms, wide enough only for a man to step outside for a smoke.

Mackeson had his hands crossed on his chest, in the pose of a dead saint put to rest, but his thoughts were anything but calm. For sleep would not come, coveted though it was. He shifted his head. Although the curtains had been drawn over each door, light from the streetlamps still seeped in around the sides. And for a long time now, he had been able to distinguish the chair, the desk, the paintings on the walls, even the whorls and swirls of the carpet's design, and the gleam of the mosaic floor. Overhead, a broad, sheetlike *punkah* moved from side to side, and a rope attached to it ran along the ceiling to the entrance door, and through a hole in the wall above the transom window. A boy sat outside, tugging at the rope and making the *punkah* move. He usually had it tied to his toe, and merely had to waggle his foot to keep the fan in motion once started.

He had fallen asleep though, Mackeson thought; the *punkah* had stopped many times, and started again when the boy awoke and remembered his duty.

The room was stifling hot. Mr. Granger, the manager, upon showing Colonel Mackeson the room, had suggested keeping the verandah doors open during the night. It was quite safe, he had said, and they had security guards patrolling the street outside. But the noises of a city fading into the night's rest had grated upon Mackeson's ears—he had spent all of his time in India in small, outlying villages and distant regimental camps. The constant sound of carriages, the harsh laughter of the coolies, the inconsequential chatter of so many people, forever and on and on, had churned inside him, given him no peace at all since he had come to Bombay this morning.

Even the hushed luxury of Watson's was painful. In the smoking room, there was the crackle of the newspapers, the smog of cigarettes, the unnerving sensation that the cut of his trousers was at least four years out of date and that the crease was not sharp enough no matter how hard Multan Raj had tried his hand at an iron. In the dining room, he had been bewildered by the array of forks and knives and spoons— which was for what? He had forgotten, so long in the army, so unused to a grand dinner party; the utensils for the fish, the fowl, the side of beef all seemed the same to him. He was conscious of having lifted the wrong one when the waiter—a native boy—had coughed by his side and gently removed all others to the side of his plate so that he could identify the correct fork.

And the women were so . . . splendid. Some were clad in real blue gowns—the up-country women Mackeson knew had long given up that color because it yellowed and aged quickly under the Indian sun—their hands were smooth and clean, unwrinkled; their hair was set by expert hands, presumably by their native *ayahs*, who were more skillful than the ones who served the Englishwoman anywhere else in India.

Colonel Mackeson had never married; that is, he had not married an Englishwoman. He did, though, have a *zenana* of native women—three of them—with whom he had lived for twenty-five years, and who had borne him twelve children. He knew all of their names, had named them himself, and taught them English and some mathematics. They lived in a house he had built on the banks of the Hooghly near Calcutta. There were some officers in the army who knew of his wives and children, but most did not, because he did not travel with them and had never introduced them to his fellow officers' wives.

There had not been enough money for an English wife at first, and then, when the promotions came in, never an opportunity to meet one. Mackeson had been forced to spend his first home leave—ten years after he had come to India—in bed with a fever through which one of his wives had nursed him, or he would have died. When the next home leave came around, another ten years later, one of his children was sick with the cholera, and the boy had subsequently died, leaving a yawning hole in Mackeson's heart. This boy he had taught to hunt, to fish, to sit on a chair, to drink tea from a cup's rim and not slurp it from the saucer. Most of the men under his command, for a very long time, had been natives. Over the years the balance had changed, as the East India Company recruited more and more men from the British Isles, promising them wealth from an Indian tour (which had to last at least a few decades before it could be realized) and faster promotions than in the King's army. This had been what had lured Mackeson also.

He watched as other, younger men, with connections on the Governor-General's Council, or the Court of Directors of the East India Company, or at court, leapt over him to higher ranks. But Colonel Mackeson was patient and unworried. Finally, he was asked to be a political agent in Peshawar while the Maharajah Ranjit Singh still ruled over the Punjab Empire. That led to other civil postings, and the final one—the one that had brought him to Watson's Hotel in Bombay, sleepless and wide-eyed—was as political liaison of the Governor-General's office during the Second Sikh War.

Lord Dalhousie had come to India as Governor-General over two years ago. It wasn't he who had recommended Mackeson for the post—he had hardly known any of the old India hands when he landed—but he soon came to rely upon the man, his dedication, his unhurried answers, his thoughtfulness, his proven bravery. Of Mackeson's harem in Calcutta, Dalhousie neither knew nor cared. And it had been two years since Mackeson had seen these women of his family.

Now this. He eventually rose from his bed, his arms stiff, his shoulders frozen, his neck muscles tense. The Punjab Empire had finally been dissolved, and there was no more pretense at the British government "holding" the throne for the young Maharajah Dalip Singh until he reached his majority. The Second Sikh War had put an end to that entire charade, and Dalip Singh had signed an official treaty giving up his lands, his right to rule over them, the jewels in his Toshakhana and the Kohinoor diamond. He had also been taken away from Lahore at Lord Dalhousie's behest, for fear that the twelve-year-old Maharajah's very presence would be an incitement to riot, to claim back the throne of the Punjab.

Colonel Mackeson walked up to the verandah doors, brushed aside the curtains, and looked out into the street. Over the tops of the buildings, in the distance, he could see the dark blue waters of the harbor, and the intermittent twinkle of lights from the boats and ships clustered there. He put his hand on the door's latch and opened it enough so that the breeze wafted in, mildly scented with frangipani flowers, and the pure breath of the sea.

As political liaison for Lord Dalhousie, he had also carried the terms of the treaty to the child king, not sure that he should have been doing this. Surely it was better that Henry Lawrence, who had been Resident at Lahore before, and knew the Maharajah well, should have performed this task?

If there was one thing Colonel Mackeson would fault Lord Dalhousie for, it had been this. The child had been brought into a room full of strangers and told that depriving him of his lands was the right thing for him, that he would be looked after, could keep some of his jewels, and would have an income for life. What more could he want?

"But," Dalip Singh had said, in the high voice of a child, "where's Henry?"

Dr. John Login had been left—when Henry Lawrence was taken away from Dalip Singh and Lahore—as the guardian for the fort, the treasury, and the child. This too Mackeson approved of; he had also thought Henry Lawrence too empathetic with the native people of the Punjab to remain there any longer . . . but Lawrence should have been there to hold the boy's hand when he signed the treaty, to explain to him what was happening, to assure him that he still had a friend.

And then Lord Dalhousie had taken charge of the Kohinoor diamond and come up with the idea that it should be presented to the Queen, that it rightfully belonged to the woman who was sovereign of British lands in Britain and abroad.

Mackeson pulled the gold tasseled rope that hung beside his bed and waited for Multan Raj to knock softly and enter, when he said, *"Aao."*

"You cannot sleep, Sahib?" he asked after he had touched his forehead in a salaam.

"No," Mackeson said with a grin. *"Tum bhi nahi so rahi ho?"* You aren't sleeping either? He didn't notice the small smile that creased the man's swarthy face, for Mackeson had learned all his Hindustani among the women of his *ʒenana,* and hadn't learned the grammar well enough to realize that he spoke only in the feminine, as the women did. "A brandy, please. No water, just ice."

"I will bring the ice, Mackeson Sahib." Multan Raj went out and shut the door. In the sudden darkness that came flooding back, and before his eyes became accustomed to the pale light filtering from the street outside, Mackeson remembered his conversation with Lord Dalhousie in the old Shah Burj, the tower in Lahore Fort. He had come upon the Governor-General holding the Kohinoor diamond, in its bracelet, and turning it this way and that in the sunlight until it looked like his hand was on fire. Mackeson had hesitated at the doorway.

"Come, please, Colonel Mackeson," Lord Dalhousie had said. "Take a look at this; splendid, isn't it?" And he'd proffered the Kohinoor.

Mackeson had taken the diamond, clutching it with both hands, afraid to drop it, overwhelmed by the sheer power that came out of a piece of rock. Kings had worn this, fought for it, held it ransom, held each other ransom for it. It had traveled all over India, had gone to Persia, had come back again to India, and he, who had started his life in the Company's armies as a subaltern, now held this gem that would at some time in the future adorn his Queen.

Lord Dalhousie had been observing him, a grave look on his face. "I think it should be given to her Majesty, *not* as a gift but as a token of surrender from Dalip Singh."

"If you say so, your Excellency."

Dalhousie's mouth had congealed in a grim smile. "I wish it were just my say-so. I'm bound, you know, by the Court of Directors of the East India Company."

"Surely not? Her Majesty nominated you?" Here Mackeson had been daring, for it was common knowledge that the Company had few powers left in India—it had all been slowly shifting into the hands of the government. But, nominally, the Governor-General of India was still, as of now, answerable to the East India Company and the chairman of its Court of Directors.

Dalhousie had run a hand through his sleek, brilliantined hair, tousling it, making him seem younger than his thirty-eight years. His face was flushed, a pulse throbbed at his temple, and his fingers interlaced and came apart—a sure sign that he was disturbed. He was so young, Mackeson thought, so fervent, so earnest, so insistent upon having his own way. So sure that he was right. Standing in front of the man who was his master—he had not yet been asked to sit—Mackeson felt aged. He was fifty-eight years old, had already lived in India since before the Governor-General was born, and had not been back to England since he left. He had looked down upon the Kohinoor and felt a pang of distress that it would not stay in the land of its birth.

When he'd glanced up at Dalhousie, however, Mackeson's face was tranquil, his thoughts hidden, even that last, fleeting, blasphemous notion banished into the recesses of his head.

Dalhousie had begun to speak between clenched teeth, the words coming out with an effort. He'd waved his ink-stained hands in the air; he wrote all the time, in his journal, documenting every idea and action, copious letters to the Queen, to the Court of Directors, to the Parliament about his duties in India, how he handled them, whom he talked to, what he said. He had no guile, nothing hidden; so much information came out of Lord Dalhousie and went on its way to almost any man, or woman, in authority, that he was as transparent as if he were made of water.

"The Court of Directors does not think I should send the Kohinoor to her Majesty," he had said. "They consider it to be spoils of war, and that it should go to the East India Company, to pay for the Second Sikh War, and it should be broken down and the money split up as prize money to the soldiers who fought in the war. But there is the three million pounds sterling worth of jewels, shawls, and goods from the Toshakhana, which will be sold off at the auction houses in Calcutta. Why this also? This jewel should belong to the Queen, not as part of the state jewels, but as her own, from *me*."

"From the Maharajah to the Queen, your Excellency," Mackeson had said faintly.

"All right," Lord Dalhousie had agreed. He hadn't stopped talking, hadn't realized the import of what he'd said and how he had said it. And that was precisely why—one of the reasons why in any case—the Court of Directors had had such strong objections to the Kohinoor diamond being given to Queen Victoria. Because Lord Dalhousie had considered that *he* was the one giving it; the Court of Directors thought they should be the ones instead. And, Mackeson thought, whether the boy king, Dalip Singh, actually wanted to give the diamond away or not, it should really come from him.

"You'll take it to England, Mackeson," Dalhousie had said suddenly.

"What?" Colonel Mackeson had backed away a few steps, the weight of the stone enormous now in his hands.

"I can trust no one else to do this. You are the best man. I'll send Ramsay along with you as a guard, an escort—two of you"—here Dalhousie had looked past Mackeson's shoulder into the sunshine in the courtyard beyond—"and it should be safe. I'll make sure it is. I would take it myself, if I could go back home right now, and I don't want it here in India any longer. The sooner it leaves, the sooner the Indians will forget it ever existed."

That they wouldn't, Colonel Mackeson had thought. He'd glanced down and cradled his fingers around the Kohinoor, and seen it glow warmly in his cupped palms. So the Kohinoor would leave India, and soon, as Lord Dalhousie had said; he made his notions into actions even as he uttered them. This, being the person who carried the Kohinoor to England, was an unprecedented honor, and Mackeson also knew that if he lost the diamond, his life would be worth less than nothing.

"You must take it to the Court of Directors the morning after you land in Southampton," Lord Dalhousie had said, his mouth twisted in disgust. "They insist upon presenting it to the Queen, as though it comes from *them*."

"Where do I sail from, Lord Dalhousie?"

"Bombay's the closest. But"—he'd pondered this for two whole minutes, his head sunk into his chin—"I will take it there myself." A sudden grin had transformed his face into that of an adolescent—he was so young, Mackeson had thought again. "At least I can take it to Bombay, if not all the way to England."

"I will guard it with my life, your Excellency," Mackeson had said.

"Of course you will," Dalhousie had said, holding his hand out for the Kohinoor and placing it upon his desk. Mackeson had saluted and slowly retreated to his quarters at the fort. He could tell no one of this, talk to no one, and he wouldn't talk with that young puppy Ramsay, Dalhousie's nephew.

Multan Raj came in with the brandy, and as Mackeson drank it, he massaged his master's feet, his skillful fingers kneading over his gouty left knee. The pain had been all right, even manageable, until he had come to Bombay that morning, when it had flared while he was checking into Watson's, and then again, sporadically, at night, keeping him awake, thinking, wondering about his first trip to England in forty years.

And then there was that little matter of the fire onboard the HMS *Medea*. Lord Dalhousie had been very insistent that the Kohinoor travel on her Majesty's warship, not on a commercial steamer. But he had been equally adamant that the diamond stay no longer than necessary in India. Colonel Mackeson had inquired; it would be at least three months before another warship could be brought to dock at Bombay, and he feared that the *Medea* had somehow been compromised. He couldn't contact Lord Dalhousie, who was on his way back to Calcutta.

So, he'd booked passage for Ramsay and himself onboard the *Indus*, and though he did read the *Bombay Herald* that morning, Mackeson had missed seeing the delicious gossip about Lord Dalhousie having been in Bombay and having deposited the Kohinoor there.

On the morning of the departure, the dock sizzled with scurry and scuttle. The smokestack of the *Indus* punched into the sky, her decks were washed and buffed, the sun glanced off the gold epaulets of the captain and the officers of the bridge.

Passengers began arriving at seven o'clock with their belongings, baskets, children, friends who had come to see them off. Horse-drawn *tongas*, *palkis*, and English carriages milled about the dock, spewing out their occupants to add to the crowd. Porters, clad in the khaki uniforms of the dockyard, scampered under the weight of the regulation boxes from the P & O handbook—twenty-six inches long, eighteen inches wide, eighteen inches deep in leather-bound wood clamped with brass. The ships would hold, easily, luggage of greater dimensions, but the outward trip to England involved crossing the desert from Suez to Cairo, and the only way to transport all the gear was to sling the boxes, one on each side, over the backs of camels.

In a few hours, the top deck was littered with baggage as the ship's crew ran around with lists. The cabins were tight, and most of the luggage had to go into the after hold. Was it all marked carefully, with the name, or at least the initials of the owner? Were the boxes numbered? Every three days at sea, the passengers would be allowed into the after hold to rummage through their boxes, so did they know exactly what was packed in each, so as to make this easier? No? Then the luggage was opened right there, repacked, the lists altered, a copy kept in the passenger's pocket book, another given to the purser.

In the midst of all the mayhem, as his porter brought up one box behind him, Colonel Mackeson first saw the young woman, serene, unruffled, her white-gloved hand resting on her luggage.

"Can I be of help?" he asked.

She raised long-lashed eyes to his face and he saw that she was not, after all, as young as he had originally thought her to be. Her waist was childishly trim, the swell of her breasts gentle under her stays, the skin on her neck unlined, but a little web of wrinkles, so fine as to be almost unnoticeable, creased around her eyes when she smiled at him. She had a small mouth, palely varnished in pink, and the pure complexion of a woman who has not allowed the sun to touch her. "My brother is somewhere, thank you; he'll come by to take care of all this."

Her voice was low, and Mackeson had to lean in to listen to her words before they were snatched away and disappeared into the general ruckus.

He bowed and offered her his hand. "Lieutenant Colonel Mackeson."

She laughed. "I'm not as accomplished, I'm afraid. Mary Booth."

"Miss Booth?" he asked.

She nodded, looking down at her gloves after she had pulled her hand out of his. Mackeson cursed himself as he saw the frown pucker her forehead. She was unmarried, she wasn't exactly young, she was returning home to England. This could only mean that she hadn't found any man to marry her in India. He took a step back. It was ridiculous that this

woman, like a freshly opened flower, full of perfume, with her
quiet movements, her candid gaze, could have been left alone
by the thousands of bachelors in the Indian regiments and the
Civil Service. There was a joke bandied about almost every
mess hall that any new woman was proposed to first and then
asked her name, before any other man got his chance. Why,
if he'd seen her before . . . He took a deep breath. He couldn't
have done anything if he'd seen her.

"Sahib." Multan Raj stood at his shoulder. "The porter
needs to know where to put the box."

"Of course," Mackeson said. He turned back to Mary
Booth. "Forgive me, I have to—"

"Yes, please go, my brother will be here soon. He's gone
to get our cabin numbers; we had to book our passage late,
you see, and they hadn't assigned us the numbers."

"Until the voyage then," Mackeson said, tipping his hat
at her.

"In a few hours," she said, with a half smile that lifted one
edge of her mouth, and in that moment Mackeson saw that
perhaps he had misunderstood the lovely Miss Booth after
all. Maybe she hadn't come to India to get married, or if she
had, she hadn't found anyone who wasn't a boor. His back
straightened, the ache in his knee seemed to vanish, and he
worked hard not to drag his foot as he moved away.

Multan Raj accompanied him to the first-class cabin,
which consisted of a long passageway, midship and upon the
topmost deck, with two berths, one on each side of the corridor. There were skylights on a slim line along the ceiling, and
light poured in. Mackeson's one box was pushed under his
berth, beside the desk, and secured to the wall of the cabin.
He looked across the passageway and saw a leather bag with
the initials W.H. stamped on it. For privacy, at night and during the day, there was a folding wooden screen slotted into
the doorway that could be pulled across. There was also
enough space for a washstand.

He sat on his berth as his servant padded around on his bare, callused feet, unpacking sheets, pillowcases, towels, and a blanket, wondering what had come over him on the crowded deck upstairs. She was pretty, that Miss Booth, enchanting even.

Just then, a man put his head around the partition. "I cannot get used to these cabins, Mackeson," he said. "They make me feel like I'm going to be crawling around on my hands and knees by the end of the voyage." His teeth flashed, white and large in his mouth.

Edward Ramsay was twenty-two years old and had grown into a bulkiness that in twenty years would cause him to be heavy-footed and slow. He had the look of his family, Mackeson thought, Lord Dalhousie's sharp nose, the jutting forehead hanging over eyes set back, and the blue eyes of their Scottish ancestors. He had the same muddy blond hair also, only in Ramsay's case it was a jumble of waves, not neatly slicked back as in his uncle.

"Where have you been?"

Ramsay came into the cabin and dragged the screen shut. He put his ear to the wood and listened, and the sound of footsteps in the corridor was plainly evident. The screen was deep enough, though, that voices were now muffled. He turned to the older man. "Did you get it?"

Mackeson smiled faintly. "Of course I did."

"I'm sorry I wasn't there earlier in the morning." Ramsay lifted his colossal shoulders. "I was . . . er . . . caught up in the arms of . . . something. I haven't been to Bombay before. Don't tell my uncle, will you? I hope he didn't expect me to sign the turnover form."

Multan Raj shut the lid to Mackeson's box and stood with his arms full of sheets and pillowcases. "Sahib," he said, "if you will rise, I can make the bed."

Mackeson edged toward the screen; there was barely enough space for all three of them. "Speak little, Ramsay," he said quietly. "Not until we are somewhere we cannot be over-heard."

Lord Dalhousie had been insistent upon secrecy. Even the Treasurer knew only that something—in a Chubb safe with its three skins of iron and tin and its detector lock—had been brought into the main safe room in the middle of the night. He had instructions to keep the room locked and open it only to Colonel Mackeson and Captain Ramsay—not necessar-ily both together, but not Captain Ramsay without Colonel Mackeson. After waiting for Ramsay to show up, Macke-son had walked from his hotel room to the Treasury in the morning, opened the room, taken the safe, put it into a large wooden box, and signed for it.

Lord Dalhousie was a stickler for paperwork. Mackeson had signed a paper stating that he had received the Kohinoor diamond (in the Chubb safe) from the Governor-General, and added his initials to another stating he had been con-tracted to take the Kohinoor to England and her Majesty, and to another which said that Captain Ramsay was to be his companion, and to yet another for all the contingencies that might befall them if one or the other was to fall ill or die dur-ing the voyage.

His pen running dry, Mackeson had asked, What if the diamond is stolen, Lord Dalhousie? The Governor-General had frowned. Surely not, Mackeson, it's a remote possibil-ity. Every precaution has been taken; no one even knows that the Kohinoor has left the Punjab, let alone is on its way to England.

In his hotel room, Mackeson had looked at the big, ugly safe, black and squat on the mosaic floor. He might as well advertise that he had the Kohinoor and let all of Bombay see him carrying this monstrosity in his arms. Mackeson had removed the key that he wore on a chain around his neck and opened the safe.

He had been assured that Chubb had come up with a

foolproof lock—if any other key was put into the lock, it jammed, and only the original key, or a regulator key, could undo the jam and allow the lock to be opened. There, in the middle of the safe, was a thin cloth packet, about four inches by two, densely embossed with blobs of sealing wax—Lord Dalhousie's seal, Mackeson's own seal, Ramsay's seal, the seal of the Lahore physician, Dr. John Login, who had been acting treasurer of Maharajah Ranjit Singh's Toshakhana. A little like Lord Dalhousie's letters, this too was done in excess. *Only* to be opened in the presence of the Director of the East India Company in Portsmouth—who had been sent a detailed list of every seal on the package.

Mackeson had always been a timid man. Well, not perhaps *timid*, since his physical courage was enormous, his head steady in situations that would have frightened most men into heart arrests. But he had always followed orders, which was, after all, the hallmark of the perfect soldier, and the perfect officer.

He spun the packet in his hands. At the other end of the room, Multan Raj had created mounds of ironed clothes and was lifting each stack and setting it gently into the trunk.

"Come back after ten minutes, will you please, Multan?" Mackeson said.

"*Ji*, Sahib," the man replied, his back still to his master, and then, without turning, he shuffled out of the room.

Mackeson took a knife and slit open the cloth. There were other layers of cloth, all wrapped tightly around, and he undid each one until the diamond draped over his closed fist, its gold chain linked between his fingers. In his trunk, Mackeson found a thin muslin bag with a loop around the top. He slipped the Kohinoor into the bag and then slid the loop into his belt. The bag he then tucked inside the waistband of his trousers and buttoned his coat over it.

"Where is it?" Ramsay asked in a whisper.

"On me."

Captain Ramsay's eyes flickered with glee. "Say, not in the pouch my aunt stitched and my uncle used to wear? Did you break all of his lovely seals? How are you going to explain that to the lordly Court of Directors?"

"Yes and yes," Mackeson said. "I think they'll be happy enough to just have it, no matter how it traveled."

Lady Dalhousie had stitched the cloth bag herself for the Kohinoor, and it was true that Lord Dalhousie had worn this purse on the waist of his trousers all through the long journey from the Punjab to Bombay. "It would have been foolish to leave it in that clunky box."

"All right," Ramsay said, pulling back the wooden screen. "Let me know if you want me to have it, be glad to relieve you anytime. Oh." This last was at the man whom the screen had revealed, standing right up against the wood, his nose a few inches from Ramsay's shirtfront.

"Pardon me," the man said. "I was wondering if you gentlemen would like to go out on the deck. It's time for the departure."

For a few minutes Mackeson and Ramsay stared at the stranger. If he had intended to knock, the only reason to be so close to the door, he did not have his hand raised. And he had been turned to the side, in an attitude of listening. Colonel Mackeson felt his collar grow tight in the closed confines of the cabin. He patted his middle involuntarily. It was there, and no one knew it was there.

"Of course," Captain Ramsay said casually. "I'm over there, two berths away. Where are you, sir?"

The man beamed. He had a round face with a shock of black hair, parted in the center of his head and combed neatly down the two sides. His chin was clean-shaven, his eyes sunken in the folds of skin on his cheeks, and when he moved his head up, both Mackeson and Ramsay saw the gleam of a short, white clerical collar. "William Huthwaite," he said. "I'm opposite."

Mackeson introduced himself and Ramsay. "On home leave?" he asked. "Where were you stationed, Mr. Huthwaite?"

Huthwaite laughed. "I found my calling at Cawnpore, gentlemen. A small church built out of funds raised in the cantonment, Sunday school classes for all—including the natives. But"—he rolled his big head on his neck—"the fever, you know. The interminable fevers in India have sapped my strength and I find it necessary to spend time back home. It will be an interesting voyage; I haven't been back in twenty-five years." He raised his thick and black eyebrows.

"Forty for me," Mackeson mumbled.

"My dear sir!"

"Three," Ramsay said easily. "My mother . . . ah . . . is unwell."

"You served together perhaps? At Lahore?" The clergyman stood back to let them move into the passageway and followed them out onto the deck. "That's been our latest victory, hasn't it, the annexation of the Punjab?"

And so his quiet chatter chased them into the sunshine. He kept talking, his voice growing louder and louder in Mackeson's ear. The ship's band had struck up a tune, trumpets blaring, cymbals clashing, and it was rivaled by the dockyard's band below. Huthwaite asked a few questions, but mostly he spoke of himself, who he was, where he had come from, how he came to be in India. Huthwaite was the son of a copper miner in Cornwall, and had somehow lifted himself from the drudgery of his father's life to attend Cambridge on a scholarship, and achieved the position of Second Wrangler there—the second overall mark in mathematics in his graduating class. He had intended to study for the bar, then changed his mind and entered a seminary to work with the Church Mission Society in India. But even that plan had had to be altered when his father died, debt-ridden, leaving his sister and him destitute. So, he had applied for the position of a clergyman with the East India Company and eventually worked his way from the bases of smaller regiments to the position at Cawnpore. It hadn't been easy for Huthwaite to gather funds for his voyage, and only three days ago, the East India Company's headquarters had sent him the money. He'd been in Bombay for a month now, waiting, having missed last month's sailing of the *Indus*.

Mackeson thought of the lovely Mary Booth—what had she said? That they hadn't been assigned their berths yet because they too had bought their tickets late. Curious, that.

The captain of the *Indus* came up alongside and said in his other ear, "Would you care to step down to the dock, sir? A word with you, if you please."

Mackeson excused himself from the voluble Mr. Huthwaite—Ramsay had long disappeared into the crowd—and followed Captain Waltham down the main gangplank. The captain had a craggy and weather-beaten face, lines everywhere, around his mouth, his eyes, on his forehead under the cap with the P & O logo. Mackeson hobbled behind until they had reached the flat of the dock's concrete paving.

A space had been cleared near the foot of the gangplank leading to the after hold, where Captain Waltham led Mackeson. They both slipped under the cordon of guards and stood in the center—here finally they would not be overheard, and the crowds on the dock were kept at bay.

Captain Waltham took Lord Dalhousie's letter from an inner pocket of his coat. "I will be candid, Colonel Mackeson. I'm deeply uncomfortable about giving control of my ship to another officer, even on the Governor-General's orders. What is all this about? My crew tells me you brought onboard only one box; it was examined at the Customs House, and there's nothing in it but clothes and personal effects."

Mackeson shrugged. "I can say no more, Captain."

The captain tipped back his cap. "I see you feel the awkwardness of this situation too, sir. The letter says I am to cede charge only 'if necessary.' And what might necessitate such an eventuality that it does not yet have clearance from the Court of Directors of the P & O? And why should I even pay heed if it doesn't?"

"Because"—Mackeson said this quietly—"if things were to come to such a pass . . . the whole reputation of the Governor-General's office depends on their"—he hesitated, searching for words to explain that would really say nothing after all—"not happening. I'm sorry; believe me when I say that this is a matter of the utmost importance. You do not question that the letter is addressed to Captain Lockyer of the HMS *Medea*?"

Captain Waltham smiled; it transformed his face, and Mackeson could see that Waltham would be charming and engaging at the dinner table. "I am not such a fool as to disregard the Governor-General's letter, sir. And not so gullible as to believe it without question. I heard about the fire in the *Medea*'s engine room and talked with Captain Lockyer. He didn't seem to know much more about this."

"Thank you," Mackeson said and turned to leave the circle of sentries.

Waltham put a hand on his shoulder. "Stay, sir. The mail is due to arrive anytime now, and it will make it seem, to anyone watching us, that you're involved in duties here." He bobbed his chin toward a man at a corner. "That's the Admiralty Agent in charge of her Majesty's mail. He oversees the loading of it on the *Indus*, and accompanies it on the voyage."

Mackeson nodded. The primary function of the P & O steamers—the very reason they came into being, and could manage a profitable existence—had been the contract signed with the British government for carrying the mail. Passenger traffic was but a small part—Mackeson's ticket, first-class, had been a hundred and twenty-five pounds sterling, and the *Indus* transported a total of some seventy passengers, not enough by far to pay for the fuel, the food, the linens, the entertainment onboard, the coaling stations at Aden and Suez in the Red Sea, Malta and Gibraltar in the Mediterranean, the camel convoy over the desert, and the steamer passage from Alexandria to England across the Mediterranean.

He drew to the side and watched as four enclosed carriages, drawn by horses, were brought up to the gangplank, accompanied by ten guards dressed in the red livery of the Postmaster General. The guards unloaded the mail—some of it was in sacks, and these would travel only as far as Alexandria, and some of it was in boxes of the same dimensions as those the passengers had been advised to use, and these would be put onto the SS *Oriental*, waiting at the Alexandria dock. The boxes were all locked securely, and Mackeson saw the keys transferred to the Admiralty Agent, who held the loop of iron against his chest. They were also color-coded—the Alexandria and Mediterranean mail was in red sacks; the mail marked "via France," to be dropped off at the island of Malta and thence to Marseille and Boulogne and by steamer across the English Channel, was in blue boxes; the Falmouth shipment (the *Oriental* would stop here before her final destination in England) was green; the Southampton mail was in white boxes.

The mail was always the last thing to come onboard, and people began shouting good-byes.

On the deck, Lady Anne Elizabeth Beaumont took out a cigarette and lit it, the breeze brushing smoke through the rampage of white curls on her head. This was the end of her Eastern adventures. She had been overland through Persia and Afghanistan, been feted at the courts of the Shah and the Amir, danced the waltz at the Governor-General's ball in Government House in Calcutta while the women, *so* provincial, had gawked at her from behind their fans. She had

been married when she was a chit of a girl, nineteen, but
Edgar was so damnably boring, so unable to do anything.
Money had never been a problem—there was an earl somewhere in her lineage, acres of parkland and hunting grounds
full of grouse—and she had a pedigree. What would have
been scandalous in a woman of lower birth, no parentage, no
estates, was overlooked as eccentricity on her part, and she
was, at fifty-two, too old to worry about whisperings behind
hands. She had ridden over the Khyber Pass on a stout horse,
wearing men's trousers specially made for her in London, sitting astride a horse as a man would.

"It's going to be quite a journey, eh?" a voice said next
to her.

She squinted through the cigarette smoke at the boy who
had addressed her. He was a thin, sallow-faced young man,
with a weak, receding chin, teeth that jutted out so his lips did
not fully close over them, spiky hair that he smoothed down
ineffectively.

"Martyn Wingate," he said, bringing his hand into the
range of her vision. "You're Lady Beaumont, aren't you? I
peeked at the passenger list. I'm opposite you in the cabin."

"Where's your father, young man?" Her voice was icy.

"Ha-ha," he said. "I'm not as young as I look. And my
father is the publisher of the *Bombay Herald*."

Lady Beaumont contemplated the end of her cigarette.
She too had read the article in the paper, and she'd booked
her passage afterward just to be onboard the *Indus*. Her
original plan was to visit the court of the Hyderabad king—
someone had wrangled an invitation for her—but she had
had to regretfully decline. A pity, she thought, for she had
not been to southern India yet, and Edgar wouldn't care if
he didn't see her for another year. He was perfectly happy in
her ancestral home, with his horses, his dogs, and his interminable mucking about in the gardens.

Martyn Wingate left his hand hanging in the air, then

withdrew it, and put it into his pocket. He waited for a long
while, shifting his weight from one foot to the other, wondering if she was cutting him.

"You think the diamond is on this ship?" she asked. They
were standing very close to each other, leaning on the deck
railing. The noise from the band blasted around their ears.
In the background, the smokestack heaved and hissed as the
Indus's engine room built up steam and sent a spiral of gray
fog into the blue Bombay sky.

"I do." Eagerly. Then, meeting her cynical gaze, he
added, "My father does. The old man booked my passage
without even telling me about it. He's a crafty one, much
under the influence of his wife and his snotty children—not
my mother, you understand; this one's much younger; he met
her at the theater."

"Who's taking it?"

"I think," Wingate said carefully, "a Colonel McGregor
and a Captain Ramsay."

"How do you know?"

"Papa," he said. "Papa knows everything."

"There's a Ramsay on the list, but not a McGregor . . ."
Lady Beaumont had reached into her reticule and drawn out
a sheet of paper. "Plenty of other army officers, but only one
colonel. Mackeson."

"Maybe he didn't come then?"

She shook her head. "Your father has the name wrong.
It's that man." She pointed at the dock with her cigarette,
where the mail was being loaded up the gangplank. "Colonel
Mackeson."

Just then, one of the guards lost his footing, and his box
fell from his hands and crashed into Colonel Mackeson. They
watched as Mackeson righted himself, rubbing his knee, and
hobbled over to the guard to pull him up and then lifted the
green box and carried it himself up the gangplank and disappeared into the hold. He was a while in coming back, his limp

more pronounced, his face ashen with effort, sweat dotting his forehead. He shook hands with the captain and then made his way up the passenger gangplank.

A few minutes later, all the mail had been packed into the *Indus*'s after hold; the mail carriages withdrew, people flapped their handkerchiefs in the air, and the ship's band stopped playing as the crew took their places.

The dockhands wheeled away the gangplanks and untied the moorings, flinging the ropes back onto the deck. The *Indus* gave a long, musical hoot with her foghorn, the paddles moved, crunching through the water, and the pilot guided the ship out of the harbor.

The night skies were enormous over the lone ship cutting her way through the Arabian Sea, spread out from horizon to horizon, the stars a pale blue glitter of diamonds strewn with a careless hand. There was no wind, not even a whisper of one, as Mackeson walked up and down the deck. Mary Booth's little hand was tucked under his arm; her head came just up to his shoulder. He could smell a whiff of jasmine in the glossy ringlets of her dark hair. They were alone on the forward deck, far from the sole lantern swinging from a post, circling its pool of light below.

"What does your brother do, Miss Booth?" Mackeson asked. He walked slowly; in the last week his knee had become more swollen, uncomfortably tight in his trousers.

She turned gleaming eyes up to him. "He used to work at Lattey Brothers."

"The Calcutta auctioneers? Used to, you say?"

Mary moved a little apart. Her lids fell over her eyes, and she picked at the lace on her sleeve. When she spoke, her voice was low, and Mackeson had to lean over to listen. "They . . . someone accused him . . . of taking one of the

Ganesha idols, a small one, from the sixteenth century. It was part of the East India Company's booty, spoils of war I think from the conquest of a small kingdom in the south, somewhere in the Madras Presidency." She looked out to the sea, her profile rigid. "He didn't do it, Colonel Mackeson. Tom's a man of great integrity and honor; the very thought of being suspected was too much for him. And so . . . we left."

Mackeson had met Thomas Booth at the dinner table that had been assigned to the first-class passengers on the very first night of the passage, and had taken an almost instant dislike to the man. He had been impeccably dressed, too foppish by far, with a care for detail that a finicky woman would take. His coattails had been brushed, his collar was pristine without a rim of sweat, his hands clean, his nails cut freshly, the gleam of a gold chain connecting his watch fob to the buttons of his ruffled shirt. His skin had been too white for Mackeson's comfort, as though he had spent his time in Calcutta under the shade of a parasol during the day, emerging only at night to show his face. And, he didn't sweat. To Mackeson, who had stewed in perspiration all through his years in India, this was the ultimate folly for a man. Booth's voice was not all that manly either; he had a mincing way of speaking, not quite opening his mouth fully, the words seeming to escape from one corner or the other. And though long grooves cut their way on either side of his lips, Mackeson had never seen him smile.

He had compared the two of them—brother and sister— seated side by side, and seen similarities in their manner of eating, of wiping their mouths at the end of each mouthful, in their dark coloring, hair and eyebrows, but what suited Mary Booth merely looked comical and unbending in Thomas Booth. Mackeson wondered if Mary had not been able to marry—if indeed she had never received a proposal at all— because of her brother. Not just for his behavior but because Tom Booth had after all been only a clerk, a minor one, at the auction house in Calcutta, and they would not have had

entry into the Government House parties or the balls held in
the regimental messes.

So he had walked away with one of the goods entrusted
to his master, he thought. Mackeson made a pretense of
adjusting his belt and felt for the bag hanging from it. There,
underneath his hand, solid and comforting, was the outline of
the Kohinoor diamond.

He looked at Mary Booth, still gazing into the waters, her
nose and mouth outlined by the stars behind her, and felt a
sudden yearning to put his arms around her and bury his face
in her hair. He had heard stories about shipboard romances,
how quick they were, how you could find yourself married
at the end of two or three weeks, the captain officiating, and
then find yourself in gentle regret for the rest of your life.

And if he had to be honest with himself, Mackeson had to
admit he was terrified of going to England, a land he had left
as a boy, of meeting his sister in Cornwall after forty years.
What would he say to her? It would be cold, and damp, the
nights long and dark in winter, no incessant shriek of the
crickets outside his window.

He had grown up in a mining town, and he could remember his father's grimy face at the dinner table, the way he
hacked off bread from the loaf, his drunken sleep every night,
a bottle of grog rolling under his chair below his inert hand.
Mackeson already missed India, and knew, even before he set
foot on English soil, he would be returning to his regiment or
his civil duties—there had been a letter for him at Bombay,
promising a posting to Peshawar. Where would Mary Booth
fit into all of this? The women of his *zenana* near Calcutta
were enough for him.

The dinner bell rang.

"Shall we go back in, my dear?" he said, and his manner
had changed, no longer the lover. He saw a flash of hardness
in her eyes, an understanding as she nodded. Perhaps Mary
Booth had indeed tried very hard to get married in India, and

she hadn't succeeded after all, and it was, just perhaps, no fault of her brother's.

An hour later, seated at the dinner table, Colonel Mackeson thought that they were all a sorry lot. Captain Waltham had stopped by his cabin on the first morning and murmured that everyone at that table had bought their tickets in the last few days before the voyage, and he had showed him the piece in the *Bombay Herald*, and the news in the other paper of the *Medea*'s fire. "It cannot be a coincidence, sir," he had said. "I would caution you to be careful with the Kohinoor."

Mackeson had stared at him, bemused. So much for Lord Dalhousie's immense secrecy and all that plotting to take the Kohinoor out of the Punjab.

"Perhaps," Captain Waltham suggested, hesitantly, "you could turn it over to me and I will place a guard around it. I could not, sir, guarantee its safety if I don't have charge of it. And I think you're seated at a table, all of whose occupants know of the diamond traveling with you."

"My dear Captain Waltham," Mackeson had said softly, "you know nothing for certain, except for your instructions. Whatever . . . needs to be taken safely to England, it is left in *my* charge. *I* am the one to guarantee its safe arrival. But, we talk too much, and the walls are miserably thin. I suggest that you do not come to visit me again; it will cause too much chatter, raise too many questions."

"As you wish." Captain Waltham had given him a short bow. But he had lingered on. "I must tell you, though I don't see how this can have any bearing on . . . ah . . . the matter at hand, but the mail in the hold was ransacked a few nights ago. The boxes were broken open, the letters strewn around—it has never happened before."

"Which ones?" Mackeson had asked. "The Falmouth boxes?"

"Yes. How did you know?"

Because it had been a green box Mackeson had taken into the after hold when the mail guard had bumped into him and fallen down. "Is anything missing?"

"There's no way of telling, sir. The mail comes onboard sealed and locked—we are never sure of the contents."

Now Colonel Mackeson sat at his dinner table and looked around at his companions. One of them was a thief. The Booths, brother and sister, were there. A young stripling called Martyn Wingate, who would not say what his business was, or why he was going to England. He had been born in Bombay, had lived there all of his life, and into his English slipped the guttural sounds of Hindustani every now and then. Lady Anne Beaumont, Mackeson knew well, and had heard of for many years, although he hadn't met her yet. But she was the local nuisance, wealthy, uncaring of proprieties, living among the natives like one of them, traveling about the countryside without a male escort—an English one that is. And yet, when she came to one of the capitals of the presidencies, she was accorded all the privileges of her rank, and entered the drawing rooms clad in lush silks and damasks that had somehow survived her travels. She was wearing one of her silks this evening, in pale green, trimmed with velvet, and around her neck glowed a string of tiny emeralds, with one stone as a pendant of a shocking size. "From the Maharajah of Jagatpur," she had said carelessly. "He was such a splendid little man, with a palace full of jewels."

Mr. Huthwaite sat back in his chair—his girth would not allow him to come any closer to the table—and smirked at everyone constantly, his collar tucked under his thick neck. His talk was, as was to be expected, pious and unrestrained, full of Major this and Captain that, and Colonel this, who had contributed to his church-building fund, and of the natives who listened goggle-eyed to the word of God. He also drank too much.

The dinners aboard the *Indus* were abundant. Soups

made the same morning, boiling in the great big cauldrons of the belowdecks kitchens—oxtail, shrimp and cinnamon, duck with chillied walnuts. This was followed by a salad of some sort, and they had been long enough at sea that the chickpea and smoked fish salad stuffed into tomato halves had given way to various bits of unidentifiable vegetables trapped in trembling aspic. A whole roast pig was brought in on most nights and carved at a large "sideboard," which was the top of the grand piano. The pig had been slaughtered just the previous night, and the meat was fresh and tender. There was curry to follow—braised quail, or duck served with a shikari sauce, which was the sauce of game hunters in India made of claret, wild mushrooms, black and cayenne peppers, and catsup. Or a proper duck curry with cardamom and cloves ground into ginger and garlic and fried in *ghee*. The desserts evanesced on the tongue, and all, invariably, were forms of pudding. The Madras Club pudding was a mixture of sponge cake with rum, raisins, suet, bread crumbs, and honey boiled in a mold and served with a Madeira sauce. The rice and sago pudding had whipped egg whites to make it fluffy. Canned fruit was served with pats of coconut pudding.

And every course came with its own liquor. Pale ale at the beginning of the meal with the soup. Champagne with the salad. Wine with the pork. Madeira with the curry. Port and sherry with the dessert, and coffee, at the end, laced with whiskey.

Mr. Huthwaite drank it all; his glass was never empty.

The eighth person at the table was a young woman with five children, Arabella-Catherine Hyde. Her quarters were in first class. Her children were in second class with their governess, a tired girl of nineteen who had come to India only to find her betrothed dead of cholera, and who had to return home to England because in the meantime her father had died and her mother had forbidden her to bind herself to any other man in India. This—working for Mrs. Hyde—was the only way she could pay for her passage.

Arabella Hyde was pretty, vapid, her head as empty as her whole being seemed to be. On the first night, Lady Beaumont had leaned over to Colonel Mackeson with the story that "the Hyde woman had to leave India, ran away with another chap, you know, the quartermaster of all people, and came back to her husband. He's shipping her home to England. It's a *divorce*."

Captain Ramsay, also at the meals, was surprisingly quiet and watchful. He was taking his responsibilities seriously, Mackeson thought with some amusement. They had come up with a system for safeguarding the Kohinoor, especially during bathtimes. All the first-class male passengers were called at the same time, so Mackeson went up to the deck in his long underwear, a towel wrapped around his middle, and stood on the portside grating while a crewman doused him with buckets of salt water he had pulled out of the Arabian Sea. A quick rubdown with his towel, and he was back again in his cabin, where Multan Raj waited patiently, his clothes laid out on the berth. Captain Ramsay sat on the Kohinoor diamond meanwhile and also waited for him to return. Mackeson put the diamond into his steamer trunk, locked it, and hung the key around his neck while bathing, and left Lord Dalhousie's nephew sitting on top of the box with the strict injunction that he was not to get up even for a second.

When Multan Raj had dressed him, pulled on his socks and shoes, and left the cabin for his own quarters belowdecks, Mackeson unlocked his trunk and took out the Kohinoor, put it back in the bag, and hooked it onto his belt again. At night, he slept with the pouch looped around his wrist, a pistol under his pillow.

Once, he had asked Multan Raj what he thought of the voyage.

"The ship rattles more belowdecks, Sahib. I fall often out

of my hammock at night," he had said. Then, concerned, "I do not mean to complain."

Colonel Mackeson looked at him affectionately. His old bearer had disappeared one day in Lahore, into the dust, never heard of again. And Multan Raj had come to him, specially recommended by Lord Dalhousie, who knew of, or knew someone whom Multan's relative had served. That had been three years ago. Multan was Hindu, not Sikh, and could have had no allegiance to the court of the old Maharajah Ranjit Singh, else Mackeson might have been hesitant to . . . take him along on this journey.

"Are you looking forward to being in England?" he asked.

"Will you be there long, Sahib?"

"I don't think so," Colonel Mackeson said, buffing the buttons on his shirt with a muslin cloth. Soon, Multan was standing in front of him, performing that duty. "I could not live anywhere other than India, Multan."

The servant's hand stopped and then went on, slowly. "You will go back then, Sahib."

"Yes, I will," Mackeson replied.

All of the servants stood behind their masters or mistresses during the meal in the saloon of the *Indus*—just as they did in India. The waiters whisked in and out, between the chairs and the attendants, served the dishes, and left. The rest was done by each personal table servant. In India, there had been different staff for each duty, including accompanying the master and his wife to dinners at other homes. Here, on the *Indus*, the P & O had restricted servants to one per person, and so Multan Raj stood behind Mackeson's chair during dinner, filled his glass when he wanted, took his plate away before the waiter could come.

The dinner was cleared eventually, coffee brought in; there was lemonade for the ladies if they wanted. The saloon crew moved the tables to the edges of the room and rolled the grand piano to the center. A few ladies sat down to play, some couples danced, slip-sliding on the polished wooden floor; the servants stood with their backs to the walls, watching, waiting to be called upon.

Colonel Mackeson leaned back and lit a cigarette. He was tired; it had been a long, hot day. He had come to the realization that he didn't want to go to England, and so, he couldn't get to England fast enough. And the Kohinoor, now that everyone seemed to know of it, was a bigger burden than he had expected. Perhaps, he thought, he ought to ask for a guard of some sort from Captain Waltham, but where to put the jewel, how to safeguard it unless he was there all the time? It was difficult to maintain the sort of vigilance Lord Dalhousie expected, and perhaps would have been equal to with his ceaseless energy, and his conviction that the Kohinoor belonged to the Queen. Colonel Mackeson did not quite believe in that; oh, he did, in the English part of his heart, but not in the, much larger, Indian one.

Just then, turning her glittering gaze upon him, Arabella Hyde tilted her well-shaped head and said, "Oh, Colonel Mackeson, all this stealth is *so* very exciting. But are you going to let us go our own way without even a *little* glimpse of the Kohinoor?"

Mackeson drew smoke in the wrong way, coughed, and said, "I beg your pardon. I don't know what you're talking about."

The others at the table had turned to look at him intently, speculation in every eye. Mary Booth had a faint, grim smile upon her face; her brother looked like a bloodhound that had just scented prey on the breeze, all quivering attention. Mr. Huthwaite was not smiling anymore; he had his hands upon the table, and Mackeson had not noticed before how gross and large they were, like the paws of an unruly bear. How did he turn the pages of the Bible when he read out of it every Sunday? Martyn Wingate had surreptitiously brought out a little notebook and was making scrawls across the page, ink splattering over the table's white linen.

Ramsay rose. "It's time for bed, I think. For me, at least. Colonel, a nightcap at my berth?"

"Yes, of course." Colonel Mackeson got up hurriedly.

Lady Beaumont, who had been watching and listening, smoke twirling out of her fist, spat out a piece of tobacco and said, "Why all the playacting, Mackeson? Show us the diamond, and we'll let you be."

At that moment, Colonel Mackeson felt something slip down along his thigh and come to a soft, tinkling rest on the floor, on the inside of his right boot. He glanced down, and the Kohinoor diamond lay there, half under the folds of the tablecloth, half in the light, worth a fortune in the world in which he lived. He froze. The cloth bag had come undone somehow. He could have put his foot on the stone to cover it, but Indian superstition was so ingrained in him, he could not step upon something that was revered and that gave life—a book, paper money, coins, food, a diamond.

He took a deep breath and bent down. Someone kicked his ailing knee, hard, and he went crashing onto the floor, a film of pain blurring his gaze. Everyone at the table rose and came rushing up. There were offers of help, arms appeared to raise him, and he found himself sitting in his chair, bent over in excruciating pain. He could feel the skin on his gouty knee expand and surge. Colonel Mackeson looked around desperately, tried to tell Ramsay to search for the Kohinoor, but the young captain's face swam out of focus in front of his eyes.

He fainted.

The vans were lined up for the passengers when the SS *Indus* put to port outside of Suez. A message had been sent from

Alexandria that the SS *Oriental* had already arrived and was waiting on the Mediterranean for the passengers from India, so the travelers disembarked with a small carpetbag each for the next three days of travel and sent all the rest of their luggage on the procession of camels, some two thousand of them, that waited in patient lines, their jaws moving rhythmically.

The vans were small wagons, two spoked wheels on either side, curved covers to shelter them from the Egyptian sun, open at the back and in the front, where the driver sat, whipping his team of four horses. Each van could seat a maximum of eight passengers, and Colonel Mackeson insisted that all the people at his table occupy the same vehicle. He supervised their boarding, then climbed in and seated himself knee to knee alongside Lady Beaumont. The driver clicked his tongue, the horses roused themselves, the wheels ground into the soft earth, and they began the journey across the desert to Cairo.

Darkness had just begun to fall when they left, and Colonel Mackeson lit the small oil lantern in the van and hung it on the rafters of the roof. It was hot inside, without even the hum of a draft, and the roving light lit all of their faces one by one.

For four hours, they traveled without a word. The movement of the wagon, the jolts and bumps along the rough road, the poor glow from the lantern, made reading or embroidery impossible. The men smoked in silence, throwing live butts out into the desert, where they were quickly extinguished by the wheels of the van that followed. The women sat, for the most part, with their hands folded in their laps. They had three canteens of water until the first stop, which was nothing more than a shack along the road, with water and bathroom facilities out under the night sky. When one of them drank, the others watched carefully, making sure that not a drop of their share was spilled in this parched land.

Finally, almost casually, Colonel Mackeson said, his hands on his knees, his gaze fixed upon the floor of the van, "Which one of you stole the Kohinoor?"

All the silence disintegrated into a babble of voices. He let it go on for a while and then held up his hand, palm outward. His voice was deliberate and cutting. "One of you, maybe more than one of you, is a thief."

Mackeson had jumped out of his bed on the night of his faint, before dawn, and gone searching for Captain Ramsay. He had jiggled him awake and told him of the loss of the diamond. Then, the two of them had rushed to Captain Waltham.

"What do you want me to do, sir?" the captain had asked, struggling into his trousers, tucking his nightshirt into the waistband.

Mackeson, white in the face, from both the pain and the shock, had said curtly, "Get them all out of bed and into the saloon. Their cabins and belongings are to be searched. Has anyone had a chance to go to the after hold?"

Waltham had shaken his head. "Between last night and now? I doubt it. This morning is one of the scheduled times, though, when the passengers can access their luggage. We're to dock at Aden in a few hours."

"Find out, will you?"

So the Booths, Lady Beaumont, Wingate, Arabella Hyde, and Huthwaite had been shaken out of their dreams and ushered into the state dining room, protesting wildly all the while. One of the female crew members, the second-class cabin *ayah*, had been dispatched to search the women thoroughly. Mackeson had made the men strip down in front of him. They'd all cursed him, but he had been immovable. He'd searched every body cavity himself. He had made them open their mouths, bend over in front of him.

Then, Ramsay and he had hunted through the cabins, the berths, agitated the bed linens, crawled under the desks and moved the sofas, unfolded every garment. He had asked Multan Raj for a knife and when it was brought looked at it in a brief moment of surprise. It was a dagger, some eight inches long, its hilt decorated in finely wrought stones embedded in solid gold.

"Where did you get this?"

"It's my father's, Sahib," Multan Raj had said. "A gift from a king; he saved his life with this dagger one night when dacoits came into the raja's tent."

Shaking his head in wonder, Mackeson had slit the silk and cotton linings of all the luggage boxes and ripped them apart. At the end, an hour before breakfast, when the other passengers were already astir aboard the *Indus,* and the six people waited, shut away in the saloon, there had been no sign of the Kohinoor.

It had disappeared into the air. Literally. There was no place Mackeson had missed, no earthly place. Unless one of them had swallowed the diamond, and it was cutting up the insides of his or her stomach. When that thought struck, Mackeson had decided that they were each to be followed to the privies, night and day, watched as they went about their business. He'd examined the contents of the bowels himself, unflinching.

And so they had all come to Suez. Everyone's nerves were ragged by now—tattered to beyond bearing.

"Mr. Booth," Mackeson said. He noticed that Ramsay had his pistol out on his lap, his fingers loosely curled around the trigger.

"What is it?" In a snarl. Tom Booth was afraid; all the blood had drained from his face, his thick eyebrows and hair stood out stark against the pallor of his skin. His knuckles, tied around each other, were knobs of bone.

"I found the Ganesha idol, and it is on its way back on the *Indus* to Calcutta and the rightful owner, the East India Company. The accusations were not false after all, were they, Miss Booth?" This last Mackeson said bitterly.

She raised her eyebrows at him, still cool, even though they were all jostled about by the movement of the van. The dirt road on which they traveled had been stamped down by many such passings, but the mud was still soft, the horses' hooves inaudible. "They might not have been, Colonel Mackeson," she said, "but that's none of your business. You're hardly in a position to send the idol back. It doesn't belong to you."

"And neither does it belong to you," Mackeson said harshly. "There were other things also; I'm sure you tapped everything you could from the auction house that had not yet been cataloged, or you thought was of small value. But tiny as this idol is, given its provenance, it's worth at least three thousand pounds. So, it goes back, and you get to keep your letter knives and silver shaving kits, snuffboxes and decorative mirrors."

Mary Booth's mouth drew back, and a hiss escaped her teeth. She did not look at her brother, and he unwound his fingers to run them through his hair and wipe a sudden perspiration from his forehead. Neither of them had known the value of the idol, Mackeson realized, or they would have tried to hide it a little better, perhaps packing it in the luggage in the after hold. He hadn't bothered to search the stowed luggage—Captain Waltham had assured him that it had not been disturbed during the night—they could have had no chance to conceal the Kohinoor. And they were only, after all, petty thieves. The temptation to steal the diamond was huge, but there was no way they could dispose of it, and if they could not realize its value in something useful—pounds sterling—it would be just a piece of stone to them.

"And what did you discover about me, Colonel Mackeson?" Lady Beaumont drawled from her corner. She had been smoking steadily all through, lighting each cigarette with the end of the last. She had her legs spread out in front of her, crossed at the ankles, uncaring that Mr. Huthwaite, seated opposite, barely had any space to put his own limbs. "Did you enjoy running your dirty fingers through my underwear; put your face to the lace of my petticoats?"

"Not particularly," Mackeson said mildly, and she flushed, red to the roots of her white hair. In the past few days, the lines on her face had become more deeply grooved, embedded into her flesh, and dark half-moons pulled her eyes downward at the edges. It was not a pretty sight. "But," Mackeson continued, "it is not every day, as you say, that an officer has the opportunity of rummaging through a titled lady's drawers, and I did find some very interesting things. Gifts, did you call them?" He put up his hand and began ticking off on his fingers. "The *sarpech* ornament from the Raja of Sitarnagar; the ruby that adorned the wife of the Raja of Palampore; the thumb ring from Emperor Jahangir's rule in the seventeenth century, which belonged to the Gujarati merchant in Bombay—I hear you stayed at his house for a while and that he was indeed very hospitable. All these were reported missing by their owners. There was also a gold brooch with a picture of our Queen; it usually lies inside a glass-topped table in the Marble Hall in Government House in Calcutta. Four native servants were charged with its theft."

Lady Beaumont spat on the floor. "They're mine; you can do nothing about this. I'm not"—she inclined her head contemptuously at the Booths, seated opposite—"*them*, nothing, nobodies. You might be able to peremptorily send back what they stole. But *I* did not steal; these were all given to me."

"The SS *Indus* will leave tomorrow from Suez on her journey back to Bombay, and she will carry all these items with her. You must take care, Lady Beaumont, not to leave such a dismal impression of the Englishwoman in India—and not just to the natives, but to the Company and the men in the Civil Service. Gifts are things that are given by someone, not taken from them without their knowledge or permission."

"You fool!" Lady Beaumont launched herself across the van and fell on Mackeson, pummeling him, kicking at his knee. When he felt that first kick, he knew that she had been the one—it was the same boot, that same intensity—who had kicked him in the state dining room and then dived to the floor. The others in the wagon did not move but sat still, watching as Lady Beaumont's petticoats rose and showed a glimpse of her lace drawers. Captain Ramsay stayed where he was also, still holding the gun, a bleak smile on his face. Mackeson struggled with the woman, and finally managed to run his arms around her flailing body. He dragged her to her seat and pushed her down. He went back to his own seat, slouching—the roof was curved tightly around the frame of the wagon and standing upright was impossible—hit his head against the lantern, and collapsed between Huthwaite and Wingate. A series of aches blossomed up his leg—she had managed to kick him every-where other than his knee, and this he could manage.

"Don't move from there, Lady Beaumont," he said starkly. "You can count yourself lucky that I didn't put you in the brig on the *Indus*."

She clicked her tongue at him. "It doesn't have a brig, and even if it did, you couldn't imprison me. I'm going to have a word with the Prime Minister when I return, maybe even her Majesty."

"You do that," Mackeson said. "And I will explain my part."

He knew that she would not dare to complain. Mackeson had only realized that these unsavory rumors had followed Lady Beaumont all around India when he opened her box. Every piece was frighteningly expensive, and small, and the losses had customarily been blamed on the servants—some of long and honorable tenures with their masters—but doubt had also, always, been cast upon Lady Beaumont. For she had descended upon obscure kings and nobles living outside the periphery of British interest, or sometimes even knowledge, because they had been known to possess this or that magnificent piece of jewelry, priceless and irreplaceable. And invariably, after supping with them, riding their horses, visiting their *zenanas,* patting their children on the head, Lady Beaumont had left with their treasures.

"I say," Martyn Wingate squeaked, "I didn't take your damn Kohinoor. And there are no skeletons in my *almirah.*" He laughed, an unpleasant, whining sound.

Of all of Mackeson's and Ramsay's tablemates, this boy was the only one who had been truly terrified by the events of the past few days. He had recognized that this was no joke, that the Kohinoor had to be found, that its loss had enormous consequences, and that if it were never discovered, suspicion would fall upon all of them for the rest of their lives. And his had barely begun.

Mackeson had found a few half-finished love letters in Wingate's box, badly written, without sentiment, just barely on this side of illiteracy. The girl was half-Indian; Wingate promised her love, but not money, not marriage. He had no intention of besmirching his own bloodline. Or letting his father know about this affair. Mackeson had read the letters with distaste, only because he'd had to. If there was one person among this sleazy lot who would return the Kohinoor to him, it was this boy, Mackeson thought. He would have taken it unthinkingly, and then not known what to do with it, and would try to slip it back into Mackeson's luggage at some further date.

"Your father is the publisher of the *Bombay Herald,*" Mackeson said softly, "and I know you're here to follow the Kohinoor to England, but you will never write about this, or talk of it to anyone."

Wingate bridled, the spots on his face blooming red. "I say—"

"Is that clear?"

"Perfectly," Wingate said, gulping, "sir."

"I hope," a pious voice said at Mackeson's elbow, "that

you will not cast your eye upon me, Colonel Mackeson. I am a man of God. I could hardly . . . Well, who will look after the poor natives at Cawnpore?"

Mr. Huthwaite's luggage had revealed, surprisingly, a sack full of banknotes which had added up to some five thousand pounds. That he too had stolen this somehow, Mackeson didn't doubt, perhaps skimming church funds or donations. And so, he too was a suspect, although Mackeson could not see how a provincial clergyman in India—or as he had been, a provincial lad in England—could possibly sell the Kohinoor. Somewhere, he too had gone wrong, despite his Cambridge education, his position as Second Wrangler, the honors heaped upon him because of his merits. In the end, the inducement to steal had been too much for him. So why not then take the Kohinoor?

The only person in the van who had not spoken yet was Arabella Hyde. She had had a box full of love letters also, and the complaints in them from her lover showed her to be self-ish, demanding, fickle. She had some pieces of jewelry that weren't of much value, and underclothing that was tattered and much darned, belying her aura of wealth. Mrs. Arabella Hyde was going back to England, and she would never again return to India—her husband would not have her. If she had indeed bought a passage to England on the *Indus* in the last few days before departure, it was only because she wanted a glimpse of the Kohinoor. Nothing more. She was the one who had asked him about the diamond at the table.

The Arabella Hydes of this world would always live in half-finished ambitions—an affair would have been jolly good fun, so she had one and didn't think of the conse-quences; a look at the Kohinoor would have been the mak-ing of her in the village to which she was returning, so she'd booked a ticket. It wouldn't strike the empty Arabella that she could actually steal the diamond—her brain was small, her belief in her abilities even smaller.

The van stopped at the midway point, eight hours into the journey, and Mackeson stepped out beyond the shack into the warm desert night. A pale moon, two days from fullness, hung in the sky, bleaching the flat land, creating dense shadows of the few sparse trees and the boulders strewn around. When they reached Alexandria, the moon would be full.

Since the day when he had discovered the Kohinoor stolen, Mackeson and Ramsay had sat alone in the saloon at mealtimes, grim and quiet, away from their fellow travelers. The ship and its passengers had been searched, every cabin, berth, desk, and box. But the diamond was not to be found. At Aden, where the *Indus* docked to take on coal, Mackeson had not allowed the six of them to disembark, even though the coaling had taken seven long hours. At Alexandria, he intended to have them followed into every bazaar and every souk. He did not allow himself the luxury of wondering what would happen if he landed in England without the Kohinoor. Self-pity had never been one of Mackeson's strong traits.

Besides, he already had a notion about who it could be.

And so they reached Cairo, and from there, at midday, a few hours after they had climbed out, weary and bone-tired from the van, they boarded the barges that would take them up the Nile. The barges were towed by horses on the banks of the river—the steamer tug being out of commission—and this took them finally to the Mahmoudieh Canal, which cut its way from the Nile to Alexandria.

Some two days after the *Indus* had docked in the Suez, the passengers bound for England straggled into Alexandria, and settled into L'Hotel d'Europe, in the Frank quarter of town, to await the boarding of their luggage on the SS *Oriental*. The mail boxes had been delayed, since the camel convoy had broken down in the desert. So the travelers had an extra day in Alexandria before the ship sailed to Southampton.

Night fell on the city, and a large moon rose and washed the skies with its hoary glow, blotting out the stars, painting deep and dark oblongs where its radiance did not touch. Golden lights sprang around Alexandria's semicircular harbor, and at one end, in the old, dilapidated lighthouse, the aged keeper doggedly lit his lamp. There was a newer lighthouse on Eunostus Point, one that approaching ships used to get their bearings and skirt around the border of land, but this older one had a history that went back many centuries, all the way to the occupation of Alexander the Great.

At Rey's, more formally the L'Hotel d'Europe, the passengers from the *Indus* slept in their rooms, knowing they would be awakened before the first glimmer of dawn to find their way through the darkened streets to the harbor and, from there, onto the SS *Oriental*. The hotel was at the end of a large street. It was built around a central courtyard, with a verandah running along the bottom and the top floors into which all the doors of the rooms opened.

As the moon climbed into the heavens, its face was blotted by a few stray clouds, like a veil drawn over a woman's pearl-like face. It sent its silver rays down on the city, over the flat rooftops, and into the room where a man sat in the darkness against a wall, just out of reach of the glimmering light.

Colonel Mackeson glanced over at the bed, jammed into one corner in the shadows. The rounded curves of the pillow made a very satisfactory image of a man sleeping. He did not smoke, although he yearned desperately for a cigarette. He had been sitting, and waiting, for three hours now, as the noises in the city quieted down, as doors slammed in the hotel, as the lamps in the courtyard were doused and carried away to be cleaned.

The door to his room opened so gently that he would not have heard it if he hadn't been listening for it. A man came in, his bare feet making no noise on the thick rugs that covered the floor from wall to wall. Mackeson did not look up; he knew who it was and why he was here. With his gaze still fixed on his hands in his lap, Mackeson heard the small creak of hinges as his box was opened, a rustle when his clothing was moved, and a little thud when the lid was shut again and the latch locked.

The man at the box then glanced toward the bed and turned slowly around, looking into each corner of the room. He found Mackeson, came up to him, and sat down on his haunches.

Mackeson now pulled his cigarettes from the pocket of his shirt and offered one to the man, his hand moving out of the dark into the square of moonlight streaming in through the window.

The man grunted, took a deep breath, and moved his own callused hand to accept the cigarette. When Mackeson lit the match and carried it to the man's face, he saw that it was calm, his movements unhurried as he bent to accept the light, his eyes closed when he took that first drag.

"Why did you do it, Multan Raj?" Mackeson asked quietly.

"Can I tell you a story, Sahib? A short one, indulge me." Multan Raj's voice was suddenly hoarse, as though he spoke in great pain, the words tumbling out in a rush.

"I have all the time in the world now."

"Many years ago, a man left his fields outside of Lahore and went to seek employment in the court of a great king, the Maharajah Ranjit Singh. For a long time he worked in the basest jobs, unworthy of his caste, but he did not mind, since they brought him into the service of a king who was a lion, a warrior, a just sovereign. Even the smallest job—like cleaning out the privies in the fort—was a pleasure to this man. And then, a few months later, the Maharajah went on campaign to Peshawar and this man was taken along as part of the entourage." Multan Raj stopped, put the cigarette to his mouth, and took in a lungful of smoke, which set him coughing. He coughed lightly, in short bursts, allowing his frame to shake as little as possible. "I'm sorry, Sahib, there's so little strength in these cigarettes of yours."

When Multan lowered his hand, Mackeson noticed that it was trembling, the glow from the butt skittering around in a small circle. "One night, while the Maharajah slept in his simple white tent, this man saw some hooligans sneak in under the flap. The sentries were all asleep, and these men were crafty and silent in their movements. He slithered in from the back himself and saw one of the men with his arm raised above Maharajah Ranjit Singh's bed; in his hand he held a long, curved sword. The man leapt at the nearby table, found a dagger, unsheathed it, and threw it across the tent, where it plunged into the murderer's heart. His dying cry woke the Maharajah and his sentries, and very soon all the other men had been captured and taken away. They were put to death outside the tent, immediately, with no trial, no attempt at mercy. The Maharajah had the dagger pulled out of the man's heart, and he handed it, still bloodied, to the man who had saved his life."

"Your father," Mackeson said. "When I saw that dagger I recognized it as something that could only have come out of Maharajah Ranjit Singh's Toshakhana. The imperial treasury had another one like it, a twin."

"True," Multan Raj said in a low, rumbling voice. He seemed to be having trouble speaking, as though his tongue had grown too big for his mouth. "The Maharajah was a just and kind man, and he asked my father what fascinated him most, what he would most like to do with his life, and my father replied that he wanted to be state treasurer one day. The Maharajah asked him if he knew the value of the dagger in his hand, from which blood still dripped onto the carpets. My father looked down upon it and said that he did not, how could he—he was just a poor peasant farmer. The very next day, Maharajah Ranjit Singh sent my father to the court jewelers, for them to teach him their trade, the valuing of stones, the setting of them, the melting of gold, the forming of it. Everything they knew. Then, after he had learned all he could, he was sent to work as a clerk in the Maharajah's Toshakhana, and very soon a day came when—"

"When he became treasurer of the vast wealth of the Maharajah Ranjit Singh," Mackeson finished for him. He turned to the man next to him. "You are the son of Misr Makraj."

Multan Raj nodded. "I am, Sahib."

And so Multan Raj had sought a job as his personal bearer, Mackeson thought; his other man had not disappeared into the Lahore night—he had been made to disappear so that a vacancy would occur. Multan Raj had come into Mackeson's employ three years ago, before the Second Sikh War, but even that early, the servants of Maharajah Ranjit Singh had known that their empire was shattered, and that the British would take over their lands. The whole thing had been a plan, in readiness just for the moment when Lord Dalhousie proclaimed in Lahore that he would send the Kohinoor to England.

"Why did you return the diamond, then? You could have gone away. I suspected . . . but didn't realize fully until just yesterday, in Cairo. You could have taken the Kohinoor back with you to the Punjab."

Multan Raj grunted again; this time it was meant to be a small laugh. "And left you with the burden of explaining where the diamond was, and how you lost it to your own servant, Sahib? A man you have trusted for three years? That . . . would not have been right. My father, who had custody of the immense treasury, never once thought of dipping his hand into it; he was upright and honest, loyal to the king, for whom he had love, and respect. He taught me no less."

In the years that Multan Raj had attended to him, Mackeson had also felt affection for the man, so quiet, so steadily intent upon serving his master, so careful of his needs. But he had really not paid too much attention beyond once asking him if he minded crossing the black waters and going to England with him. He had not thought of how sophisticated this man was, he who had said he was a farmer's son. Or how patient he had been, infiltrating Mackeson's household well in advance, not knowing when he would be needed.

But . . . something was awry here.

"Multan," he said, "you're sitting in my presence; I've never seen you do this before." He had meant this to be a joke, an amusement for both of them. Mackeson had no intention of persecuting Multan Raj, nor even telling Captain Ramsay of how he had gotten the diamond back—the incident was over, finished, brought to an end. He would travel to England with the stone, be rid of it finally, and return to his regiment in India as though this had never happened. And, in making the joke, he meant to say all of this to Multan Raj without actually voicing the words.

Colonel Mackeson rose and stepped into the light of the moon. "Come, man, stand up!"

Multan Raj put his hands out in front of him and rose awkwardly, his hands on his knees, on his thighs, embraced tightly around his waist as he straightened, half bent over. Shivers racked his thin frame as he moved into the light to stand beside Mackeson. When he unclasped his hand and held it out to his master, Mackeson saw that the dagger was held loosely in his fingers, and there was blood trickling from it.

His gaze went to the front of Multan Raj's *dhoti* and *kurta*, and there, about level with his stomach, was the black smear of blood, spreading outward. Multan Raj had stabbed himself as he sat down beside Mackeson and had talked all the while that he had been slowly dying.

Multan Raj folded his hands together in a *namaste* to his master, bowed his head, and then crashed onto the floor.

Colonel Mackeson cremated his servant's remains the next day, by the old lighthouse, having received special permission to do so. The still-warm ashes he cast upon the waters of the Mediterranean, and wished that he was on the southern side of Egypt, so that at least the waters of the Red Sea would link Multan Raj more directly to the land of his birth.

Then, he went aboard the SS *Oriental*. A few weeks later, the *Oriental* docked at Southampton, and two days after that, Colonel Mackeson presented the Kohinoor to the Court of Directors of the East India Company. They invited him to accompany them to Buckingham Palace to present the diamond to the Queen.

He declined, saying he had to return to India as soon as he could. The SS *Oriental* would leave for Alexandria in a few short days.

Diary of a Maharajah

May 1854
Four years later

> *L——'s [Login's] talk to you about the Koh-i-noor being
> a present from Duleep to the Queen is arrant humbug. He
> knew as well as I did that it was nothing of the sort; and
> if I had been within a thousand miles of him he would not
> have dared to utter such a piece of trickery. Those "beautiful
> eyes," with which Duleep has taken captive the court, are his
> mother's eyes, those with which she captivated and controlled
> the old Lion of the Punjab.*

—J. G. A. Baird, ed., *Private Letters of
the Marquess of Dalhousie*

Paris, 1893: He gropes with the catch of the grungy window,
his fingers bloated with dropsy. When the latch gives way,
he pushes open the panes, leans over, and breathes deeply
into the cool spring air. It's a few minutes before dawn, but
the street below is abustle with carts and horses, the cries of
the cheese seller, the newspaper boy hawking his wares in

the semidark. A glitter of copper as a *sou* exchanges hands. A vivid spot of purple from the flower seller's basket.

Sophia comes in. In her arms she cradles two spears of baguettes, a wheel of cheese, a pat of butter, a bunch of hyacinths from the woman below.

"Papa." Her smooth cheek touches his; the felt on her hat is cool on his skin; she smells of the morning.

She bustles around, lays the table with two white plates, a fork and a knife, a cup and a saucer on a shimmering veil embroidered with *zari* that once belonged to his mother; now it's a tablecloth.

Bamba Sophia Jindan, his oldest daughter, lights the lamp under the small stove, sets water to boil, makes his tea the way he likes it—with a crushed stick of cinnamon, no milk, a sprinkling of sugar. She stirs the coals in the fireplace; they're all almost ashes, but she coaxes some warmth from them.

They sit by the window in the light of the sun. Sophia breaks golden crusts from the bread, hacks at the cheese and lays a quivering slice on his plate, butters the still-warm bread. The soft inside of the bread holds the imprints of her fingers.

"Read to me, child," he says.

The room comes at eight hundred francs a year, on the sixth floor of a house on rue de la Trémoille, in a neighborhood that is of a fading nobility. Once, he paid that much for a night at a hotel in Paris, in London . . . anywhere in the world. This is an artist's loft, and the walls are scrawled with sketches and paintings, imposed one upon another. He has looked at them for hours, forcing his gaze to blur and soften, to sharpen, to bring into focus one scene, or another. On the mantelpiece are stacks of books, spines forward, brushed with soot from the fire below. Sophia runs her fingers over them and picks out one slender volume. The leather is old, burnished red, frayed and pitted, its gold embossing dulled.

"This one," she says, flipping open the cover.

In her father's hand are the words "My very first trip to England—this is the diary of a Maharajah."

He feels his heart stop, start again and gallop in his chest. He pushes his chair back from the table and it hits the windowsill. The jolt runs down his back. Why not? he thinks. His children have known him only as the man who pushes his bulk against the British Empire, the Crown, the Queen.

"I've never heard you speak," she says slowly, "of that time." So much has happened since. Who were you then, Papa?

"You will now, my dear."

"How old were you, Papa? When you wrote in this diary?"

"Sixteen."

Sophia is twenty-four. She knows how young sixteen can be.

She sits across the table. He lets his bearded chin rest on his chest. A man plays his violin on the street corner, and people throw *sous* into his case. But he hears only his daughter's voice, young and strong, carefully articulated.

May 19, 1854: Oh, England! My first glimpse of this scepter'd isle, this other Eden, this blessed plot, is as the SS *Liverpool* trundles toward the dock. A low band of mist curls over the water and threads through the trees. It is dim, it is gray; but it is, finally, after all these years of wanting, England!

The long arm of the pier is dotted with gaslights—each rimmed in spray, suspended midair, seemingly without support. There's no one else on the deck except for the crew, heavy-footed on the boards, shouting unintelligibly. The *Liverpool* calls out in a short, clean blast from the foghorn that cuts away into the thick beyond. The ship's engines strain and groan as she brakes to a crawl. On the pier, a man waves his lantern in a slow circle. There's a sharp bump, and I feel a frisson of vibration through my fingers resting on the deck railing.

Ropes of all sizes spiral out—from the *Liverpool*, from below; one comes snaking through the air and lies at my feet in a glistening, frayed heap, stinking faintly of the ocean, seaweed, fish, putrefied flesh.

A sailor, the stripes on his hat a gleaming white, his face a smudge, sticks an elbow in my direction. "Yer gotta move, Maharajah Dew-leep Sing."

If he speaks English, I barely understand what he says. This is not the language I began learning eight years ago from Henry Lawrence in Lahore. And, he's mispronounced my name. As usual.

"*Da*-lip Singh," I say, but my voice is overpowered by another hoot from the *Liverpool*'s horn. The man cups a palm behind his ear and grins. He winds the rope around a hook on the deck, gives it a final tug, bares his teeth, and disappears in a thump of footsteps. The *Liverpool* is at rest, though her engines still murmur. The paddle wheels drip water.

It has been only six weeks since we left Calcutta. The deepest waters I had seen before were those of the Ravi River at Lahore, and now I have traversed the Bay of Bengal, the Indian Ocean, the Arabian Sea, the Mediterranean, and the English Channel.

I'm a long way from home, a long distance from the life I was to have. I am, finally, in the land where the Kohinoor is. It used to be mine. Once. No longer. It is now the Queen's diamond.

There's a man on the pier below, chewing on a pipe; his white beard is speckled with dew, his chin is at a pugnacious tilt. He doesn't like me? Why? Bah, what do I care?

In a few days, he will still be here, and I will be meeting his Queen at Buckingham Palace. His Queen. And, now mine.

Back to bed, before my guardians awake and find me gone.

Later: They shovel all of the *Liverpool*'s passengers onto the pier—all except us—riding down the gangplank in a joyous anticipation of home. My baggage has already descended, whisked through customs by the favor of Sir Charles Trevelyan at the Treasury. Dr. Login has requested that I be granted the same privilege accorded to other royal visitors. Some of the travelers flutter their handkerchiefs at us with promises to visit, but Mrs. Login, by my side, murmurs, "These shipboard friendships are not to be considered lasting, Maharajah. We must pick and choose—there is too much familiarity on deck which will not bear scrutiny on land."

At long last, around midday, as a fragile May sun sheds a golden twilight glow over the *Liverpool*, we too are ready to depart. But, what's this? Where's the reception committee? Am I not the Maharajah of the Punjab? Am I to walk down the lengthy pier on my own?

I stumble down first, followed by Dr. and Mrs. Login and the rest of my entourage. I wear my altered robes of state— my silk trousers of an English style, though embroidered in *zari* along the seams; a long silk *kurta*, a *zari*-embroidered shawl, a yellow silk turban sitting lightly upon my head, hollow inside (the turban I meant, not my head! I've long since cut off all my long hair). The aigrette on my turban is a cluster of diamonds and rubies, a hundred and twenty gems in all, embedded in gold; the fringe is a string of dewdrop pearls. My father's pearl necklace in three strings of marble-size pearls, all perfectly matched, weighs down my chest. I have dressed my part, but there's no one to see me.

"It doesn't matter, Duleep," Dr. Login says. "You understand . . . here in England . . . But, wait . . ."

Here in England, he means, only the Queen gets a grand reception. We pass through the buildings of the Royal Pier like any other visitors.

Outside is a yellow curricle, with trim leather seats and shining wheels. A pair of well-matched roans snicker and twist their heads about.

Mrs. Login touches my arm. "I knew you would not be able to resist a ride in the open air, and you have been good during the voyage, Maharajah, so I asked Dr. Login to get you this as a reward."

I laugh. "Come with me!" I say, and when she shakes her head and mutters about the brougham instead, I ask, "How can you deny me? Am I not like your son? Come, Mama Login."

She half-turns. "John!"

Dr. Login smiles. He is paler now, not so burned as under an Indian sun. "But you wanted the Maharajah to have this surprise, Lena. Go with him. Go with Duleep."

He calls me by my name and not my title. Just as a father would. When Henry Lawrence was forced to leave the Punjab by Lord Dalhousie, John and Lena Login came in his stead. These two have taken me into their hearts, made me one of theirs, brought me to England. The Logins were made my guardians, but I think of us as a family.

We speed down the long road, past the town, out of town. Houses and hostelries give way to farms set back from the road. The wind sears my eyes. We follow the curve of the sea for a bit and then fork in landward. Here, the topography changes to smoothly humpbacked hills and hillocks, cropped close with a verdant green, stands of massive oaks dotted on their surface. A handful of clouds scuttle across the vast blue sky. This is the England I have longed to visit. After two hours we stop by the shade of an elm. When the rest of the carriages catch up with us, I relinquish my reins and ride in the brougham. Bhajan Lal is miserable; he has to sit up front near the coachman. I holler to him along the way, putting my head and shoulders out of the window, and he answers feebly, the wind snatching his words and tumbling them into the grassy plains.

At night, we stop in the village of Lowick, where our horses have been sent post to the local inn. I go to bed in a low-ceilinged room with exposed beams and quivering plaster that flakes at the slightest movement I make. The sheets are my own, the mattress has been shaken down, the carpets come from the palaces at Lahore, and Bhajan Lal sleeps on the floor, near the fireplace.

I lie in the half darkness; light filters through the tiny window that overlooks the inn's forecourt. There is a dance going on, and carriages rumble into the yard. Through the walls I hear the sound of the orchestra, the laughter, the voices, some clapping. I sleep and wake as the revelers call out their good-byes.

Tomorrow we will reach London. Dr. Login says the Queen is anxious to meet me. I wonder, will she be wearing the Kohinoor?

Paris, 1893: Sophia empties out the teapot and shakes crumbs from the tablecloth. She sets the dishes on a tray and places it outside the door. If the charwoman comes, she will wash them. There's no vase in the room, so Sophia takes the base of a *hukkah,* wrought in solid gold, fills it with water from a bucket, and sets the hyacinths in it.

"I should go get some more water," she says. There are no pipes in the room; she has to walk down six flights of stairs to the pump in the courtyard.

Her father is looking at her, his head resting on his fist; he is not really here, but far away in the England of his youth. "Let it be," he says.

"Who were they, Papa?"

"The Logins?" She nods.

"He was a surgeon in the Bengal army. I wouldn't have met him, you know, under any other circumstances. John Login was sent in Henry's place, as . . . Resident perhaps; I can't remember, they changed the titles around as they wished. He was, though, my guardian. I loved him . . . loved his wife. For a while—a very long while—they were good to me."

He gestures, and she obeys. Opens the diary. Reads.

June 2, 1854: We are settled at Mivart's Hotel on Brook Street, on the whole of the top floor. Dr. Login says this is temporary, only until the East India Company finds me an adequate house, and both Mivart's and the house are courtesy of the Company.

This is not the fort at Lahore, but my rooms are spacious, a bedroom with its own attached bath, and a sitting room which opens into two other bedrooms. Bhajan Lal is in one; the other holds my clothes. Mir Kheema unpacks the trunks, shakes out their contents, sequesters my jewels in a leather-strapped box with a lock. The key hangs around his neck.

Dr. and Mrs. Login are down the corridor; Frank Boileau is next to them. Lord Dalhousie wouldn't let Frank's brother Charles come with us, said the Company could not bear that expense. So Frank is here by himself, hoping to find both of them commissions in a Queen's regiment in India.

It is a few days before I look down from the windows. Horse buggies trawl the road below; men are in top hats, tail-coats, breeches, and boots; women in wide skirts that brush the cobbles, bonnets tied under chins, arms hung with reticules. The streets are clean, as though cut new each morning from night's dark cloth. The sun shines fitfully, glancing between tall buildings on either side—there is no openness in London, none like the most hurried bazaar street in

Lahore, where the sun blazes bright and the whole landscape seems . . . wider somehow. It is a different world, and I am here to become part of this—an English gentleman, for a while at least.

The past week is spent in fittings to make me truly one. A representative of Cotes & Sons from Savile Row is ushered in on Monday, and Mrs. Login stays only long enough to make sure that he can understand me before fleeing to her own rooms. She has known me since I was ten years old, running around in my underwear in the heat of a Lahore summer, but suddenly, I am now, at sixteen, a grown man.

The shop sends Cotes himself. He has a gloomy, white face, bred in the dark of a sewing room, and blinking, hazel eyes. His hands are immaculate, the nails trimmed, fingers tapering to pointed edges. A measuring tape throttles his neck. He gives a pencil and notebook to his assistant. When he is done, Cotes stands back, clears his throat, and orders the boy to bring out samples.

Frock coats, cutaways, morning coats, afternoon coats, smoking jackets, box coats, and waistcoats—long ones and short. So much material in which to be warm, comfortable, ill at ease, constricted under the armpits, suffocated at the waist, but above all, stylish. The English gentleman, it seems, changes his look through the day with the giddy frequency of a silly girl who cannot make up her mind on what to wear. Then come the shirts, made of silk, thin muslin, linen, starched or malleable, with pearl buttons or chunks of false gold. The vests have pockets, and so I have to have pocket watches with fobs or chains. I have to have boots, shoes, capes and winter overcoats, top hats and bowlers, trousers and pantaloons.

Where in all of this finery am I going to fit in my pearls and my turban?

*   *   *

June 6, 1854: A dinner party tonight. I wait at the end of
the yellow and white paneled drawing room at the top floor
of Mivart's for this, my first introduction to society, as Mrs.
Login breathes softly by my side.

"Why is this even necessary?" I ask in a bit of a grumble,
tugging at the waistband of my pants, which is an effort, as
I wear a *kurta* above them, and have to raise the material to
reach my trousers.

"Hush, Maharajah," Mrs. Login says. "There is nothing
to be nervous about. The guests are all friends of ours; there's
a friend of a friend, a Captain Watkins, but I am assured that
he will be good company. He's the third son of an earl. And
then there is—"

"I am all at sea with the English nobility," I say. It is
true, the very thought of keeping track of all the dukes, the
earls, the marquesses, the viscounts, and the barons, not to
speak of those knighted recently or in the past, sets my head
spinning. And if I am to fit in this society, I must know
all these orders of precedence; which sons of whom were
important, who went into the dining room first, which lady
he took in; where they sat.

"You will learn. As indeed, you must. Dr. Login has
written to the India Office and to Sir Charles Phipps for an
introduction to our sovereign, Maharajah. She has wanted to
see you for a long while; this party tonight will give you a
taste for what is to come, although you must not think that
we will be entertaining in any scale close to that of her Majesty's. It is a great privilege for the Queen to be so willing to
meet you."

Tonight, she has on something new, not the perpetual
black she wore in India but a hibiscus red. The dress has silk
roses on the bodice and is cut away from her shoulders. I
have never given thought to how old my guardians are; they
have been married for ten years or so. Their children are here

with us; in India they are looked after by the *ayahs* and the English governess. Perhaps it is a sacrifice, taking care of me, although I know that Dr. Login gets a thousand pounds a year from the Company for it. And Mrs. Login will now receive an invitation to Buckingham Palace, will shake the hand of the Queen, has already been in correspondence with her—about me.

Dr. Login comes in just as the guests enter. He takes my hand and presses me forward. This is a test for both of us, for all of us. The names pass in a haze. A Lord and Lady Bowles; their daughter, a Miss Bowles (something like Fanny? Edith? Cecilia?); their good friend, Captain Richard Watkins; the rector from Tipton (Dr. Login's home parish), a man with the most unfortunate (and consequently unforgettable) name of Mr. Sneaky; his wife, Mrs. Sneaky; a Lady Hartford and her charge, Miss Victoria.

Richard Watkins is the one who stands out. He has a big head, glistening white teeth too large for his mouth, sandy hair ironed down over one part of his forehead. We bow to each other.

"I say, Maharajah, this is a real pleasure indeed. The Bowleses were insistent that I come, and I wasn't so sure I would like it, but I see I'm wrong. There's nothing of the blackamoor about you. Why, you are as white as I am!"

Paris, 1893: They hear the charwoman's heavy tread upon the stairs, and the bump-bump-bump as she drags her pail behind. When she fills the doorway, she puts her hand theatrically on her heart. She's unlovely—matted hair pulled into an indifferent bun, sunken eyes, two teeth missing in the front. Her voice is grating. *"Maintenant, eh? Allez vite."*

The water in the pail is already filthy; the mop drips dirt

onto the floors. She begins her work even before they flee, scraping up ashes from the grate, leaving a fine plume of black dust in the air. Her face catches the soot.

He gets up from the chair. His legs are swollen, and walking is difficult. The weight that he carries around doesn't help, he thinks grimly. When he first came to England, he was slim, slender, bursting with energy and inquisitiveness. "She's no Cinderella."

"That woman?" Sophia laughs. They speak in English; the charwoman does not understand.

They crowd into the landing. April in Paris. The sun is fickle, faithless; it has already shrouded itself with clouds. What little light comes through the grimy window is of a pale, colorless kind.

For a long time, Sophia does not read from the diary. "So, it began then, so early, Papa."

She's speaking of Richard Watkins calling him a blackamoor, to his face, at the very first meeting. This was in 1854, remember, he says, three years before the Sepoy Rebellion, four years before we officially became lesser subjects of the British Crown. But . . . the sentiment was there, had been there all the while, else the Rebellion wouldn't have occurred in the first place. Now . . .

Sophia knows that now it's fashionable to make these distinctions—you're black and Indian; I'm white. Or you're not quite white, are you? Some Indian blood lurking around somewhere? A quarter of it? A sixteenth?

He shifts on his feet, moving his weight around. There's a catch in his chest; these memories are of days when he was very, very happy. Or at least he thought that he was. One thing is true, though.

"Richard Watkins was a good man, Sophia. My first true friend in England. At least, he was honest. He said what everyone was thinking. He wasn't the first to say this to me, but he was one of the very few."

She has the book open. Her finger rubs over the writing, finds the place.

June 6, 1854: When I look down briefly at our clasped hands, I see that it is true, our skins do match. I do not know how to answer, so I look at his face. It's easy, it's amicable; there is no malice here. Richard's not a bit like Dr. and Mrs. Login. Their manners are rigid, although since we've come to England, they've unbent a little. The English are more at home in England than in India—there, with so much India all around, they are likely to turn native at the drop of a hat if not careful enough to preserve their . . . Englishness.

The Bowles girl is standing next to us. "I've dropped my handkerchief," she says, in a lilting voice.

Richard and I both bend; the girl's foot comes forward and knocks him on the head. He retreats, and I pick up the piece of cloth.

"Thank you, Maharajah," she says. "I think it's time for dinner."

I take Lady Hartford in, sit at the head of the table, and place her upon my right as Mrs. Login has cautioned me to. The girl Victoria is on my left—why, if Watkins wants to find darker skin, look here, at this girl. She has brown eyes, brown hair, and a very well-bred twirl to her tongue. I can't make her out at all. She *looks* a smidgen Indian, but her mannerisms, the serene way in which she spoons the clear soup, the graceful arch to her neck, the quiet movements of her mouth, are all essentially English. However, it is Lady Hartford who demands my attention. She is, perhaps, Victoria's guardian? Or something like that? When the girl doesn't put her napkin down correctly, Hartford clinks her fork in warning against her plate. Victoria reddens, slouches; her posture shatters.

Richard's voice booms at the other end of the table. He is
seated in between the Bowles girl and Mrs. Login. Between
the soup and the fish I realize that the girl deliberately created
a diversion after Richard's gaffe. While Hartford is scolding
Victoria with twistings of her nose and gestures she thinks no
one can see, I watch Miss Bowles. The glow from the chandelier overhead sets fire to her golden head; her eyelashes
are long and cast shadows upon her pink cheek, her mouth
is a luscious pink. She's wearing a pale blue gown, trimmed
with white fur, and cloth-covered buttons ride up the slender
wrists of her gloves. Lucky Richard, to be seated next to such
a beauty.

Lady Hartford rises when the meal is over and before the
cloth is whisked off, to lead the rest of the women out of the
dining room. We stay on, light our cigars, warm the brandy
in our hands, and wreath the room in a pleasant smoke.

Dr. and Mrs. Login's little Timothy, who has been
brought in to balance out the numbers at the table, has been
intently breathing in the fog from my cigar. His father gives
him a quick glance. Go. He jumps up, regretfully, and pounds
down the corridor to his governess, his bed, his prayers.

The talk is droning, as is usual: politics in India, or the
mighty India Office in London which rules all of our lives
from its lofty heights in the Parliament buildings near Down-
ing Street.

Richard is at my elbow, smiling. "I say, do you belong to
any of the clubs?"

"What are they?" I ask.

"You don't know?" He scrubs his hands. "You're in for
a real treat. I will nominate you and get my friends to second
the nomination. A real Indian Maharajah will be an acquisi-
tion for most of them, increase *my* stock substantially, if
I may be frank. The dues will be nothing to a rich man like
you; I hear the India Office is going to settle fifty thousand
pounds a year upon you?"

Again, that honesty. Dr. Login has said nothing yet about a . . . *salary*. What an ugly word. What about the riches from my Punjab Empire? My inheritance, what was left to me as my father's sole heir. I know, I *know* that the India Office is somehow in charge of giving me the money, but am I going to be at the mercy of accountants and civil servants? I, the Maharajah of the Punjab?

Lady Hartford was sonorous and boring all through dinner. Inconsequential. Richard has already, in a few minutes, made my skin prickle. And yet, I like him.

Watkins misinterprets my consternation. "You must not mind this talk of your income, Maharajah. Here in England we are apt to do little else." His laugh rings out, causing Dr. Login to turn toward us, his own conversation briefly silenced. "We pick apart our neighbors' money, their property, their estates, how many people they employ, what they pay them, what they earn, what each promotion is worth. It is so common knowledge as to be nothing at all in terms of consequence. Even our affairs, those of the heart you understand"—and here he closes one large blue eye in a wink—"are not to be secret. But the clubs. Now"—he draws out a small notepad from his vest pocket and begins writing—"the Garrick? It's a theater club mostly, actors and such, but you need not worry about being in poor company. Do you like the theater, Maharajah?"

"Very much, what I've seen of it."

"Ha-ha, the Indian *nautch* girls are not theater, Maharajah."

When I was thirteen, at Lahore, Tommy Scott came to wake me one night, long after everyone was asleep. Tommy was the local schoolmaster's son, a year older than I, wise, and free. He did not have my restrictions, or the masses of attendants who followed me around. Dr. Login's room was across the courtyard, and Tommy and I tiptoed out on bare feet to the carriage he had waiting.

The night over the city's streets had an aroma all of its

own, smoky from the evening's fires, stinking of the gutters, of sweat, of heat. We stopped outside an old *haveli*. The front room had been converted into a music hall for the redcoats of the British army. All the soldiers I'd seen thus far were so correct, their tunics buttoned, their backs stiff, their gazes distant. Here, they roamed with their coats undone, shirts untucked, faces blotched with drink, hands roaming over and pinching the bottoms of the girls.

A man stooped and hissed into Tommy's ear, "Twenty minutes, white sahib, only twenty minutes. If your father comes to know, he will kill me."

Tommy gave him two rupees. I'd never handled money before; he did this with such ease. "Keep an eye on us, will you, Krishan Singh? The crowd looks rowdy around here, and I have the Maharajah with me. We must take good care to deliver him safely back into the arms of his nursemaids."

The men roared as the *nautch* girls came onstage. They wailed out terrible songs, took off some of their clothing. Tommy smoked a cigarette, coughing at each drag. Krishan Singh put his beefy hand on the chest of a drunken soldier who had wandered too close, and pushed him back into the crowd.

And then, the English act came on. I'd seen only respectable Englishwomen until then, collars strangling their throats, gowns sweeping the floor, hair covered in hats. These women wore nothing. Thin cotton shifts, lace panties that showed when they kicked their feet into the air. Tommy wiped drool from his mouth. I stared hard at the white thighs. Just as one of the women was raising her shift to reveal the curve of her breast, Krishan Singh said, "Out. Now. You too, your Majesty."

"Nothing like the *nautch* girls," Richard says. "But, maybe better than them." His grin is wicked. Another Tommy Scott. I hope. I hope!

He goes on writing, and I look over his shoulder. His handwriting is abominable, squiggles and scribbles. He raises an eyebrow when I point it out. "Come, Maharajah, only clerks write legibly; they're taught to, and it's their job. If you write too well—when you can hire someone else to do this for you—you'll be nothing more than a *munshi*."

Richard has done all of his tours of duty in Europe, heavily cushioned as the son of an earl against any real fighting or scrimmage, and yet his language is composed of Indian words. Two things I learn from my newfound friend: that the Indian Empire is never far from the shores of England, and that I am, with this knowledge on how to write badly, a step closer to becoming blue-blooded English.

He murmurs to himself. "The East India Club? Of course. And so also the Oriental, and perhaps the Marlborough. And . . . the Carlton?" Here, he stops to look at me speculatively. "It's a Tory club. Perhaps not quite so soon. Let's see how you get along."

"They seem like an awful lot," I say hesitantly.

He shakes his head. "You can never belong to too many clubs. Have you met the Queen?"

I spread out my hands. "Soon."

"I wonder . . ." There is a gleam in his eye as he shuts his notebook and stows it in the pocket of his vest. He reaches out to touch the rows of pearls I wear around my neck. "These look good upon you, Maharajah. Not quite the thing for men here, unless you're a dandy, but it'll do for you. Don't change this, even when you go meet her Majesty. She is sure to take to you in all of your exotic beauty."

At the other end of the table, Dr. Login makes a sign, and the men scrape back their chairs and rise. We join the ladies in the drawing room. Richard goes to sit by Miss Bowles. Lady Hartford corrals me, and pushes me down next to Victoria. The girl hiccups, she picks apart the gloves in her lap; I turn to Mrs. Login. Save me, please. Mama Login ignores me. I suppose I have to learn how to put up with the most dismal guest.

Everyone plays cards, the clock strikes eleven, coffee and biscuits are brought in. We shake hands, bow, say our good-byes.

"Did you like her, Duleep?" Lady Login says as we go to our rooms.

"Yes," I say, thinking of the Bowles girl.

"Good. I'll tell you some more about her later. Good night, son."

"Good night, Mama." I kiss her cheek.

Mir Kheema is waiting up. He takes off my clothes, buffs the pearls and folds them away in a square of silk, helps me into my pajamas, turns down the lights.

"Are you all right here, Mir?" I ask as he is leaving, framed in the doorway by the dim light in the corridor. His tall figure stoops in indecision, and then his voice comes across the yards of carpets.

"Where you are, your Highness, so I am content to be. I could not let you cross the black waters to this land by your-self, without anyone else."

"I'm hardly alone."

He is silent for a long while, and then he bows and shuts the door.

June 23, 1854: Richard takes me to the Garrick Club today. The rooms are staffed by a succession of middle-aged men dressed in black, relieved only by startling white collars.

"When you see one of these crows, Maharajah," he says as we ascend the purple-carpeted staircase to the club rooms above, "caw out aloud and they will come flying to meet your every need." He's as irreverent in daylight as he was by candlelight.

Portraits framed in gilt are pinned on every inch of wall space. Most are of men, some of women, all actors in the

Drury Lane theaters, dressed in fantastic costumes of velvet, silk gloves, pearl buttons, acting out roles from plays. I see that I was mistaken when Richard mentioned the "theater"; it's Shakespeare played out, not lively girls in little nothings converting themselves into girls in nothing!

They are all *very* respectable; at least the paintings on the main floor; but some of the other rooms have portraits of women in some diaphanous material that swirls over their bodies, cleverly hiding bits from view. Richard again in my ear, "This is art also, Maharajah."

"It is?" I ask, and then, "All right, if you say so." One woman has bright russet curls, and her gown hugs her skin, nestles between her legs. I cannot remember what her face looks like—I am not looking at her face. Dr. Login knows I am with Richard at the Garrick Club, but I think he does not know what hangs on their walls, or he would not have allowed me to come here.

Richard puts in my application for a membership.

Back at Mivart's, Mrs. Login has news. Dr. Login has been given a knighthood by the Queen; they are now to be addressed as Lord and Lady Login. Mama shakes with joy. Papa shows it less, only in a small smile that breaks out when he thinks no one is looking at him.

We celebrate with the children at tea, with extra cakes and extra icing, and at dinner with just the three of us—one of those rare evenings since the first dinner party when we are alone.

They are so happy. So much delight; it must mean more than they let on, this honor. I didn't know how much until now. We talk of Lahore, of how we met, how we came to know each other. I remember nights when I woke after a terrible dream and fled across the courtyard toward the glow of the single lamp in the room beyond. This was before Mama Login came. And Dr. Login would be there, flung into an easy chair, his hair rumpled, his pajamas and *kurta* glimmering a welcome white in the murk. He put out a hand to me, his voice gentle. "A nightmare, Maharajah? Come, sit by my side; let me read to you from *Lalla Rookh*." When I went back to my room, he would stand at the door to his and watch me, raise his hand in good night.

If the Queen can recognize the goodness of people like the Logins, and reward them, she must be good herself.

Lord Login says that I will have the privilege of paying my respects to the Queen on July 1. Our request has been approved and she is eager, willing, wanting to meet me.

June 30, 1854: A parcel arrives from Richard today, a copy of Captain Osborne's *The Court and Camp of Runjeet Sing*, wrapped in plain brown paper. Osborne was the nephew of Lord Auckland, the Governor-General of India who embarked on the First Anglo-Afghan War, deposed Dost Mohammad, put Shah Shuja on the throne . . . and ended up with thousands of British civilians dead in the effort. Osborne was in one of the early embassies to my father's court, to ask for his help in the Afghan war. This book is written about his experiences in May of 1838, a few months before I was born. I sit by the light from the easterly windows, turning the little book over in my hands. Most surprising of all is the nature of the gift; or coming as it does from Richard, the nature of the giver. He doesn't seem the type to read anything.

"What do you think, Bhajan?" I ask.

Bhajan Lal is seated on the carpeted floor thumbing through a copy of Thornton's Old Testament. "I think you should read it, your Highness. Although"—he glances toward the door—"not in front of Lord and Lady Login."

They were nothing but kind to me in Lahore. But here in England, some . . . thread is broken. How shall I put it? It is as though Lord and Lady Login have done their duty in

taking care of me in India, and done it again in bringing me
here, but now, at home, they have other preoccupations. I'm
mostly with Bhajan now; I see Richard at times. After being
away for so many years, the Logins are besieged with queries,
problems, and issues related to their landholdings in Perthshire, and numerous visits from family members. Most are
curious to see me—the black Indian prince—and I am tired
of being put on display.

Perhaps Bhajan is right; they will not approve of my reading about the history of the Punjab. Why, I don't know; I just
feel he is right.

But where else will I learn it from, all that I have long forgotten? I remember talking with Henry Lawrence about my
father, even my mother, whom he, Henry, imprisoned at the
fortress at Sheikhpura. There's no one around me now who
remembers the past, or is willing to talk about it.

Bhajan Lal was educated at the American Mission School,
and there converted to Christianity. He and I read the Bible
together, both before and after my own conversion. I learned
my English very fast after Lord Dalhousie became Governor-
General of India, because he insisted that everyone around
me should speak only that language, not Persian, not Urdu,
not Hindustani. Dalhousie imposed a fine on anyone who
spoke in a native tongue.

"I used to have great fun trying to persuade all of you to
speak to me in Hindustani," I say.

A quick smile flashes on Bhajan's brown face. He sits
where the tepid rays of the sun fall into the room, a rolled-
up ball of shawls and a gleaming white turban. Bhajan has
wanted to come to England for as long as I have, but he is
uneasy here. The almost constant gray gloom, even as we
approach July, has drained life out of him. He is fascinated
by the movement and bustle outside, but afraid to stay on the
streets too long, lest one of the carriages flashing by runs over
him, or his foot.

"You did, your Highness," he says. "By pretending to be deaf when one of us called out to you, which forced us to speak louder, and then to switch to an Indian language."

I grin, remembering. The money I collected from the "fines," I sent to one of my charities.

"Should I read this book, Bhajan?"

He scuttles on his haunches to move into the light as the sun climbs in the sky, reverently dragging the Old Testament along with him. "You should. There must be other biographies, court documents, but they're in Persian, perhaps Hindustani. You cannot read those; you've forgotten the languages, but this one you can."

The frontispiece is a sketch of an Akali soldier from my father's army, with his towering turban, his fierce expression, his circle of a quoit.

"I caution you, your Highness," Bhajan says, his words faltering, "to not believe everything you read in there. It was written . . . to be read, and must lack the honesty of something more private, like correspondence."

"Even the praise of my father?"

"Especially that, your Highness. There's no better way to tame a lion than to feed him tainted meat."

Paris, 1893: Sophia makes an omelet for lunch, dots its golden surface with the cheese she bought in the morning. They sit by the window again, shutters pulled close; the day is cool. The dull light glitters off the *hukkah* vase; the hyacinth is a splatter of bright purple and creamy lilac.

She looks around, points her fork in the air. "Why do you live here, Papa? Why not a hotel? You can surely afford it."

He smiles, coughs as a piece of bread sticks in his throat. "Not anymore, my child. They watch me, you know. I thought that in this garret I could hide from the British government."

"Really?" Her well-shaped eyebrows rise into her hairline. She's beautiful, this daughter of his. Her mother was comely enough, but this girl has the nose of the Lion of the Punjab, his gray eyes, a tint to her skin that makes a red blush rosy. He has eight children, from two wives, and none have ever before shown any interest in the past, in their grandfather, or in India. They're all English, their accents, their manners, their clothing. But this one, to whom he gave her grandmother's name—she's Bamba Sophia Jindan—has come to visit him in Paris. She spends the whole day with him, every day that she is here, is not irritated by his slowness, his coughing, his forays down the lanes of history in search of shining moments he cannot hope to re-create. Anymore.

There's a brilliance about Sophia, something he hasn't noticed before. A man, he thinks, who has captured her heart. So, she glows. She shimmers. She laughs from her heart. Even here, in this dismal studio, which he has decorated with relics—a sword, a *hukkah,* a shawl and a veil, the pearls his father wore in a distant land. If he had the Kohinoor, it too would be here on the rue de la Trémoille in Paris.

"Who?"

"Aimée."

"The charwoman? Oh, Papa, she couldn't possibly be a spy."

He expects to be disbelieved. Pushing open the shutters, he indicates the man with the violin on the street corner. "Him. He's there every day."

"It's how he makes his living, Papa."

"Yes," he agrees, "it is how he makes his living." And they're talking of different things.

She clears the table, and he helps her, limping to the sink

in the corner of the room, pouring water from a mug onto the plates and the forks to rinse them. Aimée will come again, tomorrow, to clean the dishes.

"Did you like the Queen, Papa? I mean, when you first met her?" For she knows that it has been many years since her father has met the Queen, talked to her. His letters are unanswered, or at most there's a polite, distant note from one of the secretaries saying that her Majesty is too busy right now.

"You'll see."

July 1, 1854: Surely, this is the most glorious of days! I wake to the rumble of the cleaners' carts on the street, the sweet sound of water sluiced on the cobblestones, leaving them glittering in the early sunlight. In the outer rooms, Mir Kheema lays out my clothes and polishes my jewels. And then he comes in with a tray, which holds a pot of hot chocolate, a cup, and a dish of digestive biscuits.

"What am I wearing?"

"Your pearls, your Highness," he says, approaching the bed and bowing. Then, kneeling upon the carpets, he lays his head lightly on my bedcovers. "The diamond and emerald aigrette for your turban. The diamond bracelets and four rings, also in emerald. I have chosen"—he raises his eyes to mine—"all green in your stones to go better with the embroidery in your black velvet coat and your trousers. It would befit you, as a king meeting . . . another, to wear the silk pajamas under your *kurta* instead of your English trousers?" This last is said wistfully.

I run my hand over my night wear. "Only to sleep, Mir. I have given off that part of the native dress, as you well know."

"Certainly, your Highness." He is reflective now. "At

another time, you would not have appeared in public without that glorious stone upon your arm, but now . . ." He touches his forehead in salaam, and backs out of the room.

Lord Dalhousie annexed the Punjab, and he gave the Kohinoor to the Queen. He did not ask me for permission. As with so much else in my father's Toshakhana, the Kohinoor, which Mir Kheema dares not call by its name, found its way to England four years ago. I remember so little about the last Treaty of Lahore that Sikh chieftains signed on my behalf with the British. I signed it also, but without understanding most of its clauses. I was only ten years old at the time. But it was agreed to in my name—as the reigning king of the Punjab— and I will stand by its terms. But I wonder if Lord Dalhousie knows, or guesses, what it means to me. The possessor of the diamond is the supreme ruler of all South Asia—in that fistful of stone is strength, power, glory, all the brilliance and opulence of royalty. It isn't just a piece of rock.

I go into the bathroom to brush my teeth, bathe and breakfast. It is futile to think of what is not mine any longer—especially today, when I go to meet my sovereign. For she is *my* Queen also—the Punjab Empire has been fragmented, shattered, some of its pieces sold off, and what remains is now under the crown of Queen Victoria.

Lord and Lady Login accompany me to Buckingham Palace around noon, and there we are met by a few of the Company's directors and Sir Charles Trevelyan from the Treasury.

The Grand Staircase is encased in reds, golds, and whites. Portraits of past monarchs look down upon us, though they never lived here, I am told by an equerry as we ascend; the Queen is the first to take up residence.

The equerry cannot walk in front of me, so he makes small movements by my side—first here, a right there, a left after another right. If I am abandoned in this place, I will not find my way out. And then, finally, we are at the

Throne Room. The doors are flung open and my presence announced. "The Maharajah of the Punjab, Maharajah Duleep Singh Bahadur!"

I mumble, "My name is Maharajah *Dalip* Singh Bahadur."

The equerry's backward look is one of a startled squirrel, eyes huge in his angular face. I have heard my name mispronounced so many times before, but I don't want the Queen to not know how or what to call me.

A huddle of men and women at the far end break apart to watch my progress across the lush red carpets. In the center of that group, not sitting upon the throne but standing, waiting, is a slight woman, her hair combed sensibly back into a bun, her neck festooned in diamonds, her arms bare, her gown of some glittering silver material.

She comes forward; the others bow and curtsy. The Queen puts out her hand, and I run the last few steps up to take her hand in mine.

"Maharajah, this is such a pleasure. Welcome to England. I hope, I so dearly hope that your stay here will be a pleasant one."

I bow. I kiss her hand. Prince Albert comes forward to shake my hand and add his compliments. He is handsome, with trimmed sideburns; his vest, his jacket, his pants all impeccably neat. That last word describes the two of them perfectly. The Queen is economical in all of her movements; even her smile is small, but one of such pure pleasure when she looks at me that I glow with happiness.

"Tell me about yourself," she says. "Was your journey a good one?"

"Very much so, your Majesty."

"You must feel yourself at home in England." She turns to the Company's officials who stand behind. "We must make the Maharajah welcome; he must not regret his decision to leave India."

I gulp. "I could hardly feel that, your Majesty."

"Come." And with a light touch on my arm, she pulls me to a side of the room where there are two chairs close together. "Talk to me. I am elated you are here after hearing so much about you." She gazes at me for a long time. "You are such a striking boy. I hope you will not mind my saying so; I feel as though I could be your mother, in age, of course, and I would very much like you to be a part of my family."

I cannot speak. To be accorded such an honor from her, the woman for whose well-being we have prayed every Sunday at church both in India and here, who has always seemed so distant, so magnificent. I had expected some minor notice, something done gracefully and then forgotten, but this much . . . I glance around at Lady Login. She quakes with delight. Lord Login's mouth twitches at the ends.

"You are very gracious, your Majesty."

"I had heard of your embracing the Christian faith"—and now an anxious furrow on her brow—"it was done with your full consent, I hope? You have wanted this, believed in God, knew Him to be your savior?"

"I and no one else, your Majesty."

She leans back. "I was worried, I will admit, when I heard of it, coming as it did so soon after the annexation of the Punjab. You were very young then, and I was adamant that things be done right by you. Lord and Lady Login have been good guardians? You are happy? If you are not, you must tell me."

"I could not wish for anything more, your Majesty." But there is that small memory of my conversation with Mir Kheema; I nudge it away.

She chatters as the others wait in the corners of the room. She does not say this in so many words, but I think she has been against the annexation, and would have preferred a more minor British hand in the Punjab, akin to that after the First Anglo-Sikh War, when Henry Lawrence was sent as Resident. I don't tell her that the terms of that earlier treaty

gave Lawrence more or less full ruling rights over the Punjab, even with the nominal guidance of my Sikh Council. And
that I have been, for a long while now, a king only in name,
not in deed, not in fact. But this she must have known.

She is so different from Lord Dalhousie. He had come to
the Punjab as a conqueror, with very little of the respect that
one king grants another, even a vanquished one. But then—
and now I realize the fact—Dalhousie is merely a Governor-
General; his real sovereign is before me.

A while later, the Queen beckons to a girl, introduces her
to me. "This is my goddaughter, Maharajah. Her name is
also Victoria and she is the Princess of Coorg. You will have
much in common with each other and must be friends."

It is the Miss Victoria of my first dinner party! She's quietly
sophisticated, at ease—because Lady Hartford, her guardian,
is not here.

"How lucky you are to have them," she says, nodding
toward Lord and Lady Login. "I hate mine, that woman
Hartford."

"When did you come to England?"

"A few years ago. My father brought me; he's left now
and this is to be my home."

This Victoria Gouramma had been baptized at St. James's
Cathedral—a *tamasha*, Lord Dalhousie had called it while
writing to Lord Login about my own, quieter baptism. The
Raja of Coorg had traveled to England with his daughter,
left her there to marry an English nobleman, and duped the
Queen into taking an interest in the girl. Grumble. Grumble.
Grumble. The native kings were being made too much of
at Home—if only they could see them in India as they truly
were, they would not be thought worthy of all the attention.

We have something in common then, Victoria and I, a
loathing for Lord Dalhousie. She is, suddenly, more interesting than she had been at the dinner party.

I tumble into bed late that night, so exhausted that I sleep as soon as I lie down. Mir Kheema takes off my clothes, puts away the jewels, rubs my face with a damp cloth.

I did not see the Kohinoor diamond. It has been sent to Amsterdam to be recut and reset. My father never touched the stone after he acquired it from Shah Shuja; he did, though, reset it twice, but he had always thought its cut and its appearance were flawless.

July 4, 1854: Once I have been received by the Queen, invitations flood in for dinners, picnics, and at homes! The whole of London wants to meet me. But they don't know where I fit in society. Am I an Eastern potentate? A European royal? What am I?

Tonight is the dinner at Sir Charles Inglis's home. Where I am invited, I meet Victoria Gouramma also. Lady Login says nothing, merely flings her in my way. Perhaps the Queen herself wants this—two Christians, two Indians; we could be a perfect couple.

There has always, even when we were in India, been talk of an eligible wife for me. All kings, even deposed ones, have to marry—there's no real choice in the matter. But I did say no to a girl I had been betrothed to since I was two or three years old. Her name is Roshni, and she's twelve years older than I am. She is Sher Singh's sister, and he was the adopted son of my father. I liked her very much, as a sister, as a companion, but not as a wife. Nobody protested when I refused to marry Roshni—not Lord or Lady Login, not Lord Dalhousie, who likes to object at every opportunity. It's what he does best. But with Sher Singh, the fourth king of Lahore dead, and me, the fifth king of Lahore, on the throne, Roshni has no powerful connections left in the Punjab. She has become unimportant.

When the talk of Victoria Gouramma gets to India, Dalhousie writes again to Lord Login, and he shows the letter to me. Here's what Dalhousie says: If I am to be fastidious enough not to marry Roshni, the girl I was betrothed to, I would do well to see if Gouramma was to my whole liking before I married her, since I have taken the faith myself and can no longer get "Ranees in duplicate."

Bah. Bah. Bah. *This* man is the Governor-General of India?

Sir Charles Inglis comes by in the afternoon and is closeted with Papa Login. When he leaves, I see him in the corridor. He bows, scrabbles at his collar, and almost runs out of the house.

Lord Login calls to me from the drawing room door. "Maharajah, a word with you, please."

"What's the matter with Sir Charles? Has he canceled tonight's dinner? Is there a problem?"

"The dinner's still on," Lord Login says. When we sit, he begins laughing. "You are the problem, Duleep. Sir Charles doesn't know what to do with you."

Sir Charles has invited the *ton* of London, those who are in residence, one of whom is the Primate, Archbishop Longley. Under any other circumstances, the Primate has precedence at a party such as this; he's the seniormost man in rank. But, after her Majesty acknowledged me at Buckingham Palace . . . where do I stand? Surely, the Archbishop ought to lead the way into the dining room . . . and surely I should, as a Maharajah? How to resolve this?

"And how did he?" I ask. "The dinner's only a few hours off; he had better have a plan by now and make sure he does not offend either of us."

"He suggested"—and here Lord Login collapses into his chair again, roaring—"that you both go in together, arm in arm, each of you stepping foot into the dining room at precisely the same moment so it would not be said either of you went in first."

Oh, the English and their rules in society. The man highest in rank always takes in the woman highest in rank, and so
on, down the line. And the woman highest in rank usually has
quite a few years tucked under her belt, and a mapful of wrinkles on her face.

"I'm tired of taking in old ladies," I say. "And the Primate
is an old lady, Papa."

Lord Login had convinced the distraught Sir Charles that
I would be perfectly content to enter the dining room after
the Archbishop. I have no problem with this—let him take
the oldest lady in; this time I might just get a younger one on
my arm. But when we arrive at the party, it *throngs* with old
ladies, so though I go in second, I still have to take one in. All
the younger, prettier ones waltz in with younger, handsome
men of little or no rank. I'm not sure it's that advantageous to
be a Maharajah.

The Logins and I come back in different carriages, and I
enter the drawing room first. A girl is sitting there, a shabby
carpetbag at her feet, her skin pale.

"My dear," I say. "What is the matter? And who are
you?"

She rises to give me her hand; it's tiny, fits in my palm like
a flower. Her head is bowed, and a tear trembles down her
smooth cheek to her chin. I wipe it off. "Please, tell me what
it is. What can I do?"

She looks up then, her lower lip quivering, a glitter of
tears making clumps of her eyelashes. Of course, the Miss . . .
Bowles from the first dinner party.

"Where are your parents, Miss Bowles?"

She begins to cry again; I take out my handkerchief and
hand it to her. "Please . . ." I say again. What should I do?
How does one handle a crying woman who doesn't throw
things around, doesn't shout? I've seen only my mother in
tears before, and she had splendid fits—it was more a matter
of ducking than of consoling.

"My parents are dead."

The poor child! Why, we saw Lord and Lady Bowles just a month or so ago, and now they're dead. I sit by her, clasp her cold hands. "I'm sorry to hear that. What can I do? Please, let me do something, anything."

And this is how the Logins find us, on the sofa. Lady Login comes rushing in, gathers the girl in her arms, and pushes me away.

"She says her parents are dead," I say, "Isn't that awful, Mama Login?"

Lady Login tucks the girl's head under her chin. "But they've been dead for months." When the girl heaves with another sob, she pats her on the back. "I'm sorry, my dear, but what is the Maharajah talking about?"

"How could that have been months ago?" I ask. "They were here for dinner the other night."

It turns out that Lord and Lady Bowles are her guardians. Her parents actually did die some time ago in a boating accident, and she went to live with her uncle and aunt. Yesterday, Lord Bowles was posted to Paris as the military attaché, and his wife and he left almost immediately. They tried getting in touch with Mama and Papa Login (we find the letter under the table in the front hall) and sent Cecilia (that's her name!) to Mivart's with her bag.

"Where will she stay, Lena?" Lord Login asks. He's walking back and forth on the carpet, a frown creasing his forehead. "We don't have a place ourselves."

As they talk, Cecilia Bowles sinks back into the cushions, her purple traveling habit blending with the fabric of the sofa. All I see is a white face, anxious eyes that move from Mama's to Papa's face and then back, hands knotted around my now-damp handkerchief. She's an orphan, just as I am.

"She can stay here, with us," I say suddenly.

They turn to me.

"But the Company pays our bills here," Lord Login says

slowly. "It would not be right . . . I'm sorry, my dear"—this last to Cecilia—"you know how it is, how it will look."

"Nonsense," I say. "What the Company pays for our accommodation is nothing less than what they ought to, what is due to me as the Maharajah of the Punjab. You know this, Lord Login; they aren't giving us charity."

He shakes his head, rubbing his fingers against his chin.

"I will pay for Miss Bowles's rooms at Mivart's," I say.

"No, Duleep. You're right, she can stay here, but I will pay her bill. If it wouldn't be right for me to take the money from the East India Company, it's even less likely that I will take it from you."

We argue for a while. Lord Login is being paid for his guardianship of me, and the money for it comes, in a round-about fashion, from *me,* or rather from the monies demarcated for me by the East India Company. They grabbed the Punjab and the treasures of the Toshakhana; they give back in a salary and my expenses in London.

He will not listen, though. He's a conscientious man. And so, he takes on the burden of his wife's niece, and pays for her stay at Mivart's.

Back in my rooms, I pull out *The Court and Camp of Runjeet Sing* again, sit with a lamp by the window, listen to the dying sounds of the street. In India, I had been so eager to learn English, to *be* English, but here, with England all around me, there's a craving to know my Indian self . . . albeit from an Englishman.

My father was illiterate—not uneducated—literally not able to put two words in writing. He was brought up to be a warrior, to live by the sword, die by it, kill with it. What use would a book be? Better yet to learn to look a person in the eye, take his measure, notice tics and uncertainties, smell fear running in cold veins under his skin.

In Osborne's telling, he comes across as a mountain of a man, fierce, proud, garrulous to make up for his lack of book learning, inquisitive, curious, with an astounding memory. Osborne talks of my father's generosity, of the heaps of presents given to every member of Lord Auckland's embassy, of the fact that they never had to pay for any morsel of food for the month they spent at my father's court.

When I close the book late into the night, I wonder what he would have thought of me, his infant son, grown into manhood in a place so distant that I have crossed the black waters to get here, giving up my caste as I did. There is an ache in my chest. Osborne talks of my father as a devout Sikh, though eminently tolerant of other religions and meticulous in attending other places of worship, both Hindu and Muslim. What *would* he have thought of me, a Christian? I lie down, but sleep does not come for a very long while.

At the very least, I am Ranjit Singh's son, and he, who had established the mammoth Sikh Empire, was the Lion of the Punjab.

Paris, 1893: Sophia leans out of the window suddenly and shouts, *"Viens."*

The violin player's head jerks up. He shuts his case, locks it, and runs across the street, his hobnailed boots ringing on the stones. When he's directly below, she throws a *sou* down to him. The coin spins through the air, and his hand swipes to catch it.

"Merci, mademoiselle."

"Now how did he know," she says over her shoulder, "that I'm not married?"

"He knows who you are," the Maharajah of the Punjab says.

She spins another *sou* out. This one tumbles to the street, and the man scrambles after it, before one of the ragpickers can steal it. *"Bien merci."*

Sophia hangs her reticule over her arm and goes down-stairs. He watches her from his place, as she haggles with the fish seller, who slaps a fillet of mackerel in a slice of newspa-per and takes the money from her. Then she goes into the bakery, comes out with two more baguettes. She stops by the fried-potato woman, with her heavy vat of oil, her blunt knife, her potato peelings stuffed carefully in a bag to be fed to the pigs later. When she returns, she is redolent of the aro-mas of dinner. The newspaper cone with the *pommes-frites* is dark with oil; she peels away the paper and lays the golden spears of potatoes on a plate and covers it to keep it warm.

She douses the mackerel with pepper, salt, a pinch of tur-meric, and some chilli powder, heats a pan on the stove, and sets it, sizzling, in the butter.

They sit down to dinner in the long twilight of spring. The strip of sky above them is crimson, a few thunderclouds are edged with gilt. The mackerel is perfectly cooked, flakes to the fork, melts in his mouth. The butter is already rancid, but he does not mind.

"I tried to give Lord Login an annuity from my personal income, put something aside in my will," he says, chewing. "Lady Login and he looked after me for nine years; he must have neglected his other duties. But the Company refused. No native of India could give a present or a gratuity to an officer of the Company." His smile is wry. "It was *forbidden*, by the rules of service, by an Act of Parliament."

"Do you think of the others, Papa?" she asks. "Dalhou-sie . . . Lawrence . . ."

"They're both dead."

"I can see why you hated the Marquess of Dalhousie. But Henry Lawrence."

He takes a sip of the wine. There's a wine seller in the street also, and every morning he fills the mouth of the street with his wine casks, causes a traffic jam, much yelling and cursing. His French has become rigorously fluent with these curses, some he's never heard before. At fifty-five, he's learning a new language, not the courtly French of his youth.

"Henry I loved," he says, putting down his fork and looking out of the window. And then he's back in Lahore, eight years old, still sucking his thumb. He can feel the pull of Henry's fingers as he tugs his hand out of his mouth. No, Maharajah, only babies do this. It was a difficult habit to break; but he did it because he wanted so much to please this giant, thin man, with his gentle voice, his sudden smiles. "Even though he . . . he sent my mother away to the fortress of Sheikhpura. I can understand that she had become very demanding, dangerous even. But I didn't see her for many years after that . . . my own mother. I suppose"—his voice is dreamy, still in his childhood—"they all did their duty in building the Empire. I only wish, at times, that they could have done things differently." His eyes turn to his daughter, bright, with the hint of a smile. "You have her name, you know."

She nods. "Bamba Sophia Jindan."

They don't talk of her first name. Or they do, in another way, when she asks, "Did you like this Princess Victoria Gouramma?"

"She was a silly child. I can't blame her. She was left in England so young, with no one to call her own, moved to different guardians, given no boundaries; no one cared really."

There's a curious quality to the light in the room, as though it's split into parts—pure and pale blue here, blotches of dark from the coming night there, but the pages of the diary are still visible. The ink is faded, but the writing is clear.

July 24, 1854: I take the Princess Gouramma boating on the river. We cannot be alone, so Cecilia accompanies us. They form a picture on the other end of the rowboat, laughing when I mishandle the oars, giggling when I crash into the greenery on the bank and emerge with scratches on my face. When we finally disembark, they walk arm in arm in front of me. I like the view—their figures are trim, the mass of their hair bows down their necks.

There's a frost and fire in Victoria Gouramma, almost as though she doesn't know how to control her moods. Cecilia, on the other hand, is always cheerful, ready with a smile. When we are in the drawing room, Victoria frets, sits at the piano, bangs out a few songs, paces restlessly around the room. Cecilia sits on the sofa for hours, head bent over her embroidery. Her white fingers flit across the silk, patient, until a pattern forms.

Once, I ask Victoria what she reads.

"Why, this," she says, holding out a copy of Thornton's Old Testament. I've noticed that the book goes with her everywhere.

"What else? Have you read Byron? Walter Scott?"

"Who?" she says, wrinkling her nose. "Did they write sermons?"

What sort of education has she had that she can read only religious texts? It's a narrow mind that cannot appreciate Lord Byron's poetry (to say nothing of his personal life and his arduous love affairs, exciting to know of, if not to emulate) or Scott's romantic novels?

"I've read *Kenilworth*," Cecilia says suddenly, raising shining eyes to mine. "I mean, I wasn't supposed to, it was banned by Lady Bowles, but that made me want to find a copy."

She's read Walter Scott! "How did you get one then?"

"I bribed the maid, Hannah, to buy me a copy. I had to lie to Lady Bowles for a whole month after that when Hannah went out walking with her young man at night. Oh!" She clamps her hand over her mouth. She's certainly said more than she ought to.

Cecilia plays chess with me on most nights, after Mama

and Papa Login have gone to bed. We sneak like two children into the drawing room, light a lone candle. I am in my pajamas, she's in a wrap, her lovely hair loose about her shoulders. And, she invariably beats me . . . or do I let her?

August 22, 1854: Queen Victoria submerges me with affection. I eat dinner at Buckingham Palace; we meet for picnics in the gardens. She sends me a matching pair of grays for my carriage, and when I ride in the park, everyone knows that the horses are a gift from her Majesty.

Prince Albert takes an interest in my education. I have the same music master as Albert Edward, the Prince of Wales. I tell him I want to learn German, his mother tongue, so he searches through London for a suitable tutor. He sends me a microscope; it's all black and plain, so Prince Albert suggests that I ought to have my own English coat of arms engraved upon it. Queen Victoria's husband works on fashioning a coat of arms for me himself; the court engravers hammer it into the microscope. I wish I could see Lord Dalhousie's face when he hears of this. Why does the Maharajah of the Punjab *need* an English coat of arms? Grumble. Rumble. Bumble. Laugh. I do, I mean, that last.

The royal party goes for Osborne House on the Isle of Wight soon, and I am invited to visit and stay with them. Cecilia slips a note into my hand as I'm leaving. "Read it," she whispers. "Not now, not in front of Lady Login. Later." London will have to miss me for a while!

September 17, 1854: At Osborne House the Queen and Prince Albert are more relaxed, simply parents of their large brood. There's the sound of the young princes and princesses pounding through the rooms, fighting, crying, making up. I carry Prince Leopold in my arms; he babbles for the "Maharajah" each time he sees me. He's sickly, engulfed by fussy nurse-maids, and with me at least, he has some respite from them.

We go out to shoot, splash at the beach, play hide-and-seek and charades at night. There is a real Swiss cottage at the back, near the vegetable gardens, and the princesses have a kitchen in the cottage. They pull vegetables from the patch and cook and clean like ordinary women. The princes make fun of their sisters, and so I am the only one allowed into the kitchen while they work, and at the end of each afternoon, we solemnly present their efforts to their parents.

Sometimes, I think I am dreaming here at Osborne House. The Queen and Prince Albert treat me like a son, as a member of their family. But there's a little portion of my heart left in London with Cecilia.

I keep the note she wrote under my pillow, read it every morning as I drink my chocolate. There's nothing much in the letter, some discussion about a book she read recently, a chess move she thinks I botched. The envelope is faintly scented with violets, the same perfume she wears. It's the first time Cecilia has written anything on a piece of paper for me—I mean, we aren't engaged, don't have an understand-ing; it's a daring thing to do. Mama Login would be horrified. Cecilia says that she will miss me when I'm gone—or rather she says that she's going to learn some new chess moves so that she can beat me upon my return.

Same thing.

September 20, 1854: The Queen grants me the rights, posi-tion, and order of preference of a European prince. Now I will always, *always* enter the dining room first, no matter how many other dukes, earls, and archbishops are present.

Lord Dalhousie must be sweating out this ridiculous partiality in the Calcutta heat. He said once, to Lord Login, that no matter how much favor the Queen shows me, if I returned to India, I would still have to leave my shoes at the door to his offices. Like any ordinary *chaprasi*.

But let him just come back to England, and he'll have to follow *me* everywhere. Like a commoner.

October 7, 1854: Back at Mivart's, with Cecilia. I cannot tell if she's happy to see me; she looks the same, talks the same. We still steal into the drawing room when the Logins are asleep, to play chess, or to read to each other. Sometimes, we talk, and she tells me of her childhood, her parents, how much she misses them.

I speak of my father, of Lahore, of a full moon in starry skies, of the gold of ripening wheat in the fields and the heat before the monsoons.

"You've lived so much in so little time," she says.

It's true. Compared to her restful life, mine has been anything but. I think I'm in love. I *know* I'm in love.

Victoria Gouramma has moved from the guardianship of Lady Hartford to a Mrs. Drummond, because Hartford felt that she was a bad influence on her own daughters. There's a rumor about town that the Princess Gouramma sneaked out at night to meet with the stable boy. So, she's gone to Mrs. Drummond, who has no children.

I don't know what to think of this news. Don't know if it's true, and I don't care. Because Cecilia fills my thoughts.

Lady Login says that Cecilia's portion is very small; she has no income. But I have one. The India Office will pay me fifty thousand pounds each year.

My land agent comes with details of a property in Suffolk, called Elveden Hall. Seventeen thousand acres, stocked for hunting and shooting, a lake in front of the house. I buy it, without seeing it. It has possibilities, my agent says, and that's enough for me.

If I cannot be the Maharajah of the Punjab, at least I can be the Squire of Elveden.

October 26, 1854: The Queen commissions Franz Xaver Winterhalter to paint my portrait as a special gift to herself. The sittings will take place in the White Drawing Room at Buckingham Palace. I will wear my pearls, my court dress, and the locket with her Majesty's picture.

November 1, 1854: Two sittings already for the Winterhalter portrait. Last week, Schoefft's painting *The Court at Lahore* comes up for sale. I buy it, unseen, for an ungodly sum. It is ten by sixteen feet, crowded with the important personages of my father's court, all stroked in by Schoefft's masterful brush without care for whether they would actually have been there. It is, then, a fictional piece, but one of true artistry. When I build a grand staircase at Elveden, this painting will hang over it.

Breakfast is a dull meal; Papa and Mama Login are buried behind their newspapers, and Cecilia is lying down with a headache.

When Lord Login rises to leave, wiping his mouth, I say, "Papa, Mama, a word with you please?"

"Now, Maharajah?" Lord Login asks, taking his watch out of his vest pocket. "I have an appointment at the India Office in less than an hour." He smiles. "Matters about you, of course."

Lady Login frowns. "Can you stay, John? I think Duleep would prefer if we were both here."

"Oh, it doesn't matter," I say airily. "One of you will do just fine. You'll both know in any case—the whole world will know soon."

Lord Login lingers, held to the table by his wife's hand. "Perhaps I should stay," he says, uneasy now. A pleading look at Lady Login. "Lena?"

"Go." A thin smile. "As Duleep says, I will tell you all. If it is good news, and what I hope it is to be, then we will celebrate this evening at dinner. Will you be back at all during the day, John?"

"Not until teatime. Keep the Maharajah occupied until then." He waves and leaves the room, glancing back uneasily as he does.

I pull a chair closer to Lady Login's so that the remains of the breakfast no longer span the space between us.

"I have something to ask you also," she says, drawing my hand into hers and patting it. "This is suitably serious, Maharajah; you must not smile so even before I have spoken."

"Me first," I say. "You must allow me to speak first."

"No." She half-laughs. "It's a message from the Queen. Will you listen, Duleep?"

"All right," I say gently. She's anxious about something, wants to speak her mind, doesn't know how I'll take the news. I'm not worried, either about what she has to say or about my news. They will never refuse me, I know. I kiss her hand and sit back.

Lady Login looks down upon our clasped hands. "We think of you as our son. We're your guardians now; one day you'll be on your own, Duleep. But we'll always love you. You know that, don't you?"

"Oh, Mama." The worry in her gaze frightens me. This *is* serious. "When have you given me reason to doubt it?"

She hesitates and then goes on, "I know how much the Kohinoor means to you. There have been days when we have

talked of nothing but the diamond. Do you remember your
eleventh birthday?"

"When Lord Login presented me with the cache of jewels
he had taken out of my father's Toshakhana for my own use?"

Her brow wrinkles. "Even on that birthday, glancing over your jewels"—here she lightly touches the pearls
around my neck—"one of which you wear today as your
birthright, you said to Lord Login . . . do you remember
what you said?"

I am grave. "That I had been wearing the Kohinoor upon
my arm on my tenth birthday and where was it now?"

A fleeting mask of compassion scurries across her face.
"Lord Login made sure that you were given the best of the
rest. The Kohinoor was always to belong to the Queen; it was
written into the Treaty of Lahore. You do know that, don't
you, Duleep?"

At that moment I know what she wants of me. The Kohinoor has returned to England again, after having been cut and
polished in Amsterdam. But I have not seen it yet, and no one
has mentioned it to me. Until now.

I lean over and kiss Lady Login's dry cheek. "The Kohinoor was taken from me by the annexation of the Punjab
and the Treaty of Lahore when I was but a boy, with a very
small will of my own. Then, I understood none of the treaty's
terms, and her Majesty . . . was to me a faraway creature in a
foreign land. What I wish for now, most of all, is to be able to
give it to her myself, as a gift from the Maharajah of the Punjab to the Queen of England."

Her eyes fill with tears that she does not bother to wipe
away. She holds my hand against her face. "Duleep, you do
Papa and me proud."

For a few moments we sit there, our hearts full, and then
Lady Login blows her nose in her handkerchief and looks up
at me again. "Now what is your news?"

I fumble with my words. I have some good news, and something she will not want to hear. "I cannot marry Princess Victoria Gouramma."

"Oh." She sits back in her chair. "Have you given this thought, Maharajah? It is her Majesty's dearest wish. I know the princess seems gauche in certain instances, but sophistication can be acquired with time and a little education. And the two of you are Christian now; think of how eligible this match is."

I shake my head. "I'm sorry, Mama. I truly am. I have some . . . affection for her, but I do not think she will be a good wife for me. Some other man, maybe."

"Duleep, I thought, I wished for . . . I think we all wished for this." Her expression clears all of a sudden and settles into tranquillity. "But this must be your decision, no matter what *we* wish for. Lord Login will agree with me here, just as he agreed when you wanted to dissolve your earlier betrothal. In this most important matter of marriage, your wishes must be paramount."

I take a deep breath; this is exactly what I want to hear. "Then it makes it easier for me to say this: I have found another woman whom I admire and respect deeply."

"Oh." She puts an elbow on the table and cradles her chin in her hand; the uneasiness has returned. I shift a tea-cup away. Just then, a servant comes into the room and halts uncertainly at the door.

"Later, Tait," we both say simultaneously.

"Who is she?" Lady Login asks. Her voice is faint. The room is quiet, and the clock in the corner ticks loudly through the seconds.

"Don't you have the slightest idea?"

"No," she says slowly, "I had thought . . . it was to be about the princess, but someone else, this comes as a surprise."

"A happy one, I hope." I laugh, exhilarated at being able to say her name. "It's Cecilia Bowles."

Lady Login shoves her chair back hurriedly. It catches on the carpet and tilts. I reach out, and she shouts, "Don't!"

The cracked whiplash of her voice stings my hand, burns it. I draw back, my heart pounding. I've never heard her speak like this to me, and I've known her for a very long while. She drags herself upright, leans over the table's edge, turns away from me. I stand also, hover near her. What am I to do? What is happening to her? Is she ill? Unwell?

"Are you all right?" I ask urgently.

She shakes her head violently, her breathing ragged. And then, suddenly, she calms down. She sits down again, motions me to my chair. Tears cut lines across her face. She wipes her skin and smoothes down her hair. Her voice is quiet. "I'm sorry, Maharajah. That was unpardonable of me. It's just that"—here she raises her eyes and holds my gaze firmly—"it is so unexpected. I have not noticed your paying any special attention to Cecilia."

"I haven't, Lady Login," I say with dignity. "I would not dream of doing such a thing until I had your permission to court her. As far as I know, the affection is all on my side."

She breathes audibly, a sigh of relief, I think. "That's all right then. Cecilia is, as you know, our ward, and it falls to us to look after her, take care of her, and when the time comes for her marriage, make sure that she is married respectably and into a good home."

I bristle. "And am I not a good match for Cecilia, Lady Login? I would not ever mention a woman's prospects or her income, but it is common talk here in England when it's a question of marriage. Cecilia has hardly very much to call her own. My income, my standing in London society, my familiarity with the Queen and Prince Albert—these are unsurpassed by any other man. What possible objection could you have to me? *Do* you have an objection to me?"

"Duleep," she says dimly, a hand over her heart. "You misunderstand me. I only meant that Lord Login and I are responsible for Cecilia. She is a charming girl, and I can see why you are so taken with her. But she's young, Maharajah, too young to be thinking of marriage."

"She's fifteen years old; surely that's not considered young? Or at least not too young to be engaged?"

Lady Login deliberately brushes crumbs off the table. "I've never been partial to a long betrothal. Even in cases where there has not been an income to support an actual marriage."

"Not true in *this* case," I say somberly. I wonder what Lady Login is actually saying and what she means. There's a weight on my heart, and my thoughts are all jumbled. Nothing makes sense anymore.

We are quiet for a long while. There's a clink of china as Lady Login moves the cups and plates around; rearranges the knives, forks, and spoons; lifts the lid from the teapot and swishes the cold chocolate around. I sit still, gazing at the floor.

"Can I ask a favor?"

"Anything," I say.

"I will talk with Lord Login about this. But you must not say anything to Cecilia. Write to her, once a month or so, don't mention marriage. If your affections grow over the next two years, we can reconsider this matter."

It's a middle ground, of sorts. We shake hands, depart to our own rooms. I have to rub my feelings from my face and head to Buckingham Palace. Winterhalter's portrait will give future generations a glimpse of my face; it cannot be written over with the crushed disappointment I feel.

Lady Login and I have signed a treaty. And though there are no powerful chieftains who witness it, no stiff-necked, stuffed-shirt civil servants who sign it, I intend to stand by it. Only . . . with Cecilia living in our household, I wonder how Mama will effect the letter-writing rule.

* * *

November 2, 1854: I know how today. Cecilia left early in the morning for the home estates in Perthshire. Without my knowledge, Lady Login rustled up a governess and sent her there with this woman. For two years, I think she said. I can write her a letter once a month—about chess, the rides in the park, a book I have read, but not about marriage.

I have another sitting with Winterhalter today. I didn't sleep last night.

My heart hurts and I don't know how to heal it.

Ever since I came to England, it's been like this: if my skin is dark-hued; if my mouth can form English the way it is meant to be spoken in polite society; if my jewels are indeed of a fabulous value; if I will ever take off my turban and reveal my shorn head and become a true Englishman. And now, more of the same. If Lord and Lady Login can so easily adopt a blackamoor as their son, shower him with love (and no, I have not been mistaken in this; I know them too well), why then do they recoil at his marrying into their family?

My father was the Lion of the Punjab. Today, I'm a mere, mewling kitten.

December 15, 1854: Winterhalter is a big, gruff man. Half his words, I cannot understand. When frustrated, he stamps his feet and mutters into his mustache in German. Prince Albert obligingly translates the curses for us. The painter wears a tight, fitted coat, decorated with a hundred buttons. The Queen begs him to be more comfortable, take off his coat, paint in his shirtsleeves, but he always answers, "Nein, your Majesty. Zat would not be so gut."

Somehow, with a paintbrush clenched between his teeth, dabs of paint on his face and his fingers, he still manages to keep that coat pristine.

My robes of state are stored in Buckingham Palace near the White Drawing Room, so all I have to do is arrive, get changed, and walk a short distance to the podium set up for me near one of the windows. Most days, there is a crowd sitting around, watching, talking in soft voices. When I take a break, they come up to be introduced and shake my hand.

The Queen is quieter than usual today. She wears a morning gown of some white satin, melds into the room thus, and her shining dark hair provides the only contrast.

"Do you like it, Maharajah?" she asks, stopping a little behind Winterhalter, who does not notice her approach.

He bows, and I do also. "It is wonderfully like me, your Majesty. Only Mr. Winterhalter has given me a few more inches"—I hold my hand above my head—"than I actually have."

"You will grow," Winterhalter growls.

"And if I don't, this is what people will remember most of your portrait," I say.

"It's splendid," the Queen says. "You have captured the Maharajah's beautiful eyes, Mr. Winterhalter."

"What will the background be?" I ask, curious. Others come up to mill around her Majesty and listen, interested. Lady Login is here also; she usually is. We have not talked much at the hotel after that day. There isn't much to say. I haven't forgotten, but I've forgiven her. What I cannot forget are the Lahore days when they took on my guardianship, their generosity in befriending a near-orphaned boy.

"Humph," Winterhalter says. "That I have not thought of. Maybe some minarets and domes. You know, Maharajah"— he curves the palms of his hands into appropriate shapes— "something like Lahore."

I protest. "You've never been there."

"Ah," he says, "but I have seen Schoefft's painting; the one you have in your possession. It gives me ideas, and this"—he taps the canvas with his brush—"will be much better than that one. Now, pose, please. Not like that, toward the mirror. Just your face, not your body."

In the reflection I watch as the Queen draws Lady Login to the side and they talk. About me? By now her Majesty must know that I don't want to marry Victoria Gouramma; perhaps she's heard about my interest in Cecilia also. She says nothing to me, about one or the other. If she's disappointed— I know that she also had wished for the marriage with Gouramma—her manner has not changed. She's the same. As kind as before.

The Queen summons a gentleman-in-waiting to her side; he bows, listens to what she has to say, and runs fleetly out of the room.

A half hour passes before I hear a rustle and clomping footsteps outside the room. The guards of the Tower of London come in, sleek and colorful in their livery. They hold out a tray to her Majesty. She beckons Prince Albert to her side and, turning, opens a casket and takes something out—what it is I cannot see from the other end of the room. They whisper together, and then, suddenly, the Queen comes running across the expanse of carpet, taps me on my arm, and before I can say anything, grabs my hand, puts something into my palm, and closes my fingers around it.

"Maharajah, here is the Kohinoor come from Amsterdam. What do you think of it?"

I unclench my fingers and gaze down, stupefied for a moment. And then I step off the podium and to the window, where the light is better. It snowed the day before, and the grounds of the palace are swathed in the gentle embrace of a winter's cold. The sun shows only a faint face in the gray-streaked sky, but the softly reflected daylight is luminous.

The stone in my hand draws the light inward, from the out-side, and glows within its dazzling heart.

It is set again as my father had it—as an armlet with a smaller diamond on either side. But it is not the diamond I remember. The Kohinoor lies weightless upon my hand, its heft cut away in an effort to give it more brilliance, a rose cut, I have heard Prince Albert call it. Surely the job has been bungled? Where is the Mountain of Light? The diamond cut-ters have taken away too much—this is not a mountain any-more, but a hill, a hillock, a mere bump in the horizon.

My head is bent over the stone in my hand. I place it on my heart. It isn't the Kohinoor diamond anymore, and it's the last time I will hold this stone. It doesn't belong to me.

The Queen and Prince Albert are together. She bites her lower lip; her dark eyes shine with compassion. Lady Login twists the fabric of her gown into little spirals between white-knuckled fingers. The Tower guards remain at attention, their expressions impassive, waiting for me to make a move. What do they all think I will do?

I go to the Queen, clasp her hand as she had mine a few moments ago, and place the Kohinoor in it. "It gives me immense pleasure to give to my sovereign the greatest trea-sure from the Toshakhana of Lahore. Will you accept this gift from a grateful subject?"

She touches me lightly on the shoulder. "You are truly one of the gems of my court, Maharajah."

"Will you wear it, your Majesty?" I ask. "I would like to see it on you."

The Queen slides it around her bare arm, and it blazes there on her skin through the rest of that morning, set off per-fectly by her white gown.

* * *

Paris, 1893: Night comes to the rue de la Trémoille. The gas lamps on the street are lit and throw crowns of gold in tight little circles down its length. One of the streetlights is just outside the window, and Sophia reads the last few pages with the diary turned toward this.

Her father's face lies in a deep shadow. His fingers are interlaced on his stomach, a sparkle of diamonds and rubies in the rings.

"Did you see Cecilia Bowles again?"

"No." His voice comes in a tired rumble. "Never again. I don't know who she married, if she married, if she cared at all for me."

"And so you married Mama."

She hears him sigh. "Bamba, yes, we gave you her name as your first. Sophia, so that you wouldn't feel out of place if you grew up and stayed in England. Jindan, for your grandmother."

"Did you love Mama?"

He waits a long time before answering. He wants to be honest. "No," he says finally. "I barely knew her when I married her. She was the daughter of a German merchant and his Egyptian mistress." He laughs. "She was appropriate for me, you see. Bamba had been brought up in a missionary society in Cairo; she taught at the local orphanage. I asked the missionaries to find me a wife who was Christian . . . and who wasn't British. We married at the British embassy in Cairo. I took my vows in English; she took hers in Arabic. For a long time, she couldn't speak English."

Now, it's Sophia's turn to be quiet. In the space of one day, a bit of a night, she has learned more about her father than she has known in the twenty-four years she has lived. Things haven't changed very much yet. Victor, her oldest brother, wants to marry an English girl he met at Cambridge. Her father's an earl. The Prince of Wales is pushing for the match; the Queen says nothing, and so nothing's happened yet.

She rises, scrapes a match against the side of a matchbox, turns on the gas, lights the sconces on the walls. The flames flicker, the gas hisses, the room comes into focus.

Her father has been crying. Tears soak into his mustache and his beard, his eyes are red. Sophia bends, puts her arms around him. He rests his head against her cheek. His hair is long, tied into a ponytail at his nape. He has long since become a Sikh again.

"I'm taking the night train, Papa. By tomorrow evening, I'll be back in London, if the crossing is good."

He wipes his face. "Sit, child. No, not there, all the way across the table, here, by my side. Let me look at you."

She pulls up her chair, and they sit, knee to knee. He gazes at her face for a long while. There's a shade of pain, somewhere behind her dark eyes.

"Who is he?"

She doesn't flinch, but a glow of pink covers her skin. "David Waters Sutherland. He's a physician . . . in Lahore. I met him on his last home leave."

"He's coming back again?"

She nods. "To see me. I think, Papa, that no one will care about David and me." She smiles; it lights up her face. "He isn't the son of an earl. He's nobody. Just someone I want to marry, that's all."

"And will you live in Lahore then, Sophia?"

"Yes."

"They never let me go back to Lahore. I left when I was ten years old. You will find it changed."

"I haven't been there before, Papa."

The clock in the cathedral on the next street chimes out the hour. Ten o'clock. A theater down the street empties after a play. Women come out in silks and satins, vendors roast hot chestnuts over fires, men smoke cigarettes and cast the butts on the cobblestones. A fight begins, and men push and shove against each other. There's blood on white shirtfronts, sweat on brows; bowlers roll on the ground.

Sophia gets up and pins her hat on her head. "My train's at eleven, Papa." She kisses him on both cheeks and on his forehead. "I'll come back in a week. Good night."

"Good-bye," he says. But she's gone. He can hear the sharp click of her heels on the wooden stairs, the creak of the door as she opens it, the concierge greeting her. He watches her walk quickly through the crowd, slim, upright, her hat slanted over the right half of her face. She raises her hand at the street corner, just before she disappears.

He brushes his teeth in the cold water from the bucket, turns down the lamps, and climbs into bed. There's an ache in his heart. The diary has churned up memories that have lain buried under years of distrust, dwindling hope. He has asked, in years gone by, for the Punjab Empire to be returned to him. The response was to cast doubt upon his origins, his fitness to be called the Maharajah of the Punjab. Was Ranjit Singh, Lion of the Punjab, *really* his father?

He has asked for the Kohinoor—the response was, still is, demonstrated only in the fact that he does not have it.

He massages his chest with a big hand. The street quiets down.

Paris, 1893: The next morning, Aimée heaves her pail and mop up the stairs to Dalip Singh's rooms. The door is unlocked; it opens at her touch.

"*Allo?*" she says. "*Tout ça va?*"

She enters, sees the still figure on the bed. She bends over him, puts her hand in front of his nose. And then she runs out of the room, and down the stairs, surprisingly fast for an old woman.

The violin player puts down his instrument when he sees her. She grabs his arm and drags him toward the building, filling his ear all the while. He clatters up the stairs, doesn't go beyond the doorway. He hesitates there. Makes the sign of a cross.

TELEGRAM: *From the Embassy at Paris:*
10:30 A.M. Received at Balmoral Castle, Scotland:
10:34 A.M.
      To Her Imperial Majesty. H.H. the
Maharajah died suddenly in Paris today. Please
advise about funeral arrangements.

Lord Dufferin. Her Majesty's Ambassador to
France

Afterword

So, what's fact and what's fiction? If you've read my other work, you'll know that this is where I address how all of my research and readings are woven into the text.

Shah Shuja did send his harem, along with Wafa Begam, to the court of Maharajah Ranjit Singh in the Punjab, when his brother Shah Mahmud, after having conquered Kabul, was knocking at the door in Peshawar.

The events in "Fragment of Light" take place in 1817. And, for the most part, they're accurate. For the purposes of the story, however, I've condensed the time line considerably on both ends. Kashmir and Peshawar belonged to Afghanistan when Shuja fled to the Punjab. Ranjit Singh did agree to help Shuja regain both cities, and ended up annexing them to his own Empire—the actual retaking of Kashmir (whose governor had rebelled against Afghan rule and established himself semi-independent) occurred in 1819; Peshawar fell in 1818, and was not completely annexed until 1834.

Maharajah Ranjit Singh was not quite as patient as

I portray him in "Fragment of Light" in waiting for the promised Kohinoor. He took the diamond from Shuja in 1813, after storming the fort at Kashmir to free the imprisoned Shuja at his wife, Wafa Begam's behest. After many requests, Shuja sent the Maharajah a *pukraj*—the topaz—hoping to fool him into thinking it was the Kohinoor. And Ranjit did then order no food or drink to be allowed into the mansion where Shah Shuja was being kept prisoner, starving him until he gave up the Kohinoor.

Emily and Fanny Eden left India with their hearts untouched, if the evidence of their published collections of letters is to be believed. In one such book, *Up the Country*, published in 1867, Emily mentions in the introduction that "many passages . . . written solely for the amusement of my own family, have of course been omitted." And indeed, the letters, the speaking voices of the Eden sisters, are lacking in many things—the truly personal; and even names of the main players from the East India Company at the court of Maharajah Ranjit Singh. (For these latter—the Major Bs, the Mr. Ts, the Mr. Ys—I dug into other readings from that time period.)

Paolo Avitabile, and his other foreign soldier friends, existed in the form they find in this book, for the most part. Avitabile did strike up a friendship with George, Lord Auckland, and his sisters. He didn't leave the Punjab Empire and India until 1843, four years after Maharajah Ranjit Singh's death. By February 1844, he was in Naples, and then Marseille and Paris, feted in each place. When he visited London, Lord Auckland took Avitabile around as his own special guest, and introduced him to Lord Palmerston, who was later Prime Minister of England. As a mark of favor, Avitabile—Maharajah Ranjit Singh's governor of Peshawar, the son of a peasant proprietor in Agerola—was invited to a dinner at the Duke of Wellington's residence.

I considered that it would have been Emily, the more

dominant sister, and not Fanny, who would have had a stronger connection with Paolo Avitabile at Maharajah Ranjit Singh's court—and their unusual "love" story formed the framework for Lord Auckland's visit to the Sutlej in "Roses for Emily." So, from a historical perspective, this story is possible. Would it have been probable? I was curious about what would happen if I took a very proper, intelligent, well-off Victorian lady and gave her affections for a man she would not have looked at—or met—in the normal course of her life. Avitabile, for all of his known refinement and self-taught education, was the son of a peasant, and a mercenary soldier—not at all from Emily's class.

According to a genealogical chart prepared for Maharajah Ranjit Singh around 1886, he had thirty-seven acknowledged wives. There is no detailed and reliable source on either the names of or the number of his sons. I chose to focus on the men who became rulers of Lahore after Ranjit Singh's death—Kharak Singh, the second king of Lahore; Sher Singh, the fourth king of Lahore; and, of course, Dalip Singh, who was the fifth king of Lahore, a title he enjoyed for the rest of his life, even though the Punjab was part of the British Empire.

Roshni (in "Love in Lahore"), the young woman related to Sher Singh, existed—although her name has been lost to history. And she was betrothed to Dalip Singh, even though she was much older than he. This much is true, so also the fact that Dalip Singh eventually decided not to marry Roshni.

Henry and Honoria Lawrence were married before Henry came to Lahore as Resident and met the young Maharajah Dalip Singh. To the eight-year-old king, Henry was a protector, a father figure, a man for whom Dalip formed a strong and abiding affection.

The incident with the cows and the camel artillery in "Love in Lahore" occurred during Henry's tenure at Lahore

and is described as the "Cow Row" in his biography, authored
by Herbert Edwardes, his private secretary in the Punjab.
Henry Lawrence left Lahore in 1856 and gave way to Lord
and Lady Login, who then became Dalip Singh's guardians.
Lawrence died a year later, defending Lucknow in the Sepoy
Rebellion, and is buried there.

As for "An Alexandria Moon"? The Kohinoor diamond
left Indian shores on the sixth of April 1850. It traveled not
on the SS *Indus* but on the HMS *Medea*, a Royal Navy steam
sloop. Even the captain of the *Medea* did not know that he
was carrying such precious cargo—he had only been given
orders to take Lieutenant Colonel Mackeson and Captain
Ramsay to England. On their way there, the sole sparkle of
excitement came when the ship approached Mauritius and
sent notice of cholera onboard, with two sailors dead. Port
authorities refused to allow food and water onboard the
Medea, and threatened to blow her up if she attempted to
berth. But the HMS *Medea* went on safely to England and, on
the twenty-ninth of June 1850, docked at Portsmouth.

I borrowed the story of Multan Raj's death, however,
from a similar incident that happened to Henry Lawrence's
brother. John Lawrence interviewed a man suspected of
murder who sat smoking all through their conversation.
When he rose, in deference, so as not to be seated in front of
the Sahib, there was blood on the upper part of his *dhoti*—he
had stabbed himself, and then calmly continued talking.

In England, under the guardianship of Lord and Lady
Login, Maharajah Dalip Singh fell in love with one of Lady
Login's relatives. This scene in "Diary of a Maharajah"
and Lady Login's refusal are detailed in a letter from
Lady Login to Queen Victoria. The Queen had also given
guardianship of the Princess Victoria Gouramma to Lady
Login, considering that "these two young people are
pointed out for each other. The only two Christians of high
rank of their own countries, both having the advantage of

early European influences, there seems to be many points of sympathy between them." Dalip Singh, however, did not find himself sympathetic to the Princess Gouramma and, in saying so to Lady Login, also professed his love for her other ward—an unnamed Englishwoman who was staying with them.

In all the years that the young Maharajah Dalip Singh had spent—in India and in England—under the guardianship of the various British officials who looked after him during the long process of the annexation of the Punjab, he had become most attached to Lord and Lady Login (although he always professed a deep fondness for Henry Lawrence also). Lady Login, in the same letter to the Queen, then candidly put down Dalip's thoughts on her refusal: "But if we, whom he trusted and regarded as parents, could not accept him into the family; if we, who had taken him from his own country and people, and cut him off . . . from all prospect of mixing with his own race, should refuse to regard him as one of ourselves, to whom could he look?"

Despite this plea from Dalip, Lady Login was adamant—the Maharajah might be their adopted "son," but he could not marry an Englishwoman connected with them. It just would not do. She hoped that "he will see his true position more clearly, and meet with someone more suitable in every respect . . . as we in no wise covet such a destiny for our charge."

It was the first intimation to Maharajah Dalip Singh that, although he was royal, he was still a subject of the Queen of England, and though he had the precedence of a European king in every English drawing room, he was still not good enough for a young British woman of little fortune and no pretensions to nobility.

The Maharajah's wide-eyed innocence had taken a beating; over the rest of his life it would be shattered until, knowing he would not be given back his kingdom of Punjab, he was reduced to demanding the return of the Kohinoor.

Maharajah Dalip Singh died, alone actually, in a shabby hotel in Paris in 1893. Bamba Sophia Jindan, his daughter, married David Sutherland and lived in Lahore with him. She is buried in Lahore.

The diamond is said to have held a curse. Legend had it that the Kohinoor could be safely possessed only by a woman, that no man who had it would long hold his kingdom, and that it could never be worn in the official crown of a monarch (hence, perhaps, the reason it was worn in an armlet or set in a throne). In India, Persia, and Afghanistan, during the diamond's tumultuous and bloody history, only men owned the Kohinoor.

After Queen Victoria, no male ruler of England has worn the Kohinoor on his person. Today, it is displayed along with the Crown Jewels in the Tower of London . . . in the Queen Mother's crown.

The only man to have successfully warded off the curse of the diamond was Maharajah Ranjit Singh, the Lion of the Punjab, monarch of the largest and most powerful independent kingdom in India in the mid-1800s. In his lifetime, he did not lose his lands, his Empire, or the Kohinoor. But he was, effectively, the first and last ruler of the Punjab. After his death, the Empire crumbled; some ten years later, the Punjab was annexed to the British Empire.

In 1858, India lost her sovereignty and became a British colony, and the Kohinoor shimmered on the arm of her Queen, Victoria. Perhaps, after all, there *was* a curse on the Kohinoor.

Indu Sundaresan
June 2012